T0012860

Praise for *C...*

'Jesmond explores the adrenal... original mystery... A promising debut' – *Sunday Times*
(A Best Crime Novel of the Month)

'Intriguing... The landscape of Cornwall, with its history of smuggling, makes a suitably mysterious backdrop' – *Herald*

'A gripping premise, a well executed plot and an evocative Cornish setting' – *NB Magazine*

'A surprising story filled with twists and turns' – *Living North*

'This amazing debut novel from Jane Jesmond will give you all the thrills you've been looking for and keep you gripped from the get-go' – *Female First*

'The thriller world has gained a compelling and seriously talented voice' – **Hannah Mary McKinnon, bestselling author of** *Sister Dear*

Praise for *Cut Adrift*

'Riveting... Jesmond's first novel marked her out as an original voice in crime fiction, and the new book shows how the conventions of the genre can be used to reveal a personal tragedy' – *Sunday Times* **(A Best Crime Novel of 2023)**

'Jesmond's delineation of her characters as people with plausible flaws and hot tempers adds depth and complexity to a story that might wear its sentiments on its sleeves, yet which is trimly steered and freighted with contemporary resonance' – *Times* **(Thriller Book of the Month)**

'Finding a new voice with something compelling to say in the crime writing field can be difficult. Thankfully there are people out there trying to deliver a twist on the genre, and Jane Jesmond is one of them' – *On Yorkshire Magazine*

Also by Jane Jesmond

On The Edge
Cut Adrift
Her

A QUIET CONTAGION

Jane Jesmond

VERVE BOOKS

First published in 2023 by VERVE Books,
an imprint of The Crime and Mystery Club Ltd.
Harpenden, UK

vervebooks.co.uk
@VERVE_Books

ISBN
978-0-85730-849-8 (Paperback)
978-0-85730-850-4 (Ebook)

2 4 6 8 10 9 7 5 3 1

Typeset in 11 on 13.7pt Garamond MT Pro
by Avocet Typeset, Bideford, Devon, EX39 2BP
Printed and bound in Great Britain by Clays Ltd, Elcograf S.p.A.

MIX
Paper from
responsible sources
FSC® C018072
FSC
www.fsc.org

In loving memory of my mum, Cilla Chapman 1934-2011.
I so wish you could have held one of my books.

Prologue:
Wilfred Patterson

14 June 2017
The day after the reunion

Wilf fixed his eyes on the reassuring straightness of the railway tracks, gleaming and solid in the morning sun. To his left they ran back to Coventry, where he'd come from earlier, and to his right towards Birmingham and then the north. For a moment he was gripped by the idea of taking a train north and disappearing.

Two nights without sleep had torn down the fences between his memories and let them mingle. One moment the events of sixty years ago crashed around his head, and the next minute the angry scenes at yesterday's reunion clawed them into shreds. The young faces he remembered from 1957 dissolved into their grim older versions, all talking at once. Michael Poulter, speaking through the thick tiredness of illness. Jean Storer, calm and eloquent, only her hands, clenching and unclenching, revealing how desperate she was.

He shook his head and Jack, his assistance dog, scrambled to his feet from under the bench and stared at Wilf with his odd-coloured eyes, thinking they were finally on the move. Wilf bent and patted him.

'Not yet, Jack,' he said. The movement made him wince. The brace that supported his left leg, shrivelled and useless from childhood polio, had rubbed a raw patch on the side of his knee. He'd been on his feet too much over the last two days and, anyway, he wasn't as adept as Dora at fitting it.

Dora. Her face joined the others raging round his head. And Phiney. Dora, his wife. Phiney, his granddaughter. How could he tell them about the terrible thing he'd been part of all those years ago? He sighed. Jack watched him, waiting for his next move.

The young man beside him on the bench looked up from his iPad. 'Nice dog,' he said.

Wilf ignored him. Exhaustion was draining his senses. Darkness blurred the outskirts of his vision and his fingers no longer felt the wood of the bench. He was drowning in a sea of memories. Unable to move. Unable to breathe. Unable to fight.

He'd felt like this before. After Carol, his daughter, died. The doctor had given him pills. They helped. A little. Made it possible to get through the day.

What helped most was Dora. The doctor said he should talk, so she made him. Every day, she made him talk. About anything and everything. It didn't matter, she said, he could talk about his bloody clocks. She didn't mind, but talk he would.

And he had. He talked about the clocks he loved and then about all the dogs who'd loved him. About the good bits of his childhood. And then about the bad. About the polio that had been his constant companion. About the pain. About the loneliness. About the way his legs looked and all the bad feelings that he wasn't supposed to have. He talked for weeks and weeks, and she listened and said nothing much, although occasionally she glowered or scrubbed her eyes.

And when the time came to speak about Carol, he was unhappy and angry and grieving and missing her but the awful suffocation of the depression had passed, dissolved by all the words he'd shared with Dora.

Until now.

This time, though, he'd be alone, because no one could forgive the thing he'd done. Not Phiney. Not even Dora.

But worse than the thought of Dora and Phiney were the accusing voices in his head, beating against his skull. He staggered to his feet, knowing he had to get rid of them. Except they were in him and part of him. He'd never silence them. He'd have to carry them with him for the rest of his life. For the rest of his life.

He couldn't. He knew he couldn't.

Chapter One:
Phiney Wistman

14 June 2017
The day after the reunion

The row of letterboxes ran in a neat line from the entrance door into the dusty lobby. My landlord had chosen a set in red with a white flap and they gleamed in the light from the grubby window like bared teeth. A smile or a grimace? Who knew?

One of the morons who lived in my building had dropped a heap of fliers and adverts on the floor. I picked them up and gave in to the urge to check my box, newly and clearly relabelled, *Flat 3 Josephine Wistman*, to avoid any errors. Maybe the post had come early for once.

The test centre had said it would take up to eight weeks for the letter to arrive. Seven of them had passed with me managing to focus on other things, but since the eighth week began, the test results had started to nibble away at my thoughts. I unlocked my box. Was now, in the middle of this utterly routine day, the moment when I'd know if my mother had passed more on to me than her coffee-coloured hair, her caramel eyes and her sensitivity to smell? Had she also bequeathed me the gene that would give me breast cancer?

But my box was empty.

The tight muscles in my chest relaxed and the breath slipped out of my lungs in a long sigh. Another day of normality was beginning. I set off for Coventry City Hospital, where I worked.

I always walked, even when I was on nights. It was my way of ensuring I took some exercise because, believe me, after a gruelling shift on the children's oncology ward, you don't feel like doing anything except curling up with the latest Maeve Binchy. Or having a good weep. And weeping didn't help.

No, I thought, as I sped down the familiar streets, past my old school and through the hospital car park, weeping was a waste of time; my grandad had taught me that. It was better to fight. And, with that in mind, I strode through the entrance doors and ran up the stairs to the ward and into its familiar chaos.

The door to the office was open. Meghan, at her desk, looked with disgust at a computer printout. I nipped in and put an eco-container on her desk.

'Banana bread! Homemade. Catch you later.'

She started to say something but I shook my head and sped away.

My first patient was Marnie (seven years old, early-stage lympho-blastic leukaemia, prognosis good but not reacting well to chemo), who was sitting in bed in one of the wards painted with Disney characters to encourage the kids into thinking they might be somewhere fun. Her mother stood by her with that half-bent stance all the parents had, wanting to shield her daughter from any more suffering yet knowing she couldn't.

'Good news,' I said. 'Marnie's bloods are back and they're fine, so we'll be able to treat her.'

Marnie wore a new knitted hat. A pink bonnet with pointy ears and a mane of multi-coloured wool to disguise the absence of her own hair. It framed her face and gave a warm tint to her ash-white skin.

'A pony?' I asked. 'Is it a pony hat?'

Silence from Marnie. The noise of children playing or grizzling while nurses and parents murmured to each other penetrated the curtains round our cubicle. The normal buzz of the ward.

'A unicorn.' Her mother's voice filled the gap. 'Tell Nurse Josephine, Marnie. You're a unicorn.'

Of course she was. A white knitted horn stuck out between the ears.

'Granny knitted it for you, didn't she, Marnie?' Her mother's voice cracked. She smelled of exhaustion. Of clothes worn once too often and hair not washed enough.

'You're a beautiful unicorn, Marnie,' I said in my best cheerful voice as I rubbed cleansing gel into my hands. Sharp and acid, it brightened the thick air for a few seconds before vanishing. I snapped on gloves. Marnie started to whimper. She knew what was coming. She'd been here too many times before.

The noise of vomiting reached us, followed swiftly by the comforting words of one of the other nurses. It sounded like Christine, her voice warmed by the lilt of a Scottish accent.

I leaned forward to give Marnie the reassurance she needed too, expecting the words to arrive automatically but nothing came.

What was happening to me?

I ransacked my suddenly empty brain for something to say.

It won't hurt. True enough but she'd feel it nevertheless.

It'll be over in a flash. Sort of true. But there'd be another procedure and then another, all adding up to hours of misery.

There's nothing to be frightened of. The big lie. There was everything to be frightened of. Beware the cancer eating away at your body. Beware the treatment. It might cure the cancer. In Marnie's case, it more than likely would. But it'd make her feel sick and weak as it rampaged through her body, killing everything in its path as well as the cancer cells. Its lethal effects would linger in her blood for years.

A feeling of utter blackness caught me by surprise. I needed to snap out of this.

The little girl looked at me as though sensing something was different. I smiled back. This wasn't helping her at all. From somewhere I dragged up the right air of comforting cheerfulness and found the right words. As I fixed and checked the drip, the good nurse that I was – like the smiling angels who visited every day while Mum was dying – came back.

Afterwards I leaned against the wall outside the ward and breathed in the familiar smell of detergent mingled with hints of coffee from the machine down the corridor. We all had bad days when the stresses of the job got to us. No point dwelling on it. The clock on the wall opposite told a depressing story, though. I had hours before my shift finished.

A toddler whizzed past me, followed by his mother, one hand on his jumper and the other dragging the stand with his drip behind them. She gave me a smile as she went by, happy because her son was happy. I smiled back.

Coffee. Maybe that would help. I had green tea sachets in my locker. They were much healthier but… Fuck it. I wanted coffee and, anyway, some new research showed it could protect against liver cancer. However, the machine swallowed my money and gave nothing back in exchange. A bland green message told me to take my non-existent drink and have a nice day. I kicked it, startling a trainee who was scuttling past me clutching a pile of files.

'Top tip,' I called after her. 'Never put money in this thing. The odds are worse than fruit machines.' I banged it with the flat of my hand as she turned to answer.

Meghan put her sleek head out of the ward office and caught me assaulting the machine.

'It's a thief and a liar,' I said by way of explanation.

Her lips twitched as the trainee took the opportunity to slip away. 'Nurse Wistman,' she said. 'Could you punish it quietly?'

'Yes, Sister March,' I said, and gave a sardonic curtsey.

I thought she was going to laugh but she stuck her tongue out at me instead. Its gold stud glinted in the cold light of the corridor. She came out and shut the door behind her. Sweet and spicy, the traces of her perfume warmed the air. Her amusement showed in the dark eyes she'd inherited from her mother although her stocky figure marked her out as her father's daughter. Her black hair could have come from either side of the family but her Midlands accent and determination were entirely her own. She was my best friend – had been since we first met in primary school – as well as my boss.

'Phiney,' she said. 'I was going to come and find you.'

'Well, Meghan, here I am.' I gave the machine a last smack and it vibrated for a few seconds as though moaning about its treatment.

'You OK?'

'What do you mean?'

'You seem pretty grumpy.'

'No, I'm not.'

She raised an eyebrow at the annoyance in my voice.

'You are, you know, Phiney. And you have been for quite a while!'

I looked away from her and at the clock. The one in the corridor was the old-fashioned type with hands whose movement was imperceptible.

'Work getting to you?' she asked.

'I'm fine. I love my job,' I said. 'I mean, who'd do it if they didn't?'

Meghan narrowed her eyes but let me off further interrogation.

'Going to netball tonight?' she asked as she leaned back against the door to push it open.

'I guess so.'

'How about a drink afterwards?'

I wasn't sure. My momentary inability to deal with Marnie had shaken me and I fancied a bit of time to myself to think about it. Meghan was right. I had been a bit irritable for the last few weeks. I guessed the worry about the tests had been nibbling away at my unconscious mind.

She saw the doubt in my face and misunderstood its source. 'We could go to the Zanzibar if you like,' she said.

The Zanzibar had fabulous non-alcoholic cocktails and a great range of teas plus smoking was forbidden – even outside on the terrace. Meghan knew me well.

'All right,' I said.

Maybe keeping the whole thing secret had been a mistake. I could have told Meghan and made her promise not to tell Grandad. She'd have done that for me. In fact, she still would. I'd tell her tonight.

'I mean, great.'

'You *are* OK, aren't you?'

'Sure. I didn't sleep so well.' This, at least, was true.

The hours of my shift ticked away on the ward clocks. I put in drips, checked patients, chatted to parents and took bloods. It was all fine, except the bloods. The sight of the vials made me remember my own at the test centre in Birmingham. It had looked just like every other sample of blood I'd ever seen but I hadn't been able to stop staring at it and wondering if the seeds of illness were hiding in there.

My phone rang while I was explaining the potential side-effects of chemo to a new patient's father. I'd forgotten to turn it off when I arrived. The caller ID told me it was Grandad but I knew it wasn't. It was Dora, his wife, my step-grandmother, and a right royal pain in the neck. She always rang on their landline whereas Grandad used his mobile from the privacy of his shed. She'd be back from her coach tour and ringing to nag me about coming to see them. I probably should but Derbyshire was a long way and, once again, I wished they hadn't decided to move there from Coventry when Grandad retired.

I let the call go to answering machine, knowing I wouldn't call her back, then sloped off to the staffroom – empty for once – made myself a cup of green tea and stuck my head out of the only window on the ward that opened. Anything to escape the tired smell of air that had been passed through too many sets of lungs.

'Nurse Wistman?' It was the trainee at the door. Pale and slightly sweaty, her hair had escaped from its band.

'Yup.'

'Sister March sent me to fetch you.'

'OK, thanks.' I made a huge effort. 'It's your first week, isn't it?' I looked at her name badge. 'Shona. Welcome to the madness that is paediatric oncology.'

Shona laughed. Her pointy face relaxed.

'And call me "Phiney". We're not very formal here.'

Meghan's door was open. She stood at the window, her finger tracing the trickle of a drop of moisture trapped between the panes of the double-glazing.

'Phiney. Er… sit down.'

She looked pretty twitchy compared to this morning. What had happened?

I noticed she was sipping a coffee.

'Did you get that from the machine? How?' I asked.

'There was a cup stuck. You reach up and give it a twist and it comes free. I'll show you next time.'

'Nothing works round here.'

'Have mine.'

I shook my head.

'Anyway, that's not why I asked Shona to find you.'

She shut the door and sat in the chair beside me.

'Your grandmother called.'

'I don't think so. Both my grandmothers are dead.'

It was a stupid thing to say because we both knew who she meant but I was irritated that Dora had started bothering Meghan when she couldn't get through to me. A tinge of guilt coloured my thoughts too. Maybe I should have called her back.

'Your step-grandmother, then.' A momentary blip of annoyance broke through her look of concern. 'What is her name? I can never remember it and you always call her "my grandad's wife". She's Welsh, isn't she? Like my dad?'

'Dora.'

'That's right. It's not a very Welsh name.'

'And she's not very adorable either. So her parents chose badly in every way.'

'Anyway, Dora called.' Meghan breathed in through clenched teeth. 'Shit, Phiney, how am I supposed to do this? Listen. Your grandfather is dead.' She put an arm round my shoulder and the warmth of her skin soaked through the thin material of my scrubs.

My brain came to a halt. Words with no meaning came out of my mouth.

'Don't be stupid. Of course he isn't.'

'Phiney.'

'She's lying. I'll call her. I guess that's what she wants anyway. That's why she said he was dead. Typical... Bloody typical... She'll do anything to get her own way...'

My voice stuttered into silence as a few sluggish thoughts waded into my brain.

Something had just happened. What had just happened?

Meghan's arm tightened round my shoulders. It felt like a vice rather than a comfort.

Why was she trying to comfort me?

'Phiney, I'm sorry but she wouldn't lie.' Meg's voice was soft but firm. 'Not about that. Your grandad is dead.'

I watched her mouth forming the words but the sounds were meaningless.

'And I'm afraid you can't ring her. That's why she phoned me. She was just leaving. She's on her way to see you. Her train gets into Coventry at three and she wants you to meet her.'

What was she going on about? Trains and times. Nothing made any sense.

'I don't understand.'

But suddenly I did. The words Meghan had said reached my brain and made their mark as clearly as the smoking brand ranchers seared onto the sides of their cattle.

Grandad was dead.

'Your grandad was in Coventry. I guess you didn't know. You need to go, Phiney. And now, if you're going to get to the station on time.'

My brain split into warring thoughts.

'There must be a mistake. It can't be true. He was fine last time I spoke to him.' Meghan's eyes creased with sympathy. She knew the words were automatic jabbering. Part of me knew it too. My last efforts at denial. As common as the wobbling of my knees against the fists pushed down into them.

Was Grandad dead?

Death smells of change. Of windows opened. Of clean sheets. Of undertakers in aftershave and suits with fresh, ironed shirts doing what they have to do, while the family crowd into the kitchen and stare at each other. That is death.

Was he dead?

'He was getting on, you know, Phiney.'

What could possibly make Megs think this was helpful?

'Seventy-six, wasn't it?'

She'd come to his seventieth birthday six years ago, just before he and Dora moved to Matlock, so it wasn't a work of genius to get that right.

'That's nothing these days. You know that, Megs.'

Grandad was dead.

And the stupidest thought of the whole stupid, stupid day hit me: I was really and truly an orphan now.

'Do you want me to get you a taxi?'

'A taxi?'

'To get to the station. To meet Dora.'

That was right. Grandad was dead and Dora was coming down.

'I can't see her. Please, Meghan, call her.'

'She doesn't have a mobile phone, does she?'

'Shit, no.'

One thought broke through the maelstrom in my head.

'How? How did he die?'

'I don't know. She didn't say and she was in such a state I couldn't ask.'

'Did you say he was in Coventry?'

'She said he was.'

Grandad was in Coventry and I hadn't known. He hadn't told me.

A thousand questions rose in my throat and I thought they might choke me. There was no point asking Meghan. She'd told me everything she knew. Only one person had the answers and she was about to arrive at Coventry Station.

I had to go. I had to get to the station. The station. Quickest route to the station?

'You OK?'

19

The route to the station came back to me. I forced myself to stand.

'I'll be fine. I'm going to the station.'

'I'll call a taxi.'

'It'll be quicker to walk at this time of day.'

'I'll come with you.'

'No. I'll be fine.'

I had to get moving. Couldn't hang around. The sooner I went, the sooner I'd be able to find out what had happened. I pushed Meghan's arm away and headed for the door.

'Phiney?'

What now?

'Phiney.' Meghan hesitated. 'It's a big shock, you know. Something like this.'

I waited for her to say something kind.

'So try and remember that when you see Dora. She'll be very shaken up.'

Chapter Two:
Phiney Wistman

14 June 2017
The day after the reunion

I should have taken a taxi. The lovely weather had brought everybody outside. I pushed through tour parties beside the cathedral and dodged round the students in the Esplanade, dipping their hands in the fountains and flicking water over each other. A farmers' market clogged the shopping centre. Normally, I'd have stopped to enjoy the sharp smells of goat's cheese and thyme, maybe bought a couple of soft-skinned peaches and watched the crepe lady produce lace-thin pancakes with a twist of her wrist, but today the city where I'd lived all my life felt alien and the people gathering in its streets were obstacles.

Grandad was dead.

And I wasn't going to get to the station in time. I started to run.

Grandad was dead.

My feet beat out the words on the bone-dry pavements and they started to sink into my being, leaving only the unanswered questions to trouble me. What had happened? How had he died? I leaned forward on my feet and ran faster, careering in between queues of slow-moving cars and into the station. Dora's train was pulling in on the far platform and my feet kept me running up onto the wide bridge over the track and to the top of the steps where the surge of passengers leaving the train engulfed me. I stopped.

Dora was waiting on the platform, her head darting this way and that as the crowd parted around her. She stuck out, but then she always did. Maybe it was her height, maybe the awkwardness with which she moved, or perhaps her clothes. Today she wore a massive mackintosh. She had a thing for capacious outdoor wear and big pleated skirts. She thought they disguised her hips, which were large and worried her. I knew that because she always glanced at them in shop windows and looked a bit depressed. Anyway, she didn't need the mackintosh. The sky was blue, no rain had been forecast for days and the air was full of the smells of a city summer – diesel and chips and hot skin.

She married Grandad during the years between my father's death and my mother's, although he'd known her for ages through a dog-walking service she ran. Grandad always had an assistance dog, trained to fetch things and put them away, to carry his shopping – the latest, Jack, could even open and close doors for him – but Grandad wasn't up to walking very far so Dora had exercised them.

Mum and I thought he was joking when he told us he was marrying her.

'The Welsh dragon!' she said to him. 'Ha ha. Very funny, Dad.'

'You'll have to stop calling her that. And stop Phiney too.'

'Come on.'

'She won't expect you to call her "Mum". We've discussed it.'

'You *are* serious.'

'Although it would be nice if Phiney could call her "Gran".'

'But Dad… Why?'

He narrowed his eyes and jerked his head towards me.

Later Mum told me to call her 'Aunt Dora', which was quite a surprise. I'd forgotten her real name. I'd had a childhood obsession with dragons, you see. And Dora with her green mac and the knitted scarf that hung lumpily down her back had been a casualty of it. The mac and the scarf were long gone but her protruding jaw and pointy bun hairstyle were still features.

I hesitated on the steps. The reality of her presence down below, the bony, restless fingers smoothing the unconvincing jet-black hair scraped onto the top of her head, shook me.

Grandad was dead.

If Dora was here, it must be true.

She saw me.

'Phiney,' she screamed as she pushed her way over to the steps, stumbling over people's feet and wheelie bags. 'Oh God. I thought you weren't coming. Thank you for coming. I haven't got any money. Left my purse at home. Didn't think. A nice lady in the seat next to me bought me a cup of tea.'

Nothing changed her. Not even catastrophe. She had no filter. Whatever came into her mind came out of her mouth. Annoyance and pity fought in my head. She was devastated, I told myself. The explosion of words was her way of showing it.

She tripped once again, saved herself by grabbing the handrail and swinging her body round so she landed on the bottom step with a squeal that mutated into a storm of muttering. 'The police came this morning... I couldn't believe it... Mr Wilfred Patterson, they said, dead.'

A young man helped her heave herself to her feet and she clung to the rail as she stared up at me. Her mouth quivered round each breath and she blinked her eyes rapidly. She was about to cry but was making a superhuman effort not to. My irritation faded and I walked down the last few steps to claim my one remaining link to Grandad.

She flung her arms round me, smothering me in the plastic smell of her mac until I patted her back gently and she disengaged.

'Grandad?' I said. 'What happened?'

She fumbled in her pocket, whipped out a handkerchief and patted the puffy skin round her eyes. 'Not now,' she said and staggered off over the bridge. I tore after her, anger drying up the flow of sympathy. *Not now.* How could she say that to me? I caught up as she stumbled down the steps and out into the concourse and made a massive effort to be nice.

'Please. You have to tell me.'

'Oh, Phiney. It's too dreadful.' She turned, looked back up the steps and shuddered. 'He fell off a bridge. At Tile Park railway station. I need to get out of here.'

She flung herself through the doors and out into the sunshine. I stared back at the bridge we'd just walked across. How was that possible? How could Grandad have fallen off a bridge? I ran after her.

'Tile Park?'

'Yes.' She threw the word over her shoulder at me.

Tile Park was a little backwater, set in the countryside on the outskirts of Coventry.

'But how and what was he doing in Tile Park anyway?'

A high-speed London train drowned out her reply as it tore through the station.

'What?' She stopped and faced me. 'I thought *you'd* know. Didn't he come down to see you?'

'I didn't even know he was down here.'

Her face shifted as though a horde of ants were racing around beneath her skin.

'You must have,' she said finally and started along the pavement towards the bus station. People scuttled out of her way.

'No, I didn't.' And then because I didn't want to have one of those stupid pantomime arguments. 'How did it happen?'

She gave no sign of having heard me as she strode past the bus stops, looking at the numbers.

'How did it happen?' I asked again when I caught up with her. She hesitated. She gazed at me as though she'd forgotten I was with her, then shook her head.

'He didn't even tell me he was going away. I got back this morning and he wasn't there.'

None of this made any sense.

'I went on a trip. Coach, you know. With Gillian. Scarborough and the North Yorkshire coast. Got home midday.'

'I know, I know. Grandad told me you were going away.'

'And two policemen were waiting and told me Wilf... Wilf was dead. Right. I think we'll have to get a taxi.'

'A taxi?'

'Have you got money? I don't know how much it will be?'

'I've got money.'

'How much?'

'I don't know. Anyway, they all take cards these days. So it doesn't matter.'

She charged towards the taxi rank. I raced after her.

'Where are we going?'

'The police station.'

An awful thought struck me. 'We're not going to identify the body, are we?'

The people in the taxi queue turned to look at us then swiftly turned away.

'No. They said I wouldn't need to.'

'What else did they say?'

'Nothing but a lot of rubbish.'

'What!'

'That's why I had to come down. To put them right. The two idiot police from Matlock knew nothing.'

'What needs putting right? I don't get it.'

'Just wait, can't you, Phiney? Let me sort it out and then it will be clear.'

I started to stutter some kind of answer but she swept a glance over the bystanders. Maybe now was not the best time.

'Besides,' she went on. 'They told me to come straightaway, of course.'

I asked the question I knew the listeners in the queue, despite looking everywhere but at us, were egging me on to ask. 'Why?'

'To pick up Jack.'

'Jack was with Grandad? When it happened?'

But it was a stupid question. Of course he was. He went everywhere with Grandad. And the thought of Jack alone in some crappy police station, surrounded by people he didn't know, after seeing Grandad fall to his death, almost finished me. I took a few wobbly gulps of air. 'Let's go get him,' I said.

The queue parted as one to let us pass to the front.

Chapter Three:
Phiney Wistman

14 June 2017
The day after the reunion

Jack was waiting for us in a tiny room lined with noticeboards that served as the reception at the police station. It smelled of lemon disinfectant overlaying the acid vestiges of vomit. A thump of Jack's tail acknowledged our arrival but the rest of him was focused on the entrance. He was waiting for Grandad. Dora fumbled with the catches on his harness and once she'd removed it, along with the pouches clipped onto either side, he lay down and let himself be petted without much enthusiasm.

'Lovely dog.' A policeman leaned through the hatch. 'Very distinctive eyes.'

Jack had one blue eye and one brown.

'Heterochromia,' Dora said but I interrupted her before she could embark on a long explanation of the condition.

'Yes,' I said. 'We're here to see... Who are we here to see?'

I looked over at Dora. I hadn't been able to question her in the taxi because she'd sat in the front and told the driver the best way to go, so the sooner we got on with this meeting the better.

'Could he have some water?' she asked.

'We offered him some earlier but he wouldn't look at it.'

'He was working,' Dora explained. 'Now I've taken his harness off, he knows work is over. He'll only drink when he's working if my husband tells him it's alright.' Her voice cracked. The policeman looked alarmed.

'I'll ring through and let DC McCulloch know you're here, and then I'll fetch him some water if you leave him with me. It *is* Mrs Patterson, isn't it?'

Dora nodded and blew her nose. The policeman looked at me.

'Our granddaughter, Josephine. Josephine Wistman.'

I didn't correct her. I hadn't since Grandad begged me to stop.

Grandad was dead.

I'd never again be able to take a cup of tea out to him in his shed and watch him fit the intricate parts of one of the clocks he made together while I chatted about everything and nothing. I bit the inside of my mouth and tried to breathe calmly.

A connecting door buzzed and a woman wearing spectacles on a chain peered round and looked questioningly at us. The policeman introduced us. She was DC McCulloch and, in her pale pink blouse and light blue skirt with a limp trimming of darker lace, she didn't look a bit like my idea of a police constable. She had the same vague smile as one of my tutors at uni who always believed the excuses we dredged up for late assignments. She beckoned us through, asking Dora how she was and how the journey had been. Her smile withstood the onslaught of Dora's reply – the weather, too hot – the trains, not what they used to be – the price of a sandwich, shocking. We traipsed up the corridor. Dora spied the door to the toilet and whisked inside, muttering something about too much tea.

DC McCulloch and I looked at each other.

'Your grandmother's putting on a brave face.'

I nodded. She smelled faintly of lily of the valley.

'How did my Grandad die?'

Her eyes creased. 'Hasn't Mrs Patterson told you?'

'No. She said he'd fallen off a bridge.'

'Ah.'

I waited.

'It would be better if we discussed it all when Mrs Patterson is here.'

Her lips set themselves in a firm line. Shit. What was going on?

'Do you want to go and see if she's all right?' DC McCulloch interrupted my thoughts.

I shoved the door open. It smashed straight into Dora as she came out. She staggered and put her hands to her face but claimed she was fine, although her nose was a bit red.

DC McCulloch ushered us into an office and sat behind the desk. Dora dithered between two chairs. She chose one and sat down, then stood up, removed her mac and her cardigan and straightened her skirt, sat down and then stood up again to put the cardigan back on. DC McCulloch smiled at her encouragingly. I gritted my teeth.

'Well, here we are,' Dora said.

DC McCulloch's smile stiffened. 'It must be a very difficult time for you, Mrs Patterson, and for you, er, Josephine.' She'd forgotten my surname, I thought. 'So, thank you for coming to collect your dog. If there's anything we can do to help, please say. There are organisations that can assist you with practical matters and also provide trained counsellors. Coming to terms with something like this can be very hard on the family and I'd strongly recommend you talk to someone about it. Perhaps not straightaway but sometime soon.'

Dora said nothing. In fact, she started rummaging in her bag.

'I expect you have some questions for me.' DC McCulloch gave me a look.

'How did the accident happen?' I asked immediately.

DC McCulloch sighed. It was almost imperceptible. A slight puckering of parted lips and a hiss of breath carrying a faint tang of toffee. 'I'm afraid this wasn't an accident, Josephine.' She chewed the end of her pen and looked at Dora as though waiting for her to speak but Dora had taken a handkerchief from her bag and pressed it to her mouth and nose. 'I'm really sorry,' DC McCulloch said, turning to me. 'But your grandfather took his own life. It was suicide.'

Suicide. The word hit me like a great wave, washing my thoughts away and leaving nothing but a dull roaring behind.

Dora was silent. *She knew.* That was all I could think. She knew. All the time. At the station. In the taxi. She knew and she hadn't told me. She muttered something. The handkerchief muffled it but the words were clear enough.

'It wasn't suicide,' she said. 'I told them they'd made a mistake.'

'Mrs Patterson, I understand how hard it is to accept, but there can be no doubt.'

'No,' Dora said. 'Wilf wouldn't.'

She was right. Of course she was. There was no way Grandad would do that. It was all a terrible mistake.

'Mrs Patterson.' DC McCulloch ploughed on regardless. Clearly, she'd had the same training as I'd had about giving bad news. 'Your husband walked to the barrier and climbed over it. He stood on the bridge for a while looking down and then, as the train was about to pass under the bridge, he stepped off. We have a statement from an eyewitness. It was deliberate. There can be no doubt.'

A thought flashed through my brain. 'Are you sure it was him?'

'Yes.'

'It would have been very difficult for him to climb over anything. He was disabled, you know. He had polio as a child. His legs didn't work properly.'

'We are sure. He was wearing a leg brace and had ID on him. He climbed over at a place where a car had buckled the railings.' She paused. 'Mrs Patterson has already identified him from a photo. It's just his face. If you think it would help, I can show it to you. He looks deeply asleep, that's all.'

I nodded and she passed the photo to me.

It was Grandad. No doubt about it. His eyes were closed and part of the left side of his face was covered. The skin seemed tighter over his bones than it had in life but that only emphasised the lines of his face and made him look more like himself than ever.

Dora said something indistinct through the mask of her handkerchief.

'Pardon?'

She pulled it off her face and spoke again. 'The eyewitness. I want to talk to him. Or her.'

A sweet metallic scent. DC McCulloch gasped. Blood was trickling out from Dora's nose and gathering in the corners of her mouth. The door I'd smashed into her face had actually hurt her.

Chapter Four:
Phiney Wistman

14 June 2017
The day after the reunion

When Dora's nose wouldn't stop bleeding, the police took us and Jack to a hospital close by with an A&E full to bursting even though I told them it would be fine. Dora sat dabbing at her nose and rattling through the events of the day, time after time – getting home, the police waiting for her, coming to Coventry – then turning to me and muttering how it couldn't be suicide. Over and over again. I said nothing. I was beyond speaking, beyond piecing together my shattered thoughts to produce sentences. Eventually, the bleeding stopped of its own accord and we got up and left.

'We can always go back if it starts again,' she said. 'But I can't sit there any longer.'

For once I was in total agreement with her.

'Which way?' she asked when we were back on the pavement.

'Which way to where?'

She didn't have an answer.

The midsummer sun, still high in the sky, bathed the trees in the park opposite. The world felt wrong. 'Maybe you should go home?' I said at last. 'What time are the trains?'

'I can't go home. Not until I've spoken to this eyewitness, this Matthew Torrington.'

Her hands gripped the railing outside the hospital as though daring me to get rid of her. We'd argued in front of DC McCulloch about Matthew Torrington, the man who'd seen Grandad jump to his death. I wasn't sure if I wanted to meet him. Or, at least, not straightaway. I wanted a bit of time alone to... Well, I wasn't sure what I wanted, but I needed to be alone to think and that meant getting rid of Dora. So, when I realised she wasn't going anywhere until she'd won the argument, I'd agreed to let DC McCulloch contact him and give him my mobile number in case he was prepared to meet us.

'Let's go back to your flat and have a cup of tea while we wait.'

'We can get a cup of tea in the park,' I said, unwilling to let her install herself in my flat. 'There's no point going all the way over to mine and Jack could do with a run.'

He looked up from where he was sitting on the pavement, as close to Dora as he could get.

Dora sniffed then put a panicky hand up to her nose. It was OK, although the dried blood round her nostrils combined with her darting eyes and the hair escaping from her bun made her look like a victim of domestic violence. We trudged through the park towards the café by the crazy golf course. She winced every now and then and limped. Her shoes — black leather with a heel and a shine — were the kind of thing old people think you should wear with a skirt. They're no use for walking, though, and what is the point of a pair of shoes if you can't walk in them? I had trainers on.

Dora gave up when we were halfway there and sat on a bench under the trees, easing her right foot out of the shoe.

'You wait here,' I said. 'I'll get a couple of takeaway teas and bring them back. I won't be long.'

'Take Jack. And leave me your phone.'

'Why?'

'In case Matthew Torrington calls. You said I was the one who had to talk to him.'

I handed my phone over. 'Only answer it if it doesn't recognise the number.' I didn't want her speaking to any of my friends.

She looked at me blankly and I gave up. I ran a few hundred yards with Jack then dodged behind a tree, where Dora couldn't see me. I leaned back against its warm knobbly bark and tried to organise my mushy brain.

'It's shock, you know,' I said to Jack. 'I'm a nurse, so I know these things.'

But knowing didn't make my brain work any better. It bounced around like a two-year-old after too many sweets.

Grandad was dead and Grandad had killed himself.

It made no sense. He'd spent so much of his life fighting illness and death. I couldn't believe he'd have given up.

Another thought came to me.

He of all people knew how devastating his death would be for me and for Dora. Especially suicide. He wouldn't do that to us. He couldn't do that to us.

No. I thought Dora might be right. There'd been a mistake. He must have slipped and fallen. Or his leg had given way and he'd overbalanced. We needed to talk to this Matthew Torrington person and get out of him exactly what he had seen. I mean, how could he be so sure it was suicide? He was probably old and a bit past it. Confused, even.

I bought tea for Dora and some water for me – in a plastic bottle, which was all they had – and went back. She waved me to hurry as soon as she saw me. She was talking on my phone.

'Memorial Park,' she said. 'The Earlsdon side. We're on some benches. Under the trees.' She paused. 'Ten minutes, then. Yes, of course, we'll wait.'

She gave me my phone and took her tea.

'He's coming to see us now.'

'Here!'

'Well, I didn't want to walk any more.'

She sipped at her tea, pulled a face and put it on the ground. 'Stewed,' she said and straightened the pleats of her skirt, brushing off the specks of pollen that were floating down onto us from the trees clustered around the benches. It was a stupid place to put seats. Things fell off the trees all the time: bits of twig, old leaves and the occasional cone from the huge pine whose resinous scent cut through the air. Plus the planners had forgotten that birds spend a lot of time in trees and wherever birds perch, they also shit. All in all, it wasn't a great place to meet the eyewitness to Grandad's fall.

Snarky words came to my lips but I caught sight of Dora's hands. They were still smoothing the pleats of her skirt but they shook. Tiny little tremors that blurred their outline. She was nuts. And irritating. And often impossible. But she loved Grandad and the thought that he'd killed himself was too much for her to bear.

I passed her a couple of napkins and a bottle of water. 'You've got dried blood all over your nose. Let's try and wash it off before he gets here.'

We dabbed away until the worst came off.

A tentative voice interrupted us.

'Mrs Patterson?'

Matthew Torrington wasn't old and confused. He was around my own age, I guessed, and tall, although slightly stooped as if he were apologising for his existence. He had the sort of pale skin I associate with red hair except his was light brown and massively curly, like a mane around his head. He looked vaguely familiar but I'd come across a lot of people at work.

Dora nodded and gestured for him to sit with a jerky hand but he eyed the bird-shit-spattered bench at a right angle to ours and looked doubtful. I passed him some of the wodge of napkins I'd lifted from the café and hoped they'd protect his suit trousers and white shirt from the worst of the mess. Had he changed into them as some mark of respect for us? He looked deeply uncomfortable. The trousers were slightly too tight around his slightly too large waist and his cheeks were stained red either from embarrassment or walking from the car park. He really needed to do some exercise. Didn't he know how important it was to stay fit?

'Thank you,' Dora said to him. 'Thank you for coming to talk to us.'

'Er, no problem. I'm sorry... I mean... It's not a problem.'

Dora interrupted him. 'No,' she said in a sharp tone. 'Leave it alone.'

He looked startled.

'Jack,' I said, and pointed to the dog. He was eyeing up a confident pigeon approaching us to check we had no biscuits with our tea. We'd sat here so long Jack had decided it was our space and needed keeping clear.

'My husband's dog,' Dora said.

'I know. I've met him.' He made a clicking noise with his tongue, which Jack ignored. He flushed still redder.

'Mr Torrington,' Dora said.

'Mat,' he said swiftly.

'Er, Mat. The police said you were there when – when my husband – when the accident happened.' She said the word accident very firmly and with a short, chopping movement of her hand.

Mat hunched forward and rubbed his thumbs together. The skin round the nails was dry and rough. His aftershave was overwhelming. I leaned away.

'Mrs Patterson. I'm afraid… I'm really very, very sorry but it couldn't have been an accident. I know how terrible it must be for you but it wasn't, it really wasn't, an accident.'

The police had briefed him, I thought.

'Rubbish. My husband was –'

I talked over her. 'Could you just tell us what happened? Everything. All the details. No matter how insignificant they seem to you.'

He looked doubtful.

'We're struggling to believe it,' I added.

He took a deep breath and stared with unfocused eyes into the distance. I wished I could see what he was seeing.

'I was waiting for a train into town, on my way back from interviewing someone for a story, and I was writing up the notes on the platform. I'm a journalist, you see. Only freelance although the BBC sometimes use me.'

I knew why his face was familiar. I'd seen him on TV reporting about local things. Alarm prickled along my skin. 'We're not a story, you know. If you're talking to us because you want to write an article, you can leave now.'

'Of course not. That's not why I'm here.' But a deeper red tinged his cheeks and I suspected the thought had crossed his mind.

Dora waved her arm at him as though to say, *Go on.*

'Mr Patterson sat down by me,' he continued, 'but I was so concentrated on getting the story to the *Coventry Telegraph* I didn't notice. Anyway, I finished. A couple of trains were cancelled and I made some comment to Mr Patterson about his dog.'

'Yes,' Dora said. 'How was he?'

Mat shrugged his shoulders. 'I'm sorry, Mrs Patterson. We were two people waiting for a train. I didn't pay much attention. Another train was cancelled and he... he seemed to see me for the first time and he asked me if that meant the fast train would be the next one through.' The flush returned to his cheeks and he shifted on the seat. 'Are you sure you want me to go on?'

'Yes,' Dora said. Her eyes were half closed.

'I told him, yes, the next train through would be the fast one and he... got up. And he said he'd better be going then. There was no point waiting any longer. He sort of said it to himself so I didn't pay much attention. He went out of the station and I noticed he walked with a limp.'

'He had polio as a child,' I said.

'But he didn't let that stop him.' Dora's voice was fierce. 'He wouldn't let it make a difference.'

It wasn't quite as simple as that. Grandad was often in massive pain. His life had been endless operations and procedures and tough physio to keep him walking.

'Are you sure you want to hear the rest?' Mat asked.

Dora nodded and he continued, using his body as a shield to block any curious looks from the walkers on the main path. He spoke quietly but we hung on his every word.

We learned nothing DC McCulloch hadn't told us in the police station but hearing it from Mat's mouth, in Mat's words, Mat who'd been there, who had watched Grandad drag himself up the steps out of the station and then limp along the bridge over the railway, gave it shape and solidity.

He had a journalist's eye for detail and he told us every bit of it. At the top of the bridge, Grandad had looked over the edge. Mat hadn't thought anything of it. 'People look over all the time,' he said.

'You must have been watching him very closely,' I said, clinging onto a faint hope that Mat was – well, not inventing exactly, but colouring in the gaps between the things he'd actually seen. 'Why?'

He fiddled with the rough skin on his fingers before speaking. 'I'm sorry, but it was because of his limp and his dog. I wrote some articles about polio for a local museum. People's life stories as part of their exhibition to commemorate the sixtieth anniversary of the Coventry polio epidemic. They were very interesting and I was thinking about them and watching Mr Patterson at the same time. Besides, there was nothing else to watch. The station was deserted.' He gave me a slightly sharper look. 'I'm only telling you what I saw, you know.'

I nodded.

'Then,' Mat continued, 'he walked back a bit. Tied Jack to the barrier.' He paused. 'Are you sure about this?'

'Go on,' Dora said, but she huddled into herself, pushing her hands up the sleeves of her mac.

'We need to hear the truth,' I said. 'Every bit of it.' But the image of Grandad tying Jack up had sent chills spiking up my arms. He never tied him up. Jack was too well trained to need it.

'The train appeared in the distance. Mr Patterson sort of swung his leg over and stood for a second. I thought then... Never mind. It doesn't matter what I thought. He stepped off. He folded his arms and stepped off.'

He stopped. A film of sweat gleamed on the skin above his eyebrows.

My head was full of memories of Grandad folding his arms. Folding his arms at Mum's funeral. Folding his arms when he told me he was going to need another operation. Folding his arms when I failed every GCSE the year after Mum's death. I knew what his face would have looked like when he stepped off the bridge. It would have been the same expression he always wore when he folded his arms. A look of patient determination to get through whatever had just been thrown at him. A tremor shook deep inside me. I started to believe in his suicide.

Mat leaned forward and patted Dora's arm.

She was weeping. Tears ran down her face and dropped onto her hands, for once lying motionless on her skirt.

Grandad had become a stranger. Someone who was capable of cutting all the ties that bound us to him with a single violent and uncaring stroke. I couldn't bear it. Because the Grandad I knew would never have stepped off that bridge. The Grandad I knew battled through everything without complaining. The Grandad I knew would have known how much hurt he was inflicting.

An echo of my thoughts came from Dora's mouth. 'How could he?' she whispered.

'Not how,' I said to Dora. 'Not how, but why?'

Something terrible must have happened. I clung onto the thought. Only something terrible would have made him do it. 'Why did he do it?' I said to her. 'You have to explain to me. Why did he do it?'

She looked at me for a long time, although I thought she was seeing other things. 'I have no idea,' she said, in the end. 'No idea.'

Chapter Five:
Phiney Wistman

14 June 2017
The day after the reunion

Dora came back to my flat. I didn't know what else to do. Mat's description of Grandad's last moments had made the reality of his suicide inescapable and Dora's inability to string more than a couple of words together alarmed me. Anyway, I didn't want her to go now. She must know something about why Grandad had killed himself but I could hardly bombard her with questions while she sat, white-faced and trembling, in the shifting shade of the trees.

'Thanks,' I said as Mat pulled into the area of broken paving outside my flat. 'It was very kind of you to come and meet us. And to give us a lift.'

Which it was. The spotless seats and the smell of plastic cleaning spray, together with the casual way he pointed out the sparkling white car in the car park, showed his pride in it. However, he didn't even wince when Jack scrabbled into the back and leaned his head on Mat's shoulder so his nose could stick out of the window.

'No problem.'

He opened the passenger door and helped Dora out. She headed towards the front door without a word.

'It's hit her hard,' he said. 'I guess she hoped I was... well, going to tell her something else.' He kicked the broken edge of a flagstone.

'Yes.' The flatness of my tone made him look even more uncomfortable and I tried to think of something kind to say. It couldn't have been easy talking to us.

'Well, I'll be off,' he said. 'If there's anything I can do… I mean *anything*. You've got my number.'

Dora walked back towards us. 'If you remember anything else, will you let me know?'

'Of course.'

She fumbled in her bag, found an old envelope with a shopping list and scribbled her home phone number on it.

I watched him reverse and head out into the early evening traffic, driving with a confidence that seemed to belie his diffident demeanour. A whisper of doubt crept into my mind. He was strangely awkward for a journalist. And, it occurred to me, surprisingly quick to come and see us. Was it all a front? I hoped we weren't going to feature in some story in the *Coventry Telegraph*.

Dora didn't seem to notice the mess in my flat. I called it a flat but it was really a single room with a kitchen along one side and a tiny shower room off the far corner. It contained a bed and an armchair that had come from Grandad and Dora's old house and, on hot days like today, exuded a scent of dog and furniture polish.

Normally, it was super tidy. There wasn't enough space to let things get out of control but, during the weeks since the blood test, I'd slightly lost the plot.

Dora headed for the chair, picked up the pile of dirty laundry and looked around for somewhere to put it.

'Chuck it on the bed,' I said and slid the two big sash windows open. They looked out over the ragged lawn and brambles of the communal garden. They were old, so made of wood, and were the main reason I'd rented the flat, along with the wooden floor. I couldn't avoid PVC at work but I wasn't going to live cocooned in its nasty chemicals.

Dora flopped into the chair and stared into space. Jack went over and sat down on her feet.

'I'll make you a cup of tea,' I said, feeling utterly helpless. 'I've only got long life milk, though.'

I put the kettle on, washed a couple of cups, dropped a tea bag in each and tried to assemble my thoughts. Why? Why had Grandad done it?

'Money,' I said to myself as I dripped some lavender oil into my diffuser. I had a vague idea it might be good for shock.

'What?' Dora roused herself.

'Talking to myself.'

But she'd heard. It had just taken time to travel through the numbed pathways in her brain.

'We don't have any money worries. We're not rich but we've got enough to live on. Pensions, and Harry, Wilf's father, left him quite a bit, which he'd never touched until we bought the cottage. We used some of it in the renovation. Anyway, Wilf wouldn't let money...' Her voice trailed away and she went back to staring into the distance.

Not money, then. Dora was right.

Illness, I wondered.

Illness runs through my family like a pulled thread puckering its fabric and leaving a line of holes behind it.

My grandad with his life distorted by polio.

My grandmother, his first wife, who died of cancer when I was a child, leaving me with only the vaguest memories of her. I remembered having to be quiet when we went round on Sundays so as not to wake her, and the heat in the house because she felt the cold. And the smell of violets. She ate violet sweets when she could eat nothing else.

I never knew my father's parents. The flu epidemic of 1969 carried them off within a week of each other and left my father prone to chest infections for the rest of his not very long life. It developed into chronic obstructive pulmonary disease, aggravated by his inability to give up smoking.

And then there was my mother. She had been diagnosed with breast cancer a few weeks after Grandad married Dora. We fought it every step of the way. There were months and months when we thought she'd won but they were merely pauses in its inexorable march through her body. It took five years to kill her and I struggle still to think of the last one. We'd moved in with Dora and Grandad by then and the cancer had overcome her to the point where leaving the house was only for emergencies and treatment. I tried to be an angel. Tried and largely succeeded. Except with Dora. She did everything: getting me off to school in the morning, cooking, cleaning, laundry. Plus looking after Mum, who needed more and more help with washing and eating and, eventually, with everything. I wanted to look after Mum myself and I couldn't forgive Dora for being her carer. Even now the unhappy and angry teenager from that time still occasionally escaped from the place where I kept her hidden.

'Health,' I said. 'Was Grandad ill?'

Dora looked away. I felt sick.

'Was he ill?' I repeated.

'No.'

'You don't sound very sure.'

She sighed. 'He's had a few problems in the last couple of months. His leg has been bothering him.' She lifted up her hand to stop me interrupting. 'Weakness and a bit of pain.'

She didn't get it. She never got it. For her to notice, it must have been bad.

'Post-polio syndrome,' I said.

'Possibly.' Dora dragged the word out of herself.

Ever since they'd discovered that, decades after people had recovered from polio, the muscles they'd worked on and built up through years of painful physio could fail again, I'd worried about Grandad.

'You should have told me.'

'He didn't want to. He thought it would upset you. And besides, we weren't at all sure.'

I opened my mouth to tell her that *she* should have told me anyway.

And shut it. Because it wasn't fair. I hadn't given Dora a chance to speak to me properly since I'd told them both the big lie.

I sloshed some milk in Dora's tea and passed it to her. She gulped it down, spilling some over the duvet on the bed beside her.

'Leave it,' I said as she started to lever herself up. 'It's only a few drops.'

She pursed her lips together and the familiar feeling of irritation with her rose in me. What did a few drops of tea matter when Grandad was dead?

'Don't you think,' I said, 'it might have been the thought of going through polio all over again that…' I did my best to keep my voice calm.

She started to go on and on about how they'd always known it might happen and it was why they'd bought the cottage in Matlock. Right by the main street so it was easy for Wilf to get out and see people and do things if his mobility got worse. And they'd had the cottage adapted before they moved in. Besides, Wilf was a fighter. He'd never given up and he wouldn't have now. On and on she went.

I spoke over her. 'His consultant, what's his name? The one down here. The one he saw for years.'

'Mr Standing?'

'Yes.'

For the first time Dora looked unsure. 'You think that's why Wilf came down?' She stood up, dislodging Jack from her feet, and started pacing the side of the room where the windows were. 'Maybe you're right. Wilf trusted him. He knew Mr Standing would tell him what the future held. Where's your phone?'

'Why?'

'I'm going to find out.'

She called Mr Standing's office, gazing out of the window and turning her back on me, but I heard everything. I keep my mobile on loudspeaker. It's better than holding a potential source of radiation to your ear.

Grandad hadn't been there yesterday, though. In fact, Mr Standing hadn't seen him for months. Did Mrs Patterson want to make an appointment? Dora's voice quavered when she said no and she rang off sharpish.

'See,' she said, but there was no triumph in her voice.

'So why, then?'

'I've told you, Phiney, I don't know. I don't know. I don't know.' She pushed aside the stack of recycling on the worktop and leaned over it as she spoke, digging her knuckles into the Formica. 'Except...'

'Except what?'

'Oh God, Phiney. Years ago. After Carol... your mother died. Wilf was bad for quite a while. The doctor diagnosed clinical depression, triggered by your mum's death. They said Wilf's history of illness and childhood trauma because of the polio made him more likely to suffer from depression. We got through it, though.'

One hand lifted to her mouth and she gnawed at a knuckle.

'I didn't know,' I said.

'We didn't tell you. You had enough to deal with. They say that once you've had it – depression – you're at high risk of it coming back. I always knew that. Do you...?'

The little we'd learned about depression during my mental health lectures seemed to have vanished but I was sure she was right.

'I phoned him every day while I was away,' she said, 'and he seemed fine. I was on Gillian's mobile so it was just a quick chat. Maybe he was a bit quieter than normal but Wilf was always more of a listener than a talker.'

'I don't think depression would come on that suddenly. Not without a trigger.'

'Well, I don't know,' she said, and started her pacing to and fro again. 'If anything, he was happier than he had been for ages, you know, because of your test results.'

My thoughts slid away from the lie I'd told them. Now was not the time to reveal the truth about the tests.

'If only the police had given us his things,' I said. 'We'd have his phone and we could see if he'd called anyone down here.'

Dora stared at me. 'Can you do that?'

'Of course. If you know his password.'

She marched over to the carrier bag she'd brought with her, her skirt swishing, and pulled out Jack's harness and its pouches. He came and sat by her, his eyes trained on her hands. 'Wilf only carried his wallet on him. He let Jack carry everything else.'

She emptied the pouches onto the bed. There wasn't much. His ancient mobile phone, a handkerchief, a jotter, a book, a hotel receipt and a train ticket. Dora picked up the hotel receipt.

'He must have come down yesterday. This is for last night.'

She grabbed the train ticket while I checked his phone.

'What's his passcode?' I asked.

'240392.'

It was my date of birth. When I looked, though, I discovered that Grandad hadn't made or received any calls for weeks, apart from ones to or from me.

'Nothing,' I said.

'Look,' Dora said. 'The ticket to Tile Park is a return. He meant to come back.'

She was having a serious wobble. Full on with shaking hands and tears starting to fall. I made a big effort to speak gently.

'Maybe.'

She picked up the book. I picked up the jotter. Grandad used it for lists and reminders, but he ripped each page out once finished and the only ones left were blank. I held the jotter up to the light but there were no indentations to decipher.

Dora was looking at the book. 'He bought this yesterday,' she said, examining the receipt that he'd used as a bookmark.

It was a history of astronomical clocks. Typical Grandad. I forced myself to think.

'A note,' I said. 'Are you sure he didn't leave a note? At home?'

'I didn't see anything.' She turned sharply, knocking some clothes off the bed. 'But I didn't look very hard. I should have searched the house before I left. But I was so sure it was an accident. I just wanted to get down here and put the police right.'

'He'd have left a note.'

'Of course he would.'

For a brief moment we were united.

'I'm going home.' She picked up her bag and Jack looked up at her expectantly. 'I'll have to get a taxi to the station. Will you call me one, Phiney? And you might have to lend me some money?' She looked outside at the sky, now dissolving from blue to light pink. 'Will there still be trains?' And finally, 'Phiney, do you think you could come back with me? I don't think I...'

She started to shiver.

'Of course. You can't seriously think I'm not desperate to see if Grandad has left a note too?'

It was after midnight when we stumbled out of the taxi. The last train to Matlock had long gone when we reached Derby. Dora was still fired up. She'd talked and muttered to herself the whole journey. Running through the places Grandad might have left a note, turning to me every few minutes to say she was sure there would be one. He wasn't the sort of person not to leave a note. Locked into her own thoughts, she didn't need replies from me so I watched the darkness stain the sky until outside was nothing but black, pierced by the occasional light from a cottage high up on the hills.

There was no note.

I sat in an armchair by the unlit gas fire and listened as Dora tore through the kitchen cupboards, then ran to their bedroom where the thud of drawers opening and closing and the slide of wardrobe doors revealed her desperation. No one would hide a suicide note in a cupboard or a drawer. Despite the residual heat from the long June day, I was cold. Jack retired to his bed at the far end of the kitchen.

Doors slammed and Dora's footsteps tapped wild patterns on the wooden floor as she raced back through the kitchen.

'How could he?' She sat on the bottom step of the stairs and started to cry in rasping gasps. Jack came through and stared at her and I realised I was doing the same.

I sighed. Words couldn't heal this.

I forced myself out of the chair and sat on the stairs next to her, putting my arms around her shoulders and wishing I didn't feel so utterly emptied out. Wishing things were easier between us.

'How could he?' she said again. 'I made him promise when he asked me to marry him, promise me that he'd always tell me the truth. Tell me what he thought. I don't always read people right. And I miss things. I like people to say what they mean. But they don't.'

We were crammed together on the step, the heat from our bodies soaking into each other.

'It's all so muddled,' she went on. 'I'm angry with him and then I'm angry with myself. I keep thinking I missed something. I shouldn't have gone away. I'll never forgive myself. He wouldn't have done it if I'd been with him.'

What could I say? In my deepest depths, the same thought had stirred. If only Dora hadn't gone away.

'It wasn't your fault,' I said. I dredged deep for some better words. 'I know you loved him. No one could have done more for him than you did.'

She started weeping in a noisy and snuffling sort of way and I gave her a proper hug. It was too simple to blame Dora. She was an easy target with her slightly odd ways.

After a while, her breathing calmed.

'Tissues,' she said to Jack. And then again. 'Tissues.'

He lumbered to his feet, disappeared into the kitchen and came back with a box of Kleenex in his mouth and his tail wagging furiously.

'Good boy.' And then to me: 'I'm going to bed. Give me a hand up, will you, Phiney?'

I pulled her to her feet and watched her walk slowly to their bedroom. At the door, she turned and said, 'There's bedding in the wardrobe in your room. Can you manage?'

'Of course.'

'And would you turn the lights out?'

I nodded.

'Thank you.'

She turned back at the door and her words were laced with grit. 'If we can find out what all this is about, maybe I'll be able to forgive him… and myself.'

She looked as though there was more she'd have liked to say but it was beyond her.

I let Jack out into the yard. He did his business, then nosed around Grandad's shed, checking to see which of the neighbours' cats had dared to visit in his absence, while I watched and tried to keep my brain empty. Then I went upstairs to bed and wrapped myself tight in the sheets and blanket as though they could protect me from the thoughts grinding through my head.

Chapter Six:
Phiney Wistman

15 June 2017
Two days after the reunion

In the morning, my first thought was Grandad's shed.

Dora was downstairs, already washed and dressed, dry eyed but tense, prone to wrapping an arm round her body. She was on the phone to the vicar, fixing a date for the funeral. I made coffee as she called the undertakers, who told her they couldn't do anything until the coroner released the body. She called the police, who told her they didn't know when that would be, so she rang the vicar back and cancelled the funeral. All the time striding round and round, scribbling notes on the back of an envelope and drinking cup after cup of tea. I muttered something and slipped out into the back yard. Jack followed me as though he too wanted to escape the maelstrom of efficiency in the house. He settled down on the flagstones in the sun as I went into Grandad's shed.

It was a wooden building, a tool shed with electricity and a large window looking out over the small back garden. It smelled of the grease with which Grandad cleaned the tiny parts of the clocks he loved making. He fabricated every last piece himself, cutting, shaping, pressing, filing and polishing each metal element. It took a long time, which, as Mum used to say, was a blessing in disguise because otherwise we'd have run out of wall space for the clocks years ago.

The shed was very neat. A counter running along one side was crammed with lathes and presses, sanders and even a scroll saw. On the other side, shelves of clearly marked boxes lined the wall above the work surface. Grandad had taken one down and left it out. A cardboard box with cracked corners and sagging sides. *Harry* was written on the front. In faded green felt tip. Harry was Grandad's father, my great-grandfather, famed in our family for turning to drink after years of Presbyterian teetotalism and dying from falling down some steps after a drunken night in the pub. I supposed it was a box of his old stuff. Inside was a mess of papers, as though Grandad had dumped everything back in after he'd found what he was looking for, which I guessed was the newspaper cutting by the side of the box under the desk lamp.

I picked it up, curious to see what Grandad had been searching for before he'd left for Coventry.

The cutting was old, very old. July 1957, *Coventry Evening Telegraph*. A short article and a photo showing a group of eight people outside a wrought iron gate, set into brick walls with a sign saying *Poulters Pharmaceuticals*.

Why had Grandad been looking at this? Poulters were an old Coventry firm, a big local employer and embedded in the fabric of the city through their support of local charities and sponsorship of events, although their operations had spread far beyond the Midlands over the years. My great-grandfather, drunken Harry, had worked for them all his life apart from during the war.

I read the short article.

For Poulters – It's a Family Affair

Mr Richard Poulter today announced Poulters will be doubling their staff over the next two years in preparation for the move from the company's current premises at Berkswell House into the new business park at Mitchellston. And what better way to start than bringing in the younger generation? Michael, Mr Poulter's son, (18yrs) will be helping out in the Research and Development Laboratory over summer while Mr Harry Patterson, Transport & Warehousing Manager, has employed his son Wilfred (15yrs) to help over the busy summer period.

Just a puff piece for a local business, typical of the kind of thing the *Telegraph* still published. I hadn't known Grandad had worked for Poulters one summer. After he'd left school, he'd gone to work at a local bank and worked his way up through the ranks.

Grandad was in the picture. A very young Grandad. He was sitting on a trolley on the left. If you looked carefully you could see his leg was held out straight. The middle-aged man standing behind him with his hand on his shoulder was his father, Harry. Another youngster stood on Harry's right. According to the caption under the photograph, this was Philip Mason but there were no further indications as to who he was.

Did this have anything to do with Grandad's death? Or was it a coincidence?

I'd never heard of Berkswell House or, if I had, I'd forgotten, but there was an area on the outskirts of Coventry called Berkswell, where the city gave way to the rolling countryside. And it was very close to Tile Park railway station.

I looked at the photo more closely.

Richard Poulter, middle aged and portly, was the pinstriped figure in the middle with a neatly trimmed moustache and an aura of importance. His son, Michael, stood close by but the others had left a little distance around him.

Next to Richard Poulter stood another older man. Owen Greenacre, I read, Laboratory Manager. Neither Richard nor he were smiling but, whereas Richard looked serious and important, Owen looked grim. Maybe it was his bushy moustache that made him look so dour.

Jean Storer, dressed in a lab coat, was the only woman present and, according to the caption, Poulters' Chief Scientist. She looked very young to have had such a high-powered position back in the fifties. She must have been quite something.

But it was the man on Jean's right who drew my attention. While the others were all staring into the camera, something had caught his attention and he was looking away. A trick of the light had given his face a definition the others lacked and, I saw, he was good-looking in a sort of Jude Law way – blonde, very, very blonde.

He was called Victor Leadsom. No clue as to his title, but Grandad had taken a pen, the blue biro that lay on the counter beside the article, underlined his name and put a question mark after it.

Chapter Seven:
Vivian Reynolds

2/3 July 1957
The night of the incident

The door to Victor Leadsom's office in the main building of Berkswell House slammed after Vivian as she tore in. For a moment she thought the glass pane had cracked, such had been the force of the bang still echoing through the empty building, but it was only the shadow of a pipe cast by the corridor light. The gold lettering on the glass announcing that this was Victor's office was still intact. She winced when she caught sight of it, with its reminder of everything that was wrong.

The radium dial on the clock glowed in a dark corner. Eleven thirty, it said. In half an hour's time it would be the third of July. Vivian's birthday and, also, Marie Curie's. In ten years' time, she'd be as old as Marie Curie had been when she discovered radium. Vivian had dreamed of achieving a similar feat but now, with the shirt under her lab coat still damp from the sweat of her earlier terror, and her breathing ragged from the speed of her flight, she thought she'd be happy merely to get out of here and live a dull but safe life.

She locked the door behind her and reached for the light switch, then thought better of it. There was enough light from the corridor filtering through the glass to read the records and the office lamp glaring out into the night would make her easy to find.

She forced herself to sit on the far corner of the desk, out of view of the window, while she calmed her breathing. Maybe she was mistaken; please, God, let her be wrong for once.

Half an hour later, she knew she wasn't.

The others were still out there, hunting. How long before they realised they weren't going to find what they were after in the huts scattered throughout the grounds and came looking for her in the main house instead? Through the dark window she saw the glimmer of torches as they moved from hut to hut. They'd blame her. She was sure. Panic gripped and spun her thoughts just when she needed to think clearly and decide what to do.

She should have followed her first instincts and fled. It had been a mistake to come to this small misshapen room underneath the stairs, now used as an office. It was one of many into which the larger once-elegant space had been divided by ramshackle partitions after the bombing had forced Poulters out of the centre of Coventry. But she'd had to know the truth.

Should she stay here or should she slip away?

The familiarity of the room was comforting. But it was also full of things that needed to be dealt with. The certificates bearing Victor's name on the mantelpieces above the fireplace, blocked in with hardboard surrounding a small electric fire. The cupboards and shelves that filled the alcoves containing notes for a paper on the long-term effects of mustard gas – each page headed by the title, date and Victor's name.

She felt sick. Maybe it would be simpler if Victor died.

Part of the brown linoleum had lifted in one corner to reveal the dull gold of a parquet floor. Vivian had noticed the old house trying to hold its own beneath the series of hasty alterations that the needs of each ensuing year had thrust upon it. She'd once asked Owen, who lived locally, about the history of the house but Owen had pushed his thick and rough-skinned lips up into his greying moustache and shrugged.

The thought of Owen made her force her skittering mind back to the present. Should she call Owen?

No. Owen didn't like her. She'd seen it in the way he kept his distance, as though he could smell that Vivian was different. Men like Owen hated anything different. The war seemed to have robbed them of the capacity for independent thought. They clung to their rigid beliefs as though they were liferafts in a stormy sea, never questioning anything.

She'd call Jean.

At the thought of Jean, she felt the first stirrings of hope. Could Jean save them? She'd applied for the job because of Jean. Tipped off by one of her tutors at Cambridge. Jean Storer was bright, he'd said, very bright, just spent a couple of years as a research assistant at the Connaught Labs in Canada and very well thought of there, so it was a bit of a surprise that she'd chosen to return to Great Britain and to a small company like Poulters. He could only think she'd been promised resources and funding for her own research because she was ambitious. Hugely ambitious and with a fierce determination that meant she was likely to reach the very top. Vivian could do worse than hitch her wagon to Jean's star, the tutor had said with a knowing wink. If she didn't mind working for a woman.

Of course, she hadn't minded. It horrified her that people thought she'd prefer to work for a man. Although Jean was never very womanly. She didn't wear make-up. She didn't wear jewellery. She kept her hair tied back tightly so that Vivian never knew if she'd had it cut and what little Vivian could see of her clothes revealed they were as much a uniform as her lab coat. Not for her, the excitement of new fashions after years of austerity, of Dior's changing dress shapes, of the sudden availability of lipstick and nylons and beautiful, beautiful shoes. She didn't pore over the latest pictures of Grace Kelly and Marilyn Monroe like the secretaries. Vivian wondered if Jean kept all that for home. Maybe she had a secret life strictly separated from work. Maybe she had a wardrobe full of tightly waisted, brightly coloured skirts and dresses with little matching sweaters to slip on top of them and neat pillbox hats.

But Vivian wouldn't think about that now. She shouldn't be thinking about anything but the horror that was about to unfold. Except her mind refused to focus on the reality of what might lie ahead and, instead, leapt around her memories as though they might contain a solution.

Her tutor had been right. Richard had promised Jean great things. Once the summer was over, they were moving, Jean had told Vivian, pointing to the plans and visuals lining the pockmarked and chipped paint of her office wall. A campus-like park, a temple to research and development. It was going to be stunning. And Jean would be running it. If Vivian wanted to, she could follow Jean all the way to the top.

If she wanted to. Even then, she hadn't been sure.

'It's not you, Jean,' she'd said. 'It's not Poulters either. It's everything. It's this country. I need a change. I want to go somewhere where people are freer, not so hidebound by the past. I know you don't agree but attitudes like Owen's are more entrenched than you think.'

'Owen.' Jean had dismissed him with a wave of her hand. 'Owen's star is waning. Richard's realising the reality behind the war hero. Oh, he won't get rid of him, but he'll move him somewhere he can't do any harm.' She'd stood, pushing her chair back with one violent movement, her equilibrium for once knocked out of kilter by the force of her passion. 'You should stay. I'm going to do great things here. Believe me. The future of research is with the pharmaceutical companies. They're all realising the huge profits they can make from developing new drugs and they're all investing heavily.'

Vivian had smiled and nodded her head, but she didn't think it was going to be as easy as Jean thought. She was a woman. Women didn't run laboratories, even now in 1957. Women were assistants, secretaries, helpers. People didn't want change. That was the problem.

She realised she wasn't going to call Jean. She was already thinking about Jean and Poulters in the past tense. She was starting to shut her boss away in the parts of her head where she kept the bullies from school, her friends from university and the lover she'd tried so hard to keep happy but failed.

She was going to leave now. Move on again. Get away before the others found her. She should have left straightaway.

And then the hammering on the door started.

They'd found her.

Chapter Eight:
Phiney Wistman

15 June 2017
Two days after the reunion

Dora didn't know anything about Grandad working at Poulters, she told me.

'Why are you asking?' Her manic efficiency spurt had faded and she was slumped in the leather armchair, picking at the hem of her skirt.

I showed her the newspaper cutting. 'This was out on Grandad's worktop. It came from a box marked *Harry*.'

She sighed. 'I've been asking Wilf to sort through the boxes of old stuff since we moved. Harry worked at Poulters all his life apart from the war and he never threw anything away. It was all in the attic in Coventry.' Her voice sounded as though it had been pushed through a sieve and had all the life removed.

'And the people in the photo? Do you know who they are?'

'No. Just Poulters employees Harry worked with.'

'Are you sure?'

She took the cutting and looked more closely. 'Never heard of any of them except Philip Mason. He's an old friend of Wilf's. They lived in the same street as children and kept vaguely in touch. A teacher. He moved to the Lake District when he retired. With his partner. We haven't seen much of him since.'

'I might give him a call.'

'Why?'

'In case he knows anything.'

'Phiney. This newspaper article is sixty years old. It's not going to have anything to do with Wilf's death.'

'You never know. Finding it must have been one of the last things Grandad did before he left for Coventry.'

'People don't kill themselves because of something that happened sixty years ago. It's just a coincidence.'

She had a point but I couldn't let it go. The newspaper article was the only thing Grandad had left out.

'We're going to have to let people know about Grandad's death anyway,' I said.

She picked up a battered address book from the coffee table. The kind with a slot for a pencil down its spine. 'I've been going through this, making lists of people to tell. Just I don't know what to tell them.' She flicked through the book. 'Here you are. Philip Mason. Call him if you want to. What do I know, after all? If Wilf kept his reasons for killing himself secret from me, what else might he have kept hidden?'

It was grief making her so prickly. I got that. It was doing the same to me. I took the address book and wondered if I should stay with her but she saw my hesitation and shook her head.

'Go on,' she said. 'I'm better alone. The vicar's coming round soon anyway.'

I went back to the shed and thought about calling Philip Mason. Put his number in a couple of times but couldn't quite bring myself to press call. What was I going to say? Instead, I googled him. But there were hundreds of Philip Masons. The name was too common.

I tried Victor Leadsom. It was an odd enough name to limit the results. But I found nothing. Not even a Facebook page or a LinkedIn entry.

I turned my attention to the others. Jean Storer's name came up frequently as the co-author of scientific articles and research. But it was Michael Poulter who yielded most results. He was chairman of Poulters Pharmaceuticals and heavily involved in charity work. Or he had been.

Because he was dead. He'd died yesterday morning. Like Grandad.

Chapter Nine:
Michael Poulter

3 July 1957
The night of the incident

No one spoke while they waited in the lodge of Berkswell House. To Michael Poulter, the silence felt solid, as if it was holding them in stasis until someone, Jean, he supposed, arrived and told them what to do. The exact circumstances of what had happened were unclear to him. Not that it mattered. It was clearly a catastrophe.

But he was only a bystander.

He picked his coat up from the counter in the lodge. None of this was anything to do with him, he thought. He'd go. It was one thirty in the morning. No buses at this time of night, so he'd have to walk back to his digs. He didn't mind because he was desperate to get away. The walk would take him half an hour. Half an hour of fresh night air and then a quick cup of tea and the next chapter of his book before sleep. He'd leave a note for his landlady telling her not to wake him in the morning. He'd stay in Coventry until he knew if the police wanted to talk to him and then he'd go and join some friends in Scotland who were spending the summer picking raspberries. His spirits rose. Thank God he wasn't at home. Thank God his father had said it would be more sensible for Michael to stay in digs closer to Berkswell House while he was working there this summer. His father would be too busy dealing with the aftermath to come to his digs to bully him.

The last thing Michael had wanted was to spend his summer working for Poulters but it had seemed a small price to pay in return for his father funding him through university. If there was one thing these weeks spent trailing round after Jean and Victor had shown him, it was that he was totally unsuited to the work. It would disappoint his father, who had ideas of the Poulter name becoming as well known and long-lived as Cadbury's or Clark's. But then that dream was probably dead in the water after tonight.

He promised himself he'd never come back to Poulters.

Harry, standing by the open door and tamping down the tobacco in his pipe with a thick-skinned thumb, eyed him uneasily. Owen, sitting on a stool by the counter, one hand resting on its surface amid the clutter of date stamps and bulldog clips and the brown sponges used to moisten the stamps for anything sent through the post, cleared his throat and pushed back the lank sections of hair that had slipped from their position over his balding skull. Owen's hand shook. Michael knew they'd be uneasy about him leaving but wouldn't stop him. He was the boss's son, after all.

The noise of the side gate creaking open and clanging shut broke the silence. Harry stepped away from the door as Jean strode in, waving the vestiges of pipe smoke away. Michael felt the tension in the room mount. Harry and Owen didn't like Jean and they were beyond hiding it. Their dislike, as pungent as Harry's fumes, poisoned the atmosphere.

'Where's Victor? Where's the body?' Jean cut off Owen's gruff greetings.

Of course, Michael thought, Jean would want to see for herself. She was wearing the same lab coat as yesterday and her hands clutched and released its loose folds, leaving deep and grime-edged creases.

'Still in Hut 19.' Harry answered her after a moment's hesitation.

She nodded for longer than was necessary, as though the motion gave an outlet for the stress holding her body rigid. 'I've spoken to Mr Poulter,' she went on in a voice that vibrated with some emotion Michael couldn't identify. 'He's waiting for me to call him back with the details. He was surprised you hadn't called him straightaway, Owen.'

Her needling broke through Owen's barely-held-together composure and he launched into a tirade about Victor. About how he'd always known it was a mistake to employ someone so young. How they never would have if there hadn't been a shortage of good men since the war. This was the next stage, Michael thought. The one where everybody tried to avoid responsibility by blaming each other. Thank God he was going to be out of it!

Strangely enough, Owen's rant seemed to calm Jean and she smoothed the creases of her lab coat and pushed the stray wisps of hair back into her ponytail. She cut Owen off.

'I employed Victor,' she said. 'Nothing wrong with him. The only problem here is the nineteenth-century attitudes of people like you, Owen. And, as for you, Harry, it's time you got a grip.' She whisked round and headed for the door.

'Where are you going?' Owen asked.

She gave him a cool look. 'Hut 19, of course. Richard said to deal with everything. The… the remains need to be disposed of. The hut needs to be cleaned before the staff arrive. Do you want to help?'

Michael pulled his thoughts away from what he'd seen in Hut 19. It would be a long time before he could forget those eyes, full of horror and fear. Even after death had taken away the pain.

Jean's lips stretched in a tight smile when Michael shook his head.

'You all wait here then. I'll be back as soon as I've finished. None of you were thinking of going anywhere, were you?'

She left without waiting for an answer. Owen blew into his moustache. The thick silence momentarily blown away by Jean's fierce energy engulfed them once more as they waited for her to come back and tell them what to do. Michael knew he couldn't leave. Or, at least, not yet.

Afterwards, Jean told Michael to help Harry clear up the debris in the lodge while she and Owen went up to the main house to wait for Richard to arrive. It looked as though a bar room brawl had taken place there with files and papers strewn everywhere.

The tidying took forever, mainly because Harry had a tendency to stop in the midst of the chaos and stare at the wall. When the lodge finally returned to its habitual busy-but-under-control appearance, Michael glanced at his watch. Six thirty now. The early shift would start arriving any minute. He considered slipping away without saying a word. What was there to say anyway? But just as he was thinking he would actually do it, Harry stirred himself out of his thoughts and spoke.

'You going back to your digs, then, Mr Michael?'

'I think so, Harry.'

He watched something calculating slide across the older man's face.

'Quite right too. It's nothing to do with you. Would you mind running Wilfred home? You can use one of the vans. There's no point him staying either.'

He opened the door to his inner office, a tiny room where the lodge keeper used to sit up in the old days waiting for the family to come back from balls and parties. Wilf was there, eyes shut and sitting in the only comfortable chair, with his leg in its heavy callipers resting on a cardboard box. He must have been there since Harry had sent him back to the lodge and asked Michael to help instead because Wilf was in too much pain to be of any use. Wilf really wasn't fit for a job as a porter, manhandling boxes and tanks from department to department as the different products moved through the manufacturing process, but Poulters were desperate for staff so no one had objected when Harry had taken him and his friend Philip on for the summer.

'It won't be more than five minutes out of your way,' Harry said. 'You can drop the van back anytime. There's no point both of you hanging around. Neither of you is to blame.'

It was the wheedling note in Harry's voice that made Michael pause. Harry wanted Wilf out of the way before the fallout started. It was fair enough. The lad needed to be home and in bed but Michael began to wonder if Harry had an ulterior motive.

'Philip.' Harry's shout startled Michael. Harry stuck his head out into the lodge where Philip Mason, just arrived for the early shift, hovered.

'I was looking for Wilf, Mr Patterson.' Philip's shiny face bore witness to a brutal morning cleansing routine but nothing seemed to rid him of the acne that spattered his face. Michael touched his own skin without meaning to. It felt rough and greasy but still smooth.

'What's happened, Mr Patterson?' Philip's voice cut through the silence as Harry helped Wilf out of his chair.

'You'll know soon enough.'

'But...'

'Like I said, lad, you'll know soon enough.' Harry's gruff voice snapped into angry tones.

Michael saw the puzzlement on Philip's face change to worry. He understood. Harry was going to blame Philip. That was what this was all about. The lining up of a scapegoat. And, of course, Philip was the obvious one. Poor lad. He was only fifteen or sixteen. Much too young to deal with what was coming.

'Michael?' Harry said again.

Michael put his arms round Wilf's thin body and helped him to the door, struggling at his unexpected weight.

'Let me give you a hand, Mr Michael.' Philip moved towards them.

'You leave him alone.' There was no disguising the disgust in Harry's voice. 'You've done enough damage already.'

The skin on Philip's bony face thinned and paled as though an invisible hand were cranking it tighter from behind, making his acne stand out all the more.

'I'm sorry, Phil.' Wilf's face was white and sweaty with pain. 'I've got to go home. If I move my leg, it's bad. Really bad. It feels as though the muscle is peeling away from the bone.' He hadn't been asleep, Michael thought. All those hours he'd appeared asleep, he'd been holding himself rigidly motionless, trying to control the pain in his leg.

'Don't worry,' Michael said. 'I'll have you home in a jiffy and then you can rest it properly.'

'Just drop Wilf off,' Harry said. 'He'll manage after that. Then you can go home.'

But Michael knew his bed and his book would have to wait, as would the trip to Scotland. He didn't want to come back but he couldn't let them blame it all on Philip. He couldn't walk away. And he wondered dully if this was going to be the shape of his life. If his dreams of escape were nothing more than the futile fluttering of a bird's wings beating against its cage as the door closed.

Chapter Ten:
Harry Patterson

10 July 1957
One week after the incident

Harry poked a stick into the bin, breaking up the thick piles that smouldered rather than burned. He shouldn't have put so much paperwork in at once. It was still a bit damp and the fire was sending a sullen spire of smoke up into the sky where it hung like the signals in the cowboy film he and Wilf had gone to see last night.

A couple of the lads who drove the vans came by and hung around, giving him smart-alec tips on the best way to keep it burning. He considered telling them to get back to work but thought better of it. Didn't want them wondering why he was doing this himself.

Jean came down the path towards him carrying a cardboard box. She looked tired. There were faint mauve stains under her eyes as though she'd rubbed away a layer of skin and her normally crisp walk was slower.

'Burning something, Harry?' she asked, shooting a quick glance at the lads still within earshot.

'Some paperwork,' he said, loud enough for the ears of anyone listening. 'Gutter overflowed last night and water came into the office. Full of leaves, I expect.' The rain had been an unexpected but convenient stroke of luck, breaking the spell of glorious weather they'd been having. 'Ruined. Owen told me to burn it. Nothing important, just a few consignment notes.' He nodded at the box in her arms. 'Got something there to add to it?'

Jean looked grateful. 'Just some papers. Notes from old experiments. But confidential, you know.' She raised her voice slightly as she spoke.

Harry took the box from her and glanced in. Sheets and sheets of paper in Victor's neat handwriting. Unfamiliar words interspersed with formulae and diagrams. It could have been another language.

'Things our competitors would like to get their hands on,' Jean continued. 'I was going to send them to the incinerators but then I saw your smoke.' She gave a laugh. 'No smoke without fire.'

'They don't like too much paper at the incineration plant. That's why I'm burning.' Harry had no idea if this was true and it sounded unlikely. He thought that the furnaces would be able to handle a few sheets of paper. After all, they dealt with the rest of the hazardous waste that Poulters sent them. Tissue samples and testing debris, the laboratory staff called it, carefully wrapped in sealed bags marked *TOXIC WASTE – DO NOT OPEN*. But Harry knew what was inside. Bits of flesh they'd used to grow viruses and the euthanised monkeys they tested the research on. They could have just sealed the papers in some of those bags. No one would open them to see what was inside. But Owen had insisted they burn everything on site. He was increasingly jumpy since… Harry dragged his mind back to the present.

He fed the contents of Jean's box onto the fire bit by bit. The photos of Victor's family burnt quickly but Harry waited until they disintegrated. The lads had long moved off to smoke out of his sight but people passed by all the time. Harry didn't want them to look and wonder why Victor had gone in such a hurry that he'd left his personal possessions behind.

Jean hung around for a while and watched the papers burn. Harry wished she'd go but he thought Owen or Mr Poulter had probably told her to make sure it was done properly. Once it was burned, no evidence of what had happened would remain. No taint would mar Poulters and Mr Poulter could keep on building his empire and employing hundreds of people who needed work. Young Philip would escape a lifetime of excoriation. And Harry too. There'd be people who'd blame him although he'd only been doing his best. He had a lot on his plate with the ever-increasing demands of the job on top of keeping an eye on Wilf and pushing him to make the most of himself. Wilf needed to study harder at school. Harry had hoped the porter job over summer would help him face up to how impossible any kind of manual labour was going to be for him. But he didn't want to think about how difficult Wilf had found the work. It didn't matter now anyway. Mr Poulter had come up with a solution to the problem and it was the right one. Even if it meant Wilf had lost his job, along with Philip. Harry thought about the two boys for a bit longer. He had his suspicions Philip hadn't told him everything.

Jean went once everything was on the fire, saying to Harry that this was the end of it all. She spoke quietly but a hint of anger gave force to her words.

He supposed she was right. He stirred the fire some more, smashing a bit of something that looked like a clock face, and wondered why it didn't feel like an end. Maybe because Owen kept on talking about it, coming down to the lodge at the end of the day when no one but Harry was about, clutching a bottle and a glass, even though he knew Harry couldn't countenance strong drink, and talking and talking about how they'd made the right decision. He was like a dog, Harry thought, digging up a bone every day for a final chew.

In a rare moment of clarity, Harry wondered if today really had marked the end as Jean said. Maybe it marked the beginning of something else. Maybe what had happened, what they'd done, would change their lives. Maybe its effects would echo down over the years and none of them would emerge unscathed.

Chapter Eleven:
Phiney Wistman

15 June 2017
Two days after the reunion

I skipped through Michael Poulter's obituaries. They were short on facts about his death and long on details about his career as head of Poulters. He'd taken over following the unexpected death of his father, Richard, in the late 1970s. The writers weren't overwhelmingly admiring of his leadership of the company. Most of them implied he'd missed the opportunity to take Poulters international during the mergers and acquisitions race of the 1980s, preferring to remain a wholly British company. It was only since his son, James, had taken over that things had started to look up.

Jack growled outside. I peered through the window. Only a cat, balancing on the high wall between us and next door, and staring at him through the gap between the trellis and the roof of what had been an outside loo but was now used for Dora's gardening tools. Jack growled again and then barked a few times. I banged on the window and the cat slunk away.

Was Michael's death another coincidence? Had it been suicide like Grandad? So many unanswered questions.

There was only one thing I could do. I took a deep breath and called Philip Mason. Put the phone on loudspeaker and propped it against the window.

Philip answered on the third ring. A polite voice with a faint Midlands twang. Like Grandad but without the quaver Grandad had developed in the last couple of years.

'My name's Josephine Wistman,' I said. 'I'm Wilfred Patterson's granddaughter.'

The tone of his voice smiled. 'I know who you are. Wilf often spoke about you.' Then it changed. 'Is your grandfather all right?'

'No.' Shit. It was a hard thing to tell someone. 'I'm really sorry, Mr Mason, but Grandad is dead. That's why I'm calling.'

A long silence.

I will not cry. I will not cry.

I wished he'd speak. His silence was splintering me into little bits.

'I'm so sorry, my dear. Can you tell me what happened?'

'An accident.' Something stopped me telling him it was suicide. 'He fell.'

A long drawn-in breath.

'He fell?' he said finally.

'At Tile Park station. Yesterday.'

'So, he never went home?'

It slowly sank in that this man knew Grandad had been in Coventry.

'No,' I said. 'He never came back to Matlock. You knew he was in Coventry, then?'

'I took him there.'

'You took him?'

'Yes. We went down together in my car but I couldn't bring him back because I was going on down to London.' He paused. 'Although I changed my mind once I'd got there and came home last night. Not that it matters.'

'Mr Mason, why did he go to Coventry?'

There was nothing but the sound of him breathing and then he swallowed.

'He was going to come and see you. Didn't he?'

I brushed this off, like he was brushing off my question.

'What was he doing in Coventry?'

'Oh, I was coming down anyway. Asked him if he wanted to come

71

with me. See a few old friends and obviously catch up with you. It was quite last minute.'

Too smooth. Too pat. I didn't believe a word of it. He'd had time to think and he didn't want to tell me why Grandad had gone to Coventry.

'How exactly did the accident happen?' he asked.

'He fell off the bridge.'

'I see.'

There was a thud on the roof above me followed by an explosion of barking from Jack and a thumping as he threw himself against the door. I couldn't hear Philip's voice over the racket.

'I'll call you back,' I said and rushed outside, screaming at the cat on the roof to *shoo* and grabbing Jack. He calmed down once the cat went but he wouldn't come inside the shed. His paws had picked up one too many fragments of metal shavings from the floor in the past.

'Well, you'll have to go indoors,' I said.

A woman was sitting holding Dora's hand when I dragged Jack into the house. Her collar revealed her as the vicar. I muttered an excuse and scuttled back to the shed.

Philip's number was engaged. I left it a couple of minutes and tried again but it was still busy.

I finally got hold of him half an hour later. He was as courteous as ever, apologising for being engaged, but he didn't want to talk to me. I heard it in the edge to his voice.

I steamed straight in.

'Mr Mason, I wasn't entirely truthful. Grandad's death wasn't an accident. It was suicide. He climbed over the barrier and jumped off the bridge. I'm sorry. It's not easy to tell anyone.'

There was no reaction. I went on.

'Look, me and my grandad's w… Dora, we don't understand. And we're desperate to. You can't imagine what it's like knowing Grandad felt so awful he couldn't see any other way out. Please. If you have any idea why, you have to tell us.'

'Suicide?'

'Yes.'

I let the pause linger.

'How is Dora?' he said eventually.

'Devastated. She's devastated. How was Grandad when you saw him?'

'Will you tell her how sorry I am?'

'I will, but please, what was Grandad doing in Coventry? Who were the old friends you said you came down to see?'

The sun had come round the side of the house and onto the roof of the shed. It was getting uncomfortably hot.

'Phiney,' he said. 'Do you mind if I call you Phiney? Wilf spoke about you so much and he called you Phiney.'

'Call me anything you want.' I tried to speak nicely although it was tough. 'But tell me what you know.'

'I can't. I'm sorry, my dear, but I can't.'

I started to stutter that he had to, that he had no right to keep the truth from us, but he overrode me.

'I promise you none of this is anything to do with you. Or Dora.'

'If you know something you have to tell us.'

He sighed. 'You're right, of course. But I can't. Not yet.'

'Is it something to do with the newspaper article I found? With the picture of you and Grandad when you were young?'

Silence.

'You know what I'm talking about then?' I continued. 'The one outside Poulters.' I looked at it again. 'From 1957. June 1957.'

'I know the one.'

'Michael Poulter. He's in the photo. He died yesterday morning too. Just like Grandad.'

'Yes, I know Michael's dead. I didn't know when you first rang, but I do now. Michael was ill. Very ill. His death wasn't unexpected.'

'But does it have anything to do with Grandad's?'

Long silence. And my phone bleeped. I was almost out of battery. I stared at it unbelievingly. How could that be? I put it on charge every night and it was still morning. But I hadn't last night, had I? With everything else going on, I'd forgotten. I turned off the battery-draining speaker and pressed it to my ear. Sod the radiation.

'Wilf's death. Was it definitely suicide?' Philip asked.

'Yes.'

'Are you sure?'

'Someone saw him. There was no doubt.'

'Who?'

'Who! What does it matter?'

'Who saw him? Who witnessed Wilf's death?'

'He's called Mat Torrington. He's a journalist.'

'Anyone else?'

'I don't think so. Tile Park is a quiet little station apart from during rush hours.'

'No one on the bridge?'

'I don't think so. I could ask Mat.'

'No, keep away from Mr Torrington. Nothing good ever came of speaking to journalists anyway.'

Somewhere in this conversation we'd changed places. He was the one forcing the pace. His voice had taken on a veneer of hardness.

My phone bleeped again.

'Please, Mr Mason, my phone's nearly out of battery. Please –'

'I'll come and see you. In a couple of days. In Coventry. I need to speak to some people first. It's only fair. But, Phiney, don't tell anyone about this. Wilf wouldn't have wanted anyone to know. Above all, don't speak to the journalist. Especially now that…'

'Now that what?'

'Wilf's dead. Michael's dead.' He took a deep breath. 'Two more deaths. So many deaths. There's been so much suffering and it needs to stop.' He lingered over the phrase as though feeling the meaning of the words and then he rang off.

I ran into the house, ignoring Dora and the vicar, and found my charger, but when I plugged my phone in and called Philip back, there was no answer. I gave up after the fifth attempt and thought through what he'd said.

He knew something. He said he'd found out Michael was dead in between our two conversations. Had he spoken to someone who'd told him? Did it mean the two deaths were linked?

I reread Michael's obituaries in case I'd missed some details about his death, but there was nothing. However, the name of the journalist who had written the one in the *Coventry Telegraph* sprang out at me.

It was Mat Torrington.

Philip had told me not to speak to him. Because he was a journalist? Or because of something else? Was it just a weird coincidence that Mat was the only witness to Grandad's death and wrote Michael's obituary?

I googled Mat. Article after article came up. He'd written a lot about Poulters and it was often critical, unlike the usual respectful pieces about big local employers. The most recent was in yesterday's paper.

Local Residents Furious as Berkswell House Sale Falls Through

Poulters Pharmaceuticals today confirmed they had pulled out of the sale of Berkswell House, site of the old Poulters laboratories, to the spa hotel chain Wellspring Ltd. A spokesman from Wellspring claimed that the decision had come out of the blue and seriously affected their plans to expand into the Midlands. The Council issued a statement saying that while they were disappointed the efforts they'd made to attract new ventures to the area had been unsuccessful it was entirely a matter for Poulters whether they chose to sell their own property. Locals were less circumspect. Mr Knowles, long-time resident of the area, said that Berkswell House was an eyesore. 'It's lain empty since the sixties when Poulters moved out to the new science park. The surrounding walls are crumbling away and the buildings are rotten. Everyone knows it's a hangout for local tramps and suchlike. If Poulters aren't going to use it, why won't they sell to someone who will?' When approached for comment, Poulters issued the following statement:

'We are aware of the problems with break-ins to the Berkswell House site and have taken steps to ensure that the buildings and grounds are secure.'

Berkswell House again. And if I needed any confirmation that this was the same building as in Grandad's newspaper cutting, there was a shot showing the same gated entry to the grounds. Was this the article Mat said he'd been writing at Tile Park station? Berkswell House was close by. Another thought came to me. Had Grandad been to Berkswell House as well? Was that why he'd been at Tile Park station?

Whatever was going on, I was sure the answer lay in Coventry. I shoved the chair back with my legs and stood up. A faint feeling of dizziness made me wobble. The worst of it passed as I leaned on the counter and breathed deeply. Shit. I felt quite faint.

The smell of hot butter hit me as I went back into the house. Dora sat at the kitchen table, eating an omelette, while the vicar wiped the stovetop.

'Your grandmother hasn't eaten since yesterday morning.' Her voice was as brisk as the movements of her hand. 'I don't suppose you have either. Shall I make you an omelette?'

My stomach rumbled. It smelled delicious and the vicar had cooked it perfectly with a crisp brown outside and a hint of creamy liquid inside but the eggs wouldn't be organic and, although cooking with butter was better than using polyunsaturated oils, it would still send free radicals swimming around my body.

'You're all right,' I said. 'I've got some rice cakes in my bag upstairs.' I took a deep breath. 'I'm afraid I've got to go back to Coventry. The hospital called and they're really short of staff.'

Dora stopped eating, the fork halfway to her mouth, and the vicar looked shocked, but recovered quickly.

'I'm sorry,' I said. 'You know how it is. I'll come back as soon as I can.'

There was an element of truth in this. I was due to work the day after tomorrow and we were always short of staff but Meghan would sort something out if I gave her a call. I didn't want to tell Dora about the strange phone call with Philip Mason. She'd want to pick each sentence apart for hidden meanings or try to speak to him herself. I didn't have time for it, not now I'd decided to get back to Coventry and Tile Park and the mysterious Berkswell House. Besides, Philip had told me not to talk to anyone and Dora wasn't good at keeping things quiet.

'Could you take Jack with you?'

I stared at the vicar.

'It'll be too much for your grandmother to look after him.'

Chapter Twelve:
Phiney Wistman

16 June 2017
Three days after the reunion

A day later, sitting on the train to Tile Park, I'd already learned how right the vicar was. Jack needed exercising and feeding and taking out regularly, plus he got bored very quickly. He'd started barking at the birds landing on the windowsill of my flat and I knew I was on borrowed time before one of my neighbours complained to the landlord that I had a dog.

I pulled Grandad's book on astronomical clocks out of my pocket as the train trundled along. Dora had left it behind in the mad rush to get back to Matlock and I'd brought it with me. Pretty dull stuff although Grandad had found it fascinating. The receipt fluttered to the floor and I picked it up. He'd bought it from Coventry's Herbert Museum shop, the day before he died. A memory sliced through my thoughts.

The Herbert was hosting an exhibition commemorating the sixtieth anniversary of the Coventry Polio Epidemic, one of the last of the great polio epidemics that swept the country every summer. Although Grandad had caught polio years before, he had friends who'd contributed and we'd visited together in January.

It had been fascinating and made more so because Grandad, who never normally spoke about his illness, had told me how the epidemic had affected the city. Children were shut indoors and people avoided the rivers and canals because of fears they carried the illness. People also avoided Grandad because of his limp and callipers, crossing over the road and leaving shops when he went in, despite the fact he'd had the disease years earlier.

The centrepiece of the exhibition was an old iron lung, a metal cylinder that encased the children whose lungs had been paralysed by the disease and breathed for them. I shuddered at the thought of being imprisoned in such a hideous contraption, lying on your back, facing the ceiling and only able to see what was going on around you through a mirror above your head, but Grandad said it had been a relief. No more fighting for breath. His lungs had recovered but he'd been left with a withered leg. His lips thinned as he looked at the photos of plucky children smiling and waving in the mass isolation wards and of nurses with crisp uniforms and kind, motherly looks.

It hadn't been a bit like that, he told me. Hospitals had been lonely and harsh places and his face had sharpened with memories.

Had Grandad gone back to visit the exhibition? Had I been too quick to dismiss the idea of illness being behind his suicide? Maybe the thought of more pain and weakness had been too much. Maybe...

The train arrived at Tile Park. The railway lay in a deep cutting, its steep sides overgrown with straggling rosebay willowherb and brambles. It was deserted, a quiet pool beneath the busy roads above. I left the station and walked up the steps to the road bridge across the railway line. The narrow pavement offered little protection from the lorries that thundered past, spewing out foul fumes. Jack shivered and pressed himself against my legs, and I buried my face in my T-shirt even though I knew the material was worse than useless at filtering out pollution. I found the mangled barrier Grandad had stepped over at the centre of the bridge and peered down. A blast of hot dust-filled air from the track below blew into my face and for a few brief seconds I felt giddy. Only the bite of the metal barrier on my skin and the tremble of Jack's body pressed against my legs steadied me.

It was horrible in every way.

And it was all wrong.

Even if Grandad knew his future held only pain, he'd have seen suicide as a betrayal of his life. He'd have been determined to live every last minute left to him: spend time with old friends; reread his favourite books and find new ones; finish another clock.

No. Something utterly unforeseen had brought my beautiful, wonderful Grandad to throw himself off a bridge without a second thought for the grief it would bring to the people he loved most. It spoke of an action driven by a sudden and terrible blow.

Why, Grandad? Why?

There was no answer for me here.

Horns blared. Jack whimpered. I was too close to the road. I walked away from the bridge and the station and turned down a quiet lane that cut through the flat, open fields. I was going to find out why Grandad had jumped and I'd start with the place I was sure he'd visited earlier that day.

Berkswell House.

The wall round Berkswell House was too high to see over, with great bulges where the bushes and trees in its grounds had pressed up against it and pushed the bricks out of alignment. Jack wanted to linger and investigate the weeds growing along the bottom but I hauled him on until we reached the entrance.

The 1957 photo had definitely been taken here in front of the wrought iron gates, now rusty and sagging on their hinges. Someone had boarded them over, blocking the view into the grounds, and done it recently because the boarding was clean and the weeds at the base freshly crushed. Poulters said they were taking steps to ensure the building was secure in Mat's article. Clearly, they hadn't hung about.

The roof of a low building peeked over the wall at the side of the gates. A lodge, I guessed, dating back to the days when the house was privately owned, long before Poulters occupied it.

The gates were locked and chained and adorned with razor-sharp barbed wire but a bit further on, another door – a side door for staff, maybe – was cut into the wall. Half hidden under the branch of a beech tree, it was lower than the wall and without barbed wire. I looked quickly around. The road was quiet. The houses opposite – 1930s, semi-detached – were set back from the road behind mature gardens of trees and bushes. No one was about. It was too good an opportunity to miss.

I told Jack to sit, then crouched and prepared to jump, grateful for the years I'd spent playing netball. I leaped and grabbed the top of the door and pulled myself up and over, landing close to a mess of barbed wire. Jack barked and kept on barking. Shit. I called out to him through the door as I tried to untangle the barbs from my jeans.

I wasn't the first person to get in this way. The barbed wire on the ground had recently been cut from the top of the door, presumably by the same person who had also cut through the shiny new chain and padlock on the inside and left it hanging loose. Only an old bolt held the door shut now. I pulled it open and let Jack in, seizing his collar to stop him bounding off, then closed it firmly behind us.

We were in.

I thought I was going to find a tangle of thorns and entwining plants – like Sleeping Beauty's palace – but, apart from the perimeter of overgrown bushes and undergrowth where Jack and I crouched, the wilderness had been tamed. And very recently too. Grass, weeds, shrubs, bushes had all been hacked down to an overall height of a few inches and the debris had been left to rot in heaps, filling the air with an acrid tang.

I stayed in the bushes in case there was anyone around, but it was deathly quiet. There wasn't even a wind today to rustle the tree branches. Sweat trickled down my neck. But no one seemed to be there despite the signs saying security guards patrolled regularly. To my side was the lodge with its windows boarded up and doors chained shut. In the centre of the grounds, Berkswell House rose with a clump of stained one-storey prefabs around its base.

My phone bleeped, breaking the silence and startling me. A text from Meghan, checking I was still coming in to work tonight. Yes, I texted back. Was I sure, she asked. I was sure. I couldn't sit at home and do nothing.

I stepped out of the bushes and took a few cautious steps into the open. No one appeared. I walked a little way along one of the concrete paths that criss-crossed what must have once been the lawn. All was still quiet. I was fairly sure the place was deserted and, with growing confidence, I started exploring.

The old house was impenetrable, every window freshly boarded and every door with a new chain and padlock. So, I wandered round the buildings scattered all over the grounds. Some were old, dating back to when the local gentry lived there and needed stables and outhouses; others newer but uglier and in worse repair with stains or mould or ivy covering the brickwork and the panels. A few of them still had rusting metal plaques with a number. Like the main house, they too had newly boarded windows and every door was securely locked or chained shut. Mat's article had said the site was used by local 'tramps'. Poulters had clearly made good on their undertaking to secure it. Because there couldn't be anything worth protecting inside these long-disused buildings that were slowly rotting back to nothing.

At the far side of the grounds, I found another entrance, newly filled with a rolling steel gate. A building stood a short distance away. It was larger than many of the others. I rubbed a finger over the plaque by the door. This was number 19.

The windows weren't boarded but blocked by rusted bars. I shone the torch on my phone through but there were too many shadows to make much out apart from broken furniture and a pile of square metal cages at one end. For keeping animals? For testing? I shuddered.

Jack barked. Behind me the gate gave an ominous click. Something whirred and it started to slide open. Too late I noticed the camera glaring down at us from the roof. Shit. And it wasn't the only one. Two others were fixed to the gateposts.

I turned and ran for the bushes along the perimeter wall, grabbing Jack's collar and giving it a yank to make sure he came with me, diving for cover as the gate opened. A white van with a security firm logo drove in.

Was this a routine patrol? Or had cameras elsewhere caught me?

Two men got out. Muscled and hot in their uniforms. They went round the back of the van and let a dog out. A German Shepherd. A big one. A ridge of hair along Jack's back rose but he kept quiet.

The van drove off down the path round the perimeter, leaving the two guards. One of them headed towards the house but the other – the one with the dog – started searching around the building I'd looked into, coming closer and closer to our hiding place. Shit. Would the German Shepherd smell us through the dry scent of pine needles and the stench of rotting grass? Thank God there was no wind.

It's only a security patrol, I told myself. I'll be chucked out. Or get a rap on the knuckles from the police. Nothing more. But I couldn't bring myself to step out of the shadows. Something about the speed of their arrival and the thoroughness of the search worried me. It was over the top for a routine check or even a suspected trespasser.

My luck held.

The man and his dog finished poking around the building and headed round the perimeter away from us. As soon as they were out of sight, I slipped off in the other direction, back to the side gate and escape, staying in the bushes by the crumbling bricks of the wall. But as the low roof of the lodge came into sight, Jack stopped. His ears lifted and the hair on his back rippled up into a crest again.

I heard the voices too.

'Stay, Jack,' I muttered firmly and he responded to the intensity of my whisper and sat. I peered round a thick stand of bay trees. The van was parked by the old gates and the driver stood in front of the side door. No way past him.

The guard with the dog came into sight from behind the lodge. He'd beaten me here. I put a warning hand on Jack and promised my soul to the God of dogs if he would keep him quiet.

'Any sign?' the driver asked.

'No.'

'They got in here.' The driver pointed towards the side door I'd climbed over. 'I've called it in. You better do another sweep. In the bushes round the wall this time.' He jerked his head in my direction. 'Anything could be hiding in there. Let the dog flush them out.'

The handler bent down to unclip the dog's harness. I felt sick. Jack gave a low growl. But he'd be no match for the German Shepherd. It was a big and aggressive-looking beast. He might get badly hurt. I should give up. Reveal myself.

The radio crackled. A distorted voice shouted that he'd got him.

Got him? Got who?

'We're at the old entrance,' the driver snapped back. 'Bring him round here.' And then to the guard beside him. 'You can keep hold of Vulcan unless you want him to have a run.'

'Nah. You're all right. He can be a bugger to get back if he finds anything interesting and there are rabbits everywhere.'

Two figures appeared in the distance.

I relaxed a little. They'd been after someone else. Hopefully, they'd leave now they'd caught them. We just needed to lie low and wait.

But as the two figures picked their way over the stubble towards us, my skin prickled. One was the third guard. Recognisable from his uniform. But I knew the other too. I was sure I did. Even from a distance, with his curly hair and apologetic stoop. I stopped breathing. And as he came closer, I was sure.

It was Mat.

What was he doing here?

He didn't look the least bit bothered about being caught trespassing. In fact, he was chatting and laughing with the guards. Nasty, prickly thoughts bounced about inside my head. Mat – the only witness to

Grandad's death. Mat, who'd been so willing to come and talk to me and Dora. Mat, who Philip had told me to keep away from.

A horn blared, loud and insistent from the other side of the wall. Radios rattled with voices. The driver headed towards the old lodge gates, shouting down the radio that he was on his way. The dog handler shut Vulcan in the van while Mat talked to him. I couldn't hear what they were saying over the creaking and scraping of the old gates opening.

A van drove in and two men leapt out, went round to the back and pulled out barbed wire, chains and a padlock.

Shit. They were clearly going to make the side door impenetrable. Staying hidden until they'd gone wasn't an option. And I really, really didn't want to get caught here. Not now that Mat had showed up. Something was going on and it felt bad. Very bad.

The old gates were wide open now. If we were quick, we'd get away before they thought to come after us. Thank God they'd shut their dog away.

Jack stuck by me as I edged close to the old gates. Until only a few straggling rhododendrons lay between us and escape. I took a deep breath and as soon as the men were occupied in untangling a roll of barbed wire, I shoved Jack forward and ran.

I was out of the gate and into the road before they started shouting. My feet pounded the ground. My breath tore holes in my chest. My eyes filled with water. More cries came from behind me, but no thudding feet. No noise of engines firing up.

I didn't stop until I was far away. Until pains leapt like electric shocks through my shins every time my feet slammed into the ground.

Stopping was worse than running. My breath was sandpaper in my lungs and my legs shook. My stomach sent throat-tightening spasms up through my body and the green tea I'd drunk that morning shot out of my mouth and splattered the long grass at the side of the road.

I looked around. Jack wasn't with me.

My legs wobbled, crumpled beneath me and I sat down with a thump.

Had they caught him? Maybe he'd stopped to say hello. Sweat trickled down into my eyes and stung them. Stupid dog, I raged, trying to fight back the tears at the thought of the guards grabbing him. I'd have to go back. I couldn't leave him. Not with the guards and the nasty-looking Vulcan.

I forced myself to my feet, blew my nose and wiped the sweat and tears from my face. My breathing was nearly normal but my legs hurt and it took me an age to limp back to Berkswell House.

There was no one there. The old gates were shut and locked. The side door I'd climbed over had new barbed wire fixed along the top. I peered through the gap at the bottom of the main gates. Nothing. No feet. No van wheels. I called Jack until I was hoarse and despairing.

There was no sign of him either when I staggered round to the steel gates at the far side of the grounds and called. All was quiet. No Jack. No guards. Not even Mat.

Chapter Thirteen:
Phiney Wistman

16 June 2017
Three days after the reunion

I rang the police in the end, the local station, not 999, although the number went through to some central answering facility. The man on the other end was pleasant but uninterested. A lost dog lacked urgency. He told me to call Poulters' security firm in the morning. There was bound to be a sign giving details. There was. I called the number and left a message on an answering machine saying my dog had gone missing in Berkswell House and I thought they might have picked him up. I left another one half an hour later, begging them to call me. And again fifteen minutes later. None of them produced a response.

I went back to my flat, picked out my cleanest uniform from the laundry basket, checked my phone for the millionth time and went to work. I'd missed a few calls from Dora but I couldn't face ringing her. She'd ask me how Jack was and I didn't think I'd be able to lie.

Finally, I called Mat as I walked round and round the car park, waiting for my shift to start. I hadn't had time to think about why he'd been at Berkswell House nor why he'd seemed so relaxed with the guards. I didn't trust him. But right at this moment it didn't matter because he'd know if the guards had caught Jack and he didn't know that I was suspicious of him.

There was no answer.

I left him a message saying I'd lost Jack at Berkswell House and

I knew he'd been there. I was on night shift but would check my phone regularly, so to please let me know if he knew anything. Then I turned off my phone and went in.

Night shifts used to be a favourite of mine. They mess your body up a bit, so you eat odd things at odd times and tiredness catches you out when you least expect it, but on the whole the work itself is routine checks of children throughout the night. It left time to chat to parents who, despite their exhaustion, couldn't sleep. They roamed the corridors, leaving a trail of stress and anguish behind them as they let their façade of coping slip while their children slept. Time to hold their hands, to make them cups of tea and listen. That was what they most wanted. Someone to listen to their words, coloured dark with the bitter red of anger and the blackness of despair.

Normally, I took their words in and absorbed them but I couldn't tonight. Grandad's death had stripped away the armour that protected me; their misery cut into my heart and I couldn't take it. So, I found other things to do. I tidied our stations, watched the clocks tick round slowly, checked equipment, watched the clocks some more, ran errands that took me away from the ward, watched the clocks again and hid in the staffroom.

'You OK?' Meghan asked when she found me there, wiping a table for the tenth time. 'Sorry I've not been around. Meetings, you know.'

I'd seen her when I arrived, escorting a mother to her office with a look on her face that told me she had bad news to break, and her office door had stayed firmly closed on them both ever since.

'Thought you might have liked a bit of time off,' she continued, twining a loose strand of hair round and round her finger. 'I know how close you were to your Grandad. Maybe spend a bit of time with Dora.'

This was the moment when I should tell her about Grandad jumping off the bridge but I couldn't find the words.

'Dora's fine without me,' I said shortly.

'Oh, OK.' She pulled out the drawers one by one and slammed them shut. Crap. Now I'd upset Meghan with my prickliness. Why couldn't I just tell her?

'How come we have no teaspoons?' she said. 'We have enough knives and forks to stop the five thousand having to eat with their fingers, but no teaspoons.'

My nose started to ache as the weight of all the unsaid things forced the tears to my eyes. I had to say something.

'Sorry,' I started. 'I didn't mean to snap. My legs hurt. Went running today.'

'Is that why you're creeping around like an old woman and sitting down all the time?' She sat on the lumpy couch and scooped out her yoghurt with a fork.

'Probably. And Jack's gone missing.'

'Ah, sorry. I'm sure Dora will find him.'

'No. I'm looking after him. Or I was. She couldn't cope.'

'Oh.'

'And now I've lost him.'

The tears I'd been trying to hold back trickled out of my eyes.

'Phiney!'

She put her yoghurt on the table and came over and hugged me.

I told her most of it. About Grandad and about not knowing why and about how it was torturing me. She listened and hugged me again and occasionally turned to wave nurses at the door away.

'I should get back to work,' I said, in the end. 'And let the others come in and get their food.'

'No, go home. There's only an hour left. We can cope. Get a bit of sleep and I'll come round as soon as I've finished and help you find Jack.'

I knew I should refuse. We never had enough staff but I wasn't much use hiding in the staffroom. For once I would have liked a taxi. My legs were screamingly sore from the run but it was six o'clock on Saturday morning and already light – a dead time for taxis. Too early for workers but too late for even the most persistent Friday night partygoer. I'd have to walk.

I stumbled as I got to the steps leading to the passage under the road outside the hospital and waited for a minute, clutching the rail. Going down hurt more than anything else. Rapid footsteps came up behind me and a sixth sense made me clutch the railing even harder. Something hard smacked into my head and hands shoved my back. The force of the push dislodged my grip and I heard myself screaming into the darkness as my legs gave way and I tumbled down the steps, scrabbling at the damp stone.

I woke to the smell of blood. Metallic and sweet, mingling with the chalky scent of dry concrete. And stickiness on my hands. Someone was bleeding. I reached out for them but my hands met only air as I realised I was on the ground. I must have slipped in the blood.

Footsteps. The ground stabbed pain into my head with each one. Someone groaned.

'Run to A&E. Tell the paramedics to come here. Tell them someone's fallen. Badly. Head injury and bleeding. Tell them Sister March from Foster Ward sent you.'

It was Meghan's voice.

I tried to do what she told me but I couldn't move and the patient's groans got louder. My head hurt too much to move.

'Keep still,' Meghan said. And then to someone else. 'Just go. Leave the dog here.'

More footsteps, running away this time, and Meghan's hand held mine.

She held my hand as we waited for the paramedics. She held it as they put a neck brace on me and inserted a line and carried me up the steps to the hospital. She held it as I was poked and prodded and rolled over. She held it until the moment I disappeared in the scanner and took it again as soon as I emerged. Her hand in mine was the thread that held me together through all the noise and confusion and the not being sure of what had happened. It was the last thing I remembered as my bandaged head sank into cool pillows.

Chapter Fourteen:
Phiney Wistman

17 June 2017
Four days after the reunion

Meghan was the first thing I saw when I came to. Curled up asleep in an armchair next to me, she was clutching a book with a cover showing a woman in a long and frilly pink dress walking beside a lake. Storm clouds brewed overhead and I thought the woman would soon regret leaving home without a coat.

'Meghan.'

She opened her eyes. 'Finally! You took your time waking up.' Her left cheek was creased where she'd rested it on the chair.

'Where am I?'

'In hospital.'

I looked around. She was right. I was in a ward of eight beds. Afternoon sun shone in through the window and bounced off the white sheets. Trolleys squeaked. Machines bleeped and the familiar scent of disinfectant filled my nostrils.

'Our hospital?'

'Of course. You were kind enough to fall just outside. Didn't even need an ambulance.'

I remembered the sensation of tumbling down steps. The sunlight faded a notch and the background noises became more intrusive. Someone in a bed near me was complaining.

'How are you feeling?' Meghan asked, pushing herself up and stretching, her voice taking on its professional tone.

'Rubbish.' My head hurt. I put up a hand and felt a bandage. 'It's too tight.'

'It's all agency on this ward. You'd think some of them had never seen a bandage before.'

I felt an overwhelming sense of despair and tears started to trickle down my face.

'What is it, Phiney?'

'I don't want to be here.'

'Of course you don't. No one in their right mind would.'

'Take me to a proper ward. Please, Meghan.'

She laughed. 'Try and get some rest. You're just feeling the after-effects of shock. You can go home tomorrow. You know the protocol.' I still felt wobbly but her voice was soothing and I did know the protocol. Twenty-four hours observation after a head trauma, and then take it easy for a week or so.

'Have I had a CT?'

'Of course. Nothing damaged.'

'Then I want to go home. I can't stay here.' I knew I was clutching at straws. No doctor would let anyone in my condition go home.

'Come on, Phiney. You know the score. Just stick it out until tomorrow.'

She stroked my hand.

I wasn't going to be able to get out of bed anyway. Even the slightest movement sparked ripples of agony round my skull.

'OK,' I said.

'I'll take Jack home with me. My parents will love him.'

'Jack?'

'Yes. You really don't remember, do you?'

I tried to shake my head but the pain dislodged more tears from my eyes.

'A bit of memory loss is normal. You know that. It'll come back and you're going to be fine. A guy called Mat brought Jack in just after you left. I ran after you to let you know. Lucky for you I did.

You fell down the steps outside and you could have lain there for ages. There aren't many people around at that time.'

As she told me, some memories came back. Grabbing at the steps as I fell. Footsteps running, Meghan's voice and Jack sitting still, good as gold, only his head whisking back and forth as he watched the paramedics and returned his eyes to me, anxious, watchful.

'Where is he?'

'With the porters. Having a huge fuss made of him. I'm going now, Phiney. I'm working tonight and I've got to get some sleep. I'll pop in tomorrow morning after I come off shift.'

'I'm supposed to be working too but I don't think I'll make it.'

She laughed. 'I've signed you off for the foreseeable future. I bought you some food.' She held out a bag with the name of my favourite organic deli on it. 'I knew you wouldn't eat anything otherwise. I'll put it in the locker with your bag and your phone. Dora rang you, by the way.'

'You didn't answer it?'

'Of course I did. What are you like! I had to tell her that you'd had a fall.' She put the book back in her bag and stood up. 'She was very upset but sends her love.'

Some memory stirred at the back of my aching head as she put her coat on but she had gone by the time the thought had touched the part of my brain that gave words to ideas.

I didn't fall.

I remembered the footsteps coming up behind me and the smack of something hard echoing through my skull and the *ooof* of sharply exhaled breath as hands shoved me over.

I didn't fall, I was pushed.

My legs had been sore and wobbly but I didn't fall. And if I hadn't already been gripping the rail for support it would have been so much worse. I'd rolled down the steps rather than falling headlong.

A nurse came over. The colour of her uniform gave her away as agency.

'Your bandage. They said it was too tight. Shall I have a look?'

94

I pushed her hand away. 'No, it's all right.'

'Sure?'

'Sure.'

I didn't fall I was pushed.

The day outside began its long stretch into night. The ward darkened and the evening routine rolled into motion. My head buzzed with thoughts that wouldn't settle long enough for me to grab them and pin them down.

Someone had pushed me down the steps.

When did Meghan say she was coming back? I needed to talk to her. Find out if she'd noticed anything.

'How are you feeling?' It was the same agency nurse as before. A waft of anti-perspirant hit my nostrils as she bent to slip the blood pressure cuff on my arm.

'What's my BP? I'm a nurse, you know.'

'Sister March made that very clear. It's lower than I'd have expected and your pulse is quite high.' She showed me the results.

'I don't like being here.'

She laughed. 'Nurses often don't.'

But it was more than the awfulness of being a patient. I couldn't forget the blow on my head and the sharp impact of hands shoving me. And then I remembered Meghan had said Mat had been there. I shivered despite the heat in the ward and suspicions hurtled round my brain. Had Mat pushed me? He'd been there. But why would he do that? Was it because I'd been at Berkswell House? Because he knew from my phone call that I'd seen him there?

I called a nurse.

'Is the ward door shut?'

Occasionally, when they were short-staffed, the nurses wedged the door open so they wouldn't have to answer the buzzer every time someone wanted to come in.

'Of course.' She checked my pulse again. 'Why?'

'Don't like the idea of strangers wandering in and out.'

'It's locked, don't worry.'

But I still couldn't sleep. Every time I closed my eyes, I felt myself falling down the sharp-edged concrete steps and the words came back into my brain: I didn't fall, I was pushed.

Like Harry.

I opened my eyes. Where had that come from? My great-grandfather, Harry, hadn't been pushed; he'd fallen after a drunken night in the pub. My poor, shaken brain was misfiring, making connections that didn't exist. Yet I couldn't stop thinking about him and wondering why he'd turned to alcohol so late in life.

Chapter Fifteen:
Philip Mason

20 October 1977
Twenty years after the incident

Philip pushed open the bar door and went into the little pub on the corner. Normally, he didn't drink so close to his flat and so close to the school in case he met parents or even sixth formers sipping gingerly at a half pint of beer with their eyes on the door. The pub was crowded, with the rapid-fire commentary of a horse race on the radio barely making itself heard above the raucous laughter and chatter, but he was too tired to go further afield. The day had been long, finishing with a fractious staff meeting after an afternoon spent drumming the motives of the conspirators in Shakespeare's *Julius Caesar* into the heads of the lowest stream of English Literature O-Level pupils – a few of them might even pass – and persuading a particularly bolshie sixth form group that their comments – mainly disparaging – on Jane Austen's *Persuasion* needed to be rooted in an understanding of the time it was written and related to the actual words of the novel. God knows he had some sympathy for them. It might be twenty odd years ago but he remembered the hormone-driven confusion of his adolescence and the awfulness of standing out in the crowd, either because of his opinions or the dreadful acne that had plagued him. *Persuasion* was a difficult choice of text for a group of sixteen- and seventeen-year-old boys to study anyway but there'd been no persuading his new head of department.

'Time to open their minds to something new,' she'd said, brushing her shaggy fringe out of her eyes. Why didn't she get it cut? 'They can't avoid women writers forever. Besides, Austen is quite radical. Try and get that across to them, Phil.'

There was some truth in what she said, although he wished she wouldn't call him Phil, but she didn't understand how a refusal to consider anything outside its narrow sphere of interest was the overriding impulse of a teenage boy's mind. The amalgamation of the all-boys grammar school Philip had taught in for the last six years with the local secondary modern to create a vast comprehensive school had meant the mingling of boys and girls in the same building for the first time. This had stirred up a maelstrom of hormones which did nothing to promote pupils' interest in academic work.

It had also brought about the uncomfortable cohabitation of two sets of teachers. Uncomfortable until, by tacit agreement, the secondary modern staff had taken over the staffroom on the third floor of the newer building and the grammar school teachers had confined themselves to the original staffroom on the ground floor. A kind of partition that, according to Benson, was doomed to disaster. Benson was the head of History who'd held onto his headship even though the subject had been amalgamated with Geography and was now called Humanities, much to his disgust. Peaceful coexistence wasn't possible, he claimed. History was littered with examples. Sooner or later there would be war. Philip rather thought it had already started and the battlefield was the monthly staff meeting, the one occasion when both sides saw the whites of each other's eyes.

Tonight's meeting had been nothing out of the ordinary. Long and tedious with both sides jostling to score points. One win for the Marxists, as Benson called the old secondary modern staff, with a demand that girls be offered the chance to do Woodwork as well as Needlework. A victory in name only, as far as Philip could see, since none of the girls had shown the slightest interest in anything other than scouring the range of boys available for good boyfriend material. And one win for the Imperialists, as Philip knew the

Marxists called them. A win that Philip was happy about. After an impassioned speech about choice and opportunity in education, Lee had won his case for the Classics to continue to be taught from the second year onwards. Philip had seen a couple of the softer Marxists nod in agreement with his words. If only the partition wasn't so rigid, the two sides could have done much good together. He had sympathy with a lot of what they said about equality, about smashing the hidebound status quo and so on, but he thought they were laughably out of touch with the need to ensure the youngsters left school with a modicum of useful education.

So, he was tired and doubtful and needing a drink.

He edged round the side, away from the densest part of the crowd, muttering greetings, and pushed his way through to the bar. He ordered a pint and drank the top of it quickly, enjoying the slight bitterness and the sense of fitting in. He might not come in here very often but he was known and unremarkable. Young Philip, whose father had been one of the unlucky ones that had not survived the war, who'd gone to the local school and done well for himself, now a teacher, but still part of the neighbourhood.

The horse racing came to an end. People started to drift out into the night. Over in the corner, someone started singing, and Pete, the barman, looked over Philip's shoulder and sighed. Philip looked round. It was Harry, Wilf's dad. A few of the regulars shouted at him to shut up and most of them moved away, clearing a path between Harry and Philip. Philip sighed too. The last thing he wanted was a drunken rant from Harry.

'Should I call Wilf?' he asked, nodding over to the payphone attached to the wall by the Gents.

'No, leave him be. It's a long way for him to come and fetch his father since he moved. How's he doing?'

Wilf had moved to a new ground-floor flat on the Harper Estate built in the countryside surrounding Coventry.

'Loving it, I think.'

'And the family? All well with them?'

Philip nodded. Wilf's daughter Carol was a bright little thing and, if Wilf's domestic happiness meant he had less time for Philip, he was fine with that.

'And you, Philip? Nice young man like you. Good job. When are you going to settle down?'

'Not found the right person yet, Pete.'

'Oh well. No rush, I suppose.'

Philip nodded and drank more beer. He was thirty-six. He wondered at what point his carefully cultivated persona would cease to be an adequate disguise. At school, he was a tweed-jacketed philosopher, one of a little group who discussed Sartre and Foucault in break time and attended talks and exhibitions in the evenings. At home, in the streets where he'd been born and brought up, he was still 'a nice lad, done well for himself but kept his feet on the ground', always willing to clear the snow away from his elderly next-door neighbour's steps and tell the local kids off for dropping litter in the park. But at some point, his single status would become more important than anything else and people would start to wonder.

Harry started singing again, a bellowed version of Frank Sinatra's 'My Way', despite the glares of the remaining people near him.

'Simon,' Pete leaned out over the bar and called out. 'If you can't keep him quiet, he'll have to go.'

The young man talking to Harry stopped his singing by dint of passing him his beer, much in the same way mothers shoved dummies in the mouths of their babies.

'Who's that with Harry?' Philip asked. 'I haven't seen him around.'

'You don't come in often enough, then. He's from Liverpool, used to work over at the Longbridge Plant.'

'Laid off?'

Pete nodded and pursed his lips.

The mass redundancies in the automotive industry in and around Coventry were a source of worry to them all. Most of the locals owed their employment one way or another to British Leyland and the other car manufacturers.

'One of the first,' Pete said. 'Bit of a troublemaker, if you get what I mean.'

Philip did. Local feeling was polarised. Some, angered by their essential powerlessness in the face of poor management and economic forces outside their control, were supporters of 'Red Robbo', as the press called him, and his striking colleagues. Others felt the continual industrial action was harming British Leyland's chances of ever returning to prosperity. Philip stayed on the fence. Like he always did. Like so many others did.

He looked over at Simon, now steering Harry away from a dartboard. There was a blandness about him that Philip mistrusted given what Pete had said. An unobtrusiveness. He was medium height and medium build, his shabby trousers and shirt making him indistinguishable from many others in the pub. He was balding, despite his youth, and his round face looked like a balloon on which a child had drawn a face. Two eyes, a nose and a mouth, but nothing more.

As Philip watched, he leaned over to ask Harry a question and Philip wondered what the two had in common.

'Does he often do this? Chat to Harry, I mean?'

'Probably the only person who will,' Pete said, as he emptied the ashtrays on the bar and gave them each a quick wipe. 'Harry pays for the drinks but Simon's seen him home a couple of times because Harry's fallen in the road, you know. Nothing serious. He's had the luck of the very drunk so far but one day it'll run out.' He gave Philip a sharp look. 'Or his money will.'

'What do you mean?'

'You tell Wilf that, if he's giving his dad money, he should stop. It's not doing him any good. In fact, it'll kill him, because it's not just a few pints here of an evening. I can smell it on his breath when he comes in.'

'I'll tell Wilf but I don't think he gives his dad money. Harry got a good pension from Poulters on top of his state pension.'

Pete raised his eyebrows. 'See what I mean? The luck of the drunk. Half of mild, Colin?' he asked the man counting his pennies into a pile on the bar. He poured the drink as he spoke to Philip. 'Never understood how Harry kept his job at Poulters. Everyone said he was half-cut most of the time towards the end. I suppose he knows where the bodies are buried. At least, that's what he says.'

A trickle of unease ran over Philip's skin like icy water. He rarely thought about the disastrous summer he and Wilf had spent working at Poulters.

'And here's the man himself. We were just talking about you, Harry.'

Harry stood next to Philip, surprisingly steady on his feet, as Simon came up behind him, carrying their glasses. Harry was drunk, very drunk, Philip could tell. His wandering eyes gave him away and his joy at seeing Philip. Harry had never been a mean drunk. He saved that for his occasional moments of sobriety. Alcohol bathed him in happiness.

'Philip,' he shouted. 'Is Wilf with you?' He peered round Philip's shoulders as though expecting Wilf to pop up.

'No, Harry. I'm on my own. How are you?'

'Never better, lad. Never better!' He turned to Pete and slapped some coins on the bar. His hand shook slightly and his voice too. 'Two pints of your best bitter, landlord, and whatever my young friend Philip here would like.'

'No more, Harry. You've had enough. Take him home, Simon.' Pete crossed his arms.

Harry ignored him. 'Simon,' he shouted. 'This is Philip. My old friend Philip.' And for some reason only known to him, he started singing 'We'll Meet Again', quietly at first but his voice swelled with the tune. 'Don't know where. Don't know when,' he bellowed into Simon's ear.

Simon shrugged. 'Come on, Harry. Time for a walk.'

'We going for a walk? Wonderful.'

'Say goodbye to – Philip, was it?' Simon turned to Philip with a smile that sat uneasily on his face, as out of place as lipstick would have been.

'Yes.'

'Philip Mason?'

'Yes.'

Simon held out his hand. 'Pleased to meet you, Philip. Friend of Wilf's, aren't you?'

Philip nodded and shook the proffered hand for as short a time as possible.

'I'll come back once I've seen Harry home and buy you a drink,' Simon said. 'I'd like a quick word.'

'Well, aren't you the lucky one,' Pete said, as the two of them watched Simon usher Harry out through the door. 'He doesn't often put his hand in his pocket, like.'

Chapter Sixteen:
Philip Mason

26 November 1977
Twenty years after the incident

Philip checked the address he'd noted in his pocket diary. This *was* Owen's house. He hadn't expected it to be so grand. True, it was close to its neighbours, the garden at each side a mere strip of grass bounded by an old brick wall, and the building itself was smallish, but it was beautiful. There was no other word for it. Double-fronted with three storeys and painted white, one of the houses built by the wealthy industrialists who had dominated Coventry's growth in the nineteenth century.

How on earth had Owen ended up living here?

There could be no doubt he did because the brass plaque next to the bell was engraved with the name *Greenacre* as well as *Coventry Chronic Illness Support*, the name of the charity Owen had set up when he'd left Poulters.

Philip almost expected a maid to usher him in but the door was opened by a woman in her early twenties. Definitely not a maid.

'I'm here to see Owen, Mr Greenacre,' he said in response to her pleasant smile. 'Philip Mason. He's expecting me.'

She was as beautiful as the house but nothing like as old-fashioned. Her long hair was curled and waved in the style of the moment. Very Farrah Fawcett-Majors. Looked natural although one of his female colleagues had told him it took a lot of time and hairspray to reproduce. She wasn't wearing the jeans and loose shirts beloved by the fashion icon, though. Her dress was sharply cut and canary yellow, and the high heels of her matching shoes clicked on the floor as she turned to call back into the darker reaches of the house.

'Dad, someone for you.'

She was Owen's daughter then. With a graceful smile, she left him standing outside with only a cloud of perfume, Rive Gauche, he thought, to indicate she'd ever been there. How on earth had Owen ended up with a daughter like this?

Unlike his house and his daughter, Owen was still resolutely unbeautiful. The twenty years or so that had passed since Philip last saw him had turned his moustache and springy hair white although they were still as bushy as ever. He didn't look at Philip as he shook hands. He ushered him into a back room that, despite the gleaming wood and burnished leather of its antique furniture, was clearly used as an office.

Philip sat himself in an armchair with carved legs and brass studs round the seat and discovered it was as uncomfortable as it looked. Owen stood by the old fireplace whose elegant proportions were marred by the gas fire rammed into its centre and hissing gently.

'It's been quite a time, hasn't it?' Owen said. 'Must be all of twenty years.'

'Twenty years and three months, Owen.'

A typewriter started clattering in the room next door.

'And how have you been? You're looking well. Teaching, I hear. Drink?'

Philip shook his head. Owen seemed determined to dress their meeting up as some kind of pleasant reunion. Surely he must be aware Philip would only have sought him out because of that summer twenty years ago.

Evidently, he was, because his next comment was about Jean and how well she was doing in the States.

'She's part of the team developing the vaccine for meningitis and I hear there are other things in the pipeline,' Owen continued, as he opened the large globe by his desk to reveal a bar. 'And I like to think

I've achieved something too. You probably haven't come across my charity.'

Philip looked around the room with its thick carpet, its antique desk and chairs, the bar of cut-glass decanters with their sparkling gold and deep-red liquids. He began to understand where all this wealth had come from and the knowledge only hardened his resolution.

'I suppose Poulters supports your charity, Owen?'

'Richard has been very kind, yes.'

Owen pulled the stopper off a decanter of scotch. Its peaty aroma mingled with the smell of polish as he poured himself a large glass.

'And the charity employs you, does it, Owen? It must pay you a good wage for you to be able to afford all this. On top of what I suspect is a very generous pension from Poulters.'

'Poulters gives us a large donation every year but all the pharmaceutical companies give to charity. There's nothing out of the ordinary about that.'

His smugness grated on Philip's already stressed nerves.

'Can't you see what it's for, Owen? It's to keep you quiet. It's to keep you happy. It's blackmail.' Philip's voice had begun to rise. The noise of the typewriter in the distance stopped.

'It's not like that. Richard looks after us, it's true, but –'

'Us? Your daughter works for the charity too?'

'Laura's a very good typist,' Owen said.

Philip sighed to himself. How could Owen be so blind?

'Richard likes to help,' Owen said.

Help was one way of putting it, Philip thought. The secret of how Harry had enough money to drink himself into an early grave was revealed. Philip felt sick.

'How do you think Wilf got his flat?' Owen continued. 'They're like gold dust. But Richard put in a good word for him. He knows a lot of people. It's like a club, big businessmen. Everybody knows everybody.'

'I suppose Harry asked him because I'm sure Wilf didn't.'

'Harry asked me and I asked Richard,' Owen said proudly, as though Richard's benevolence had somehow rubbed off on him in his role as go-between.

'Well, Harry's not keeping his side of the bargain,' Philip said. 'He's not sticking to your nasty little arrangement. He's said too much and someone has listened too hard. Someone with his eyes open for an opportunity has put two and two together and realised they might add up to hundreds of pounds. And he came to me.'

'Who?'

'It doesn't matter. I didn't come here for that. I didn't come here to ask you to pay him. No, I came to tell you that it's time for the truth.'

Owen started to stutter a response, then sat down suddenly, sloshing his whisky over the leather top of the desk. He ignored the splashes and put his head in his hands. Was it fear of the truth coming out? Or the same mixture of shock and nausea Philip had felt when he realised Simon was blackmailing him. Simon's words, muttered into Philip's ear through the smoke and laughter, rang in his head.

Mr Poulter, now, he's done well for himself. Big flashy offices in London and all that. Bit of a toff, isn't he? MBE now, Harry told me. But such a kind man. Looks after Harry. I'm sure he wouldn't want Harry spreading silly stories around the place.

I'm happy to keep quiet. It's in no one's interests for the truth to come out. Not now. Not after all this time. But I'm not a rich man. No chance of another job. Not here, not after the rumours those bastards at Longbridge have spread about me. I'm sure Mr Poulter'd see his way to helping me out. In return, like, for my keeping an eye on Harry. I'm not asking you, Philip. I know you're just a working man like me. But you pass the message on. You can do that, can't you? Just pass the message on.

Philip had given himself time, keeping a semblance of calm as he told Simon nothing would happen quickly. All the time he had longed to drive his fist into the smiling face that seemed to claim kinship with Philip, dirtying him with the assumption that Philip would condone his demands.

Then Philip had gone away for the half-term holidays to the Lake District. He'd been promising himself he'd visit it for years. He took Wilf's dog, Bouncer, because Wilf had just come out of hospital following another operation on his left leg. He'd been worn and white when Philip had visited. His wife looked equally tired and was struggling to find time to walk the dog.

The effect on Wilf of the truth coming out was another thing to think about. Philip had argued with himself for days as he'd climbed the hills and hiked alongside rivers and lakes. Gradually, the beauty of his surroundings had seeped through the noise of the voices in his head and, one late afternoon, sitting on a stone wall overlooking a meadow of long grass, his hand on Bouncer's collar to stop him from chasing the rabbits, he'd come to an awareness of the need for truth. For truth regarding the past and for truth about himself in the present. Its absence was warping his life. That was as close as he could get to explaining. And he thought he could tell a little lie or not tell a little truth and keep Wilf out of it.

He looked down now at Owen whose head was still hidden in his hands. Philip would have to try to make him see how important the truth was.

'Owen,' he said. 'I know it'll be bad. But there is no other option. Believe me, I've thought and thought about it.'

Owen lifted his head.

Philip was shocked. Owen was crying. Really weeping. Tears filled his tired eyes and spilled out, rolling down over old and crumpled skin. His hand shook as he wiped them away and cleared his throat.

'No,' Owen said. 'No. You can't. I won't let you.'

'It's the only option. Even if you pay this man off, there'll be others. With Harry like he is, there'll be more. Besides, I honestly think it's time for the truth. We should have done it then. Time has only made it worse.'

'We made the right decision then. I've always known that.'

Philip sighed. He thought he understood. Owen needed to think they'd done the right thing all those years ago to be able to live with himself. The past still haunted him, though. Plus, the revelation of what had happened would involve him giving up things that had become woven into the fabric of his life.

'I'm sorry, Owen. You can't stop me revealing the truth,' he said.

But Philip's statement seemed to settle Owen, who smiled and took a sip of his whisky, letting it swill round his mouth before swallowing it.

'No one will believe you. You were a lad and only at Poulters for a few weeks. We'll say you got confused. We'll all deny it.'

'And Harry? Will Harry deny it?'

'I'll make him.'

'You might be able to make him keep his mouth shut while he's sober but…'

'Leave Harry to me,' he said.

'Owen, you're not listening to me.'

'No. It's your turn to listen and listen well, Philip.' He clinked his nail against the crystal glass of whisky, watching the dark liquid ripple. 'Richard has a lot of responsibilities. He's grown Poulters from the small company it was after the war, with a single factory in Coventry, to what it is today, with labs all over the country and major processing plants too. That's a lot of people he gives work to, and a lot of money he ploughs back into the community. Next step for him is to go multinational. You'll read it in the papers soon, so it's no secret. Richard's got big ambitions.'

Philip wondered where this was going.

'We've stayed close, you see. Richard and I. He still lives locally. Of course, he's got a flat in London, but he likes it here. It's where his roots are. But don't make the mistake of thinking he's sentimental. He's far from that. He'll do whatever it takes to keep Poulters a success. And he's not stupid. He's a planner, is Richard. So he's kept an eye on you all, you know. Jean, over in America. Wilf and his family.'

'And Harry? He hasn't kept a very good eye on Harry.'

'Never you mind about Harry. You need to think about yourself. Richard's kept an eye on you, Philip. That's what you need to think about. And when I say an eye, it's a very far-seeing one. It can see all the way into a certain sort of club in London.'

Philip's thoughts drained away, leaving him empty and numb. Just one remained. He mustn't react. He wouldn't react. Not in front of Owen, he wouldn't.

Owen looked at him sadly. 'Bit of a shock, is it? Sorry. But you brought it on yourself with all your talk about the truth. The truth goes both ways you know.'

A wave of anger broke over Philip.

'I've not broken the law. Everything I've done is legal.' Was that his voice? It sounded like it came from a fourteen-year-old struggling to master the shift from boy's voice to adult. He cleared his throat and tried again. 'You've got nothing on me.' No, that really wasn't what he wanted to say.

Owen stood and walked over to the window where he stared out at the bare trees dripping from a recent shower.

'I know it's legal. It'll be ten years now since they passed that Act, but there's the law and then there's public opinion and, in a profession like yours, the latter counts as much as the former. Especially as you're planning to change schools.' He turned to face Philip. 'St David's, isn't it? Yes, Richard asked around when I told him you'd contacted me out of the blue. It's a wonderful school, so I've heard. Private, of course, so a better class of pupil. Children who want to learn. You'll do well there, Philip. Of course, they might not be so keen on you if they knew about Jonathan.'

Philip didn't know what was worse. The realisation that Owen was right and he might lose everything. Or hearing Owen's tones of disgust as he mentioned Jonathan's name. Because Owen wouldn't be the only one. All his old friends, the families in the streets he'd grown up in and where he still lived, his own family, his mother... He couldn't bear the thought of even a fleeting revulsion flickering through their minds. He wanted to scream to the world that there was nothing disgusting about any kind of love and there was nothing wrong about his and Jonathan's.

Owen sipped from his drink and watched him curiously. Whatever he saw in Philip's face must have reassured him. He walked back to the desk and clapped Philip on the shoulder. 'You leave Harry and his new friend to me. You've nothing to worry about. You've done well, Philip, and Wilf has too. Good job at the bank. Pillar of the community, he is. An example to us all with what he's achieved.'

Philip waited for the familiar words: *despite his crippled leg, despite his polio*, but, of course, Owen swerved from mentioning them.

'Richard agrees with me. Proud of both of you. He'd help, you know, if you needed anything… if I asked him.'

Philip shook his head. He had to get out of here. Find somewhere quiet to think. Somewhere away from Owen's words twisting his gut into knots. Somewhere away from the relentless hiss of the fire.

'Well, the offer holds good for the future because Richard and I both know you weren't to blame. You were covering for Wilf, weren't you? Harry was so edgy about everything, I eventually worked out why.'

Philip couldn't listen anymore. He looked away from Owen and down at his shoes. He'd scuffed one of them and he bent to rub the mark.

'It can't have been easy for you to shoulder the blame,' Owen said. His voice was kindly now, like that of a benevolent uncle slipping a tenner into his nephew's pocket. 'You should benefit from it. And, of course, it would be a pity for Wilf if any of it came out. After all he's achieved. No, we must all of us protect Wilf.'

Philip stood up. Owen's last words sickened him more than anything else he'd said.

'Do you need to get off, Philip? I'll get Laura to see you out.'

But before Owen could call Laura, she was there, standing at the door with her lips curved into a smile. She must have heard their conversation, yet no concern nor curiosity disturbed her composed features. She knew it all already. Of course she did. At some moment in the intervening years, Owen had told her. Philip had a sense of the secret like a virus, slipping insidiously from one person to another. There'd been seven of them originally. How many other people knew now? How many other people had been infected with it?

He pushed past her and ran to the front door, pulling it open and escaping into the chill of the air outside. As he turned to shut it behind him, he saw Laura's face, gazing at him from the study door down the corridor. His precipitous exit had disturbed her imperturbable beauty and she looked annoyed.

Chapter Seventeen:
Phiney Wistman

18 June 2017
Five days after the reunion

Dora was the first person to turn up the next morning, weighed down with bags, as she pushed past the tea trolley and dislodged a basket of biscuits. A feeling of huge irritation made my mood even blacker. I'd never be able to question Meghan closely about my so-called fall with Dora listening in avidly.

'You're not going to work?' she asked as she plonked the bags on my bed.

'No. These are the only clothes I've got.' I was dressed in my uniform and waiting for the doctor so I could get away as soon as possible. 'What are you doing here?'

'I thought of clothes.'

She passed me a bag. Inside was a pair of my favourite brand of jeans along with a white T-shirt and some underwear.

'I'm dressed now,' I said, passing the bag back to her. Her face closed up like it always did when I said something mean. I cursed my grumpiness. Dora was making a big effort and she was still shaky with the shock of Grandad's death. It showed in the trembling fingers plucking her skirt.

'I mean, thank you, but I don't have the energy to change.' I remembered the absence of clean clothes at my flat. 'Actually, I will take the clothes. Er, they're great.'

'How are you?'

'I'm fine. You didn't need to come down for me.'

'I didn't.'

Dora had the intent look on her face that meant something was bothering her. I waited for the onslaught of words but none came.

'Why did you come down then?' I asked. Might as well get it over with sooner rather than later.

'I'll tell you. But not here.' She looked around and shuddered. 'Too many people. Never liked hospitals. But then who does!'

Dora was right. It wasn't the place for a revealing conversation. Not with the woman in the bed on my left watching our every move. I could practically see her straining her ears in our direction. Old cow. She'd had the nurses up and down all night with demands for cups of tea and painkillers and help to go to the loo.

'Let's go then,' Dora said.

'Can't. Got to wait for the doctor to tell me it's OK.'

'Worse than getting out of prison.'

'How would you know?'

'What?'

'I mean you've never been to prison.'

'You know what I mean. Don't be so... difficult, Phiney.'

The snarky comments had slipped out before I could stop them. Why did Dora always bring out the worst in me?

'Anyway, I've got to wait for Meghan,' I said. 'Her parents are bringing Jack in for me.'

'They already have. He's downstairs. Meghan's parents took her home for some sleep. She's shattered after yesterday. She said she'd call you later.'

I double-cursed Meghan. Firstly, for answering my phone to Dora and bringing her down to check I was all right and, secondly, for slipping off before I could interrogate her about last night. I might as well go back home and try to sleep myself. I felt pretty shitty to be honest, a bit sick and my head throbbed relentlessly. I'd have to lie to the doctor if I wanted to get out.

Dora fidgeted around the cubicle, fingering everything. A snappy comment about spreading germs rose to my lips but I bit it back.

'You haven't left Jack alone?'

'No.' She pursed her lips. 'Mat's waiting with him. He picked me up at the station and drove me here.'

'Mat's here!'

I added feeling faint and very shaky to the list of symptoms not to tell the doctor.

'You called Mat to give you a lift!'

'No. He called me. He wants to see us. Oh please, Phiney. Just wait until we get out. Please.'

She was right. Mrs Nosey on the left was making no effort to hide her enjoyment of our fierce whispers and the rest of the ward had grown suspiciously quiet. Luckily, the doctor chose that moment to swan in. He signed me out with a lot of jolly comments about nurses being the worst patients and how lucky I was to have my gran to look after me. I contented myself with a glare.

'What a numpty,' Dora said, as soon as we got out of the ward. 'Are they all as annoying as him?' She took one look at my face and charged on ahead down the corridor to the way out. I tried to keep up but the muscles in my legs were in agony.

The glass doors at the exit swung open for Dora but I held back. Mat was outside, walking up and down and talking on his phone, while Jack watched him.

He couldn't do anything to me, I told myself. Not in broad daylight with a gentle stream of visitors and porters trudging past us. Besides, I was with Dora, although I never thought I'd see her as protection.

He gave me a wave. I lifted a hand in return. He'd tied his curls back into a stupid ponytail but half of it had escaped and the remaining strands looked like a huge tangle on the back of his head. I guessed he thought it looked cool. My quivering insides settled a little. No one so moronic-looking could be a threat.

Maybe it was a coincidence that he'd been at the hospital when

I'd been pushed down the steps. I still wanted to know what he'd been doing at Berkswell House. And why he wanted to talk to me and Dora.

There was only one way to find out.

I left the shelter of the hospital and went out to join them. Jack bounded forward and shoved my poor legs in a way that he never would have if Grandad had been in charge. He was a lovely dog but he needed a master and Dora and I weren't up to it. I ignored my aching shins and bent down to cuddle him.

'What happened to you, boy? I told you to run.'

Mat finished his phone conversation. 'He stopped to say hello to the men fixing the side gate.'

'You silly boy,' I said to Jack. And to Mat. 'And then?'

'Well, I was there.'

'Yes, I saw you chatting away to the guards.'

I tried to keep the suspicion out of my voice.

'I told them Jack was mine. He recognised me anyway and came over.'

'Why didn't you call me straightaway? I've been worried sick about him.'

'I called your grandmother as soon as I got away from the guards. It's her number on Jack's collar. She said she'd call you…'

I thought about all the calls from Dora I'd ignored.

'And then you left me a message and I realised she hadn't managed to get hold of you. I called you but your phone was switched off. Anyway, I wanted to see you so I got up early and brought Jack over to the hospital. Lucky for you I did. Your friend, Meghan, said you might have lain there for ages, bleeding, if we hadn't come looking for you.'

His eyes stared beyond us as though remembering the scene.

'I expect it was horrifying,' Dora said. 'Head wounds bleed so much.'

I realised she was talking to Mat.

'Meghan knew exactly what to do. She was amazing,' he said.

116

'It must have been awful for you, though.'

'It wasn't great for me either,' I said.

'No, of course not. What happened? Did you slip? Meghan said the steps can be very slippery but it's been so dry recently –'

'I tripped and fell,' I said, cutting her off.

Something flitted across Mat's face. A hidden thought clouded his eyes for a moment. Was it relief that I didn't seem to remember what had happened? If only my head didn't hurt so. If only my shaken brain would settle down. I needed to go back to my flat and sleep but I wanted to know why Mat had been at Berkswell House and what he'd said to Dora that had brought her back down to Coventry so quickly.

'What were you doing at Berkswell House anyway?' I asked. 'You looked mighty friendly with the guards.'

'It's complicated,' Mat said. 'What were you doing there?'

I ignored the question. 'And why did you want to see us?'

'Yes,' Dora said. 'Have you found something out? About Wilf's death?'

'Can we go somewhere?' Mat said as he looked around at the scores of people skirting our tight group to get into the hospital. He was right; it wasn't an ideal place for a discussion about Grandad's death but I felt safer with people around.

'Can't you just tell us quickly? I need to go home and rest.'

'You do look a bit pale.'

Actually, I was wondering how much longer I could stand up.

'How about my car?' he said. 'It would be private, at least. It's in the car park.'

I nodded and wished I hadn't.

We trailed round the outside of the hospital to the car park – a piece of waste ground where some private contractor charged patients a fortune to park. Mat walked slowly with me as the muscles in my legs protested every step. Dora took Jack and kept on charging ahead, her coat flapping and making her look more like a crow than ever.

117

'How did you get into Berkswell House?' he asked.

I told him about shimmying over the gate and then letting Jack in after me. He looked impressed.

His car was at the far side of the car park, away from the cluster of visitors' cars near the exit. 'Sorry about the walk,' he said to me as I stopped to give my legs a rest. 'I keep away from other cars if I can. Don't want to get mine scraped by a careless driver.' He glanced anxiously round the sides when we finally got there. 'It's fairly new.' He wiped a smear of mud off a gleaming wheel arch.

'It's the two-litre version, isn't it? With limited slip differential?' Dora asked, tapping her finger on the pristine bonnet.

Was she winding him up? No, she wasn't capable of it. She wasn't capable of any kind of humour. There was a feverish quality in her voice anyway that made me think she was trying to hold it together. They went on discussing the merits of limited slip differential – whatever it was – as we clambered into the car. Me in the back with Jack. Dora in the front. The inside smelled painfully of air freshener and plastic cleaner. I thought of all the naphthalene they emitted, known to cause lung cancer in rats although the manufacturers claimed it was safe for humans.

'Enough of the *Top Gear* chat,' I said. Every bit of me was starting to hurt. 'What do you want to say to us?'

'Tell me why you were at Berkswell House first,' he said.

But I'd had time to think of a reasonable answer.

'I wondered if Grandad went there. It's close to Tile Park station and…' I cast a quick glance at Dora, praying she wouldn't remember the newspaper cutting. I didn't want to tell Mat more than I had to. 'His father worked there for years.'

Mat breathed in audibly and tapped his fingers together.

'What were you doing there?' I asked.

'I wanted a quiet look round. Some odd things have been happening with Poulters and Berkswell House.'

I schooled my face into a blank expression.

'What odd things?'

He told us the stuff I already knew about Poulters pulling out of the Berkswell House sale at the last minute.

'Why,' he asked, 'do they suddenly want to hang on to a derelict building they have no use for? And then there's Michael Poulter.' He squirmed round in the seat with the steering wheel wedged into his side so that he could face us both. 'He's the chairman of Poulters. Or he was. Because he's dead and he died on the same day as Mr Patterson.'

I didn't let on I already knew about Michael Poulter's death.

'Nothing surprising about Michael's death on the face of it. It was common knowledge that he was very ill and that he'd refused treatment. The *Coventry Telegraph* asked me to update his obituary. But... '

He dabbed a trickle of sweat running down from his scalp.

'Something was wrong. Normally with an obituary, people are bursting to talk to you but Michael's secretary was cagey, very cagey. She would only tell me he died in the Ramada Hotel in Coventry; housekeeping found him in the morning. And that he'd come for a meeting with one of the charities Poulters supports. At The Herbert.'

I flinched. I couldn't help myself. The Herbert?

Mat gave me a quick look. He must have seen my reaction.

'It's very hot in here,' I said. 'Could you turn the car on so I can open a window?'

'The ones in the back don't work. Some electrical thing. I'm taking her in tomorrow for them to sort it.' He opened the front windows and the sharp odour of dust and grit fought against the air-freshener.

My brain was focused on the news that Michael Poulter had been at a meeting at The Herbert the day before he died. Grandad had been there on the same day. The receipt in his book showed that. Was it a coincidence? The following morning they were both dead. Another coincidence?

'Michael was always heavily involved in Poulters' charitable work,' Mat continued, 'but either his secretary knew very little about the meeting and who'd been there or she wouldn't tell me. And it made my journalistic antennae start to quiver.'

He gave a little cough and looked faintly pleased with himself.

'And then, Mr Knowles – he lives right by Berkswell House and has strong feelings about the way Poulters have neglected the place – he called me and told me Poulters had tidied up the grounds and installed massive amounts of security. It seemed amazingly speedy and sudden. The place had been left to rot for decades. So, I thought I'd take another look yesterday morning.'

Dora, who had so far listened with a faint look of puzzlement on her face, cut in. 'But what has this got to do with –'

I interrupted her.

'How did you get in?'

'Mr Knowles lent me a ladder – he's not averse to taking the law into his own hands and he's very angry with Poulters – and I went over the side gate.'

'I didn't see a ladder,' I said.

'Mr Knowles took it away. No point advertising my presence. Although the bolt cutters I used to cut the barbed wire at the top of the gate and chain are hidden round the back of the lodge. Anyway, I didn't realise they'd installed security cameras round the house. They must have acted bloody quickly to get them up and running so fast. So, the security firm turned up and nabbed me. Just as I'd found a loose board on the window by the back door.'

'But they let you go.'

I tried as hard as I could to keep the note of accusation out of my voice.

The sun shone straight in through the window on my side, exacerbating the chemical odour of the car and my headache.

'What else could they do? I wasn't a vagrant, just a perfectly respectable newspaper reporter – which they checked – following up on a story I'd written about the sale of the house falling through – which also checked out. I told them I'd come across the side gate open – which they couldn't check – and wandered in to have a look. Sure, they could have tried to do me for trespass but I knew they wouldn't. Firms like that, they value their relationship with the police too much to bother them with a nice, polite chap like me. Besides, as soon as I said I was a journalist, it was kid gloves all the way.'

His story hung together but I still doubted him. There were too many coincidences. He was the only witness to Grandad's death and the only person who'd been around when I'd been pushed. What would have happened if Meghan hadn't come looking for me? And why had I been pushed? Was it because I'd been at Berkswell House? If so, Mat was the only person who knew that. Unless…

'Did you tell the guards who I was?'

Mat blinked at me. 'No,' he said and then, after a pause, 'I did tell them you must be the person who'd broken in though and that my dog must have sniffed you out. I knew they'd never catch you. You ran like a bat out of hell.'

'But what has this got to do with Wilf?' Dora asked. 'His dad worked for Poulters for most of his life but Wilf had nothing to do with them.'

The light of the sun was deeply unflattering on her sallow skin, picking out the redness round her eyes that faded into mauve shadows beneath.

I suspected I didn't look much better. I certainly felt like shit.

'Mr Patterson went to Berkswell House,' Mat said. 'On the morning he… the morning I saw him at the station. That's why I wanted to see you.'

We both stared at Mat.

Dora found her voice first. 'Why didn't you tell us before this? We begged you for information.'

'Because I only found out yesterday when I was there myself.'

Dora's voice barged in. 'How do you know?'

'When the guards let me go,' Mat said, 'I went back to see Mr Knowles and apologise for leaving his bolt cutters behind. Also, to tell him about the cameras because I'm sure he goes into the grounds.

JANE JESMOND

Well, Jack was with me, of course, and Mr Knowles recognised him because of his eyes. He'd seen him with Mr Patterson the morning he died. Mr Patterson was at the gates trying to get in. Mr Knowles thought he was one of the vagrants who slept there and went out to tell him to move on.'

'A tramp.' Dora's voice throbbed. 'I told him not to wear that awful old mac of his but he would never throw anything away.'

'A lot of them have dogs apparently.' Mat tried to placate her.

But I thought it was as much Grandad's shuffling gait and limp that had decided Mr Knowles.

'I don't think he'd have remembered but for Jack, you know. Plus the fact that Mr Patterson was weeping.'

'Weeping?' Dora and I spoke at the same time.

'Wilf never cried. Did he, Phiney? Are you sure it was him?'

Of course, Mat was sure. The dog. The limp. The timing.

'Yes,' Mat said.

A van pulled in beside us and drove backwards and forwards as it straightened up, sending showers of loose gravel pinging against the side of Mat's car. He gave the driver a quick glance then continued.

'I wanted to tell you that Mr Patterson had been at Berkswell House but I also wanted to know if you knew why.'

Dora thought for a moment and then shook her head. 'No idea.'

'Phiney?' he turned to me.

'No,' I said.

Mat looked disappointed. 'Nothing at all?'

Dora shook her head.

'Could it have been something to do with his father? Maybe he told him something...' Mat's voice trailed off.

'Which charity was it?' I asked. 'The meeting Michael Poulter went to at The Herbert. Which charity?'

'The CCIS. Why?'

I started to say something noncommittal but Dora interrupted me.

122

'Where did you say the meeting was?'

'The Herbert,' Mat said.

'Could we have the air con on?' I asked quickly. I had a feeling Dora had seen The Herbert on the book receipt and was about to reveal that Grandad had been there on the same day as the meeting. I gave her a fierce glance and shook my head as Mat leaned forward to turn the air con on. Her mouth opened and closed a few times but she kept quiet.

'It's probably all a coincidence,' I said.

'I don't think so,' Mat replied.

'Why not? You said Michael Poulter's death wasn't unexpected. And as for Berkswell House, maybe Poulters have other plans for it and that's why they took it off the market and started looking after the place.'

'There's more,' Mat said. 'I got the tip-off that the sale had been pulled from a contact in Poulters.' He bit his lip. 'He said it had been very sudden. That there'd been a panic. And that the order had come right from the top of Poulters. There's something going on and my instincts tell me it's something big.'

I only half listened as he rattled on about Big Pharma being a bit of a hobbyhorse of his because of the scandalous amounts of money they poured into advisory groups that help governments to decide their drug-buying strategies. I was starting to feel sick but I didn't know if it was from the heat or trying to get my aching head round what Mat had told us.

'Most people think big business is dull,' he said.

Dora opened her mouth to speak. I wondered if she was going to tell him it *was* dull, but he spoke too rapidly even for her to get a word in.

'But there's always been a whiff of the Wild West about the pharmaceutical industry. Salesmen at fairs selling snake oil and so on. Cocaine made into tablets and sold as a cure for hay fever, headaches, toothache – anything for a quick buck. Unregulated and full of charlatans.' His voice had come alive as he spoke. 'You know, less than a hundred years ago the production of the smallpox vaccine involved strapping a calf to a table, scratching it to introduce small amounts of the disease, and then killing it and scraping the growth off. So, although you might be vaccinated against smallpox, you ran the risk of picking up some other illness the calf had.'

Dora looked horrified and I felt even sicker myself.

Why was he telling us all this? Surely no one could be genuinely interested in this stuff?

'They don't still scrape animals, though?' Dora said, fingering her shoulder where, I was sure, her smallpox vaccination scar would be.

Mat laughed. He sat straight now, no longer diffident and awkward. Energy sparkled through his voice. 'No, they grow viruses on cell cultures in glass dishes in sterile conditions. But only because governments make them jump through hundreds of hoops to get their products approved. They're still in it for the money. Otherwise, they'd invest in finding cures for illnesses that affect the developing nations rather than drugs for the rich west. Make no mistake – scrutiny is what keeps them honest. Scrutiny from governments and the press – journalists like me.'

'I need to go home,' I said. 'I think I might be going to be sick,' I added for good measure. 'Concussion does that.'

Both Mat and Dora looked as though they'd have liked to say something but they could hardly insist I stayed. Besides, I wasn't at all sure I was lying.

Chapter Eighteen:
Phiney Wistman

18 June 2017
Five days after the reunion

Mat dropped us back at my flat and drove off. Dora had been mercifully quiet during the journey but I knew that wouldn't last. It would be easier to let her say her piece now, so I could get rid of her, crawl into bed and wait until the ache in my head and legs faded.

'Wilf was at The Herbert the day of the meeting,' she said, her hands chopping the space in front of her like a deranged martial arts expert. 'The receipt for the astronomical clock book. He bought it –'

'I know, I saw it. He bought the book at The Herbert.'

'Why didn't you tell Mat that Wilf was there? Maybe he went to the meeting.' Dora said. 'And that newspaper article you showed me. With the photo of Wilf at Poulters. That was Berkswell House, wasn't it?'

'I want to think about it first.'

She stared at me, her mouth once more opening and closing like a demented goldfish.

'I'm not sure I want Mat to know,' I added. 'He's a journalist. He's after a story. You don't want Grandad splashed all over the press.'

'But you can't think that... that Wilf would have done anything to be ashamed of?'

'Of course not.' But Philip's words about Grandad not wanting anyone to know came back to me. I had to get hold of him. Force him to reveal what this was all about. 'Please, can we talk about this tomorrow? I promise I'll call you. My head's about to fall off my shoulders.'

'I still think we should tell Mat. He'll be able to help us.'

'No!' The word burst out of me in an angry explosion.

Dora recoiled as though I'd hit her but I was beyond caring.

'Listen. You don't understand. About Mat. Look, I didn't fall. Last night. Outside the hospital. I was pushed. Someone came up behind me, whacked me on the head and shoved me down those steps.'

'Are you sure?'

'So, you don't believe me. Well, there's a surprise.'

'Head injuries can –'

'I know. I'm a bloody nurse. Head injuries can cause confusion and memory disturbances. But I am sure. Absolutely sure.'

'But why would anyone do that? Unless it was an accident. Someone bumped into you by mistake?'

'It was hardly bustling with people.' I forced myself to calm down. 'The only person definitely there was Mat.'

She gulped a few times as the meaning of my words sank in.

'You're probably right,' she said at last. 'You should get some sleep and we can talk about it tomorrow.'

I knew she thought I was out of my mind but there was no point arguing.

'What are you going to do?'

'I booked into the Travelodge round the corner.'

'Not going home then?'

She brushed her skirt flat and muttered to herself while I waited for a reply. I knew I was being curt but I'd had enough. More than enough. And I really did need to rest.

'I can't go home, Phiney,' she said at last. 'Not while there's a chance of finding out why Wilf killed himself. It'll be…' She paused as she searched for words. 'Well, it'll stay with me for the rest of my life if I can't find out.'

She stared at me, her eyes painfully wide.

'We'll talk about it tomorrow,' I said. 'I'm going to lie down. My head's splitting.'

I couldn't keep the sharpness out of my voice and she looked as though I'd slapped her but she nodded.

'All right. You get some rest. I'll take Jack if you like. He needs a walk and I'll keep him tonight. The hotel accepts pets.'

This was kind. I managed a thank you and a nod. 'Tomorrow, then. When I'm not so tired.' I made a big effort. 'Sorry if I'm a bit abrupt. My head is killing me.'

The front door grated over the tiles as I pushed it open. Not even the hot weather had made it fit any better. The row of letterboxes along the wall caught the light.

My results. Were they waiting for me?

My fingers fiddled with the bunch of keys in my pocket and found the one for the letterbox.

Oh God.

Suddenly I wanted Dora to stay. To put off the moment when I'd have to open the letterbox for a little while longer.

'How do you know so much about cars?' I called after her.

She smiled as her eyes flicked into the past. 'I grew up surrounded by them. Pa had a garage. Just a big workshop, really, with a couple of petrol pumps and a flat over it where we lived, but we all helped out. I would have liked to be a mechanic but women didn't do that sort of thing in the little village I lived in, so my brother runs it now.'

I tried to imagine her young, in overalls, clutching a spanner, but it was impossible. She strode off down the road with Jack walking patiently behind her. There was a lot I didn't know about her past. She talked a lot but it was all about the present. Or maybe I just hadn't listened.

I waited until she'd gone and opened the letterbox. Nothing. Except a couple of woodlice scuttling for cover.

My body sagged with relief. I couldn't face anything else today.

A sudden noise from above splintered the silence. I jumped. Shit. I should have got Dora to wait until I was safe in the flat. My neighbour opened his door and thundered down the stairs, nearly knocking me over.

'Sorry. I didn't see you in the gloom.'

I smiled at him. 'No worries. Just catching my breath,' I said, and ran up the stairs into my flat, locking the door behind me.

I phoned Philip. He didn't reply. Probably ignoring my calls. I tried again and again until tiredness overwhelmed me and I crashed out.

My head was clearer when I woke in the evening. A light breeze ran in and out of the windows, bringing a scent of dried grass and barbecues. I shuddered at the thought of all the carcinogens coating the singed meat and prepared myself miso soup, fragrant and savoury, and a marinated tofu and sesame seed salad, then picked up my phone to try Philip Mason again.

Still no answer. Was he avoiding me? Or had he gone away? He'd said he had to speak to some people and would come to see me afterwards. Maybe he'd needed to visit them? Or maybe he was on his way to see me now? I should have asked for his mobile number. Even people his age normally had them now.

I had two missed calls from Meghan, both around half an hour ago. I called her straight back.

'Phiney,' she said. 'How are you feeling?'

'Much better since I've had some sleep.'

'Good. But don't start doing too –'

I cut her off. 'Tell me what happened yesterday.'

'What do you mean?'

'It's not all clear in my head and I just want to know.'

'I've told you already.'

'The details, I mean. Everything that happened after I left. You know, Mat arriving and you coming after me and all that. Every bit of it. It's all a bit hazy in my head.'

'Well, the porters rang up to say that someone was there with your dog so I raced down. I met Mat and told him you'd left early but he might be able to catch you up.'

'Did he find me, then?'

'No, I tried to explain which way you'd have gone but, in the end, it was easier to go with him.'

'So you left together. You're sure about that?'

'Phiney! What is this about?'

'I didn't fall, Megs. Someone pushed me and I wondered if it was Mat.'

'What? I mean, are you sure? You know –'

I cut her off before she could start on the guff about head injuries making people confused.

'I'm sure. One hundred per cent. Could it have been Mat?'

She took a moment to let that sink in.

'No,' she said finally.

'How do you know?'

'Because we were together all the time when we went looking for you. Besides, why would he do that? I mean he's really nice. He was really upset that you'd got hurt.'

'Maybe he pushed me before he came to the hospital?'

'With Jack in tow? How could he have done that? Besides, we were together when you fell.'

'I was pushed.'

'OK, when you were pushed.'

'Are you sure?'

'We heard you shriek, Phiney. And then the sound of you tumbling. Mat was with me.'

Some of the tension in my shoulders slipped away. I realised I was glad it hadn't been Mat. Except if it wasn't him, who had it been?

'It must have been kids having a laugh,' I said, but even as the words left my mouth I knew I didn't think it had been.

'You should tell the police.'

'They won't do anything.'

'I guess not. But how could you think it was Mat? He seemed lovely. Quite cute really and very concerned about you. He wouldn't leave until he was sure you were going to be OK. And he rang me last night to make sure I was all right. So sweet of him.'

'Did you see anyone else hanging around?'

'No.'

'Are you sure?'

'Yes.'

'So, it must have been a random thing.' I was beginning to believe it myself. 'After all, if it was deliberate, they'd have had to know I was on night shift and been waiting for me.'

Meghan was silent.

'Meg? You still there?'

'Yes, just thinking. I need to go, Phiney, but you take care of yourself.'

After she'd rung off, I thought about putting some laundry on but instead I used the last of my diminishing energy to explore the internet. I was looking to see what I could find out about the charity that had held the meeting Michael Poulter and maybe Grandad had attended. If I knew what Grandad had been doing in Coventry, I could start to get the answers to some of my questions.

CCIS stood for Coventry Chronic Illness Support. They were often in the local paper during the 1960s and 1970s but there was nothing recent except a couple of references to them as sources of aid on other charities' websites.

They weren't a registered charity so I couldn't see their accounts nor who was on their board but some things were clear. They were funded by Poulters. Richard and later Michael turned up at dinners and galas in the early days and the charity was run by the Greenacre family. At first by Owen Greenacre (the man with the bushy moustache in the 1957 newspaper cutting) and, after his death (marked by a large and glowing obituary in the local paper), by his daughter, Laura.

Owen Greenacre's involvement was a bit of a blow. I'd almost convinced myself the whole 1957 newspaper-cutting thing was a coincidence. I wondered if Grandad had been asking the charity for help in some way and pulled out the article to show his connection to Poulters. Then why would he have left it behind? Maybe he forgot it? I made a decision.

I'd try Philip again in the morning. If I couldn't get hold of him, I'd go and visit the charity. What harm could it do?

My head still ached the following morning but my legs were starting to ease so I walked to the street where Laura Greenacre lived, in a house that was also the address for CCIS. It was one of the grand old buildings not far from Memorial Park where Dora and I met Mat for the first time. I hesitated outside the house, regretting the smart shoes that pinched my feet and the black wool trousers and jacket I'd chosen as a suitable outfit. I was sweating slightly already.

Come on, Phiney. You can do this.

The gravel on the path leading up to the front door crunched beneath my feet, lodging a stone under my sole. I shook it out, hopping up and down, conscious that anyone might be watching my progress through the huge bay windows that dominated the front of the house. Too late to turn and scarper.

Laura Greenacre answered the door. Still recognisable from the photos of her as a young woman with Owen at the charity's galas, everything about her screamed money. Her skin was free of lines in the way only a lifetime of remorseless moisturising and top-range treatments could ensure. Her hair colour (shades of blonde) and make-up were considered and expensive. Very expensive. As were her maroon blouse and skirt and the glorious shoes she wore. God, they were lovely. Utterly plain but perfectly cut and with the muted gleam of expensive leather.

'Josephine Wistman,' I said and held out my hand. She smiled and extended hers. I became instantly aware of my rough skin and unmanicured nails. I launched into my prepared spiel. 'I'm here about the charity you run, CCIS. I'm a nurse at Coventry General.' I flashed my hospital ID. 'In the paediatric oncology ward. We're compiling a list of charities that might be able to offer help to our patients and I wondered if you might have a few minutes to chat to me.'

Her eyes glazed and I guessed she was wondering how to get rid of me.

'I won't take up much of your time. Or I could come back later?'

She produced a tight smile that showed only on her lips. 'Come in, Josephine,' she said and I followed her into a large, elegant sitting room, smelling of furniture polish and a hint of stale cigarette smoke, with the kind of sofas that look spectacular but are too low to sit on gracefully. She, I noticed, remained standing. Maybe the beautiful cut of her skirt didn't let her sit comfortably.

'What would you like to know?'

'Could you tell me a bit about CCIS? The parents of the children on our ward are beyond doing research into available help and need steering in the right direction.'

She rattled off a brief history of the charity. How her father had started it in the 1960s to improve access to new therapies for the chronically ill. How he'd set up local facilities, physiotherapy and advice centres with visiting specialists. 'Wonderful work, he did,' she said. 'Of course, now the prevailing thinking has caught up with him and much of our work has shifted to families needing support at home.'

I pretended to look at some notes. 'You're funded by Poulters, aren't you?'

'Yes. We always have been. My father used to work for them and the charity was his and Richard Poulter's brainchild. Richard was a great philanthropist.'

'Terrible news about Michael,' I said.

'Ah, you heard about that. Mind you, he's not been well for years.'

She crossed to the mantelpiece and picked up a packet of cigarettes. Surely she wasn't going to smoke? Indoors and in front of me?

'Do you mind?' she asked. 'I'll open the window.' She pushed the bottom sash window up and sat down on the window seat in front of it. It must have been a favourite spot of hers for smoking because a creamy onyx table lighter lay on the windowsill. She picked it up and cast me a quick look. Fuck. I couldn't say no. She'd finish the conversation super quick if she was desperate for a cigarette. And wrapping my scarf over my nose was hardly going to encourage her to chat either.

I nodded.

The lighter rasped and she held the flame to the cigarette and sucked in, her cheeks hollowing and magenta lips forming a perfect ring, then blew the smoke out of the corner of her mouth towards the window. Very little of it went outside.

'Dreadful habit,' she said. 'But I love my ciggies.'

The smell of the smoke was choking but I smiled.

'Where were we? Oh yes, Michael. It's very sad but it won't make any difference to CCIS. Poulters will carry on supporting our work. James Poulter has promised.'

She smiled, took another deep drag on the cigarette and made the same halfhearted effort to blow the smoke outside.

'And what sort of criteria do you use in deciding to award grants?' I asked, remembering my role as inquirer in this conversation.

'These days we don't make grants direct to families. We work through other charities. I'm afraid there's no point any of your patients contacting us.'

So, it was unlikely Grandad had been at The Herbert meeting to ask for financial help. Unless…

'You never give money direct to anyone – even if they've been referred to you via another charity?'

'No. Our grants are all for projects rather than individuals.'

'Even if the individual had a connection to Poulters?'

Her eyes narrowed and she paused mid-exhalation, letting the smoke trickle out of her nostrils.

'No,' she said again. 'Why do you ask?'

'We have a family where the father works for Poulters,' I said smoothly, as I wondered what else to ask. I could hardly demand to know the purpose of the meeting at The Herbert. Not without having to tell her everything and I didn't want to. I didn't like her one bit and, anyway, I wasn't one hundred per cent sure Grandad had been at the meeting at all. Maybe he'd only gone to The Herbert to look at the polio epidemic exhibition undisturbed.

'Poulters would more than likely offer help themselves,' she said, launching into what was clearly a prepared spiel. 'We find it's best to adopt a coordinated approach with other charities. The applications process is very time-consuming for people needing help so better for them if they only have to do it once. And for us. Vetting applications took up most of my father's time.'

My nostrils burned with the sharpness of the smoke and the list of carcinogens I was breathing in ran through my mind. PAH; N-nitrosamines; aromatic amines; 1, 3-butadiene; benzene; aldehydes; ethylene oxide; these were the worst. I tried not to picture them coating the cells of my lungs and slipping into my bloodstream. But she didn't seem to care, leaning back against the window frame with the hand holding the cigarette waving as she spoke and disturbing the smoky haze. I started to think about getting out.

'So, you run the charity now?'

'Yes.'

'It must take up a lot of your free time still. Accounts and paperwork. Meetings… and so on.'

I smoothed my trousers and picked up my bag as though readying myself to leave but she carried on, happy enough to chat while she smoked.

'I don't mind. I enjoy that side of it. I took over after Dad died. I'd helped him for years anyway.' She took another deep pull and held the smoke in her lungs. They must be black if she smoked like this all the time. 'I can send you a list of the charities we've given money to this year if that would help? Your patients could approach them.'

'Of course.'

'Give me your email address.' She stubbed the cigarette on the stone ledge outside the window and threw it out onto the gravel, got up and picked up a pencil and notepad from the coffee table.

'Phiney.wistman@gmail.com.'

'Phiney?'

'With a P-H, not an F. It's short for Josephine. Everybody calls me Phiney. Most people don't even realise my name is Josephine.'

She stopped writing and looked at me closely through narrowed eyes. Something about her face reminded me of the cold stare of a snake eying up a mouse.

'Well, Phiney,' she said, after a long pause. 'I'll be in touch with the list of charities and if you have any other questions send me an email.'

She rose, shook my hand and opened the door to usher me out. Before I knew it, I was standing on the drive, looking out into the road I'd walked up only a few minutes before.

My phone rang. It was Meghan. She started talking as soon as I answered.

'The night you fell down the steps, someone called the hospital asking for you.'

'What? What are you going on about, Meg?'

'When we spoke yesterday and you asked about Mat, I remembered Christine mentioned someone had called for you.'

She had all my attention now. 'Go on.'

'I'm back on days now, if you remember, but I went in early and spoke to her before she left. A man called and asked for you the night you were pushed. Christine said she'd get you to call him back but he told her it wasn't important and he'd send you a text. She thought it was odd.'

Despite the heat of the day and my woollen clothes, a shiver of ice ran across my skin. Had the man been checking to see if I was there? So he could hang around and wait for me to leave?

'Maybe it was Mat?'

'No, I called him to find out. And, anyway, he already knew you were working because you'd told him.'

A twitch of movement caught my eye. Laura was standing at the bay window looking at me. The expression in her curiously immobile face impossible to read. Botox, I thought. She'd given herself away earlier, though. The name Phiney meant something to her. She knew who I was and she'd got rid of me straightaway. What was going on?

As I watched her, she picked up her phone and started dialling before turning away from the window.

'I have to go, Meg. I'll call you later.'

I stumbled down the road, wanting to get as far away from Laura as possible.

Chapter Nineteen:
Phiney Wistman

19 June 2017
Six days after the reunion

I never took the bus if I could help it but, after leaving Laura, I couldn't walk home. Not in the shoes I had on and with my head starting to pound again. Besides, the look in Laura's eyes when I told her my name, and Meghan's discovery someone had been asking for me the night I was pushed, had shaken me up. I fancied being surrounded by people.

Dora and Mat were waiting for me outside the flat. Mat leaned against the driver's door of his car, with a hand shading his eyes while Dora talked, the force of her words bobbing her head up and down. Doubtless relating the finer points of something arcane to do with engines. Jack lay in a patch of weeds and looked bored. I was surprised by how pleased I was to see them. Especially Mat. His awkwardness now seemed slightly endearing rather than a mask covering something malevolent.

'What *are* you wearing?' Dora gestured towards my thick wool trousers and matching jacket.

'Nothing else was clean. It was that or the dress I wore to Susannah's wedding.'

We both shuddered.

'What are you doing here?' I asked.

Dora started pulling the ends of each finger in turn. A clear sign that she wasn't sure how I'd react.

Mat gave her a quick glance as though expecting her to speak.

'Can we go to your flat?' he asked in the end. 'We've got something to tell you.'

'Just tell me now. My flat's a mess.'

Mat heaved himself off the car. 'Your grandfather was at the meeting at The Herbert.'

Shit. I wasn't surprised, though.

'You better come up then.'

The postman arrived as I was unlocking the front door. Please let my results not arrive now! I couldn't open them with Dora and Mat here and I didn't think I could bear to wait knowing they were in my letterbox. But he shoved a pile of brown envelopes through my next-door neighbour's slot and walked away.

I trailed up the stairs after Dora and Mat.

'Are you all right?' Mat asked. 'You're very pale and sweaty.'

'Well, apart from the fact that I smashed my head falling down a flight of stone steps, I'm absolutely fine. Never felt better. You should try it yourself sometime.'

He flushed and looked away, and I felt a stab of guilt. I really needed to stop being so grumpy all the time.

No fairies had come and tidied my flat while I'd been out so it was strewn with the clothes I'd looked through trying to find something both clean enough and serious enough for my visit to Laura. I sniffed. The flat always smelled a bit if it wasn't aired. The carpet and curtains were impregnated with the previous tenant's late-night curries. But there was something else. I sniffed again. Cigarettes! God. It was me. Laura's cigarette smoke trapped in the heavy wool of my clothes was sneaking its way back out again.

I opened the windows and cleared the space by stuffing all the dirty clothes in the washing machine. Put the dial onto the speediest cycle. Then remembered I had no detergent. Shit. I poured in some conditioner and the tiniest amount of washing up liquid instead and put it on anyway.

'So, tell me what you found out, Mat,' I said.

Dora took a deep breath. 'He didn't,' she said. 'I did.' She skittered her hands over her skirt. 'I couldn't sleep last night for thinking about Wilf so I went to The Herbert this morning and spoke to the receptionist. I told her my husband had been at the CCIS meeting and dropped his wallet somewhere. She was very helpful. She remembered him and Jack.'

Of course she did.

Dora rattled on, avoiding meeting my eyes. 'She let me look round the room the meeting took place in while she checked with the cleaning company to see if his wallet had been found in the toilets. She promised me the staff would have handed anything they found in. I doubted it myself. Not that the lost wallet actually existed but, I mean, no one can be that sure about their staff. Especially with –'

'Yes, yes, yes. I get it. Are you sure it was the same meeting that Michael went to? It's a big building. There could have been lots of meetings.'

I was sure it was. I was only buying time while I decided what to tell them.

'Aha. I thought that too. So, I wondered out loud if anyone at the meeting might have picked my husband's wallet up. I said I'd ring round but I wasn't sure exactly who had been there, so she very kindly gave me a list.'

I held out my hand. It shook slightly.

'Mat has it,' Dora said. 'I called him and told him what I'd discovered. Phiney, we need help.'

Her eyes begged me to tell Mat about the 1957 newspaper article. She was right. We did need help and Mat was used to looking into things. He knew who to talk to. As a journalist, he'd have access to databases and stuff like that that we didn't.

'Mrs Patterson's done as well as I could,' he said. 'I wouldn't have found out any more than she did.'

'Give me this list, then?' I said.

Mat handed it over, and leaned against the windowsill, the light making a halo of his hair as he watched me read.

Seven people had been expected at the meeting. Michael and James Poulter and Grandad. Plus Jean Storer, Susan Storer, Laura Greenacre and Philip Mason.

Not quite the same people who had stood outside the gates of the Poulter factory and had their photo taken in 1957 but not far off. Michael and Jean had been there along with Grandad and Philip. Owen Greenacre was dead, as was Harry, my great-grandfather, and, of course, Richard Poulter. But they were represented at the meeting by their children. The only person without a presence was Victor Leadsom.

I handed the list back to Mat but he shook his head.

'Keep it. I've got a record on my phone. I photograph everything straightaway. It's much safer that way.'

'Who are they all?' Dora asked, as she lowered herself into my chair and stretched her legs out before her. Her feet were slightly swollen and her patent leather shoes with the little bow dug into the flesh. 'I know Philip Mason. He's an old friend of Wilf's, and you told us about Michael Poulter yesterday. But the others?'

'I don't know,' Mat said. 'Apart from James Poulter, who is Michael's son, CEO of Poulters and a business powerhouse. A very busy man. A man with big plans and a reputation for achieving them. "A chip off the old block" is how my contacts in the City describe him. With the old block being Richard, his grandfather, not Michael. So, what was he doing here, in Coventry, at a tiny charity meeting?'

My feet were killing me. I kicked off the stupid shoes I was wearing and put a pair of battered and comfortable sandals on.

Dora gave me another imploring look.

'Jean Storer rings a bell,' Mat said. 'And I guess Susan Storer is a relation. But I've never heard of Laura Greenacre.'

'Laura Greenacre booked the meeting,' Dora said. 'It started at three and was supposed to be over by five, but it went on until after seven.'

I made a decision. It was time to tell them everything.

'The connection is Poulters,' I said.

Chapter Twenty:
Susan Storer

30 May 2017
Two weeks before the reunion

The front doorbell rang, cutting through the thickness of the afternoon heat and briefly drowning out the endless, droning clicks of the cicadas. Susan Storer sighed. Auntie Jean had gone for a walk, seemingly impervious to the sun, despite her age, so she'd have to go to the door herself.

The doorbell rang again and Susan levered herself to her feet, tying a scarf over her sweaty hair. It was hot, hot, hot. She'd closed the shutters and the large French windows earlier, hoping that the temperature in the ochre-washed sitting room she'd chosen as her writing domain would go down a couple of notches.

It hadn't.

A man in a Panama hat and a linen jacket leaned against the stone wall of the porch, his back to Susan when she opened the door as he stared out into the countryside. He turned. He looked tired, she thought. Well, maybe not tired but ill. His skin lifeless and papery.

'Beautiful,' he said. 'I can see why Jean loves the south of France so much.'

Susan looked beyond him at the grey-green hills shimmering in the heat haze against the relentless blue of the sky. It was beautiful but a bit samey and empty if she was honest. She wouldn't mind a few days of garish hoardings and buses and people and even rain falling on grimy pavements. Anything with a bit of life and energy.

'You could never get tired of looking at that view, could you?'

Susan smiled and nodded. 'I'm afraid Jean's gone out for a walk. She always does around this time of day.'

'I'll wait. I've come a long way to see her. Michael Poulter.' He held out his hand.

She knew who he was from listening to Jean's patient retelling of her life. She had worked for Poulters way back in the 1950s, not long after she had left university. Not that Jean had gone into much detail about Poulters, which in itself was interesting. Susan shook his hand and wondered if she should invite him in. But he sat himself on the stone bench lining the porch and announced he'd wait there, so she fetched him a glass of water and went back to her writing, wondering what Jean would make of this unexpected visitor.

When Jean returned, Susan heard her exclaim, 'Michael! What are you doing here?' But they went into the main sitting room and Susan could hear no more.

She finished typing up her notes from this morning, then replied to a couple of emails from friends in London. *Yes, she was having a wonderful time. Yes, Auntie Jean's memoirs were fascinating and she was enjoying writing them. No, she wouldn't be back for quite a while. Auntie Jean preferred to work here rather than in her flat in London.*

And to a more businesslike one from Auntie Jean's publisher. *No, they hadn't got as much written as they'd hoped and what they had was very bitty, jumping around in time, so, no, Susan couldn't send her anything as yet but hopefully she'd have something in the next couple of weeks.*

Privately, Susan thought that alarm bells would ring as soon as the publisher read the sample chapters. She'd expected Jean's life to be – well, more interesting. Shades of Rosalind Franklin, perhaps, because her experience had been very similar. A life at the forefront of scientific research at a time when women still had to fight for recognition. And she'd worked all over the world. In makeshift camps in Africa and on the outskirts of the Amazon rainforest in Brazil. But, somehow, Jean's accounts of it were very dry. And

Susan, who was normally so good at inserting life and drama into the rambling accounts of her less noteworthy clients, couldn't get hold of Jean's personality. Without it, she was missing the thread to pull the reader through the story. She suspected the problem was a secret Jean wasn't telling her.

It was a pity. She'd been quite excited when Jean had rung her out of the blue and asked her to come to France and help write her memoirs. They were due to be published next year, Jean had told her, and, as Susan had ghostwritten a fair few celebrity autobiographies, she'd be the perfect person. She'd pay her, of course. She wouldn't dream of anything else.

Susan had jumped at it. God knows she needed the money and if the book was successful, Jean had promised her a share of the royalties. A big share. A big share of nothing, Susan thought, as the chances of the memoirs selling well seemed unlikely.

Afternoon became evening. The door to the sitting room where Jean and Michael were closeted stayed firmly shut. Susan stopped working and stepped out onto the patio. This was her favourite time of day, when the heat faded and the air seemed to relax. She thought about helping herself to a glass of wine, white and ice cold. Jean wouldn't mind. In fact, Jean would assume she'd help herself, but somehow she couldn't.

She lit the coils that kept the worst of the mosquitos at bay and scratched the bite on her leg. It bled a little but was still very itchy. Maybe she should fetch the lotion Auntie had given her but she was still sitting when a local taxi came up the drive. Michael left a few minutes later.

She expected Jean to come out and join her; instead, her voice cut through the evening air from the open window above. She was on the phone in her bedroom. At first, Susan could only hear the occasional word. 'Michael' was one. And 'Poulters'. The writer in Susan whispered that something interesting was going on and, when she moved out from under the shelter of Jean's balcony, the conversation became clearer.

'He is. In fact, he's dying.' Jean's voice grew louder. 'And he wants to go out in a blaze of moral glory. Without a thought for anyone else. I'm going to lose everything,' she said, biting off each syllable. 'Everything I've worked for. All the years of battling against the system. All the years of being grateful for the crumbs. For my name as co-author on research papers where the work, the ideas, the methodology were all my own. After all that, I'll end up with nothing.'

Whoever was on the other end started speaking and there was silence while Jean listened.

Susan looked up at the stone walls of the villa and thought of Jean's stylish flat in Chelsea, of how Jean hadn't hesitated to agree to the amount Susan had suggested as payment for her work. Jean wasn't rich exactly, but she was very comfortable. How could she lose it all? Despite the warmth of the evening, Susan felt cold. At the back of her mind had always been the knowledge Jean was childless and Susan her only relative. Jean's money would more than likely come to her, so she'd never worried very much about pensions and savings.

Jean's voice rang out again. 'But that's the thing. He's wrong. Wrong in every way. Maybe if we all get together, we can make him see sense. Because he has to be stopped. There's no other solution. Michael has to be stopped.'

The other person must have started speaking because Jean grew quiet and, when she spoke again, her words were impossible to make out. She'd shut the window against the night-time mosquitos, Susan realised.

A little while later, Jean came out into the garden, glass of wine in one hand and the bottle in the other, and switched on the outside lanterns with her elbow.

'Has Michael gone?' Susan asked.

'Susan! I didn't see you sitting in the dusk.'

Something had definitely happened. Even the soft glow of the light couldn't warm the chalk white of her face and she gulped wine from the glass without tasting it.

'Susan,' Jean said again but this time her voice was calm and thoughtful. 'Actually, there's something you could help me with. I need to track some people down.'

Chapter Twenty-One:
Laura Greenacre

30 May 2017
Two weeks before the reunion

After Jean Storer had rung off, Laura Greenacre gazed through the window into her dark garden. She noticed the cleaner had left a smear on the glass but most of her thoughts grappled with Jean's news. She turned it over and over in her mind, like a child trying to guess what lay beneath the gaudy paper of a birthday present.

It would be a disaster for Jean. No question about it. But she wasn't so sure it would be for her. It was her father's mess after all, and she'd played no part in it.

CCIS would have to close. The charity wouldn't survive the storm of condemnation in the press. The implication that it owed its existence to a massive cover-up. But she was sick of the endless begging letters and the meetings, telephone calls and forms anyway. She'd tell Michael to shut the charity at the meeting Jean had asked her to host. As though Laura had nothing better to do with her time than organise refreshments and so on for what would definitely be a ghastly reunion.

She looked at the list of people Jean was going to summon. They were the names she remembered from Dad's tearful ramblings after a few too many whiskies. Jean assumed they'd have their reunion here but it would be better somewhere else. The Herbert Museum. She'd hired rooms there before for charity board meetings.

A little smile curved her mouth at the thought of it.

She'd leave when the shouting and arguing started. It was nothing to do with her. She'd spent enough of her life nursing Dad through the depression the guilt had caused. She'd leave and come home.

She looked around the house with some satisfaction. She'd had it remodelled recently, emptying the graceful Edwardian rooms of their dark furniture and painting everywhere in light and airy shades. It had cost a lot but, of course, Poulters had paid.

And then the thing that should have occurred to her straightaway arrived and stopped her wandering from room to room and enjoying the beauty of her home.

It wasn't her home.

She didn't know why she hadn't thought of that first of all. Maybe because she'd lived here since she was seven. But it wasn't her home. It belonged to Poulters and was leased at a peppercorn rent to the charity. Somehow she didn't think Michael, with his present determination to undo the past, would let her stay or keep on paying her a salary after the charity closed and the news was out.

And then she really started to think it all through. Words like 'conspiracy', 'accessory after the fact' and, of course, 'murder' flicked through her brain. Good, solid words with centuries of legal meaning behind them. None of them was going to escape what those words meant unless they could make Michael keep the long-buried secret quiet. Yes, Michael had to be stopped.

She scanned the names again. Jean had been sure they'd all back her. Well, Laura would. And she rather thought James Poulter would as well. It was a pity Michael had made Jean promise not to talk to him until he'd broken the news but nothing Michael could say would mitigate the fact it was going to be a disaster for Poulters.

She sped through the other names and started to feel a little better. Everyone would help them to stop Michael. One name jumped out. Philip Mason, the one whose fault it all was. How had he managed to live with what he'd done? Jean had said she'd write to him and Laura wondered how he'd feel when he read the letter.

Chapter Twenty-Two:
Phiney Wistman

19 June 2017
Six days after the reunion

'The connection between all the people at the meeting is Poulters,' I repeated.

'I think so too,' Mat said.

'I know it is.'

Mat's eyes narrowed but he waited to hear what I had to say.

'The people at the meeting at The Herbert all worked, or are related to people who worked, for Poulters in the late 1950s. Michael and James, obviously. Jean Storer and Laura's father, Owen, worked for them, as did Grandad's father, Harry. And one summer, Grandad and Philip Mason too. It wasn't so much a meeting, more of a reunion.'

I took the 1957 article out of my bag and passed it to Mat as the washing machine started its cycle.

'Grandad left this out in his shed.'

I told them my story of finding the newspaper cutting and realising it was the last thing Grandad had looked at before going to Coventry. I told them about my strange conversations with Philip Mason. About finding Mat's article on Berkswell House and realising Grandad might have been there on the awful morning he killed himself. I told them I'd been pushed down the steps and, since Meghan had told me about the phone call asking if I was working, that I was convinced it was linked to Grandad's death. I told them everything including my visit to Laura Greenacre this morning and how she'd recognised the name Phiney Wistman.

Neither of them said anything throughout my story. Mat made a few encouraging noises when I paused. Dora stared at the arm of the chair, her hands tracing the outlines of its swirling pattern, stopping only when I reached the part about Laura Greenacre.

'You shouldn't have gone,' she said, heaving herself out of the chair. 'It was a stupid thing to do.'

She was probably right.

She picked up the list of people who'd been at the reunion from the counter by Mat. 'We need to know who all these people are.'

'Let me see what I can find out.' Mat started tapping on his phone.

'Well, I can tell you about Harry. Wilf's father. He was a drunk and a waster. Died in an accident after a few too many. Wilf never said much about it but a couple of his friends told me it was a blessing.'

'An accident? When?' Mat asked and the hair prickled around my scalp at the sharpness of his tone.

'Oh, years ago. Before I met Wilf. When he was married to his first wife.'

Mat looked disappointed. 'It's all such a long time ago,' he said. 'I mean everyone in the photo is dead or really old now. Even the people at the reunion were old. Except James. The others must all be over sixty.'

'That's not old,' Dora said.

This was obviously untrue but I didn't say anything.

'I know what you both think. You think the same as the vicar's infuriating daughter. She gave me a lift to the station and I could tell she thought Wilf's death didn't matter as much because he was old. Because I was old. The young think only they feel things deeply. What a load of garbage. We know we haven't got much time left, so every drop of life tastes sweeter or harsher or sadder, and all the things we haven't done are much more important. You youngsters, you put everything off until tomorrow. Well, you won't when you're my age.'

She shook her head several times and filled Jack's water bowl from the tap, spilling half of it over the counter.

'You're quite right,' I muttered.

'So find out who these people are. Please, Mat. I have to know if they're anything to do with why Wilf killed himself.'

'It would be quicker if I went down to the newspaper offices and logged on from there.' He glanced at his watch. 'Five minutes in the car at this time of day.'

'Then go,' Dora said. 'We need to know.'

The washing machine whirred into a rattling spin as Mat left. A couple of rinses and then I'd have clean clothes. The smell rising from my outfit was starting to drive me mad. I took the jacket off and shoved it on a hanger, hooking it by the open window. Dora paced up and down the room.

'I smell,' I said. 'That Laura woman smoked.'

'Why don't you have a shower?'

'Nothing to put on afterwards. It's all in the washing machine.'

'I could take your wet clothes to the launderette and dry them if you'd like? There's one round the corner. Next to the supermarket. I'll get some milk.'

'Would you? That would be wonderful. Thank you.'

She looked startled. I guessed she'd been expecting a snappy refusal. Note to self: must try harder with Dora.

The shower was ecstasy. It was one of the few things in the flat that worked. Always hot and powerful. I breathed in lungfuls of steam and coughed them out, and afterwards I made myself a cup of green tea to help cleanse away any lingering chemicals. I rinsed the woollen trousers I'd been wearing and hung them on the towel rail to dry and remembered the clothes Dora had brought to the hospital for me. I put them on.

And then I sat and waited.

Dora came back first, lugging the black bin liner that had been all I could find to put the damp clothes in.

'Mat's just parking,' she said, dumping the bag on the bed and putting a carton of milk in the fridge.

Mat came in, a wodge of papers shoved under one arm and a

laptop in the other. 'I don't think it's a good idea to leave the door open,' he said and kicked it shut behind him.

'Cup of tea?' Dora said. 'I've bought some milk. And biscuits.'

'Please.'

'No,' I said. 'Later. Tell us what you've found out first?'

He laid the papers in separate piles on the counter. 'Quite a lot, actually. Some of it is interesting. Where shall I start?'

'Jean Storer,' I said. I wanted to know about the lone woman in the picture.

He picked up a pile of paper.

'But just give us the important details,' I added.

'She's quite a person. Cambridge graduate. First Class degree and all that stuff. Worked in research for the last forty or so years. Mainly in the States. She's mentioned as co-author in a vast number of medical research articles. Reading between the lines, though, I'd say she never quite got the recognition she deserved.'

'Because she was a woman.' Dora was about to launch herself into a tirade but Mat smiled at her and agreed, and she subsided.

'Things are changing,' he continued. 'A lot of women are suddenly being recognised. Jean has recently been given an award by the Tasker Foundation in honour of her life's work. What else can I tell you? She splits her time between London and the south of France since she semi-retired, although she's on the boards of a couple of universities and advisory bodies and I imagine she'll be asked on a few more now that she's been honoured. I rang some people and no one had anything but good to say about her. Recognition long overdue and all that sort of thing.'

'When did she leave Poulters?' I asked.

He leafed through the papers, his stubby fingers deft as he scanned each page rapidly. He was good at this. The slightly awkward demeanour had vanished and I wondered again how real it was. Maybe it was something he cultivated to make himself easier to talk to.

'I'd say Jean left Poulters in the late 1950s. She's named as a research assistant on a paper published in the US in 1962.' He tapped the piece of paper. 'I'm surprised she left Poulters for a job as an assistant. She was Head of Research there, with brand-new, state-of-the-art facilities for the 1960s. And doing great things. Poulters went on to develop, patent and license a number of new drugs that formed the basis of the company's prosperity throughout the rest of the twentieth century. Mind you, she's not short of a few quid. She's on the list of Poulters' shareholders. Has been since the early 1960s.'

'Isn't that a bit odd?'

'Maybe a reward from Richard for something she developed before she left?'

Dora and I both shrugged. Mat went back to his papers.

'Susan Storer is Jean's niece. Her brother's daughter. Studied English at university. She writes. Biographies mainly. Solid but uninspiring stuff under her own name and she ghostwrites celebs' books under another. Doubt she makes much of a living from either of them.'

He looked up at us and we both nodded.

'Owen Greenacre now,' Mat continued. 'He worked for Poulters before the war and went back afterwards. He was in charge at Berkswell House but took early retirement at the end of 1958 and set up the charity. There's a lot in the archives about it up to his death in...' He checked his notes. '1982. Laura must have taken over then. Which is lucky for her because the charity owns the house she lives in.'

'Is that allowed?' Dora asked.

'It is,' I said, 'if the charity isn't a registered charity. I suppose it pays her a large salary as well?'

'Possibly. No way of checking. Not officially.'

'She didn't look as though she was short of money.'

'Owen and Jean seem to have done very well out of their time at Poulters.'

'And Harry,' Dora said. 'Wilf always said his dad's pension was very generous.'

'Victor Leadsom,' I said. 'Did you find anything out about him?'

'But he wasn't at the reunion,' Dora said.

'No, but he's in the photo.'

'Just because he's in a photo taken over fifty years ago doesn't mean he's got anything to do with what's happening now. For all you know there could be people involved who aren't in that photo.'

'But Grandad underlined his name.'

'Looked more like he crossed it out to me.' Dora put the kettle on before I could stop her.

'Shit,' I said. And the power went out.

'Was that me?' Dora asked.

'Yes. You can't have the towel rail and the kettle on at the same time.' I made a superhuman effort not to snap. 'But I should have told you. Never mind. I'll go downstairs to the fuse box in a minute and put it back on.'

'I did look Victor up,' Mat said. 'There's very little. A record for the birth of a Victor Leadsom in 1936. His name is included in a 1956 Cambridge University list of graduates – First Class with Honours, so he must have been a bright boy. I guess he went to Poulters straight from university. But after that, there's nothing. Absolutely nothing.'

'Is that normal?'

'It's possible. Especially if he left the country like Jean. Lots of opportunities for scientists in the US at the time. Maybe he went and worked for another pharmaceutical company rather than in research, which would explain why he's got nothing published. And his generation often don't have much of a social media presence.' Mat shrugged.

I picked up the 1957 photo and looked again at Victor. Was he dead too? Or merely living a quiet life in some backwater? A little breeze came in through the window and blew a couple of Mat's papers onto the floor. Jack stirred and barked at them idly before settling back down to sleep.

'I need a cup of tea,' Dora said.

'Michael?' I said. 'How did he die?'

'They're waiting for post-mortem results but it looks like a heart attack while he slept. The maid found him in the morning. He was ill and old, though. It wouldn't have been difficult to kill him. You should know, you're a nurse.'

He was right.

'It wouldn't take much if he were frail and with heart problems,' I said. 'Suffocate him with his pillow and sit on his chest at the same time. It would look like heart failure. In fact, it would be heart failure.'

We fell silent for a few seconds. I thought none of us wanted to say the word 'murder' but it was clearly in our minds. Finally, Mat spoke.

'So, maybe something did happen in the 1950s that's come back to life now. It would make sense of a lot of things that have happened. Like the way Berkswell House was abruptly taken off the market and heavy security put in place to stop anyone getting in after years of letting the place fall apart. Why else would these seven people meet in an anonymous room in The Herbert? Seven people with no connection other than Berkswell House and Poulters in the late fifties – a connection that some of them seem to have done very well out of. Twenty-four hours later, two of them were dead, and one of them, Philip, is very mysterious about why he was there and what happened. Phiney goes to have a look round and someone pushes her down some steps. I'd say something deeply wrong happened all those years ago and has been hushed up ever since.'

Was he right? It certainly made sense. It just seemed impossible that Grandad had been involved in anything deeply wrong. Even sixty years ago. Dora looked troubled. Was she wondering if the secret had made Grandad kill himself?

'Philip Mason?' Mat broke the silence. 'He said something about deaths to you, Phiney. What was it?'

I thought back, trying to remember Philip's exact words.

'It was when he'd found out about Michael dying. "Two more deaths," he said. And then, "So many deaths."'

'Did he?' Mat's voice darkened. '"Two more deaths". So, there have been others.'

'What did he mean?' Dora said. '"So many deaths"?'

We stared at one other, each trying to make sense of it.

'I think your Philip Mason needs to answer some questions. He hasn't been in touch since, has he?'

'No. I keep trying but I've only got a landline number and I get his answering machine every time.'

'Give me his number. Let me try.'

The call went to answering machine.

'It's been like that for days. He said he needed to talk to some people before he could tell me anything, so I think he's gone away.'

'What people?'

'He didn't say?'

'Well, if the reunion at The Herbert is anything to do with it, he must have meant the other people there.'

'I guess he spoke to Laura. She didn't know who Josephine Wistman was. It was only when I told her everyone called me Phiney that she reacted. Philip called me Phiney.'

Mat thought for a moment.

'It makes sense. Philip spoke to the others. He told them you wanted answers. That you'd seen the 1957 newspaper article, and then you turned up at Berkswell House.'

'But you didn't tell the guards who I was.'

'They'll have reported your presence all the same. A woman. With a dog. Someone might have put two and two together.'

I remembered the cameras around the building with the bars. 'They probably got a good view of me too.'

'You've stirred something up. Panicked someone?'

'Who?' Dora asked. 'Who's panicking?'

'Someone who doesn't want us to find out why Grandad died.'

'I don't like this,' Mat said. 'I'll keep trying Philip.'

'Could you sort the electricity out?' Dora asked me.

We left Mat to it and went downstairs to switch the power back on at the fuse box. Jack woke up and pattered along with us. Dora took him out onto the dried-out patch of grass at the back that claimed to be the communal garden and waited while he did what he needed to do.

When I went back up, Mat was staring out of the window and drumming his fingers against the frame.

'I'm going there,' he said.

'What? Where?'

'Where do they live?'

'They?'

'Philip Mason. Where does he live?'

'Ullswater. Lake District. Dora has the address.'

'God. That's three or four hours away.'

'Why? Did you speak to him?'

'No, I didn't speak to Philip. His friend answered in the end. Jonathan?'

'I don't know him.'

'He said Philip had gone out for a walk. He didn't have a clue when he'd be back because Philip hadn't said. Could be hours if the mood took him. Although Jonathan was surprised as the weather was miserable. Drizzly and grey.'

I looked out of the window at the burnt and yellowed grass below. Jack snuffled in a corner and Dora strode backwards and forwards talking to herself. We could do with some of the drizzle ourselves.

'I'm going up there,' Mat said. 'Philip has all the answers. It will be easier to get them out of him face to face.'

'I'm coming too.' The words surprised me. They'd come out of my mouth automatically. But the more I thought about it, the more it seemed like a good idea.

Mat looked doubtful.

'Philip Mason knows who I am. He'll speak to me more than he'll speak to you.'

Dora struggled in, dragging an unwilling Jack behind her.

'I'm heading off,' Mat said to me. 'Now.'

Shit.

'We're going to drive up and see Philip Mason.'

'Of course. Excellent idea.'

'The thing is… Would you take Jack with you?'

'Where?'

'Back to Matlock. We can't take him with us.'

Dora's voice had steel in it. 'I'm not going to Matlock,' she said. 'I'm coming with you.'

Chapter Twenty-Three:
Philip Mason

6 June 2017
One week before the reunion

The letter arrived late morning, dropping onto the doormat together with a gentle reminder that Philip hadn't paid his annual subscription to the Fellside Walkers and an invitation for Jonathan to attend the opening night of the summer season at the Theatre by the Lake. Philip walked through to the kitchen, placed Jonathan's invitation on the mantelpiece where he'd see it as soon as he came back from his Cornish tour, and put the reminder on the kitchen table. He looked at the letter thoughtfully.

He knew who had sent it. Jean Storer. But only because she'd written her name on the flap in blue ink and with a fountain pen. Only people of a certain age did that. People as old as he and Jean were. He didn't open it straightaway. It was as though he knew it would draw a line in his life. There would be a before and an after, much in the same way the events of that day sixty years ago had marked an ending and a beginning. Jean wouldn't have written to him if it wasn't serious. Not after sixty years of silence.

So, he made himself a little pot of coffee and fussed around with a tray and a jug for milk before going to sit in the conservatory that he and Jonathan had built on the front of the cottage so they could enjoy the view over Ullswater whatever the weather.

And he read Jean's letter.

Afterwards, he watched a flotilla of dinghies scud to and fro across the lake. The wind was perfect, whipping the surface of the water with white-topped ripples and hurling the boats forward. He let his thoughts go where they wanted, churning through the implications of what he'd just read.

Michael Poulter came to the surface first. After all these years, how strange that it should be Michael, of all people, who rocked the boat. Michael, who'd said the least at the time but whose life had seriously diverged from where he'd planned it would go. Every time Philip read about Michael Poulter, Managing Director of Poulters, opening a new facility or announcing a new product, he'd struggled to relate him to the Michael he'd known for that brief period of time. The young man who'd talked of university and travelling and writing but never of picking up his father's reins and running the family firm.

The meeting was next week. Jean hadn't given them much time to organise themselves. She must have decided the threat of revelation would bring them all running. But she was mistaken if she thought Philip would try to stop the truth coming out. If Michael wanted to tell all then he was fine with that.

He put the letter back into the envelope, went upstairs to his study and added it to his 'to do' pile. Not that there was anything to do. A reply to Jean would arrive in France after her departure for Coventry. No need to book a train. He'd drive and afterwards he'd go to London and spend a couple of days there, see an exhibition and enjoy a short spell of city life. Then maybe he'd go to Cornwall, spend some time with Jonathan. Or maybe not. Being with Jonathan was never very satisfactory when he was working. He could think about nothing but his play and how the performance had gone the night before.

But as the morning progressed and he pottered round the cottage doing a few chores, the reality of what would happen started to come home to him. There would be an investigation, bound to be, even after all this time. It would probably last months and months with the press picking over the lurid details.

He put on his coat and headed along the path to one of his favourite walks over the hill and down beside the streams that became the Aira Force waterfall. Each step of the familiar path seemed more beautiful than ever with the lake glimpsed between the swaying trees. He stopped on the bridge at the bottom of the waterfall and let his eyes follow the cascading water down over rocks and ferns. There was no one else about. It should have been a magic moment but nothing could drag his mind away from Jean's letter.

He wondered who else would come to the meeting. Michael's son, he supposed. James, that was his name. After all, he was running Poulters now. Jean had mentioned that Laura was organising the Coventry end. Owen, of course, was long dead. As was Harry. The old doubts about Harry's death resurfaced but he pushed them away.

And then he thought of Wilf.

Had Jean written to Wilf? He hoped not. God, he hoped not. Didn't she realise that Wilf knew nothing? That he'd been in so much pain at the time that any knowledge of the terrible mistake he and Philip had made had passed him by. But the more Philip thought about it, the surer he was she'd written to Wilf. He'd been there, after all.

And then he understood that it didn't matter what Jean had done. As soon as the news was out and Wilf learned that it involved Philip, he'd work out he must be implicated too. And from there it was only a short step to the truth.

A streak of determination shot through the grey of Philip's mood. Michael had to be stopped.

Chapter Twenty-Four:
Arch

6 June 2017
One week before the reunion

Arch manoeuvred the Rolls between the bollards with the ease of long practice, ignoring the blare from the horn of the taxi behind him, forced to wait a few seconds while James got out.

'Thanks, Arch. I'll be ten minutes.' James Poulter shut the car door and walked smartly up the steps and in through the imposing entrance to Poulters' London headquarters. From the driver's seat, Arch watched the stir James's arrival caused. Heads looked up, the receptionist stood and Mary, his secretary, waiting for him by the door, turned and headed towards the lift.

It wasn't worth trailing round the block and down into the underground car park for ten minutes so Arch went and filled the Rolls up. Poulters had an account at the garage round the corner and the owner was more than happy to let Arch wait in the bay by the air hose.

They were off to the Shrewsbury factory after this quick meeting with James's father, Michael Poulter. It was a lovely day for a drive, dry and cloudy with the sort of clouds that stopped the glare of the sun but didn't threaten rain. Arch whistled a little tune. Life was good and only going to get better.

He'd worked with three generations of Poulters, first driving for the old man, Richard, still the benchmark at Poulters for successful if ruthless management despite being dead for nearly forty years. Michael, his son, the unlucky beneficiary of comparisons to Richard, had refused to be seen in a chauffeur-driven Rolls and Arch had been reduced to picking up visitors from the airport in a series of smart but dull saloons. To be fair, Michael had been in charge during difficult times for the UK economy and had probably been right to ban ostentation, although much of his reign had been marked by the wrong decisions. He lacked the killer instinct his father had and it was only since James had taken over that things had looked up.

James had dragged Poulters out of the doldrums and into a shiny new future. James thought the appearance of success was a good thing, so a new Rolls had been purchased. Arch wiped a mark off its gleaming windscreen. Bloody pigeons. That was the only problem with waiting here.

He glanced at his watch. Over half an hour had passed already. Most unlike James to take longer than the time he'd scheduled. Even for his father. Arch gave the windscreen another wipe and then the nearside door. He'd go to the car park and wait for James in reception. Something must have happened.

Ninety minutes later, he was still in reception when James burst out of the lift. Arch took one look at him and went to get the car.

'Shrewsbury, Mr Poulter?' he asked, once they were on the road. He was still slightly out of breath from running down the stairs to the car park.

James nodded, shut the soundproof glass window between them and made several calls. Arch listened through the gap in the bottom corner that no one ever noticed as he crawled through the traffic towards the M1. Something was definitely up. Something to do with Berkswell House. He wished he could hear both sides of the conversation because James was maddeningly curt, barking instructions about the sale. He heard enough, though.

James did nothing for a long time before he made his final call and, when Arch glanced in the mirror, he was rolling his upper lip between his teeth.

'Jean,' he said when the phone was finally answered. 'It's James.' And then after a short pause, 'Yes, he told me.'

A long silence while James listened. So long that Arch began to wonder if the call had finished without him noticing but then the quiet was broken.

'Absolutely,' James's voice was harsh and taut like a piece of elastic stretched so tight it could barely vibrate. 'He has to be stopped.'

After that, James buried himself in a report until they reached the Shrewsbury factory.

He rapped on the glass and Arch opened it.

'I've got a meeting in Coventry next week, Arch. I'll need you to drive me up. I'll text you the details.'

'Don't worry, Mr Poulter. I'll get them from Mary.'

'Mary doesn't know about it. It's confidential, Arch. So keep it to yourself.'

Chapter Twenty-Five:
Phiney Wistman

19 June 2017
Six days after the reunion

There was no stopping Dora coming with us to see Philip so we all bundled into Mat's car, along with Jack, and headed north. Mat was a good driver. He drove smoothly and fast, very fast, but without frightening me. Unlike Meghan's old boyfriend who'd taken us up to a festival near Leicester last summer, darting in and out of the traffic like a billiard ball ricocheting off the sides of a table.

The sky became darker and a few drops of rain spattered the hot, dusty tarmac. The hot weather was finally breaking and, when we stopped for Dora to go to the loo, a damp tar smell, gritty and sharp and strangely pleasant, came in through the window.

While we waited for Dora, Mat made a call with the phone still fixed to his dashboard and on loudspeaker and put up a warning hand to me to be silent.

'Arch,' he said. 'It's Mat.'

'I can't talk.' Arch, whoever he was, had a nasal twang to his voice and the background hum of car noise told me he too was en route somewhere.

'When then?'

'Leave it for a while, Mat. Things are complicated.'

'Complicated. How?'

'Not now, mate.'

'Sorry, Arch, it doesn't work like that. I can't leave it. You confirmed that the sale of Berkswell House had been stopped. What did you say?' Mat flipped back through the papers in his file. '*All hell broke loose today*' he read. '*Mr James shut in a meeting with Mr Michael for hours. Face like thunder when he came out. Called the agents and told them straight off to pull the sale.* Someone offered you more money than me, Arch? Because I could make your life very difficult, you know. It's a two-way thing. I'm sure Poulters would like to know how I got the information in the first place.'

Despite the blandness of Mat's voice, a threat tightened its core. I was surprised. I hadn't thought he had it in him. Silence from the other end. Mat raised his eyebrows at me and continued.

'You know I'd never ask you for anything that would make your life difficult, Arch, but there was a meeting last week at The Herbert in Coventry. I know James went, and Michael. Did –'

The phone went dead.

Mat phoned straight back. Twice. Both times it went to an automated voice asking us to leave a message.

'Who was that?' I asked.

'James Poulter's chauffeur, Arch. Ratty little man but with a nose for money. I met him at some civic do and he told me a few interesting things about the Poulters. So, I slipped him a few quid and my phone number. He understood. You see, people like James don't hang about when they've made a decision. They come out of meetings, into their cars and they make calls to set things in motion. Even if it's only to their secretaries. Something's put the wind up Arch. And he didn't like me mentioning the reunion. I don't like it. I don't like it one bit. The sooner we get to Ullswater and see Philip Mason the better.'

Dora approached us through the parked cars with Jack following reluctantly. Mat turned the engine on as soon as they got in. He edged his way out of the car park and back onto the motorway. The engine noise rose up a notch and I felt the car pick up speed.

'You're in a hurry.'

He was quiet for a while and then he muttered something.

'What?' I asked.

He looked grim.

'I said, I am. I am in a hurry.'

The further north we drove, the darker the skies became. The rain continued, fitful and sulky, spattering Mat's windscreen for a few minutes then stopping. It did little more than loosen the motorway grime and smear the glass. It wasn't until we left the thundering motorway traffic and drove down quieter roads that it settled into a misty drizzle with glimpses of high mountains breaking through from time to time.

Philip and Jonathan's cottage was a low stone building at the end of a cul-de-sac overlooking the lake below. The rain was gentle but penetrating, seeping through my T-shirt in seconds and making me shiver. We flung waterproofs on and raced for the door. Only Jack took his time, sniffing round the pavement before joining us.

A slim but elderly man answered the door, his look of expectation fading as he looked past us into the dark evening and realised we were alone. He had his coat on but it was dry, unlike ours, which dripped all over the red tiles of the porch as we took shelter inside.

'Dora Patterson,' Dora said, in answer to Jonathan's puzzled scanning of our faces. Clearly, he hadn't recognised her. 'Wilf Patterson's wife. We've come to see Philip.'

She started a long account of the last time they'd met while I tried and failed to stop Jack from shaking himself and spattering the walls with muddy drops.

The phone rang, and Jonathan darted in to answer it. We followed him into a long, low-ceilinged room that ran across the front of the cottage and would have had a fabulous view of Ullswater if the mist hadn't been obscuring everything. Inside was what you'd expect: wood-burning stove, tweedy soft furnishings and polished old wood. Only the far wall struck a discordant note. It was covered with photos and, unable to resist, we went as one to look while Jonathan spoke on the phone.

There was no order to them. Initially, I thought they might have been hung in three blocks but over the years the blocks had joined and pictures had been hung in whatever spaces were left and in whatever frames came to hand. The passage of time was marked by the greying and thinning of hair and also the shift in print colour from the orange-tinted shots of the 1970s to the clean colours of recent pictures.

There were photos of Jonathan on stage in costume and posing with groups of people outside theatres. His angular face had softened over the years, its sharp lines blurred by gentle folds of skin, but his body, muscled and lithe in photos of him holding yoga poses on beaches, in forests and on mountain tops, seemed taut as ever.

If I'd been in any doubt whether Philip and Jonathan were friends or lovers, the pictures dispelled them. A whole section showed them at the early Gay Pride marches. It seemed strange to think of the courteous elderly man on the phone as a right-on radical but clearly Philip had been. He waved banners and shouted with the best of them and one shot showed him and Jonathan kissing underneath a banner claiming *Homosexuals Are Revolting.*

Jonathan finished his call and came over to join us. 'I'm sorry. Was Phil expecting you? He went out for a walk this morning and he hasn't come back.'

'Not really,' Dora said. 'We were… Well, we wanted to see him.'

'The thing is, he's not answering his phone either although that's not unusual. The reception here is pretty poor. But he's been gone a long time so I called Mountain Rescue. That was them calling me back. They're sending searchers out. Just in case. They're going over the slopes below Helvellyn if the cloud lifts enough to be safe. It was one of his favourite walks.'

He pointed to a shot of them both walking along a steeply curved slope of green which towered over them like a huge wave about to break.

'How lovely,' Dora said. 'But I expect there are lots of nice walks round here.'

I gritted my teeth.

'Can we help look for him?' Mat said.

The urgency in his voice took Jonathan aback. 'I'm sure he's fine,' he said. 'I called Mountain Rescue as a precaution. Phil's an experienced hiker. I did think I might drive over to a walk he loved just along from here. Up by Aira Force. It's easy but you never know, he might have slipped and fallen, and there won't be many people about with the weather like this.'

Slipped and fallen. Mat and I looked at each other. This was why he'd been in such a hurry to get here.

'But,' Jonathan continued, 'I didn't want to leave in case he phoned. In case he got some phone reception and needed picking up.'

'I'll come with you,' Mat said. 'We can go in my car. Phiney and Dora will man the phones.'

Dora looked at her black patent shoes with the bow and didn't argue. Neither did I. I just ignored Mat and went with him and Jonathan. Dora could man the phones by herself.

The road to Aira Force wound round the lake. There was no mist down here just greyness with the rain-streaked water reflecting broken fragments of sky. Aira Force, according to the sign as we turned off into the car park, was a waterfall further up the valley. Mat and I followed Jonathan up a path that criss-crossed the stream as it tumbled down a rocky bed. He was fit, almost running up the gentler stretches. Fitter than me and, judging by the sound of panting coming from Mat, far fitter than him. Only Jack kept up with ease.

Jonathan stopped and let us catch up when he reached a spot where the trees crowded round the path and the stream lay far below us.

'It's slippery here,' he said when we arrived. I knew that. The sandals I was wearing had already slid from under me a couple of times and my feet were covered in mud. Mat was coping better in his trainers.

We traipsed on in silence for a few minutes, until I slipped again and Mat grabbed me before I fell. Jonathan gave us a minute to recover as I tried to wipe the worst of the mud off my feet and onto the grass at the side of the path while Mat leaned against a tree and breathed heavily.

'You're Wilf's granddaughter, aren't you?'

I nodded.

'Phil was very upset about his death.'

'Did he talk to you about it?' Mat heaved the words out between gasps for air.

Jonathan shook the drops of water out of his hair. 'A bit. I've been away you see. A little tour in Cornwall with a one-man show I do, about Wordsworth. He's on the GCSE curriculum this year and I'm very much in demand. I told Phil to get on the train to Cornwall when he called me after Wilf's death but he wouldn't. He said he was going away. He had to find someone and talk to them. Someone he knew a long time ago.'

Fear nibbled at my thoughts. Fear for Philip. He'd promised he'd come and tell me the truth after he'd spoken to some people and I was growing increasingly sure the someone didn't want me or anyone to know what the truth was.

Jonathan turned and trudged up the slope. Mat scrambled after him.

'Did Philip find them? The person he wanted to talk to?'

'I don't know. I only got back very late last night and Phil went out before I woke up. He knew I wouldn't surface till after lunch.'

A sound like the thundering of a train in the distance made the wet air vibrate.

'What's that?'

'The waterfall. We're not far from it.'

'Do you know where Philip went?' Mat persisted.

'No. Maybe abroad. He said something about Manchester Airport being horrendous. It's always snatched phone calls and texts when I'm away. We catch up when I come home.'

The path flattened for a while but the going was no easier. Water had collected in its dips and left thick mud behind. Clearly, Ullswater hadn't been suffering from the dry weather we'd had. My feet were so muddy now I couldn't tell the difference between my sandals and the skin. And they were cold.

Mat carried on probing Jonathan. Picking up the thread after each pause as we dealt with a particularly muddy bit of the path or a point where the bushes, weighed down with wet, blocked our way.

But it was hopeless. Jonathan knew nothing. He'd thought about nothing but his show over the past few weeks and struggled to switch off from it now, telling us little anecdotes about the different theatres he'd visited in Cornwall.

Throughout it all, the relentless thud of the waterfall grew louder and louder until it seemed to slap the air. Jonathan shouted a few words over the noise and, as we turned the corner, Aira Force came into view. It was spectacular. Far taller than I expected. A torrent of water poured over the ridge high above us and fell into the foaming waters of a pool beneath, emitting shock waves of noise that hit the stone cliffs and echoed all around.

The path split here. One part carried on up the left side of the gully and the other descended in a long run of steps down to a mossy stone bridge. This crossed the pool at the base of the falls and climbed steeply again up the other side.

Jonathan shouted instructions into Mat's ear. I understood that we were to go down the steps and take the path up the far side while he continued up on the left. But when Mat and I reached the bridge, and I looked at the path snaking back up through the trees and rocks, I knew I was finished.

'I'll have to wait here,' I said. 'I've had it.'

'Will you be OK?'

'Just need a rest. Feeling a bit wobbly.'

'I'll leave Jack with you.'

'I'll be fine. You take him. He's enjoying this. He hasn't had a decent walk for days.'

He was too. I watched him bound up the path in front of Mat, stopping to explore the smells and to let Mat catch him up.

Strangely enough, it was quieter on the bridge although the bottom of the waterfall was only yards away. It was out of range of the clashing echoes and the noise was gentler, as though the water's energy was dispersed by the spray that shot up into the air and then lingered before falling back again, hidden in the light rain.

I leaned over the bridge to gaze into the pool. At its edges, away from the fierce current, the surface was only disturbed by light ripples. Leaves and twigs bobbed and swayed there, caught in a temporary stasis until the flow swirled them under the bridge and away downstream.

The ache in my head calmed and the warmth created by the exercise faded. My T-shirt was clammy underneath my coat and chilling my skin. I should have asked Mat for his car keys and gone back down to the car park.

The sky cleared a little, brightening from dark grey to light grey, and when I looked back into the water it reflected a blurred silhouette of myself. I leaned over and waved and the rippling figure in the pool waved back. Something caught my eye. A dull green, a bulbous dull-green mass floating alongside my dark reflection.

It took a while for me to understand what it was. A long time of staring and blinking as understanding penetrated the fog that seemed to have taken over my brain. And when I knew what I was looking at, it took even longer to work out what to do. And then I screamed. I screamed for help. For someone. For anyone. But mainly for Mat. Staccato shouts picked up by the echo and flung into the droplet-laden air. All the time my eyes fixed on the body in the water, praying that the current wouldn't pick it up again and wash it under the bridge and further downstream.

Jack came first, tearing down the path and skidding to a halt before me. Thrusting his nose into my legs, nudging me and barking until I turned away from the pool. Then Mat appeared. And I wasn't alone anymore. Jonathan arrived a few minutes later.

They climbed down to the pool while I called 999. I tried to ignore the awful sounds of grunting and the grate of pebbles as they dragged something wet and heavy over them. I couldn't ignore the keening. Jonathan wailed and I buried my head in the raised hair of Jack's coat and wished I was somewhere else. It was Philip's body. Jonathan's grief only confirmed what I'd guessed.

Philip was dead. In what looked like an unfortunate accident. Except I was sure it wasn't. Someone had killed him. Someone who was desperate to stop him talking, who wanted the secret I was now sure had killed Grandad kept buried under the weight of the years that had passed. And I was also sure that, if I'd never phoned Philip and asked him why Grandad had jumped off the bridge, he'd still be alive.

Chapter Twenty-Six:
Phiney Wistman

19 June 2017
Six days after the reunion

Once the ambulance had taken Philip's body away, we drove Jonathan back to the cottage through the night. We were all drenched and shivering and, although Mat turned the heater up to full, it had made little difference by the time we arrived at the cottage. A few cars were parked outside. Jonathan's friends, called by him during the long wait for the ambulance, peered through the windows and came out of the door to envelop him and take him inside.

'We should go,' I said to Mat. 'We're in the way.'

'Yes.'

'And we can't ask him any more questions. At least, I couldn't.'

'You think I would?'

'It's what journalists do, isn't it?'

'Some might, but not me.' He wrapped his arms around himself and looked cross. 'You go in and get Mrs Patterson, so I can avoid the temptation to interrogate him. I've got some dry clothes in the car.' He stomped off into the dark.

Dora and another elderly lady were sitting on the sofa, surrounded by people who were either weeping or hugging or doing both. Dora shot uneasy glances round the room. I caught her eye and she came over, knocking a pile of books to the ground as she passed. The other lady followed.

'We're leaving,' I said.

'Good. Where did I put my bag?'

'I'll get it,' the other lady said. 'I think you left it in the kitchen when we were making tea.'

'Thanks, Edwina,' Dora said. We watched Edwina thread her way back through Jonathan's friends with considerably more grace than Dora would have. 'She's their next-door neighbour. She came over to see what was going on and stayed to keep me company. She's a widow.' She paused for a moment. 'Like me.'

'Should we try and say goodbye, do you think?'

Dora looked again at the people. 'No. I don't think he'll notice. I'll ask Edwina to explain.'

Outside, it was dark and cold. The mist and cloud had cleared apart from a faint haze that veiled the pinpricks of starlight. I shivered in my damp clothes and my feet were numb under their muddy coating.

Dora thanked Edwina and we got into the car and drove down the hill onto the main road round the lake. Mat stopped the car in a little layby.

'Why have we stopped?' I asked.

'To decide where we're going,' Mat said.

'I need something to eat,' Dora said.

'You'll be lucky. At this time of night.'

Mat thought for a minute. 'Motorway services is our best chance. I guess we're going to be heading south eventually. Yes?'

But the thought of deciding where we were going after we'd eaten was too much for both Dora and me.

'Let's do that,' I said.

None of us spoke after that, not even when we levered ourselves out of the car at the services, stiff with cold and shock and also hungry. I spent a long time huddled under the hand dryer in the Ladies', trying to remove a layer of damp and chill and wondering if I had the nerve to wash my feet in a basin. I didn't. I sponged off enough of the mud with paper towels to get rid of the smell that took me straight back to the awful sight in the pool at the bottom of the waterfall. I bought a pair of novelty socks and put them on under the damp sandals. Now was not the time to worry about fashion.

There was a choice of burgers or sandwiches. The burgers were the kind that come from a large factory dedicated to extracting every bit of meat from a cow. Organic only in the sense that every single organ was used. They were served with chips whose relationship to a potato was dim and distant. A sandwich was the healthier option but the savoury smell of the burgers was too much. I was starving and desperate for something hot.

Mat polished off his burger and chips then devoured a rum baba, sticky with synthetic syrup and without a single atom of nutritional value. I was tempted. Sugar was poison. The cake would be full of chemicals. But I couldn't tear my eyes away from the teaspoon carrying each glistening morsel to his mouth. I let my finger dip into a pool of syrup on the plate and lift itself to my lips. The sweetness danced on my tongue and soothed away the last of the chill. Mat pushed the plate towards me and handed me another teaspoon. Sod the chemicals. Once wouldn't do any harm. I ate half of it while Dora's eyes watched me with the brooding stare of a cat observing a hamster in a cage. God, it tasted good.

When we'd eaten everything and Dora had fussed around – taking Jack water in the car, clearing the debris and wiping the table with a serviette, and then deciding she wanted another cup of tea – Mat finally dragged us back to the question none of us wanted to answer.

'What are we going to do?'

I didn't want to think about it now. I wanted to curl up in a lovely bed and sink into oblivion. Pull the sheets up over my head to block out all the horror of the past few days and become nothing but a shadow in the dark.

'They killed him, didn't they?' Dora spoke first. She of all of us looked the least shattered. She hadn't been out on the path by the waterfall and she hadn't heard Jonathan wailing. The food and the tea had revived her and the warmth had flushed her cheeks so she looked positively cheerful to a casual onlooker.

'It could have been accident,' I said.

They both looked at me.

'OK, it wasn't an accident.'

'I think someone pushed him,' Mat said. 'It's the pattern, isn't it? You and now Philip. People stick to the same way of doing things.'

'Two doesn't make a pattern.'

'What about Harry?'

'But that was years and years ago,' Dora said.

'You think someone pushed Harry?'

'I don't know. I don't know anything. But it strikes me that Harry, with his drinking, might have been unreliable. This is all about keeping something secret.'

'What about Michael?' I said. 'No one pushed him.'

Mat didn't answer but stared into the distance where a tired-looking woman was trying to persuade a toddler to sit and eat rather than throw his food on the ground.

'Someone tried to kill you, Phiney,' he said finally. 'Michael Poulter and Philip Mason are dead. And all of this follows on from a strange reunion of people whose only connection is that they or a family member worked for Poulters in the late 1950s. It has to be a cover-up. A secret all those people know about. And I think it's to do with something that happened at Berkswell House. Nothing else ties all these people together.'

Despite his tiredness, his eyes gleamed and the muscles in his face and body tightened like Jack's did when Grandad pulled his harness off its hook.

'I need to do some research.' He spoke almost to himself. 'Late 1950s. What were Poulters working on? What was going on in the world?'

The 1950s meant nothing to me. Apart from vague images of Bakelite phones and women washing clothes with mangles. I pulled the old newspaper article out of my bag and smoothed it onto the table, seeing if it would conjure up something.

'The USSR launched Sputnik,' Dora said. 'Donald Campbell

broke the world water speed record again on Coniston Water. Fangio won the F1 Championship.'

Mat stared at her.

Something glimmered at the back of my mind. Some remnant of local history from school. 'The new cathedral was being built after the old one was bombed in the war.'

'The boom years of car manufacturing in Coventry,' Mat picked up the thread. 'Housing estates popping up everywhere. High wages. The "you've never had it so good" era. But none of this is very relevant. What was going on in the pharmaceutical industry?' He wiped his finger round the rim of the bowl that had contained the rum baba and licked it as he thought. 'Not so much Wild West by then – more the Gold Rush. With new drugs and treatments flooding the market, there were fortunes to be made. Poulters developed a lot of drugs during that period – antibiotics, blood pressure and heart treatments, drugs for tuberculosis and cancer – and Richard Poulter made a lot of money.' He paused, his eyes alight with thoughts. 'Yup. Richard Poulter made a lot of money. And he probably wasn't too careful how he went about it. I'm sure he took a few risks along the way and got away with it. Other companies weren't so lucky. Some of their developments killed rather than cured or had serious side-effects.'

'Like Thalidomide?' Dora said.

'Well, yes. But there were others.' His voice sped up. 'What if something went wrong with one of Poulters' new drugs? What if one of them was toxic –'

'But we'd know,' I said. 'There'd be people damaged or dead all over the place. Like Thalidomide.'

Mat ignored me, his attention fixed on his phone.

'How could you cover up something like that, Mat?'

'I don't know,' he said. 'But we've got to start somewhere.'

'Well, I know where we should start. With Jean Storer. She must be behind all this. She's now the only one of the people in the 1957 picture still alive.'

'Well, it isn't her.' Mat had found whatever he was looking for on his phone.

'Why?'

'Because I had the same idea. Jean is in Boston and was giving a speech to the International Biochemical Research Foundation yesterday. She couldn't have been in Ullswater today.'

I looked at his phone. Another photo. Jean Storer surrounded by a lot of men but somehow standing out even more. Maybe because she wasn't wearing a lab coat to disguise the fact that she was different. Instead she wore a sparkly blue kaftan-type thing while the men wore black suits. She looked like someone's wife.

'I think I'll wear a black suit if I ever get an award,' I said, and passed the phone back to Mat.

He laughed. 'And I'll come with you and wear a nice dress,' he said.

He got it, I thought.

Dora looked confused. 'If it isn't Jean, who is it?' she asked.

'Whoever's doing this isn't necessarily one of the original conspirators,' Mat said. 'Take James Poulter. He wouldn't want the world to know his family had connived at hiding a disaster. Word is he's trying to buy his way into the US through the acquisition of a company over there. The bad press generated by something like this would kill it off. And Laura Greenacre, Owen's daughter. She's ended up with a very cushy life, hasn't she? Thanks to the charity her father started, supported every step of the way by Poulters. She wouldn't want to lose that.'

'Find out where they were yesterday,' Dora said.

'It's not that easy. I might be able to find out about James but Laura? And Jean's niece? What's her name?'

'Susan.'

'They'll be a lot harder. Besides, there could be others involved. Secrets have a habit of leaking out. People drop hints to their friends and family like Owen must have to Laura. We don't know who else has been kept quiet with judicious payments and wouldn't want to see the source dry up.'

Dora picked up the newspaper article. The time it had spent in my bag had not improved it. Crease lines obscured Grandad's face and cut Richard in half. She touched each face in turn as though trying to feel what each one had been like.

'And Victor,' she said. 'Why wasn't he at the reunion?'

'We decided he had nothing to do with it. Remember?' I said, trying to be patient. 'You were the one who said it looked as though Grandad had crossed his name out.'

'I was wrong.'

She took her bag from the seat next to us and rummaged in it. 'I had a look round while you were gone. Found Philip's desk upstairs in one of the bedrooms. More of a box room really, but they've turned it into an office. Quite nice, with a view –'

I interrupted her before she could blather on any more about Philip's living arrangements.

'What did you find?'

'This.' She brandished a piece of paper.

'You took something from the house!'

'I didn't steal it. It was in his bin.'

This was probably true. The sheet she'd pulled out had crumple marks.

'What is it? Let's have a look.'

'Philip wrote lists of things. People do that, you know. On paper. Or on the back of envelopes.'

'I know. Shopping lists and so on. I use my phone.'

'Some of us prefer paper. And some of us doodle while we think. You can't do that on a mobile phone.'

She ignored my outstretched hand and passed the paper over to Mat. He laid it between us. It was exactly what Dora had said. Lists of things to do. Many neatly crossed off but still legible. And doodling. And in between the reminders to buy milk and cat food and call the doctor's surgery and the squares shaded in to form a chessboard and the other random scribbles, were nuggets of gold.

Book flight was in there and I thought I recognised the word *hotel*. A couple of phone numbers that looked foreign. *Jean* was written several times and *Wilf* as well, although it was hard to tell if they were part of the lists or just doodling.

'Looks like Jonathan was right,' Mat said. 'Philip went out of the country. I wonder where he went.' He started typing the phone numbers into his mobile.

'France, I imagine,' Dora said.

'Why?'

'Because that's what Edwina said.'

Mat put his phone down and stared at her. 'What else did Edwina tell you?'

'He asked her to feed the cat. Said he was going away for a couple of days. She knew it was France because he'd left the ticket on the coffee table. He was flying to Nice. That's on the Mediterranean, isn't it? When she asked if it was a holiday, he was quite short with her, which she thought was a bit steep seeing as she was the one doing him a favour. She doesn't much like cats.'

'He must have gone to see Jean,' Mat said. 'She lives somewhere in the south, retired down there.'

He tried the numbers but neither answered.

'What about Victor?' Dora asked.

'What about him?'

'Philip wrote his name down.' She turned the paper over.

On the back, *Victor* was written lightly in pencil. Several times. With a question mark after it. Nothing else.

'Maybe he's the one killing people,' she went on. 'Maybe they had the reunion to discuss how to stop him.'

'No one died until after the reunion.' Mat stopped his phone research for a minute.

'Only as far as you know.'

I looked very carefully at Philip's crumpled scribbles.

'Leadsom is an unusual name,' I said. 'We should have been able to track him down easily. Surely that tells us something.'

180

'Like what?' The rims of Mat's eyes were red with tiredness.

'I don't know. Like he's dead.'

'No death certificate. I checked when I looked up Owen's.'

'It doesn't mean he isn't dead,' I snapped back at Mat. 'Maybe that's what they were covering up. Victor's death.'

Dora's eyes flicked between the two of us. I knew we were bickering stupidly. A reaction, I thought. That's all it was. The aftermath of the awfulness of finding Philip's body. And tiredness. And everything else. This horrible place with its too-bright flickering lights and red Formica tables, smelling of stale coffee and grease. And fear. I made a big effort.

'Please, Mat. Let's at least try and find out about him. Even if he isn't involved, he might know something. Because I'm sure you're right. This is to do with the past. With 1957.'

'And Wilf knew about it?' This was Dora.

'I think he must have,' Mat said, his voice gentler now he was speaking to her.

I kept my face blank and I didn't look at Dora. I was terrified she'd read my mind. Because I couldn't see how a careless or negligent drug trial would make Grandad kill himself decades later. He'd been fifteen or sixteen at the time. How could he have had anything to do with scientific research? This was all about something that happened at Poulters while Grandad was there. Something terrible. But something much simpler. Much, much simpler. Like murder. And I couldn't stop wondering about Victor and why there was no trace of him since 1957.

We left the service station and headed back to Matlock. Going there was the only decision we took. We were too tired and shaken to make any others.

I slept in the back with the wind from Mat's open window whistling over me. Mat had decided that a gale in the car was a small price to pay to be able to drive without Jack's chin on his shoulder. Besides, he and Dora had the heater on full. I was OK though, buried under their coats and with Jack's warm body as a pillow.

I woke from time to time to hear Dora's voice interspersed with grunts and murmurs from Mat. She was telling him about her childhood in Wales. Her grandfather speaking Welsh to her as they searched for mushrooms in dew-wet grass on the Brecon Beacons. She loved the mountains.

I woke completely when we turned onto a twisty road through the Peaks but I stayed quiet, soothed by Jack's regular breathing and the soft lilt of Dora's voice which had lapsed into the cadences of her Welsh childhood. She was talking about meeting Grandad. How she'd lost her job and started doing anything to make ends meet. Dog walking had been one of them.

'The dogs obeyed me,' she said. 'Maybe because I don't particularly like them. Now, Jack doesn't obey me and I like him.' She sighed. 'He's a one-man dog and that man was Wilf. He's waiting for Wilf to return but putting up with us in the meantime.'

Mat said something I didn't catch but his voice was soft with understanding. He was so good at getting people to talk to him.

'From the start, Wilf and I got on,' Dora continued. 'He was pleased that I spoke my mind. Refreshing, he called it, although most people don't like it.' She paused and then added, 'Or me.'

A scream of brakes and a swerve cut her off.

'Sorry,' Mat said. 'What was it? Did you see?'

'Fox. Did we wake Phiney?'

I shut my eyes tight and breathed calmly.

'Dead to the world,' Mat said. 'Both of them.'

Jack was asleep so he'd shut the window and it was the absence of wind noise that had let their voices penetrate my sleep.

'So,' Dora said. A long drawn-out *so*, redolent with memories. 'I wasn't surprised when he said he had something to ask me. I guessed it might be marriage. I thought he'd point out its practical advantages for both of us. It would take the responsibility of caring for him away from Carol, Phiney's mum, and let her get on with her own life and it would provide me with a secure home. Except it wasn't like that.' She paused for a long time and, when she started speaking again, there was a lilt in her voice I hadn't heard before. 'Wilf took me out for the day to the Malvern Hills,' she said. 'He told me they were the closest thing to mountains near Coventry. He knew I loved the mountains and we walked until there was a bit of a view. Not far, of course. And then he asked me to marry him. Said he couldn't go down on one knee or, if he did, I'd have to help him back up but would I be prepared to take him on, disability and all, because he thought we'd be very happy together and he loved me.'

She paused and I realised I'd stopped breathing.

'There are tissues in the glove compartment,' Mat said.

The noise of fumbling and Dora blew her nose. 'And,' she said, 'he pulled the most beautiful ring out of his pocket. This one. Rose quartz, it is. He said I could change it if I didn't like it. He knew his tastes were old-fashioned but he'd seen it and thought it was perfect for me. Nobody had ever given me anything pink before.'

'It's beautiful,' Mat said. 'Really lovely.'

Silence filled the car, broken only by the hum of the heater fan and rattle of the wheels on the uneven road, echoed by the whirr of thoughts in my head. Poor Dora. She loved Grandad so much. I knew that. I'd always known that really, like I knew how much he loved her. Everything she'd done had been with him in mind. Maybe, I thought, as sleep started to drift my brain down random lanes, maybe I needed to remember that when she drove me mad.

Chapter Twenty-Seven:
Phiney Wistman

20 June 2017
Seven days after the reunion

Mat was making coffee when I came down the following morning. It smelled good. He waved the pot at me and I grunted a 'yes'. He looked quite at home in Dora's ultra-modern kitchen, wearing one of Grandad's old dressing gowns over his jeans, his hair still wet from the shower.

'Where's Dora?'

'Gone to get some bread and milk and some of the organic cereal she said was the only thing you would eat in the morning. The milk's off, by the way.'

'I prefer it black.'

He put a mug on the breakfast bar and sat down facing me, a large pile of toast dripping butter on a plate in front of him. He had that irritating look of someone who'd been up for hours.

I'd thought exhaustion would plummet me into sleep last night but the napping in the car put paid to that. As soon as I started slipping into unconsciousness, the memory of Philip's body floating in the pool jerked me awake. I'd ended up dozing on and off and I felt like shit.

Mat carried on ignoring me, tapping away at his phone and scribbling notes, only stopping to slather his toast with Dora's dark and fragrant marmalade.

'You eat too much sugar, you know,' I said.

He said nothing but a faint flush on his cheeks made me think my gibe had hit home.

'Really,' I said, 'it's not good for you.'

'Give it a rest, Phiney. We're not all as fanatically health conscious as you.'

'I've got my reasons,' I snapped back.

Mat considered the mug of coffee in front of him and carefully fished out a crumb of toast.

'Why are you ignoring me this morning?'

'I'm not. I'm just giving you a moment to come to. Dora told me you're not a morning person.'

'Dora, is it now? Not Mrs Patterson? Well, Dora shouldn't have,' I said, ignoring the unpleasant ring of truth in his words. I *am* pretty grumpy in the mornings.

His Mr Smiley façade slipped and he looked quite annoyed. 'OK. So what are the reasons for your manic healthiness?'

I sipped my coffee. It wasn't too bad. A bit bitter round the edges but I preferred that to bland or creamy.

My phone rang. I answered it without looking.

A pleasant female voice. 'Is that Josephine Wistman?'

'Yes?'

'It's Marie Stannard here. Just a follow up call to see how you are.'

Oh God. The counsellor I'd seen before the genetic testing.

'I'm fine, Marie.'

'I expect you've had your results by now and I wondered if you wanted to make an appointment to see me.'

My results. Shit.

'I haven't had them. Not yet.'

'That's quite strange. They should have come through by now.' She paused. 'It would be fair enough for you to chase them, you know. The waiting period can be very difficult.'

'I'm not at home,' I said. 'So they might have come through. They're probably waiting for me.'

'I see. Well, do call me when you get them if you want to chat. Whatever they show.'

I said I would and thanked her.

'Shit.' I realised I'd said it out loud.

Mat raised an eyebrow.

Something shifted in me. Meghan's words, saying I kept too much to myself, echoed in my head. Why not tell Mat? What did I have to lose?

'I can be a bit… terse,' I said. 'But I've got a lot on my mind.'

'I understand. Your grandfather's death…'

'It's not just that.' I took a deep breath. 'You might have noticed that illness seems to be the trademark of my family.'

He narrowed his eyes.

'Grandad with his polio and my dad with chronic bronchitis, then there's my gran, my real one, and my mum – both died from breast cancer.'

He looked as though he was starting to put it all together.

'And if I tell you that my gran's sister also died from breast cancer and, we think, a cousin, I guess you'll know where I'm going.'

'It's a gene, isn't it?'

'Several, to be exact. But I expect you've heard of BRCA 1 and 2.'

He nodded again.

'The knowledge sort of crept up on us during my teens. That I might have the gene, I mean. And that's why I'm so careful about what I eat and so on. It all helps cut down the risk.'

I'd focused on cutting out everything linked to cancer but the older I got, the more I was aware of the potential poison in my blood as a force running under my life.

'You can be tested for it, you know?' Mat's voice was tentative.

'I know. I'm a bloody nurse.'

It was Grandad who mentioned it in the end, spurred on, I'm sure, by Dora. He'd told me they'd pay for the testing if I wanted to have it done privately. He left it at that but Dora couldn't. She kept on asking me until I snapped at her to leave it alone.

It was all so simple to her.

It just wasn't so simple to me. And the more pressure she put on me, the more I put it off. I didn't want it to be so important. I could only cope with it if it wasn't so important.

And in the end, I did something very stupid.

'I have been,' I said to Mat. 'Tested, I mean.'

I was quite proud that nothing in my voice, unless it was the total flatness, gave away how hard it had been. It opened the box on all the fears I didn't want to face.

The butter on Mat's toast had congealed, forming white and yellow patches, as he waited for me to carry on. I wondered if he would have the courage to ask the question. He didn't let me down.

'And the results?' he said, in the end.

'I don't know.' It came out like a wail. 'But they're probably sitting in my letterbox in Coventry.'

He pulled his car keys out of his pocket.

'I'll take you back now. It's no more than a couple of hours away.'

'No,' I said. 'No. Actually, it doesn't matter.'

He didn't sit down, though.

'Honestly, Mat. I can wait. It won't change anything anyway and this is more important.'

He nodded like he understood.

'One more thing, Mat. Well, two actually. You'll have to forget I told you because I won't be able to cope if I see it in your eyes every time you look at me.'

'Sure,' he said. 'Forgotten already.'

'The other thing is that you can't mention it to Dora.'

'OK.'

If he'd demanded to know why he couldn't, I wouldn't have told him, but his quick acceptance unlocked something I'd been holding tight.

'You see… they… she thinks I've already been tested.'

I'd cracked one Sunday lunchtime when I'd come up to see them. Every time Dora spoke to me I could hear the big unasked and unanswered question at the back of her voice and see it in her eyes. Had I got myself tested? And, if not, why not?

The lie had burst out of me before I could stop myself.

'They were so worried,' I said to Mat. 'I told them I'd had it done and that I tested negative for the gene. It was stupid and I regretted it immediately.'

But I couldn't tell them I'd lied because Grandad had been overjoyed.

It was like a weight had been lifted from him straightaway. A weight I hadn't even realised he was carrying. Dora was wrong to say he never wept because he did then. While she was bustling round finding champagne and the special glasses that had been her mother's, his tears dripped onto the glass top of the table and he wiped them away quickly.

Afterwards, his happiness showed in the cadence of his voice when he chatted to me on the phone. He was sleeping better than he had for years, he told me, now that he knew I'd escaped the illness that seemed an intrinsic part of our family life. So, how could I spoil that? Dora had been right. I should have had the test ages ago. If I'd known how it would affect Grandad, I would have. And after the lie, it was doubly difficult because I knew the horrors that faced me if the results were bad. I'd have to keep them a secret and deal with it on my own, because the alternative was impossible. I could never tell Grandad and watch his new-found happiness collapse.

It was all too complicated to explain to Mat. I shook my head at him.

'Do you want toast?' he asked. 'Your gran's homemade marmalade is fantastic.'

He *did* understand.

I nodded. I was hungry and the smell of toast made my mouth water.

His phone vibrated briefly and he read the message. 'Now that's interesting,' he said.

'What?'

'Word is the coroner isn't happy about Michael Poulter's death and there's going to be an inquest.'

'Isn't happy? In what way?'

'No details.'

'What else have you found out this morning?'

He rammed bread into the toaster and told me that he'd been researching Poulters in the 1950s. Berkswell House had mainly been used for manufacturing drugs, particularly those that needed careful supervision. 'Some of the new antibiotics and vaccines, for example,' he said. 'It made perfect sense because the science department, as it was called then, was based there. The research side of Jean's work was small, just early experiments in the labs and some testing on animals. They were waiting for the move to the science park for the big expansion to take place. So, no new drugs came out of Poulters in the late 1950s. The cover-up has nothing to do with a drug having unexpected side-effects.'

The toast popped up and he palmed it onto a plate for me, brought it over and sat down.

'Besides, I've been reading up on Jean Storer and she doesn't strike me as the sort of person who'd do something risky. She wouldn't cut corners. She'd want to be sure new drugs wouldn't do any harm before she gave them to anyone.'

'Maybe she took it herself first.'

Mat paused with a piece of toast halfway to his mouth. The butter dripped over his fingers. 'It's possible. Researchers did test things out on themselves,' he said. 'All the time. Horace Wells with anaesthetics, Jonas Salk with the polio vaccine, can't remember his name who deliberately gave himself cholera –'

'Victor?' I interrupted him. 'Maybe he took something, or Jean gave it to him, and he had a bad reaction to it? Maybe it killed him? Maybe that's why we can't find anything out about him?'

The sound of a key in the lock and Dora burst into the room, dragging a barking Jack behind her.

'That dog,' she announced. 'He chased a cat. Tore the lead out of my hands and jumped over a wall into someone's garden. Smashed a whole bed of hollyhocks. Never been so embarrassed in my life.'

Jack pattered over to the back door and stared at her fixedly. When she didn't move, he barked.

'He's impossible. Just impossible. I don't know what I'm going to do.'

She marched over to the kitchen, still talking non-stop about Jack's sins, and started unpacking her bag, slamming tins and bottles down onto the counter. I slipped off my chair and let Jack out into the back garden. He raced around snuffling in the gaps between the paving and the shed.

'He's bored,' I said. 'He's used to working all the time. To being with Grandad and following his instructions.' And being loved and paid attention to, I thought. Jack must be missing Grandad desperately.

Like Dora.

She was having a bad moment, barely holding back the tears as she piled tins into the mug cupboard. I went over and patted her shoulder tentatively, like someone checking an electric fence isn't live.

'Look, we'll have a think about Jack.'

Dora looked hopefully at me. A bright idea pinged into my mind.

'The charity he came from. They'll know what to do. Maybe they'll rehome him.'

'That's a good idea.'

With the problem of what to do about Jack temporarily sorted, she unpacked her shopping and put the kettle on.

'And what are *we* going to do?' she said, in that abrupt way of hers.

'We think Victor might have died from a drug he and Jean were developing and they covered his death up.'

'And that's why he wasn't at the reunion? His death is what started all this?'

'I didn't say that,' Mat said.

Dora ignored the doubt in his voice. 'You should go back to Berkswell House,' she said. 'Search the grounds. He could be buried there.'

'They're massive,' I said. 'We'd never find...'

'I'm sure I read something about a sort of scanner that can detect long-buried bodies? Look it up, Mat.'

Mat shook his head slightly but obligingly went back to his phone.

I couldn't get Berkswell House and the expanse of wilderness that had once been its garden out of my mind. Why abandon the house to rot and crumble over the decades if there wasn't a secret hiding in its grounds? Large companies weren't sentimental about property.

'And we need to find out more about Victor,' Dora said. 'What about his family?'

'I have,' Mat said, a note of exasperation creeping into his voice. 'I got someone at the *Telegraph* to look him up this morning.' He started reading from his phone. 'His parents are dead – no surprises there – but he has or had a sister. Elizabeth Hindmarsh. Quite a bit younger than him. They came across her because she reported him missing in...' Mat scrolled down. 'In 1978.'

'Missing! But only since 1978?'

'Yes, a tiny little article in the *Telegraph*. But, get this: missing since the early 1960s.'

'Can we get in touch with her?'

'There's a phone number in one of the original listings but whether it's still functioning...' He tapped his pen to his teeth while he thought.

'I think we should call her.' Dora turned to me.

'Of course.'

But neither of us wanted to make the call. Neither of us knew what to say to her. So, in the end, Mat phoned her. Smooth but friendly, he was brilliant, explaining to Victor's sister that he was a journalist with the *Coventry Telegraph* and writing an article on long-term missing people. She'd reported her brother missing in 1978. If he was still missing, would she be prepared to discuss the case with him? He could call back at a time convenient to her, of course.

Elizabeth Hindmarsh was more than happy to talk at length. She brushed aside Mat's offer to let her call the *Telegraph* switchboard and check his credentials and, for the next ten minutes, Dora and I had to listen to Mat occasionally interject with 'I see' or 'Uh-uh' and the odd 'when?' or 'where?'.

He scribbled unintelligible notes as he listened, waving us away when we leaned over him and tried to decipher them. Eventually, he took pity on us and wrote in capital letters, *SHE THINKS HE IS DEAD.*

Finally, the voice at the other end ran out of things to say.

'Would you have any photos of your brother?' Mat asked. 'Or anything else? Letters, maybe? It always brings an article to life.'

And then he was back to short comments again. Dora and I wandered over to the window and looked out through the dark bushes that clustered against the house. She sighed.

'Everything needs cutting back again. We should have taken out the rhododendrons and the camellias when we had the path widened. They stop the light coming into the house. And it's not as though they're particularly attractive. Oh, they're lovely when they flower but it's for such a short –'

Mat waved his free hand at us.

'Maybe I could send one of our researchers over to have a look,' he said into the phone. He scribbled a note on the paper and pointed to it. I went over.

Could you go and see her?, he'd written.

I nodded and gave him a thumbs-up sign. And then wrote, *Where? Not far. Leek.*

I'd never heard of it but Dora nodded.

'Tomorrow afternoon, then. Around four. Of course. I'll email you a confirmation and the researcher's name and phone number.' He paused. 'No, they won't remove anything. They'll just take pictures. Yes. Quite.'

'So?' Dora said as soon as he ended the call.

He glanced at his notes and rattled off a résumé of what he'd learned.

There was a twelve-year age difference between Victor and

his younger sister, Elizabeth. The Second World War had come between their births and the age difference had meant they'd never been close. Victor had left home for university when she'd been eight and had only come back occasionally after that so she couldn't remember when she'd last seen him. There'd been a big falling-out but she didn't know why.

'How come she doesn't know?' I said. 'That's weird.'

'Maybe not,' Dora said. 'It was a long time ago. People didn't talk about things like they do now. Especially not to children.'

'Anyway.' Mat picked up the thread. 'At some point, her parents told her Victor was dead.' He glanced at his notes. 'When her father died in 1977 – her mother had died a few years before that – the solicitors wanted a copy of Victor's death certificate and she couldn't find it or any record of his death. So, that set her wondering if he actually was dead and if she'd been lied to or misunderstood her parents. And I guess suddenly finding herself alone made her want to know, so she started looking for Victor and reported him missing to the police and to the various charities. She got the *Telegraph* to run the article because the last place she knew he'd been was Coventry. There was an old card from Victor among her parents' things, postmarked Coventry. She knew nothing about him working for Poulters, though.'

'When did he send the card?' I asked.

'She couldn't remember. It's been a long time since she thought about it and she'd rather given up but she'd like to know what happened and she said she'd find the card. She's got photos as well. She offered to send me copies but it will be quicker and better if you go to see her. Chat to her. She might well remember some more.'

'You can't come then?'

'No, you go and see her and I'll explore a couple of other avenues. I want to try and find out what the others were up to yesterday.'

'You think we're wasting our time, don't you?'

'You might find out something useful. And, anyway, it would make a good story. If I could find a couple of other missing Coventry people from long ago…' He looked at his phone as he thought. 'Not much battery! I've got a spare one in the car.'

But when he came back his face showed he'd had second thoughts. 'I'm not sure you should be going anywhere,' he said. 'I got carried away earlier. You should stay here and… well, keep safe.'

I remembered the feel of hard hands shoving me down the steps and hesitated. But I had to do something. As Mat clearly didn't believe the mysterious Victor was worth following up, it was down to me. And Dora.

'I'm going,' I said.

Dora looked worried.

Chapter Twenty-Eight:
Phiney Wistman

21 June 2017
Eight days after the reunion

Leek might not have been far away as the crow flies, but getting there by public transport was almost impossible unless you were prepared to stay the night and wait five hours in Buxton the following day. So Dora drove me.

'What if she realises you're not a researcher?' Dora said, signalling right and moving smoothly to overtake a car belching grey smoke from its exhaust.

'I've only got to take a few photographs on my phone and chat to her. It can't be that difficult. She's not going to ask to see my CV, is she?'

Dora sighed and pulled back into the inside lane, touching the brakes lightly as we slotted in behind a black car with a 'Baby On Board' sign.

The alarm on my phone went. Like it had every hour on the hour since we left this morning. I texted Mat as I'd promised.

We're OK. Not far from Leek now.

There was no reply but he'd said he might not be able to answer when he headed off yesterday. He'd been very vague about his plans but insistent that we both kept in touch.

'I'll try and keep it short,' I said to Dora. 'Get her talking about Victor. And leave as quickly as possible.'

'Do you want me to come in with you?'

'Probably best not to. I expect researchers don't generally bring their grandparents with them.'

I remembered Mat's words: 'Let her ramble on and, above all, don't fire questions at her. People like to chat when they're face to face, especially if you give them time and space to fill. And now we've put Victor into her head, her subconscious will start dredging up old memories. Let her ramble and look interested. You'll see.'

I hoped he was right.

Elizabeth Hindmarsh lived in a modern bungalow on a new estate just outside Leek with lovely views over the moors. There were ornaments and photographs. Lots of photographs. Family holidays and weddings and babies and christenings. If Mrs Hindmarsh had lacked family after her father died, she'd certainly made up for it in the intervening years.

She was about the same age as Dora but there the similarity ended. Small but portly, she was held together by expensive underwear. Probably a lot of it. I'd helped women like her undress and been amazed at what you could buy to give shape to recalcitrant flesh. Dora, bless her, was strictly a Marks and Spencer sensible underwear buyer, not that her large but bony frame needed any support.

'Thank you for seeing me,' I said, as we sat down on the sofa – me with ease and her with a slightly ponderous majesty due, no doubt, to the rigidity of her underwear. A cut-glass bowl of potpourri on the coffee table gave off a faded scent of dead flowers. Two photos and a yellowed envelope were laid out beside it.

'I don't have much to show you and, to be honest, I'd rather given up on ever finding out what happened to Victor. Perhaps Mr Torrington's article will jog a few memories.'

I picked up the first of the photos. It was a black-and-white snap, showing a group posed round a Christmas tree, adults standing and children sitting cross-legged on the floor. Girls in plaits and dresses and boys in those longish shorts they made them wear even when the weather was freezing. A young man stood slightly to one side with the same face as the one in the newspaper photo. I looked at the back. *Christmas 1956.*

'That's me,' Elizabeth said and pointed to one of the children on the floor in front of a man with a ferocious look and eyebrows to match. 'And that's Victor at the side. That's how I remember him. He was sort of caught in between the adults and the children. There was no one his age among our friends. And no one clever like him. Not that any of us were stupid. But he was in a different league.'

'And the others? Who are they?'

'Family friends. I remember the children's names but I've lost touch with them all. None of them were close to Victor, though.'

'Nice photo.'

I took a couple of shots on my phone.

'So, you don't remember when you last saw him?' I asked.

'Sorry. As I said to your boss, I was very young.'

I realised by my boss she meant Mat and picked up the other photo.

It was another group around a Christmas tree. Just the family this time. Victor stood out again. Not because of his beauty but because of the dressing on his face. A wodge of lint around his chin and lower lip held in place by a bandage and more lint and sticking plaster on his cheeks. I flicked it over and looked at the back. *Christmas 1958*. Shit. Eighteen months after the summer of 1957. He'd been alive eighteen months later.

'Victor had been in an accident that Christmas,' Mrs Hindmarsh said, while my thoughts raced, trying to make sense of it all.

'What sort of accident?'

'A car accident. I mean, I think it was. I don't really remember.'

She bent down and picked up a speck of something from the carpet. It looked suspiciously like one of Jack's hairs. Had I brought it in with me? I cast a stealthy look at the carpet round me. It was clear but there were a couple of black hairs on the arm of the sofa where my hand was resting.

I tried another question.

'Someone must have told you about his death. Can you remember who it was?'

Mrs Hindmarsh stared past me and out of the window. 'When the police asked me that question in 1977, I couldn't recall anything. It was as if I'd always known. But a couple of months later, I was in a friend's garden and she had big bushes of lavender. When I was a child, my mother grew lavender by the washing line. Said it scented the sheets. And, all of a sudden, the memory flooded back. I suppose I'd been searching for it unconsciously after all the questions the police asked. I remembered taking sheets off the line and folding them with her. Those lovely white linen ones we used to have. Stiff until they were ironed. It must have been summer because the bees were humming round the lavender and I was worried they might sting me. And Mummy said, "Victor is dead." And I remember she looked very cross.'

Her eyes lost their glazed look.

'Not that it was much help. I had no idea when it happened or what we were talking about before. And, since then, I've wondered if it was just Mummy being dramatic. She could be very emotional. Made life so difficult for Daddy.'

She was right. It wasn't in the least bit helpful. Nevertheless, I took a couple of pics of the photo. Front and back.

She sniffed and wrinkled her nose. I began to wonder if she could smell something. Me? I lifted my arm and breathed in surreptitiously. Was there a faint smell of dog, dragged out from the clothes I was wearing by the warmth of the room? One I hadn't noticed because I was so used to it?

'Are the dates on the back of the photographs accurate?'

She looked at me as though I was mad. 'I think so. Why wouldn't they be?'

'Do you have anything from Christmas 1957? Any pictures?'

'No.'

'But he spent that Christmas with you?'

'I think so. I mean, I don't remember him not being there. But it's possible.'

She looked flustered and I made myself rein in my questions.

'Do you want to read the card?' She picked it up and handed it to me.

I looked at the envelope. It had been sent to Victor's mother in March 1959 from Coventry and it wasn't much of a card. A picture of primroses and a few scrawled lines in blue ink.

Happy Birthday Ma.

I hope you're well.

Sorry about Christmas.

V xxx

'What does he mean? "Sorry about Christmas"?'

'There was a family falling-out. I told your Mr Torrington.'

'What about?'

'I never really knew. Maybe about the car accident? I remember my father and mother discussing it. At the bottom of the garden by the fuchsias. They always went there when they wanted to talk privately but I could hear bits and pieces if I opened my bedroom window and stood behind the curtain.'

She went very still, staring into space. I tried not to fidget, remembering what Mat had said about the benefit of giving people time if you wanted them to speak.

'Father was furious. I remember that. Called Victor an unnatural son. Said what he'd done was wicked.'

'Mmmm,' I said. I'd been hoping for a bit more than that.

I waited a few seconds and loosened the top button of the blouse I'd borrowed from Dora. It was stuffy in this plush sitting room with all the windows closed tight against the outside. But she couldn't remember anything else and she was starting to get restless, casting quick glances at the carriage clock on the mantelpiece and pushing the photos and card into a neat pile.

I asked her if there might be any other papers. She insisted she'd been through everything when she'd first reported him missing, turning her father's house upside down to find any traces.

'Do you think Mr Torrington's article will help?' she asked me as I left.

'I don't know. It can't do any harm.'

'I'd like to know what happened. I don't remember much about him but the few memories I have are nice. He was a kind brother. He bought me things I really wanted for Christmas and birthdays. Dollies I could dress and frivolous things whereas my parents always gave me books and sensible clothes.'

'Well?' Dora said as soon as I got back into the car. On the other side of the road, a couple of neighbours clearing apple tree blossom from their otherwise immaculate lawn stared at us.

'Let's get out of here.'

'What did you learn?'

I told her, explaining how the dates on the card and second photo meant Victor was still alive after 1957. 'Mrs Hindmarsh's parents called Victor "wicked". "An unnatural son". Do you think it was to do with whatever happened in 1957 at Berkswell House? Would he have told them? It seems unlikely.'

Dora thought for a while. 'Yes, it does. I expect they fell out over something else.'

'They called him wicked, though.'

'That's only what Mrs Hindmarsh thinks she remembers, and anyway, it was much easier to be wicked then. Everything was much more rigid. My pa called me unnatural, you know, when I asked him if I could become a mechanic.'

'But you didn't fall out about it and never see them again.'

'No, but that was because I gave in and took typing lessons instead. It's a pity Victor rowed with his family, though. It meant no one cared much when he died.'

'Or someone knew about the family rift and saw an opportunity?' I said.

'To do what?'

'I don't know. To kill him. To keep his death quiet.'

'If he is dead. We've no proof.'

Dora had let the car slow down as we talked, to the irritation of the driver of the black car behind us. He flashed his lights and pressed on the horn, before overtaking us.

'BMW drivers.' Dora sniffed but she pulled into the next car park and I showed her the pictures.

'1958,' I said, as she looked at the second photo. '1958 and Victor was alive.'

The knowledge filled me with unease. It turned every idea we'd had upside down.

'And injured,' Dora said. 'But not because of something that happened in 1957. It's too long after. Like Mrs Hindmarsh said, a car accident, maybe.'

She passed me my phone back and I zoomed in as tightly as I could on Victor's face before the picture started pixelating. 'It's quite strange. If he'd been in a car accident you'd expect his nose to have been damaged and more swelling round the eyes. It was something else, I think. You know, there are injuries that take a long time to heal. Full thickness burns can take months. Chemical burns can be very tricky. Especially if they get infected. Mind you, anything can be difficult if it gets infected and they didn't have the range of treatments back then that we do now.'

'So, it could be the result of something that happened in 1957?'

'It's possible.' But I wasn't sure. Nothing was sure. That's what was so difficult. We knew so little and the few facts we had seemed to contradict each other.

'What I don't understand is why all this is happening now?' I said. 'After all the years of silence?'

Dora was uncharacteristically quiet for a few minutes.

'Didn't Mat say Michael Poulter was very ill anyway?'

'Dying, I think.'

'Maybe that's why. Maybe he felt the truth should be told?'

There were too many maybes about everything.

'Maybe he wanted to put it right,' Dora said, after a pause. 'Things change as you age. You don't have years and years stretching in front of you and if you want to do something, you need to do it now. Because time is running out.'

It sort of made sense.

We didn't talk much after that. Apart from Dora muttering about Jack.

We'd left him behind at the cottage. He'd come out of the house willingly but, as soon as we'd approached Dora's car, he'd refused to budge an inch. We'd both tried to drag him in, separately and together, and failed. He'd had enough of car journeys so we shut him in the back yard with food and water. I knew Dora didn't want to leave him too long because she told me countless times. She told me as we crawled along in tailbacks created by an accident involving a lorry. She worried about him in between her comments about the other drivers as we drove the second part of the journey with the evening fading into a criss-cross of headlights and cat's eyes. I tuned her out in the end and tried to make sense of what I'd learned. And wished Mat would call in answer to my texts so we could chat.

It was very dark by the time we got back. There were no streetlights in Dora's road and the only lights peeked from between the tightly closed curtains of the terraced cottages.

'I forgot to leave the porch light on,' Dora said, as she manoeuvred into a parking space a few houses up from hers. 'Didn't think we'd be back this late. You'll have to watch the path up to the front door. It can be slippery.' She paused. 'We were going to get it resurfaced but I suppose it's hardly worth it now.' A whole world of regret echoed in her voice.

I squeezed her hand. 'I'll use the torch on my phone.'

But there was no need. As we approached the cottage, Dora's next-door neighbour flung open his front door, switched on his porch light and marched down the path in his dressing gown, tightly belted round startling yellow-and-blue checked pyjamas.

'Mr Dolling,' Dora started to speak.

'Mrs Patterson! You're back. Your dog —'

The noise of barking and whining interrupted him.

'He's been like this ever since it got dark. I'm sorry but we couldn't take it anymore. I'm afraid I called the police. About twenty minutes ago. I expect they'll be here soon.' He turned and strode back down his path.

Sure enough, a police car crawled down the road towards us. A sudden movement by the house caught my eye. I swivelled round to see a black figure detach itself from the dark corner where the house and porch walls met. It dodged behind a camellia and leapt over the brick wall that separated Dora's front garden from the alleyway running between her house and the next-door neighbour on the other side from Mr Dolling.

I stopped breathing. My brain not quite sure what I'd seen although my body knew. A ripple of shock coursed through my blood. Understanding came and with it my breathing returned. Rapid, shaky grabs of air. Dora gasped too. I shot her a quick glance. She stared at the wall beside the camellia bush. She'd seen it too.

Two policemen got out of the car, one bearded and chubby, the other slight and with a smattering of acne on his shiny forehead around the line of his helmet. Never had I been so glad to see the police. Dora too. She launched an incoherent, trembling stumble of words about an intruder but they got the gist fast and Beardy charged down the alley while the other took Dora's keys and went into the house.

'You saw it, didn't you?' Dora said.

'Yup.' And, because her voice shook, I put my arm round her shoulders and wished she wasn't so much taller than me.

The police found nothing and, after they'd ushered us into the cottage and I'd let Jack into the house, Beardy made tea and heaped biscuits onto a plate. Dora ate them mindlessly, taking a bite between each sentence, chewing and swallowing, then gulping tea. She poured everything out to them. She told them about Grandad dying. About how we didn't know why. About the mysterious reunion he'd been to before his death. As she talked, Beardy's note-taking slowed and Spotty rubbed his forehead and glanced at his watch surreptitiously.

203

They wound the conversation up as Dora started on about Michael's death in the hotel room the same morning.

'Come into the station tomorrow morning and report this to the duty sergeant,' Beardy said. 'There's nothing we can do now. We've checked the premises. And we'll go round the outside once more. Make sure you lock up well. But it is very possible the figure you saw was someone come round because of the noise your dog was making.' He leaned down and patted Jack who was lying on the rug, tightly pressed against Dora's legs. 'Lovely dog, Mrs Patterson. We won't report it as it's the first time. But you'll have to keep him quiet.' And with that, they left.

'Well,' Dora said. 'I expect Jack was barking because someone was hanging around. They thought I was mad, didn't they?'

'Yes.' I was beyond lying.

'You saw him, though, didn't you?'

'Yes.' I could still see it. It was imprinted on my brain. The dark figure vaulting over the wall and away.

'What shall we do?'

I had no idea.

'Sleep,' I said. 'And discuss in the morning. The house is safe. Thank God the neighbours are close and Jack will wake if anyone tries to get in.'

We locked up together, each of us checking that every key was turned and every bolt shot firmly into place, and went to bed.

I called Mat but he didn't answer so I sent him a text. *We're OK. But someone was waiting for us at the cottage. Call me. No matter how late.*

But he didn't.

Chapter Twenty-Nine: Phiney Wistman

22 June 2017
Nine days after the reunion

Dora was ironing with grim concentration when I forced myself out of bed in the morning. A faint cloud of steam hung about her as she determinedly pressed each crease out of a stack of linen napkins. A packet of organic muesli lay out on the breakfast bar along with a bottle of rice milk. She nodded when she saw me but said nothing.

'You can speak to me,' I said. 'Surely I'm not that bad in the mornings.'

'How did you sleep?'

'Not great, if I'm honest. And you?'

She shook her head. She wore the same dark-green blouse with a pussy bow as yesterday. It could have been the same skirt too because all of hers looked identical to me. Her hair was scraped back into its normal bun but the hairpins were roughly inserted and strands were already escaping.

'Phiney, I can't stay here.' The words burst out. 'Not like this. I couldn't sleep at all last night. Every noise startled me awake.'

She yanked the iron's plug out of its socket and thrust the napkins into a drawer.

'Are the doors still locked?' I asked.

'Yes. I unlocked the back to let Jack out this morning but I locked it up again immediately.' She hung the ironing board in the cupboard under the stairs and slammed the door shut.

'Can you go and stay with someone?' I said.

'I could stay with the vicar. She's already offered. She's got a big family and there are church people in and out the whole time.'

'Do it.' And before she could suggest I stayed at the vicarage too, I said, 'I'll go to Meghan's. She's living at home at the moment, with her parents.'

'The vicar won't have Jack, though. Her youngest is allergic to dogs. Could you call Mat and tell him what we're doing? I'm going to speak to the dog charity.' Dora went into her bedroom clutching the phone.

Mat didn't reply so I sent him a text, telling him what we'd learned from Mrs Hindmarsh and how we wondered if Victor's injuries were the result of something that had happened at Poulters. I attached the photos and spent a few minutes staring at the bandaged figure in the second one.

The dressings were very odd, bulky and concentrated around his lower face – not like any bandaging I'd ever seen. I began to wonder if they were a disguise rather than a covering for a wound. But disguising what? Some disfigurement? Caused by whatever had happened in 1957? Maybe.

Maybe Victor had been left alive but badly damaged. I remembered what Dora had said about old people realising how limited the time left to them might be. Had he decided, as he reached the end of his life, that he wanted revenge? Was that what lay behind these deaths?

Why would Victor want to kill me, though? I had nothing to do with the events of 1957.

I washed the breakfast dishes and wiped down the kitchen surfaces. Looked up the times of the trains to Coventry. Called Meghan and asked if I could stay. Tidied all the papers Mat had left behind, saying he had copies on his phone, found a file and put them in it. But the thought of Victor out there, angry and scarred, wouldn't leave my mind while I waited for Dora to finish her call.

'They'll take Jack,' she said. 'Straightaway. In fact, the sooner the better. They've got several people they could rehome him with.'

But she looked doubtful.

'It's the best thing for him,' I said. 'He needs to work. He needs to devote himself to someone.' I smiled at her. 'I'll take him with me.'

It was a rush to catch the train, what with packing all Jack's stuff up and forcing him into the car to get to the station. I managed to find an aisle seat at a table in a silent carriage and flopped down thankfully, closing my eyes.

A nudge in my arm stopped me drifting off. It was the man opposite. My age. Tight black T-shirt showing he worked out regularly. A couple of discreet tattoos. Quite tasty.

'Is he allowed in here?'

He pointed to Jack and I revised my opinion of him. He was an ignorant lout.

'He's not making a noise, is he?' I said and shut my eyes again.

Unfortunately, the train was busy and Jack was a big dog. Or, at least, he took up a lot of space when lying in the aisle so, after the tenth time of getting him to stand up to let someone past while Tattoo Man opposite glared, we went and stood in the bit outside the toilets. I found a little pull-down seat and Jack lay on the floor.

I texted Meghan my train time. She replied at once.

I'll meet you.

Thanks

Is Mat with you?

No. Why?

Just wondered.

'Plenty of seats in the carriage, Miss.' The ticket inspector held out his hand for my ticket.

'I know but my dog gets in the way.'

'The train will fill up at Birmingham International with people going to London. This area will be crowded then.'

'I'll go back to my seat before that.'

My phone rang. He gave me a disapproving look but couldn't actually say anything as I was outside the silent carriage.

'It's my gran,' I said, as though that excused it.

Dora was worried. She'd called Mat but there was no answer. I calmed her down, said I was sure he was OK, just busy, and promised her I'd call the *Coventry Telegraph* to see if they had any news of him.

The first whispers of concern nipped at the corners of my thoughts. I hadn't heard from Mat since yesterday afternoon. Even if he'd been busy he'd have sent a quick text by now. Had something happened to him? The memory of Philip's body floating in the pool came back to me. I felt sick.

The *Telegraph* didn't know where he was. A harassed-sounding man, trying to answer someone else's questions at the same time, told me Mat wasn't there. There was nothing in the diary for him, and anyway, he was freelance. He organised his own time.

I called Mat again. The phone went straight to voicemail again. Like it does when you've switched it off. Or when you've run out of battery.

I thought of Mat and his supply of battery packs. I thought of Mat always with half an eye on his phone. Checking the news feeds in the middle of a conversation. Texting replies to people at every available moment. I remembered him making me promise to text him wherever I went.

A wave of worry swept over me.

How could I have thought he was too busy to keep in touch? Something had happened to him. He'd never have ignored us for so long. I had to do something. If we'd gone to look for Philip earlier, he might still be alive. I couldn't risk the same thing happening to Mat.

What was I going to do?

Police?

Of course. I'd report him missing.

But the memory of the police's polite disbelief last night made me hesitate. Even if they took me seriously, they'd want to check everything and they'd tread cautiously as soon as I mentioned Poulters. We might not have time. Mat might not have time. I had a better idea. I'd get Dora to report it. She'd have more success than me anyway. Once Dora decided to do something, she stuck with it and she'd drive them mad until they did something.

I texted her. I told her I was really worried about Mat too and she should go to the police.

Of course. I'll go now.

And what would I do?

I dragged Jack back into the carriage and ignored the sigh Tattoo Man emitted, forced him to retract his legs enough to let me sit down and spread the contents of the file over the table.

Think, I said to myself, think. What would Mat have done?

I reread everything in the file, trying to imagine I was Mat poring over it all and looking for the next step. The list of people who'd attended the reunion sprung out at me. Mat had talked about finding out what they'd been up to the day Philip had died.

Next stop is Birmingham International. Birmingham International. Change here for...

A clatter of feet and cases and people lined up in the aisle waiting to get off, stepping over Jack who stuck his head under my legs and ignored them. Poor old boy. He'd had enough of travelling to last him a lifetime.

This is the London train. Calling at Coventry, Rugby, Watford Junction and London Euston.

Ideas raced through my brain.

Twenty minutes to Coventry.

I spent them trying to make up my mind what to do.

As the train pulled into Coventry, I fought my way to the door with Jack trailing behind me. A few people got off before me. When they'd all left, I leaned out of the door and waved until Meghan saw me and came over.

'Meghan,' I said. 'Take Jack.'

I bundled him out of the door, then shut it.

'What are you doing?'

'Emergency. Sorry. I'll text you. No time to explain.'

The train pulled out and Meghan's face with its open mouth disappeared. I went back to my seat.

My phone rang two seconds later. Tattoo Man glowered. I put it on silent. Then a text.

What is going on?

Sorry. Got to meet someone. I'll be back later. But I can't take Jack.

Call me.

Can't. In a silent carriage.

Go somewhere else.

The train is rammed. Just wait.

I sent her a text telling her I had to go and talk to someone about Grandad's death and, because I wasn't stupid, I sent her their name and address.

Then I put the phone in my bag so I wouldn't have to read her messages trying to dissuade me.

Chapter Thirty:
Phiney Wistman

22 June 2017
Nine days after the reunion

Susan Storer, according to Mat's notes, lived in a flat in a little pocket of Edwardian houses in the tree-lined streets of south-east London. It wasn't far from a park with a small café selling designer coffee and cakes whose irregularity made them appear homemade. I sat there gathering my thoughts and watching the mothers and toddlers play among the swings and slides. Now that I was here, the thought of questioning Susan was daunting and I felt as inadequate as the lone pigeon darting under tables in a fruitless quest for crumbs. And as fearful.

I looked again at Mat's notes.

Susan Storer, Jean's niece. She was forty-four. Not old. There were women in my netball team older than that. Fast, strong women, more than capable of pushing me over. We knew Jean had played no part in Philip's death, so had Mat thought Susan was also in the clear? Had he decided to come and ask her about the reunion? I thought it was possible. He wouldn't have approached James. Nor Laura after my experience with her.

I called him again, praying he'd answer and show me that my worry was unnecessary. He didn't. So, I made myself get up and walk to Susan's flat, ring the bell labelled *Storer* and stay there when I heard the sounds of her coming to the door.

With faded blonde hair straggling out of a floral scarf that held the rest of it back in a ponytail, and a loose dress whose faded colours gave its age away, she looked totally unthreatening. She'd been laughing, I thought. The traces of it hung around her eyes and in the curve of her mouth gradually settling back into calmness.

'Sorry,' she said. 'Did you have to ring a few times? You're earlier than I expected and I was in the garden. I'm a bit slow.' She gestured towards her leg. Her other arm leaned on a stick and there was a bandage round her left shin. I relaxed a little. She wasn't going to be chasing down the street after me if I decided to run.

But when had she hurt her leg? I remembered the slippery path leading to the waterfall and told myself to be careful.

'I'm supposed to be working.' She smiled. 'But I've been mainly chatting to next door if I'm honest. It's too nice a day to work.'

She was so friendly and open, I couldn't think what to say.

She looked at me more closely. 'Oh. How stupid! You're not the nurse, are you? Sorry. I was expecting one. Listen, if you're here to sell me something, I'll tell you now, I'm not interested.'

It was too good an opportunity to miss.

'No, no, I am the nurse. A locum.' I pulled my NHS pass out of my bag, flashed it at her and followed her in.

Hers was the downstairs flat and she led me through the sitting room and into the kitchen at the back. French windows opened onto a paved garden that was lush with flowering shrubs and jasmine climbing the old brick walls. A garden chair with a footstool and a little table with an open book, a cup and spectacles on it showed she'd been speaking the truth about working. But we stayed in her kitchen by a table with a computer squeezed in between piles of papers. She took a box of dressings down from a shelf and made a space on the table for it by putting one pile of paper on top of another.

'I'll wash my hands first,' I said. 'Where's your bathroom?'

'Through the door in the sitting room and on your left.'

I slipped out before she could ask me why I didn't use the sink in the kitchen and found the bathroom, washed my hands and checked her bedroom on the way back. There was no one but us in the flat. Not Mat. Nor anyone else.

Under the bandage, the wound on her leg was infected. Badly infected. Her leg was red and swollen and the area around the sore was yellow with pus. Clearly, she hadn't climbed the steep path at Ullswater to the top of the waterfall three days ago and pushed Philip into the pounding waters below. I thought getting to the shops would be a struggle.

'How did that happen?'

'An insect bite. I thought it was nothing at the time. Very itchy, though, and I might have scratched it a few times.' She gave a deprecating laugh. 'So *mea culpa*, really.'

'How long has it been like this?'

'A week or so. But it is looking much better since I've been on antibiotics and you and your colleagues have been cleaning it every day.'

She chatted away as I prepared the new dressings, telling me that it didn't hurt too much provided she kept off her feet. The faint noise of cars in the street and the neighbour cutting back the honeysuckle on their joint wall lent everything an air of normality. It would have been easy to finish the dressing and leave.

I waited until I was swabbing the wound with antiseptic, the moment when she was most vulnerable, because gentle as I was, the pain made her hiss her breath in between clenched teeth.

'Did Mat come and see you?'

I stared at her face as I asked the question, hoping her reaction would give something away.

'Mat?'

'Mat Torrington.'

She had no idea what I was talking about. No idea at all.

'Ah. Is he one of the nurses?'

'No. He's a journalist.'

Her mouth started to form questions and then stop. She looked like a goldfish grabbing after food. If I hadn't been so desperate for information I'd have felt sorry for her.

'A journalist? Why would a journalist come and see me?'

She could have been lying but I didn't think so. Wherever Mat had gone, it hadn't been to see Susan.

Shit. Where was he then?

Still, Susan must know something. She'd been at the reunion at The Herbert.

'I'm Josephine Wistman,' I said. 'But everyone calls me Phiney.'

The name meant nothing to her. Confusion and concern chased each other across her face. Her eyes darted to the telephone on the windowsill behind the table.

I'd blown this.

'You've got nothing to worry about,' I said quickly. 'It's complicated but I need your help.'

Her face hardened. She reached out and smacked my hands away from her leg.

'Who are you?'

I stepped away from her, leaving her lots of space.

'I *am* a nurse, you know. Look.' I gave her my pass and gave her time to read it and compare my face with the photo. 'Just not the one you were expecting.'

'What do you want?'

'Just to ask you a few questions.'

'Questions? I don't think so. Please leave. Leave now.'

She stretched out to the windowsill and grabbed the phone.

'Look, I promise you I'm not here to hurt you. Your neighbour is still out there. If you call, he'll come.'

Her hands tightened round the phone. Clearly, she thought I was a madwoman but wasn't sure of the best way to handle me.

I spoke swiftly, desperate to get the words out before she evicted me.

'Last week, my Grandad – who was perfectly fine before – jumped off a bridge. We don't know why and I can't explain to you how terrible that feels. Before he did it, he went to a meeting at The Herbert in Coventry. A sort of reunion, I think it was. And you were there. So you must have met him. His name was Wilfred Patterson.'

'Wilfred Patterson.' A memory lightened her face.

'He'd have had his dog with him.'

'Yes. I remember him. Your grandad?'

'My grandad. But, like I said, he's dead now. He killed himself and I think something happened at the meeting that made him do it. So, please. Please, please, please, could you tell me what it was all about?'

I wanted to grab her shoulders and shake it out of her. Except she'd call the neighbour and then I'd have no chance. Besides, something told me it would be better to appear as sane as possible so I waited and tried to look normal. Tears prickled my eyes and I blew my nose.

She eyed me up and down and glanced through the window to check her neighbour was still there. She seemed to reach a decision.

'I'm really sorry about your grandad,' she said. 'I only met him briefly but he was charming. But, you see, I don't know what happened. I didn't go into the actual meeting. I waited outside.'

After all that, she hadn't been there.

'You think your grandad... You think he killed himself because of the meeting?'

I nodded.

'I never knew what it was all about but I can tell you it all started when Michael Poulter came to see my aunt, Jean Stofer, in the south of France. I could call her. She would know what happened but she's on a plane coming back from the States.'

A fly buzzed in from outside, breaking the silence.

'Could you just tell me what you do know?' I scrubbed my eyes dry. 'And I really should finish your dressing. It's not good to leave something so badly infected uncovered.'

She nodded.

I snapped clean gloves on and tore the wrapping off one of the gauzes. She took a deep breath and started to speak.

Chapter Thirty-One:
Susan Storer

13 June 2017
The Reunion

Jean and Susan took a taxi from Birmingham Airport to The Herbert in silence. Jean stared out of the window at the rows of terraced houses interspersed with bus stops and clusters of small shops and, once again, Susan felt that her presence was a problem Jean couldn't resolve. Since Michael's visit, Jean had spent hours walking the hills surrounding the house, seemingly impervious to the heat and the mosquitos, and focused relentlessly on her memoirs during the time she and Susan were together. She retired early to her room with a tray of food in the evenings, claiming to be preparing material for Susan although there'd been little evidence of this.

'What is this meeting about, Jean?'

Jean looked surprised, as though she'd forgotten Susan was there again.

'A problem with an old piece of research. Didn't I tell you?'

'I don't think so. What was the research to do with?'

'You wouldn't understand.'

This was a bit much. Susan had grappled her way to an understanding of the basics of what Jean did. It wasn't as difficult as Jean made out. People always thought their fields were too complicated to share with outsiders but Susan had yet to discover a subject she couldn't master sufficiently to write about.

'Try me,' she said, with a laugh. 'It always helps to have a few pointers in advance so I can follow.'

'Not now. I need to collect my thoughts. Anyway, I won't need you in the meeting.'

'I see. But I thought it would be useful to sit in. For background material.'

'No.'

'Oh.'

'Some of the research is quite sensitive. Ethical considerations, you know.'

'Ah.'

'So, you go off and explore. I believe Coventry Cathedral is stunning.'

But, after they'd taken the lift up to the second floor, where a poker-faced and immaculately made-up woman, whom Jean addressed as 'Laura', met them and whisked Jean into the meeting room, Susan set herself up on one of the desks in the grey-carpeted and anonymous lobby area outside the meeting room. The bite on her leg was swollen and it hurt when she walked. The cathedral could wait for another time. Besides, Jean's refusal to reveal anything about the meeting had piqued her interest.

It was cool and quiet up here on the second floor and she quickly lost herself in writing. She was reaching the point with Jean's memoir where the initial desperation to get words onto paper was fading and she wanted to start exploring the times Jean hadn't spoken about. Susan's clients rarely told her their life stories in chronological order. She'd write up whatever they said and insert it in the right place. Once the word count started to be respectable, she'd read it through and ask them what had happened in the gaps. And, often, that was where the key moments were. The months towards the end of Jean's employment at Poulters were still a blank but Susan's writer's instincts had twitched when Jean claimed nothing much happened. The nuggets of gold always lay in the areas clients were most evasive about.

Two elderly men came out of the lift, one of them with a pronounced limp and a dog. They went into the room together but the man with the dog came back out after a few minutes and walked up to Susan.

'I believe you're Dr Storer's niece.'

'Yes.'

'I'm Wilfred Patterson.'

Susan didn't bother to tell him she knew. And that she'd guessed the man who'd come with him was Philip Mason, whom she'd only managed to trace via the last school he'd worked at.

'Dr Storer thought you wouldn't mind if I left Jack with you. Apparently, Miss Greenacre doesn't like dogs. I promise you he won't be a bother.'

She loved dogs but she wouldn't have refused anyway. He was such a nice old man. So courteous, offering to get her a cup of tea from the meeting room.

Michael Poulter arrived next and he too had gone straight in with barely a glance in her direction.

Susan carried on working. Her fingers typed up notes but her thoughts were on what was going on behind the shut door. And then another man arrived, a little younger than Susan, she thought. From the glorious leather of his shoes to his discreet but beautifully cut suit, he oozed money and confidence. He stopped and looked around, nonplussed, as though he expected someone to greet him. A second man followed him, slightly out of breath and wearing a silver-buttoned jacket. In his hands was a cap. A chauffeur? Crikey, did normal people still have them?

'I'll call you when I'm finished, Arch,' the first man said. 'But it will be at least an hour.'

'I'll wait here, Mr Poulter.'

'Fine.'

Michael put his head round the door.

'Ah. We're in here, James. Come in. We've all been waiting for you.'

This must be James Poulter, Susan thought. Michael's son.

'Dreadful traffic.'

'You drove?'

James nodded towards the chauffeur. 'Arch drove me.'

The chauffeur nodded to Michael. 'Mr Poulter,' he said, by way of greeting.

Something about the chauffeur's face was wrong. As though it had been assembled from two different sets of features. A smooth and hairless expanse of forehead, with pale, wide-open eyes, topped a bland nose and round jaw. He would have been inoffensive and unremarkable if he hadn't grown a pointed beard that bisected his chin. It looked as though it belonged to a different face.

Michael stared at the chauffeur as though he too was trying to sort out the puzzle of his face.

'You'd better join us, Simon,' Michael said to him eventually. 'I hadn't thought to ask you to come, but as you're here.' A look of distaste wrinkled his face.

He went back inside without another word but Susan had the impression Simon's presence had upset him in some way.

'Simon?' James Poulter said.

'It's my name. Simon, Mr Poulter. Simon Archibald. Everyone at Poulters has always called me Arch.' He looked after Michael. 'Except Mr Michael.'

'And you know about this?'

Susan had the impression that the calm surface of James's voice hid a strong emotion. Anger?

Arch, or Simon, gestured towards Susan with a jerk of his head. She went back to her typing.

'Yes,' he said. 'I do know about it.'

'How?'

'Someone told me. A long time ago. Back in the seventies. But you don't need to worry. I've never breathed a word to anyone.'

The meeting began for real as soon as the two of them went in. Susan could only hear the noise of words, their pitch and speed and intonation, while the individual consonants and vowels were blurred, no matter how near to the door she went. Jean's voice stood out. But the rest of them were indistinguishable. At first, they spoke in turn but, later, their voices rose together and drowned each other out.

Jack settled himself under her desk. Clearly, he was used to waiting, although his eyes remained fixed on the door. After a particularly heated exchange, it opened abruptly, James stormed out and Jack scrambled up. James stopped when he saw Susan and the dog. A jumble of words followed him out of the room. For a brief moment, Jean's voice rose above them all. 'Remember the cutter,' she was saying before James shut the door sharply. He hesitated for a second as though he were going to say something to Susan. Whatever it was, he thought better of it and headed across the lobby towards the lift, taking a circuitous route to avoid passing near her desk.

The chauffeur came out too. 'Mr Poulter?' he called and hurried after him.

'Bring the car round,' James said. He spoke quietly but the force of his voice carried the words to Susan.

'Are we going back to London?'

'Yes.' He paused. 'No. I need to talk to you. Let me think.'

Susan started typing again, her ears straining to pick up their conversation. James wanted to go somewhere else first. Something house, she thought he'd said. But he'd have to get the security company to meet them there and give them the keys and the security code.

The lift doors opened and they disappeared.

Jack sighed and settled back down under the desk.

'I feel a bit like that too.' She bent and patted his back. 'Shall we go and get a breath of fresh air?'

When they came back, the meeting room door was open. There was no noise and, for a moment, she wondered if they'd all left, but Jean was still there, sitting at one end of the big table that all but filled the room, her head buried in her hands. At the other end, Wilfred and Philip stood up when Susan appeared. Laura and Michael had gone.

'I'm sorry,' Susan said. 'Have you been waiting for us?' She let go of Jack's leash and he rejoined his master, wagging his tail and pushing his nose into the hand reached down to greet him.

'Only a few minutes,' he said. He looked pitifully white and tired. 'Thank you for looking after him.'

'Come on, Wilf,' Philip said. 'Let's get out of here.'

Jean took her hands away from her head and laid them flat on the table. 'Think about what I said, both of you. You know I'm right.' She was as white and strained as the man called Wilf and her hands trembled.

'It isn't going to make any difference what you or I think, Jean. Michael is on a mission.'

'We can deny it.'

'There's evidence. You heard him,' Philip added.

He went to help Wilf to his feet but Wilf shook off his hand and walked by himself out of the room with Jack glued to his side and Philip hovering behind.

'Aunty?' Susan said.

But Jean shrugged off all her questions and offers of help, insisting she was fine if a little tired. They took a taxi, neither of them speaking, to the hotel Jean had asked Susan to book and Jean went straight up to her room.

Honestly, Susan thought, she might as well have gone back to London from the airport for all the time Jean had spent working on her memoir.

Chapter Thirty-Two:
Phiney Wistman

22 June 2017
Nine days after the reunion

'In the morning,' Susan said, 'Aunty was back to her old self. Up early and going for a long walk before she met me at breakfast. Whatever she'd been worrying about, she'd put it behind her. We came back to London, and I spend most mornings with her, or did until she went to the States.'

I barely listened to her talk about how wonderful it was that Jean's accomplishments were finally being recognised.

Part of me acknowledged that Dora had probably been right. It sounded as though Michael Poulter's desire for the truth to be finally told had started the chain of events. But, mainly, I was consumed with worry about Mat. His contact, Arch, James Poulter's chauffeur, had been dragged into the meeting by Michael. He was part of the conspiracy. And Mat didn't know. Or hadn't known. It was all too possible Mat had gone to see Arch.

'What is this all about?'

Susan's question brought me back to the here and now. She was watching me with narrowed eyes and there was a sharpness in her voice I hadn't heard before. Her brain was ticking over the ramifications of what she'd told me. She wasn't stupid. She'd realised there was more to it than a disagreement over some piece of research.

The few bits of information she'd overheard made nothing any clearer. Something about a cutter. And evidence. I was sure the house

James had gone to visit was Berkswell House. Was the evidence there? Was it a dead body? Victor's? Maybe I was right and he had been injured in 1957 – badly enough to keep his face hidden – but he hadn't died until 1959. Or been killed…

Susan's voice interrupted my thoughts. 'Of course, Michael died after the meeting. But it was a coincidence, wasn't it?'

The doorbell rang, saving me from answering. Susan reached for her stick and started levering herself out of her chair.

'I'll go.'

But on the way to the front door, a thread of fear tightened round my throat. Mat had disappeared while investigating and I was doing exactly the same. I put the chain on the door, opened it and peered through the gap.

Meghan stood on the doorstep.

With Jack.

I removed the chain and opened the door all the way. She ran her eyes over my body.

'Sod you, Phiney,' she said. 'I thought you might at least be injured. You know, a black eye or a few broken fingers.'

Oh God, I was so glad to see her.

'Give me two minutes and I'll be out.'

Her eyes glowered with a mixture of rage and relief and worry. She shook her head at me.

'Hurry up. Some of us have jobs. I'm working tonight and I can't be late.'

'Fine.'

'And Phiney,' she said, as I turned to go back in. 'You owe me a hundred and thirteen pounds for the last-minute, super-expensive ticket I had to buy to get here.'

I almost laughed.

'Well, what did you expect me to do? You sent me her address. It sounded as though you thought it might be dangerous. Did you think I'd wait meekly at the end of the telephone?'

'No, Meghan. Never.'

Back inside, I told Susan that I didn't know what it was all about. I told her to be careful. I told her that people had died because of what happened at the meeting but there were questions in her eyes that I thought she'd be tempted to find the answers to. I'd probably thrown a bomb into the hornet's nest, or whatever the saying was.

I told Meghan everything, muttering it into her ear as we stood on the crowded train from Euston back to Coventry, hands grasping the backs of the seats of the lucky few who'd reserved them. Jack crawled into the luggage space and slumped at the back.

'Mat's missing?' she said when I'd finished. The colour had drained from her face.

'Yes. Since yesterday afternoon and I have an awful feeling he went to see Arch, who is much more involved than we thought.'

'You need to tell the police. Now, Phiney. Or do you want me to?'

'Dora went to see them. I'll call her.' I looked round at the carriage rammed with people. I couldn't call from here. I'd have to shout over the background noise of laughter and chatter.

'I'll go to the loo,' I said to Meghan and fought my way through the hordes.

There was a queue and the woman in front took ages, irritating the man behind me to the point where he started making sarcastic comments and barking instructions at me to knock on the door. It was tempting but I didn't.

I called Dora as soon as I'd locked the door.

She'd gone to the police in Matlock but it had been a waste of time. A waste of breath. A waste of everything Dora could think of. So now she was at Derby Police Station.

Correction: she was outside Derby Police Station and she was furious but it was an anger stiff with worry.

'They're not going to do anything.'

'What?' I whispered. If Mr Angry outside realised I was calling someone it was going to enrage him even more.

'They listened. They were polite. Insufferably polite and they said they might check up to see if Mat is really missing, although I doubt it.'

'Right.'

'Why are you whispering?'

'Too complicated to explain.'

'They asked me for Mat's address. I don't know it. Do you?'

'I think he said he lived out near Binley,' I muttered.

'His car registration?'

'Nope.' It wasn't the kind of thing I noticed. Who does?

'Details of his family and friends?'

There was no point answering this. I was beginning to see what Dora had been up against.

'What are we going to do?' Dora's question came out like a wail.

'Did you tell them everything?'

'Yes. All the convenient deaths and your accident and Wilf. Maybe I shouldn't have told them about Wilf. That was when they lost interest. I was just a hysterical woman driven mad by grief.'

I could imagine it. In other circumstances, I'd probably have felt the same.

'I'm sorry, Phiney. I tried. I really did. Maybe you should have gone.'

A voice outside asked if I was going to be much longer.

'You're going to have to go back in and talk to them again,' I hissed.

'Phiney, I can't.'

I gave her the brief outline of what I'd learned from Susan. I tried to talk quietly but it was impossible and taps on the door punctuated the latter half of my story.

'Do you know this Arch's address?'

'No.'

'Well, it's the first thing they'll ask me.'

'Tell them he works for Poulters. Please. Try. For Mat.'

She gave a huge sigh but I knew she would.

225

Another knock. More forceful.

'I'll have to go.'

'Where are you?'

'On the train to Coventry.'

'There's something I need you to do. It won't take long.'

Her voice was tentative. I knew it was going to be something I didn't want to do.

'Yes.'

The door rattled this time with the force of the bang.

'The charity have found a new owner for Jack. But I want you to go and check her over this evening before I agree. Take Jack with you.'

'I can't.'

'Please. Unless you've got something else to do. He needs a new home. I promise you I'll go back to the police now. I don't see what you can do.'

Neither did I. My mind was a blank.

'Wilf would have wanted us to be sure he was OK. I told them you'd be there around seven.'

I knew I didn't really have a choice.

Chapter Thirty-Three:
Phiney Wistman

22 June 2017
Nine days after the reunion

Jack's potential owner, Mrs Oliver, was in a wheelchair. She could walk with sticks, she told me, but it was tiring, so she saved it for when she absolutely had to. Her children had paid for the bungalow to be adapted. I stared around the bright modern space and murmured the right things. It was practical, floored throughout in easy-to-clean tiling and linoleum, with a big grassy garden out the back. Perfect for Jack. As was Mrs Oliver herself. Mid-sixties, I thought, intelligent and lively, pleasant and smiling, but no pushover. She'd had a dog before and she understood that a working animal was different to a family pet.

I couldn't really believe I was here, going through the motions of introducing Jack to a potential owner. Not that I was doing the introducing. A Mr Holden from the dog charity, who'd met us at the station, showed Jack round while Mrs Oliver and I sat and chatted. Or, at least, she chatted to me and I thought about other things.

Dora was still with the Derby police and Meghan had gone to the *Telegraph*'s office to get Mat's address so she could go and check his flat. At least they were doing something useful.

'He's a lovely dog,' Mrs Oliver said, after an awkward pause.

I nodded.

'Your grandfather's, Mr Holden said?'

I nodded again. Meghan wanted us to go to Coventry Police together. Maybe we should.

'Was he in a wheelchair too?'

I dragged myself back to the present.

'Only from time to time.'

We descended into silence once again. I had to say something. I was supposed to be checking her over.

'It's all been a bit upsetting for Jack. So much change.'

'I promise you he'll be happy. My younger son and his children live round the corner and they'll come every day and take him out.'

'He'll like that. He loves children.'

Another silence. I should be full of questions.

'Have you been in a wheelchair long?'

'Pretty much all my life.'

'Oh, I'm sorry.'

'Polio. Like your Grandad. I hope you don't mind but Mr Holden told me.'

'Of course not.'

She wore trousers but underneath I knew her legs would be thin with little muscle. Mainly bone covered by skin and probably scarred from numerous operations to cut or stretch shrinking tendons and graft new bone.

'I was only four when it happened. One of the last cases of the Coventry Polio Epidemic.'

'Yes,' I said. 'I saw the exhibition at The Herbert commemorating its sixtieth anniversary.'

'Of course, you'd be interested because of your Grandad. So many youngsters aren't. So many of them are anti-vaccination too. If they'd lived through the fear of polio that was everywhere when I was young, they'd feel differently. No one really understood how you caught it and I remember long summer days staring through the front window and wondering if we'd ever be allowed outside again.'

I made a sympathetic noise but she cut me off.

'I'm fine about it. No one's perfect. You have to move on. My mother never could. She blamed herself, you see. The vaccine had just become available but she dilly-dallied. The queues were long and she was busy. Of course, when the epidemic started that summer, she took me for the first jab at once, but you need three to have complete immunity.'

My mind drifted back to Mat and what might be happening to him as she chatted away. My phone bleeped. I shot a quick look at it. A text from Meghan. I needed to get this meeting over and done with so I could read it.

'It must have been hard,' I babbled.

Mrs Oliver smiled. 'Not really. I was unlucky but the rest of my life has been good. Things happen and you have to make the best of them. My mother didn't. She let the fact she hadn't had me vaccinated poison her life. Even on my wedding day. I couldn't walk down the aisle and that spoilt it for her, whereas everybody else just enjoyed the day.'

When we left, I told Mr Holden that we'd be happy for Jack to go to her.

He helped me bundle him into a taxi and I headed off for Meghan's parents' house. I looked at Meghan's text.

Telegraph won't give me Mat's address but had idea.

I called her.

'Can't talk, Phiney,' she said straightaway. 'Just going into work. Going to see if I can find Mat's address via PIP.'

PIP was the platform we used at the hospital to access patients' GP records. Looking in them to get someone's address was massively illegal and unethical.

'Brilliant idea,' I said and left her to it.

The driver took a route that passed by my flat.

'Could you stop a minute and wait for me?' I said. 'I just need to pick up a few things from here.'

I tore upstairs, Jack bounding after me, and threw some clean clothes into a bag. On the way out, the row of metallic red letterboxes in the dim lobby caught my eye and I stopped.

The results must have arrived.

I found the key and looked inside the box.

There was a letter.

Correction. There was tons of crap: fliers from local takeaways; adverts for window-cleaning services; a reminder from the dentist that my check-up was overdue; a postcard from someone I studied with who'd gone to work in Australia.

And a letter.

Jack sat patiently by the front door, looking at me as though wondering why I stood without moving in this windowless space with its odour of damp paper and rust.

So, it was going to be now.

This was going to be the moment when I found out and it was not in the least how I'd imagined it would be. It was a moment grabbed while I was rushing somewhere, caught up in other imperatives. I wasn't even sure I had the strength to deal with it.

Maybe I should wait.

The feel of the paper in my hands undid the last ties holding me together. It was all too much. Grandad jumping off the bridge. Tumbling down the stone steps outside the hospital. The lump in the pool at the bottom of the waterfall gradually resolving into a body. Mat vanishing. And now this.

The light on the lobby timer went out and the faint green from the fire exit sign coloured the skin on my hands. I couldn't move. I couldn't feel my chest. I wasn't breathing. My diaphragm wasn't tightening and releasing to drag the air into my lungs and push it out. I forced myself to breathe but the air didn't seem to contain any oxygen. Black specks buzzed before my eyes and the rasp of panicky gasps filled my ears. Then the still, small voice of my training pierced the confusion.

Anxiety attack, it said. It's an anxiety attack. Nothing more. Sit the patient down. Reassure them. It's only temporary. Encourage them to breathe regularly and gently. Three seconds in and four seconds out.

I sat on the stairs. Who cared how dirty they were? And breathed. Three seconds in. I put the post in a neat pile beside me. And breathed. Four seconds out. This would pass. Breathe. Jack came over and shoved his nose into my hand and I breathed. Thought about the air. Thought about it pouring into my lungs and enriching the blood with precious oxygen until the panic passed.

And then I opened the letter. Skimmed through the tables with their lists of figures, blessing Marie Stannard for telling me exactly what to look for. And found it.

Negative.

I'd tested negative.

I checked again.

Negative.

When my parents' genes had combined to create me, the poison from my mother's blood had passed me by. I was clear and free.

And it meant nothing to me. I wasn't ecstatic. I wasn't bursting with joy. I wasn't even relieved. It should have been a gift but instead it felt as though I'd opened a box and found it was empty because I couldn't tell Grandad. We couldn't hold each other's hands and cry together with joy and relief.

At least he knew, I told myself. It might have been a lie when I told it and I might not have been able to share in his happiness, but he had been happy and it wasn't a lie any longer.

I went back to the taxi with Jack. For once, he followed me in without protest. Waves of fatigue shook my limbs as I leaned back and shut my eyes.

My phone rang.

Not Meghan.

Not Dora.

Not Mat.

A number I didn't recognise and I nearly didn't answer.

But then I thought it might be someone with information about Mat. Or Mat using a different phone. Maybe his had died. Maybe he'd lost it. Maybe that was why he had been out of touch.

A light voice asked if I was Josephine Wistman. I shook off the shadows of tiredness and said yes.

'I believe you've been looking for me.'

Fear prickled over my skin.

'Who is this?' I asked.

Silence.

'Victor?' I said.

More silence.

'Are you Victor Leadsom?'

'Yes. I suppose you could say that. But I'm more interested to know who you are.'

'I'm Wilfred Patterson's granddaughter. Phiney.'

'Ah, I thought you must be.'

Another silence. If my brain would work I'd say something. Ask all the questions I needed answers to. But nothing came to mind or, rather, too much came in a mad onslaught that I couldn't pummel into words.

'I suppose we'd better meet,' Victor continued.

'Where are you?'

'It doesn't matter.' Then a strange noise that could have been a laugh. 'But I can be in Coventry tomorrow. Never thought I'd go back. But there you are. Back at the beginning of it all, you could say. Where shall we meet?'

Somewhere absolutely safe, I thought. Doubts crowded my mind. Was it a trap? Was this really Victor? Was Victor actually still alive after all?

'Let's meet at the Cathedral. Tomorrow. Two o'clock?'

'Fine.' I dredged up one last thought. 'How will I know you?'

'Sit about halfway up on the left-hand side and wait. I'll come and find you.' There was another sound and this time I was sure it was a laugh. 'I'll wear a blue scarf with dolphins, so you can be sure it's me.'

Chapter Thirty-Four:
Phiney Wistman

23 June 2017
Ten days after the reunion

I came early to the cathedral, slipping past the woman on reception, who offered me a welcoming smile and a leaflet on the cathedral's architecture. I responded to the smile but refused the brochure. I hadn't visited for years, not since I came on a school trip, but I remembered the concrete walls and pillars, narrow at the bottom and widening until they branched into stylised trees supporting the golden-brown wood of the roof. The stark simplicity of the design held me still for a few minutes, forcing my mind away from its turbulent thoughts. The main nave where I'd arranged to meet Victor was a vast open space, dwarfing the few people standing beneath it and the rows of wooden chairs. I walked up the central aisle, towards the massive tapestry of Christ that dominated the structure, but I didn't look at it. Instead, I checked the people, dotted here and there, little islands among empty swathes of chairs. Most were women or too young to be Victor.

A priest, kneeling and praying, looked up at me as I passed and I had a brief impression of a tailored cassock and a face dragged down by gravity. He crossed himself and stepped out into the aisle as I passed, sending a jolt of fear down my back.

He was the right age.

I slowed and let him pass me, then followed him as he walked up to the altar, crossed himself, before heading into the passage that ran behind the chancel. He walked past the little chapels lining the back wall until he reached one behind a screen of iron spikes. He went in and knelt before a mosaic, showing a golden angel holding a cup, and buried his head in his hands. I dawdled by the entrance, reading an information panel. The spikes on the screen represented the crown of thorns and the mosaic depicted the angel of agony visiting Christ the night before his crucifixion but not to offer comfort. The chalice in the angel's hands contained suffering.

Gruesome.

The priest stood and hurried out of the chapel. He'd been crying, I noticed, as he pushed past me. I trailed after him but when he reached the vast nave he headed straight for the exit and disappeared.

There was no one else who could be Victor, so I found a place against a pillar at the side of the pulpit, half hidden behind the choir stalls with their canopy of crosses soaring into the air like a cloud of birds, and looked back over the almost empty interior. The sun poured through the great windows of stained glass that were invisible until you looked back. Vivid colour from floor to ceiling, they were a hidden glory painting a rainbow of colours on the concrete walls and floor but, after the first glance, I fixed my eyes on the entrance and watched the arrivals.

My phone vibrated. It was Meghan calling.

Text me, I wrote. *I'm in the cathedral. Waiting.*

Am at Mat's. No sign of him. Is his car white with a grey leather interior?

Yes.

It's here.

I thought a while.

Bit weird. Let Dora know.

OK. Going to the police now myself.

Good Luck.

My back-up. Dora and Meghan. Both knowing where I was and who I was meeting. Meghan, who'd found Mat's address on PIP, gone to check it out and was now headed to the police in Coventry. And Dora back at the police station in Derby again.

I stuffed my phone back into my pocket and waited. The time ticked down towards two o'clock. A few people entered and left. A coach party of tourists wandered round following a whispering tour guide. A teacher sat a group of children down on the floor of the nave and handed out sheets of paper for them to sketch the ruins of the old cathedral viewed through the vast clear window of the new cathedral. No one who could be Victor arrived, unless he was the white-haired man almost bent double with arthritis, or the unshaven one in a grimy mackintosh who clutched a couple of battered carrier bags full of what looked like old clothes. He fell asleep behind the screen of the side chapel nearest me.

Two o'clock came. I took a deep breath, walked to a chair on the left-hand side of the nave as instructed and sat down.

An older woman, tall but graceful, leaning against the stone in between two towering verticals of blue, violet and green windows on the other side of the cathedral, stood a little straighter as I sat down. She smiled at me when our eyes met and walked in my direction. A long, slow walk but definitely heading towards me. She didn't look like a tourist wanting to ask a question and she didn't have the apologetic look of someone about to disturb a stranger. A messenger from Victor? Slim and elegant, her grey hair streaked with white and beautifully styled, she walked with confidence. It struck me that Dora could look like her. They were both tall with angular frames but this woman was happy in herself whereas Dora looked as though she constantly apologised for existing. Dora would have looked good in the narrow black trousers and the turquoise and green blouse that the woman wore. And the bright blue scarf...

A bright blue scarf.

I watched the woman walk towards me.

My brain whirred and clicked.

At the last moment, she veered into the row of chairs in front and sat down. Then turned. Her blue scarf was dotted with grey dolphins, leaping and playing. Her eyes asked me the question.

And I knew the answer.

I wondered if the prolonged walk towards me was to give me time to understand. There were clues, if you looked hard enough. I could still see the sharp planes of the beautiful face in the photo taken outside Poulters in 1957. She'd had work done. No doubt about that. And I understood what had lain beneath the bandaged face of the 1958 picture.

'It is you, isn't it?' I said. 'Victor…'

'Vivian,' she said.

'Leadsom?'

'Reynolds. My mother's maiden name. Not that I had anything against my father but I wanted a break with the past.'

No wonder we'd found no record of Victor since the 1950s, nor of his death. Vivian ran the scarf through her fingers. She wasn't as comfortable as she looked.

'You certainly succeeded in disappearing. We'd decided you were dead. But why?'

'Because of all this.' She gestured to her body. 'I never fitted in, you understand, but it took time to grasp that, despite my DNA, despite the outward appearance of my body, my blood circulated to a different beat and carried the thoughts and desires of a different gender. And when I did understand, I realised I could never be Vivian Reynolds here. Not where people knew me as Victor. Where I'd have to run the gauntlet of their stares as they tried to reconcile their memories of me with the present, and tick off all the changes.'

Like I had, I thought, when I first realised who she was and I understood how much it had cost her to meet me.

She put her arms on the back of the chair and leaned forward. 'Besides, the 1950s were a different world. A different time. You're so young, you can't imagine what it was like. Being transgender was a concept that didn't exist. Even my parents saw me as something perverted and evil. So, I left. Went abroad to a place that was more accepting of who I am.'

The light from the stained glass caught her face and hair, casting fleeting shadows of red and gold over it. She gestured to the cathedral.

'This wasn't built when I left. They'd started but it had barely emerged from the ground. And look at it now. It's so beautiful.

Something glorious that's risen from a terrible time. It made me want to cry when I got here. Everything has changed. I didn't realise it would. In my mind, Coventry has stayed the same and I'm the one who's changed.'

I thought about Berkswell House. That hadn't changed. It was trapped in the past by the secret it sheltered. It wasn't Vivian's corpse, so what could it be?

'Listen,' I said. 'I get all this. I understand why you disappeared but, before you did, something happened. In 1957 at Poulters. I need to know what it was.'

She gave a deep sigh. 'Philip wrote to me via a mutual friend. Someone whose family I boarded with when I was at Poulters and on and off for a couple of years after I left. When I started the process of changing. Philip went to university with her. They've kept in touch over the years. He went to see her.'

'In France?' I said, remembering Philip's mysterious trip to Nice.

'Yes. She married a Frenchman although they split up years ago but she works in a hospital over there. She forwarded a letter from him to me.'

She reached in her bag and passed me the letter. It was written by hand and dated six days ago.

Dear Victor,
I hope this finds you well.

Julia, who has promised to forward this letter to you, assures me that you are happy although she would tell me nothing else about where you are and how you've been. However, the smile in her eyes when she talked about you makes me feel life cannot have been all bad.

You have not been an easy man to find. In fact, without Julia, I think I would have failed. We have kept in touch. She stays with us when she comes to the UK and we have taken advantage of her living in Grenoble for a couple of winter holidays. I should have asked her how you were years ago. I hope life has been good to you. It certainly has to me although not in the way I thought.

My career was not the glittering success I hoped it would be when I was young. No headmastership of an illustrious school, but I have been happy enough teaching and I think the stress of pretending to be other than I am would not have been worth it.

Until recently, I thought I was going to finish my life in contented retirement in the Lake District where Jonathan, my partner and the love of my life, and I have a cottage overlooking Ullswater. Maybe when all this is finally over, you might come and stay and we can catch up properly. Because, of course, the purpose of this letter is not to reacquaint myself with an old colleague after all these years.

Michael Poulter is ill. Heart disease. He's had it for a long time. There were things they could have done but Michael has never liked taking medication. It would be amusing, wouldn't it, given that he's spent his life running one of Britain's premier pharmaceutical companies, if it wasn't both tragic and ironic.

Anyway, I think he knew he didn't have much longer and he wanted to set the record straight. Of all of us, he's been the one who struggled most with what we did all those years ago and as I've realised, and I'm sure you have, your outlook on life changes as you grow old. It's the realisation that the tally of one's days is finite. We all know it but the young can forget about it. In Michael, I think it sparked a crisis.

He went to see Jean. Maybe he wanted to see if his intentions could withstand the blast of her intellect. Maybe he was being honourable and giving her a chance to prepare herself for the inevitable scandal. I don't know. But she persuaded him that everybody must be told first and got us all together.

Everyone except you. She didn't know how to get in touch with you, she said, when I asked her. She'd had no word from you since you left Poulters and couldn't find any trace of you. But the rest of us got together. Michael and Jean, Owen's daughter Laura, who Owen told years ago, and Michael's son James, who Michael only recently told. There was me. There was a nasty piece of work called Simon Archibald who found out from Harry, Wilf's father, years ago and wangled himself a job for life at Poulters, as a chauffeur. And there was Wilf.

I wish Jean hadn't written to Wilf. She thought he knew about everything but the reality is he was in so much pain that day that he was aware of very little else and Harry sent him home before the decision was made. He called me as soon as he received Jean's letter and I had to tell him what had happened on that awful night in 1957 and, of course, he blamed himself. The job was physically beyond him with all the walking and carrying. Harry should never have forced him to do it but Wilf didn't have it in him to tell his father, so I covered, racing around and doing all the lifting and carrying, taking the tanks to the furthest units, while Wilf did the labelling and the nearer huts. Between us, we made the fatal mistake, but Wilf saw it as entirely his fault, because his disability put too much pressure on me. It was a huge shock and he was devastated – because if anyone could understand the effects of our mistake, it was him. All the pain. The long years of suffering. The deaths. The grieving families.

Summoned by Jean, we all went to The Herbert and tried to discuss what had happened. We rehashed all the old arguments and in the end, when we couldn't agree, Jean forced a vote.

There was a time when I wanted the truth to be told but at the meeting I voted against the secret coming out because I wanted to spare Wilf. As I've grown older, it's the individuals that matter to me most rather than the big issues. In fact, everyone voted against, except Michael, of course, and Wilf.

It was only afterwards that Michael said he wouldn't be bound by the vote and he was determined to reveal the truth.

Michael's dead now. And for the life of me, I don't know if it was a coincidence or something worse.

But it's because of Wilf that I'm writing.

He wanted the truth to be known. He shook Michael's hand and told him he was right. And then he killed himself.

So I've decided to do what he wanted. I feel as though I owe it to him. Besides, Dora, his wife, and Phiney, his granddaughter, are desperate to understand and, at the very least, I have no right to withhold the information from them. I've spoken to the others and they'll do everything they can to actively thwart me and there is a lot they can use. I was sixteen in 1957, still at school, a lad doing a temporary summer job at Poulters. They'll question my memory and my credibility.

That's why I need your help.

Michael mentioned some evidence that you had. Some tangible proof of what happened. If you still have it, will you give it to me?

If you won't stand with me, if you think the old arguments hold good and the choice we made all those years ago was the right one, then so be it but, please, remember Wilf and his family before you make a hasty decision.

Very best regards,

Philip.

She didn't watch me while I read but turned round and looked towards the vast figure of Christ on the tapestry that dominated the far end of the cathedral. Once I'd finished the letter, I stared at it too, trying to process the information. Then I touched her on the shoulder and she turned. Deep lines of tension and age showed through the immaculate make-up.

'I should have contacted him straightaway,' she said. 'But I hesitated and when I finally called, Jonathan told me he was dead. An accident, he said?'

'We don't think so.'

The echoing space seemed to have shrunk to cocoon the two of us. Nothing outside mattered anyway.

'Because of 1957?' she asked.

I nodded.

'I wondered,' she said. 'I always thought the truth might refuse to lie dormant. I came over once I knew he was dead. I planned to talk to Jean, but she was away. Then I rang my sister.' She blinked rapidly for a few seconds. 'She was... She was so pleased to hear from me. But she thought at first I'd rung in response to a newspaper article about missing people and, when she explained, I wondered if the researcher who'd visited her might be something else. It seemed too much of a coincidence. Elizabeth gave me your number and I rang you.'

'What is the secret? What did Grandad find out he was responsible for?'

'Are you sure you want to know?'

She meant it. She actually meant it. I opened my mouth to tell her it wasn't even a case of wanting. I had to know.

She spoke quickly. 'Once I've told you, you can't unknow and you'll have to decide what to do with the knowledge.'

'I have to know.'

She shook her head slowly. 'It doesn't work like that,' she said.

'Look, something made my Grandad hurl himself off a bridge. I need to know. I can't let it go.'

'Would it help if I told you it wasn't your Grandad's fault? He and Philip were teenagers who should never have been put in the position they were. Even Jean and I were too young. We knew what we were doing with the science but we lacked life experience, people experience. I look back now and it doesn't seem possible that we were left in charge. But Richard liked youngsters. Especially ambitious ones like me and Jean. We were cheap and energetic and forward-looking while the older generation, the men like Owen and Harry, were stuck in the past. The war had left them determined to cling to old ways that didn't work anymore.'

I shook my head. 'It's not just Grandad. There's someone else involved. Someone who's disappeared and I think it might be because of this. So please, tell me what happened.'

She looked through me in the way people do when they're remembering the past and began to speak.

'Like all tragedies, it was a cascade of little things going wrong and it's hard to say which was the first. The problem had occurred days before, but the first I knew of it was a monkey.'

'A monkey?'

'Yes,' she said. 'A monkey caught polio.'

Chapter Thirty-Five:
Vivian Reynolds

2/3 July 1957
The night of the incident

A *monkey caught polio.* Vivian knew as soon as she saw it, lying in a corner of its cage unable to move, its eyes begging her for something she couldn't give. What else could it be? That was the whole point of the monkeys. Inject them with the vaccine and then wait to see if, despite all the protocols and checks, some of the live poliovirus had survived. Mainly, they picked it up from blood tests but just occasionally, as now, the monkey actually developed symptoms. Nevertheless, Vivian took blood and tested it to be sure. It was polio. She logged the result, noting the time and the vaccine batch number (Batch #2006) at the top of the paper and signed it, *Victor Leadsom*, at the bottom. She'd get Harry to return the contaminated vaccine to the lab for destruction before he went home. Quarter to six, it was. Harry should have time before he finished.

At nine thirty, she sent Michael, who was lost in a book in a corner of her office, to chase it up while she finished writing up the research she and Jean were working on. And at ten forty-five, realising the wait couldn't be down to Harry's infuriating habit of taking as long as he could over anything Vivian or Jean asked him to do, she went to hunt Harry and Michael out herself.

They were in Hut 34, a prefab put up after the war but already showing signs of age with green mould discolouring its painted panels and rust creeping up the metal frame. It was one of a row close to the main house and linked by a path just wide enough for the porters to wheel their trolleys. Harry and Michael, in duffel coats and gloves, were in the refrigerated interior, heaving a large steel canister of vaccine from one side to the other. Vivian winced as they let it fall to the ground with a thud.

'Harry, I really need that batch of vaccine,' she said. 'Batch #2006. I asked for it ages ago.'

'We're trying to find it,' Harry said shortly. 'Some bugger's put the wrong label on it.'

'What do you mean? The labelling is checked before it leaves the lab.'

Vivian looked at the canister Harry and Michael had shifted. The label on it said Batch #1997 but it was torn and parts of it were obscured by the remnants of another label that had been on top. And as Vivian looked around the rest of the hut she realised that most of the canisters on the left had been double labelled too. The floor was littered with ripped scraps of paper.

Harry had been relabelling the vaccine.

The canisters on the right bore witness to this. They all were marked with a *34* followed by another number. Nothing like Jean and Vivian's careful, sequential allocation of numbers.

'What are these labels, Harry?'

Harry glanced up from the clipboard he was running a finger down. He looked grumpy and tired. Vivian wondered how long he and Michael had been working in the chill, which was already penetrating her thin lab coat.

'Harry?'

'It's easier this way. Every available space that can be refrigerated is full to the gunwales with your bloody vaccine. There is barely enough room so the porters started putting the tanks wherever they could find a space. And it was a bugger to find them when you called down and told us to ship them to the ampoule-filling facility. So now, when a batch is ready to go into cold storage, I make a note of your number.' He waved the clipboard with columns of figures in his cramped writing. 'Then I allocate it a storage code depending on which hut has room, give the labels to the porter and send him off to get it. It stops the porters squeezing it in anywhere and makes it much easier for me to keep an eye on what's gone where.'

Christ, Vivian thought, they should have checked what Harry was doing.

'Don't worry,' Harry went on. 'We remove the storage label before they're sent out.'

She tried to think through the ramifications but her brain was sluggish, as though the icy surroundings had slowed its working.

'Anyway, Batch #2006 should have been relabelled *34/5*.' Harry continued to explain, oblivious to the growing horror invading Vivian. '34 for the hut and 5 because it's the fifth batch in here. But it hasn't been. Or, at least, not all of it. Michael tore one of the labels off to check. Only half of it is Batch #2006. So, now we're having to rip all the labels off to find the missing canisters. I should have been home hours ago.' Harry seemed affronted, as though the ruin of his evening was all down to Michael's actions.

'So, 34/5 is half batch #2006 and half which batch?'

'Batch #1997,' Michael said shortly and pointed to the canisters with the labels now visible. 'We've nearly finished this hut,' Harry said. 'If we can't find the missing vaccine here, we'll start on the others. We've got a system now, me and Michael. Go on, you leave us to it. We'll come and tell you once we've found it.'

'What was Batch #1997 supposed to be labelled as, Harry?' Michael asked. 'Surely it's just those two batches that have been mislabelled. Everything else we've looked at has been correct. Might they have gone into storage at the same time?'

Vivian answered as Harry clearly had no idea.

'It's possible,' she said. 'We number them sequentially so there should have been nine other batches in between. But we often have problems with contamination and have to destroy several lots. We keep the vaccine in the labs until we run out of room because we know Harry doesn't have a lot of space, so #1997 and #2006 could have gone into storage at the same time.'

Her brain was beginning to stir into action. Michael was probably right. Batches #1997 and #2006 had been muddled.

Harry looked at his clipboard. 'The storage label for #1997 is 22/3. That means it should be over in Hut 22. We'll head over there now.'

A chill rippled through Vivian's body. What if she'd ordered #1997 to be released already and somehow they'd sent out half of #2006 with it?

She turned and went out into the night.

Harry called after her. 'And you can let me know which of the bloody porters signed for your Batches #1997 and #2006 because he'll be the one clearing up this mess in the morning after I've given him a piece of my mind.' He laughed grimly to himself. 'Don't forget to shut the door. Owen is always on at me about the amount it costs to keep these huts cold.'

Outside, the terror Vivian hadn't let herself show in front of Michael and Harry seized her. She thought she was going to vomit but she only retched over one of the rubbish bins while sweat dripped off her face and drenched the shirt she was wearing under her lab coat.

Please, God, let her fears be groundless.

She thought then about leaving. About going back to her digs, packing a bag and disappearing because, if her fears were right, they'd set a catastrophe in motion. But she had to know the truth.

The door slammed after Vivian as she tore into her office in the main building of Berkswell House. For a moment she thought the glass pane had cracked such had been the force of the bang still echoing through the empty building but it was only the shadow of a pipe cast by the corridor light. The gold lettering on the glass announcing that this was Victor Leadsom's office was still intact. She winced when she caught sight of it with its reminder of everything that was wrong.

The radium dial on the clock glowed in a dark corner. Eleven thirty, it said. In half an hour's time it would be the third of July. Vivian's birthday and, also, Marie Curie's. In ten years' time, she'd be as old as Marie Curie had been when she discovered radium. Vivian had dreamed of achieving a similar feat but now, with the shirt under her lab coat still damp from the sweat of her earlier terror and her breathing ragged from the speed of her flight, she thought she'd be happy merely to get out of here and live a dull but safe life.

She locked the door behind her. She reached for the light switch but thought better of it. There was enough light from the corridor filtering through the glass to read the records and the office lamp glaring out into the night would make her easy to find.

If her suspicions were right, she wasn't sure she wanted to be found.

She rifled through the records. And there it was. She'd ordered Batch #1997 to be sent for packing into ampoules five days ago.

Did they check the batch numbers when they filled the ampoules? She didn't think so. The checks were supposed to happen here.

The filling wouldn't have taken long. A day at the most and from there the vaccine would have gone straight to the Health Authority, who phoned every day begging for more. The question was what had been sent in place of the canisters of Batch #1997 that were still in Hut 34. She had a terrible feeling it was the missing Batch #2006, which contained contaminated vaccine.

The thought of it overwhelmed her and she sat for a long time, with horror shaking her bones, trying to work out what to do. Should she call Owen? Or Jean? Or should she slip away? Her mind went round and round in circles so, when Harry and Michael came hammering on her office door to tell her Batch #2006 was nowhere to be found and every other batch was correctly labelled, she'd done nothing.

She called Jean.

Harry called Owen.

Jean arrived around two in the morning and dragged Vivian out of Hut 19, where she'd been dealing with the dead monkey, and back to the lodge.

'Richard wants me to check the consignments notes,' she said. 'To be sure which batches went out when. I need your help, Victor. The others don't understand.'

Together, they hunted through the files of paperwork, with shaking fingers running down lists of consignments until Jean found it. She couldn't speak for a moment. Only the sudden stillness of her hands alerted Vivian, poring over another pile of paperwork. She looked over and saw where Jean's finger had come to rest. A delivery to the ampoule facility five days ago. Batch #1997 was among the list of numbers at the top in Harry's cramped but neat writing. At the bottom of the list, another hand, less neat but equally clear, had added Batch #2006. Clearly, someone had noticed the discrepancy when they'd removed the storage labels.

'Why didn't they check with me?' Harry blustered when shown the piece of paper.

Jean pointed to the time. The van had picked the consignment up at eight in the morning.

'I start at nine. They should have waited.'

But they all knew the porters lived in fear of Harry's temper. No wonder they hadn't wanted to incur his fury for holding up a delivery, especially when it had been drummed into them that the consignment had to be kept chilled and couldn't linger in the summer heat.

Jean had been right. All those months ago, when they'd set up the vaccine manufacturing processes and trained the staff. She'd argued for everyone, even the porters, to have the whole protocol explained to them. Owen had been against it, saying it would cause confusion. They only needed to set in place strict instructions for each stage that would be overseen by Jean. Except Jean couldn't oversee every step of every process. She certainly couldn't oversee the porters wheeling fifty-litre containers of vaccine around the site on their flat trolleys into the different refrigerated storage buildings. The old house, with its scattered outbuildings and hastily constructed prefab huts, was vastly unsuited to the careful storage of the vaccine at its different stages.

It might have been alright if they weren't trying to manufacture the vaccine five times faster than the labs were set up for. In the midst of the summer polio epidemic, the press was scathing in its accusations that the government had failed the people. Huge pressure had been put on the labs, and Richard Poulter had seen an opportunity to make a quick profit and ingratiate himself with a government who would doubtless reward him with research grants later. No point, though, pouring money into improving the facilities because in a couple of years, once everyone was vaccinated, demand would drop a hundredfold.

Vivian and Jean had done their best. They'd driven the manufacturing and testing departments to their limits but neither of them had thought of the impact on the storage facilities, which were crammed to bursting with the vaccine as Vivian had discovered last night.

Jean called Richard again and broke the news that they had proof. Vivian didn't wait to hear the rest. Instead, she went out into the dark and sat on the bench outside the lodge, breathing the cool night air with its scent of something green and sharp. She'd woken with a stuffy head and itchy eyes this morning. She'd nearly called in sick. It was only the thought of all the work piling up that had driven her out of bed and to the bus stop.

The door to the lodge opened, its light casting a shadow on the grit path. Jean stood there, her eyes hollow as though only her body were present and her essence were a million miles away.

'Richard's on his way. I need the paperwork.'

Jean had the consignment notes in one hand, and Vivian handed her the results she'd been clutching that confirmed the presence of the virus in the monkey's blood.

She nodded and left, and Vivian slipped away to her office, glad she wasn't the one who had to speak to Richard.

Light came. The day started. Vivian heard the lab assistants chatting as they came out of the changing rooms clad in their overalls, gloves and masks, ready for another day of mincing kidney cells and mixing them with nutrient-rich liquid in the lab next door where they grew the poliovirus. Normally, she left the door open, enjoying the banter and laughter, but today she kept it closed and waited for the summons to Richard's office.

The knock, when it came, startled her out of a doze. She couldn't believe she'd fallen asleep but her clock showed half an hour had passed. Wiping the damp from the side of her mouth, she staggered to her feet and opened the door. It was Michael.

'Do you mind if I sit in here, Victor?' he asked. 'I've taken Wilf home and Harry's shut up in the lodge with Philip. I suppose he was the porter who signed –'

'Yes.'

They didn't speak for a while after that. Not that there was anything much to say. Outside, the hustle and bustle of a normal day continued but it felt as unreal as a bright dream waiting to be burst.

She thought Michael had fallen asleep. He was sitting in the far corner of the office on the floor, his head resting on a bunch of lab coats he'd wedged between his neck and shoulder, out of sight of casual glances through the door's glass window. So, when he spoke it was a surprise.

'How did you know?' he asked.

She looked up from the results which she'd been using to distract her thoughts. Anything rather than think of syringes of batch #2006 being plunged into children's arms.

'One of the monkeys,' she said. 'Showing signs yesterday afternoon. I tested its blood but I knew what I'd find straightaway. So, I recalled that batch of vaccine for destruction, and the rest you know.'

'I don't, actually. I know a monkey caught polio. I saw it before you euthanised it. And I know there's something wrong with a batch of vaccine, but I don't know what.'

How was it possible that Michael hadn't grasped the most basic facts of what had happened?

'And keep it simple, Victor,' Michael said. 'I studied English Literature, Latin and Greek for A-level. You and Jean talk in a code I don't understand. You said, "A monkey caught polio". Was that because the vaccine failed? Do you test it by injecting the monkeys and then exposing them to the virus?'

'God, no. Haven't you understood anything? The vaccine gave the monkey polio.'

A shudder ran through Michael's body as though it fought against understanding her words. Vivian gave him time to work it out for himself.

'I thought… I thought we'd sent out a dud batch. I never dreamed we'd… Do you mean it will give the children…?'

'Yes. Any child who is vaccinated with Batch #2006 will have the poliovirus circulating in their blood.'

'But how? How can that be?'

She thought for a while. 'You understand that a vaccine works by stimulating the body to produce antibodies against a particular disease? Such as polio. So that, if you do come into contact with it, you've already got defences to kill it. You understand that?'

'I suppose so. I've never really thought about it.'

'Edward Jenner discovered the first vaccine when he realised people who'd had cowpox were immune to smallpox. In other words, cowpox left antibodies in the blood which could fight off smallpox.'

'I see.'

'However, the vaccine for polio uses an inactivated form of the poliovirus itself to leave antibodies. We grow the virus and then we kill it, if you like. The problem is it's very difficult to be sure you've killed it all. Have you heard of the Cutter Incident?'

'You and Jean sometimes talk about it, but not really.'

'It was a disaster. Just two years ago, in the United States. In the desperate rush to get as many children vaccinated against polio as possible, Cutter Laboratories weren't careful enough with their manufacturing processes. The result was that over 200,000 children were injected with live virus.'

'And we've done the same?'

Vivian felt her anxiety and horror grow into an explosion of anger. She hurled her pen into the corner of the office, where it ricocheted off a wall and rolled under the wooden filing cabinet. 'No, *we* bloody haven't. Harry and his damned porters have. Look around you, Michael. Walk through the labs with your eyes actually open rather than focusing on where else you'd like to be. You're not stupid. You must see how carefully we keep each step of the process separate to avoid any contamination. Listen to the staff muttering about how fussy we are. Ask your father how much the filters we use to strain out the dead monkey cells we grow the virus in cost. Have you not noticed how many tests Jean and I do, day in and day out? We keep testing the vaccine until there's no trace of live virus left and then we continue the inactivation process for a few more days to be absolutely sure.'

Michael reached under the cabinet from where he was still sitting on the floor and retrieved the pen. 'I know how careful you are. But the vaccine still contained live virus. And I honestly would like to understand.'

Vivian calmed down. It wasn't Michael's fault.

'It can happen,' she said quietly and held up a hand to stop Michael from interrupting. 'That's why we store the vaccine and run a final check by injecting a sample of each batch into the monkeys and waiting to see if they...'

Michael finished the sentence for her. 'Get polio.'

She nodded.

Michael was silent for a while, staring into the distance, running his fingers through the dust particles dancing in the shafts of sunlight.

'How many children have we killed?' he asked. 'Can you work it out with your formulas and your calculations? I'm sure you can, Victor.'

Of course she'd worked it out. She'd hated herself for doing it but she needed to know. She might as well tell Michael. He was Richard's son, after all, a member of the Poulter dynasty. It would be all over the newspapers anyway.

'Probably only a couple of hundred will get it badly enough to be severely crippled or paralysed or...'

'Die?' Michael's voice was shocked.

'Initially, anyway.'

'What do you mean initially?'

'The children we've given the disease to will infect other people so there will be more. That's the difficult figure to calculate. There are too many variables.'

Vivian stopped as Michael pushed himself to his feet and started walking up and down the small room. 'How can you sound so calm about it?'

She felt a momentary irritation. Michael had asked the question and the maths was the maths. She was saved from answering by Jean's entrance.

'Victor,' she said. 'Can you join us upstairs?' She caught sight of Michael. 'You too,' she said to him and turned without another word.

Bright sunlight, inappropriate and uncaring, cast the windows' outline onto the floor of the graceful room Richard Poulter used as an office on the rare occasions he was at Berkswell House. His main office was in London but he spent most of his time travelling around the country visiting the health authorities, doctors and chemists who bought Poulters' products. It was one of the few rooms to retain its original proportions although the sparseness of its furnishings reflected its lack of use.

Harry and Philip were already there. Philip perched in a solitary chair in front of Richard, who sat in state behind his desk, flanked by Owen and Jean, both standing slightly behind him. Harry stood in the far corner of the room. It looked like a moment from a West End play, a tableau of the climax. Judge and lawyers about to condemn the guilty party while a guard looked on.

'Is that everyone?' Richard said. 'Everyone who's aware of this... incident?'

'Yes,' Jean replied. 'Just the seven of us.'

Richard nodded. He sat back in his chair and surveyed the room. Choosing his words, Vivian thought, as though he were at a board meeting and someone was taking notes. She realised how much she hated the man. From his slicked-down but thinning hair to his starched white shirts and pinstriped jacket. He was a pompous toad. And a stupid one. It was only his ruthlessness and a certain understanding of how to manipulate people that had got him so far.

'I've called you here,' Richard announced, 'because we've reached a decision.' He paused. 'We've reached a decision,' he repeated. 'But only after much consideration. As you know…' He cleared his throat and picked up a piece of paper with Jean's neat writing on it.

Surely, he wasn't going to go over the whole horrific discovery. They'd all lived every detail of it during the night hours and needed to make use of their fast-receding stores of energy to deal with the crisis. Exhaustion tickled the back of Vivian's eyes and pumped her heart faster and faster. From the look of them, the others were the same. The sunlight was harsh on Harry and Owen's faces, aging them. Philip had the advantage of sleep last night but shock had flattened his skin to his skull and drained all colour from his face apart from the lumpy outbreaks of red acne. It was his few seconds of carelessness that had started the catastrophic chain of events but they would all be caught up in the aftermath. Each of them bore some responsibility. It would be a black mark against them forever. She'd be known as Victor Leadsom, one of the scientists involved in the Coventry Scandal.

Victor Leadsom, she thought. And an urge to turn and walk out the door gripped her.

Only Jean retained some semblance of normality but, as Richard started to speak again, she lifted a hand discreetly to her forehead and massaged it.

'As you know,' Richard restarted. 'Yesterday afternoon, er…' He cast a quick look at his notes. 'You are, of course, all aware of the strict protocol put in place to ensure that the polio vaccine is safe. It is an inactivated vaccine and contamination can occur –'

'Richard,' Jean interrupted him gently. 'I think we know all this. We all know that, no matter how careful we are, the filtering process doesn't always extract all the dead cells and that these can harbour the live virus and protect it from being inactivated.'

Vivian saw the blank look on Harry's face. 'Killed,' she said to Harry. 'We can't always be sure that all the live virus has been killed.'

'Utmost vigilance,' Richard said. 'It requires utmost vigilance.'

Harry looked horrified. 'So, my lads have been transporting poliovirus around the site?'

Richard had been right, Vivian thought, to go over everything. Clearly, in the panic of last night, Harry had not grasped the detail of what had happened. No more than Michael had.

'We've reached a decision,' Richard said again, twisting his thick gold wedding band round and round the full flesh of his ring finger and glancing round at them all.

The strangeness of his words struck her. No decision made by Richard was going to change what had happened and what was going to happen. It was out of their control now.

'It hasn't been an easy one. We have had to consider the far-reaching implications of the choices we make today.'

Her skin prickled. She looked over at Jean. What was all this about? Jean's eyes were fixed on her.

'It is already too late,' Richard continued. 'The, er… the damage has been done. Nothing we can do will change that. What we must do is look further down the road at the damage that *would* be done if the public lost faith in the vaccination process.'

Richard paused. No one moved.

'What do you mean?' Vivian asked.

Jean stood still and straight. The sun caught the curly tendrils of hair that had escaped from the tight ponytail and framed her head with a fuzzy halo.

'Think, Victor,' she said. 'We've both studied the Cutter Incident.'

This was true. They had pored over everything, ensuring that their protocols avoided any of the errors that had been made.

'But I don't see what that has to do –'

'The Cutter Incident was widely publicised. The public were informed, Victor, and even though the mistakes in manufacture were corrected, parents turned their backs on the vaccine. The following summer, there were seventeen hundred cases of polio in epidemics in Massachusetts and Illinois alone. All of them among children who would have been vaccinated if there hadn't been a backlash. Seventeen hundred cases that could have been avoided.'

She paused, giving Vivian time to think about what she'd said. Richard was silent, recognising that she was the one who could best explain.

'So,' Vivian said, catching up with her at last. 'You're suggesting… You're advocating we do nothing? Nothing at all? Keep it quiet?'

Jean smiled, pleased at her quickness, but she'd often been able to follow Jean's mind when it went leaping after a solution, brushing away the irrelevancies and dead ends that got in other people's way and slowed them down.

'To stop a worse catastrophe, yes,' she said. 'It's the best thing we can do.'

'But…' Surely it couldn't be as easy as that?

'It's happened, Victor. It's horrific but we're too late to stop it.'

'Too late for every dose of it?'

'I rang the Health Authority this morning.' Owen interrupted them. 'I asked if they wanted an additional supply of vaccine. They practically bit my hand off. They said they could use every drop of it we could send. They said that they had absolutely none left.'

The vaccine was administered as soon as it arrived. They'd seen the queues waiting outside the vaccination centres. Batch #2006, with its cargo of poison, was already swimming through the veins of Britain's children, multiplying as it went and encircling their hapless nerve cells. Some of the children would be feeling ill. Some of them might already be showing the first signs of paralysis. Many of them would be gifting the virus to their friends and family. Vivian wondered if Jean had done the maths too. More than likely. If so, she'd know the appalling worst-case figures for paralysis and death. Her hand was massaging her forehead again and Vivian noted that it shook.

So, the conspiracy of silence had already started. Owen had called the Health Authority but said nothing about the lethal vaccine.

There was no need to second-guess what motivated Richard to keep everything quiet. Poulters, the family pharmaceutical company he'd dragged out of the age of herbal remedies and laxative pills into the dynamic world of today, would never survive the scandal of giving polio to Britain's children.

Owen and Harry would do as they were told, whatever their personal feelings. Two world wars had bred in them a sense of common obedience that overrode any individual feelings. Michael would do what his father wanted and Philip, the boy responsible for the mislabelling, would leap at the chance for it all to be forgotten.

'But won't someone notice that children who have been vaccinated are falling ill with the disease?' Harry said.

Jean answered. 'Unlike Cutter, we're in the middle of a polio epidemic. Children are catching the virus anyway. Besides, the vaccine takes time to be effective and you need three shots to have full protection.'

That was also true. The magic vaccine the press were crying out for was never going to solve the immediate problem. It was in the years that were yet to come that its effects would be felt. And that, of course, was what Jean meant about avoiding a worse catastrophe.

'Next year,' Owen said. 'Next year, if the vaccination programme continues, and only if, there won't be a polio epidemic in Coventry. There won't be a polio epidemic anywhere in Britain. That's what we have to keep sight of. We're all working towards the total eradication of the disease.' He sat down heavily on a chair propped against the wall, pulled out a handkerchief and wiped his nose. Jean nodded in agreement.

It was all so logical. Say nothing and save countless numbers of children's lives. Vivian was sure Jean believed it was the right thing to do. But somewhere there was a human angle Jean had missed. She looked out at the glorious summer day. Jean had forgotten the youngsters they'd condemned to a life of shrivelled limbs, lugging around pounds of heavy steel strapped to their legs, or worse, trapped in an iron barrel that forced their chests in and out, viewing the world through a mirror above their heads. Surely they owed them the truth?

Or did they? Would knowing the truth help? Might they not be better believing they'd been unlucky?

It was an impossible decision. Suddenly, she was sick of it. Sick of trying to choose. What was better? Living a lie that hurt no one? Or insisting on a truth that would create huge grief – in every sense of the word?

'Victor?' Jean asked.

She dragged her eyes away from the green and blue and gold outside and to Jean's face. She believed in Jean. She believed in her ability to extrapolate the best solution to a problem. Time and time again, during the limited research they'd been able to do, she'd seen her mind reach through a tangle of confusing results and pull out the thread they needed to follow. And she believed in Jean's motives. Was that enough?

Richard grunted and looked over to Harry. 'What do you think, Harry?'

Harry looked startled. Startled at being asked, Vivian thought. Startled that Richard would think he needed to ask. He muttered something about being sure they were right.

Richard's shoulders relaxed a fraction of an inch and the exquisitely tailored cut of his jacket slipped back into its normal state. He was once again the epitome of the tycoon. 'Right,' he said. 'I'm sure you're all very tired and I'll leave Owen and Jean to –'

'Wait, Richard,' Jean said. 'We need to know what Philip thinks.' She gave Vivian a quick glance but forbore to mention that she'd also said nothing.

Jean was right, Vivian realised. They'd all discounted Philip. He was the man in the dock waiting for his sentence to be pronounced rather than a jury member actively considering a verdict.

'I'm sure Philip will agree it's the only solution.' Richard's voice was tinged with disgust. A man who'd ordered oysters and found one that had gone off.

'Do you agree, Philip?' Jean asked.

It was hard to know what Philip thought. He'd been staring down through most of the conversation, seemingly transfixed by the gently moving shadow of a tree cast by the sun on the floor. Vivian wanted nothing more than to get out of this room and leave this moment behind. She thought Philip must feel the same way but the boy was strangely quiet.

'Philip?' Jean's voice prodded him.

'I agree,' he said, but he sounded forced, as though the decision had cost him dearly.

Richard ignored him. 'Owen, Harry,' he said. 'I think we can let Philip go home now and it's probably best for everyone if he doesn't come back.'

Owen and Harry nodded but, before they could say anything, Philip rose from his chair and walked past Vivian to the door. He looked calm, Vivian thought, and intact.

'Owen,' Richard said. 'Just see Philip off the premises, will you? Make him see what a lucky escape he's had and check he takes nothing with him.'

Owen left without a word.

'A friend of your son's, isn't he, Harry?'

Harry nodded.

'I think your son should leave too, Harry. Wilfred, isn't it? We'll pay him until the end of summer. He's off to college then, I believe. Expensive business, isn't it? I'm sure we can find a bit of a scholarship to help him. Bright young lad like that.' This was Richard at his most gracious.

It was that more than anything that strengthened Vivian's resolve. The casual offer of money tainted everything. Jean, she noticed, had turned away. 'I don't agree,' Vivian said. 'I'm not happy about your plan.'

Their heads snapped round to stare at her. It would have been funny in another situation.

'But I'll accept your decision.'

Jean looked at her through narrowed eyes.

'I'm not going to tell anyone,' she added, in case they hadn't understood. 'I'll keep quiet about it, but I can't go along with it. I'm leaving.'

Chapter Thirty-Six:
Phiney Wistman

23 June 2017
Ten days after the reunion

Vivian's voice ground to a halt as the guide leading a group of tourists stopped in the aisle near us. I was glad of the pause. I needed a moment to get my head round what she'd told me. It was so enormous, I struggled to pummel it into some kind of shape. Children with desperate parents queuing to have death and disease injected into their veins. The nurse in me shuddered. I buried my hands in the pockets of my coat, unable to bear the muscle memory of my fingers plunging syringes through soft skin.

This was what had killed Grandad. I was sure. Discovering he was responsible for inflicting polio on hundreds of children had finished him. He understood what they'd been through. Waking up to sickness, with legs and arms that no longer worked. Torn from everything familiar – home, parents, families and friends – to spend weeks shut away on an isolation ward with barely coping and often uncaring nurses. The months of painful rehabilitation. The endless operations to break and stretch and cut and bend distorted limbs into temporary working order. The lifetime of being unable to do things everyone else took for granted. Watching friends play football. Watching them dancing, then walking their dates home. Grandad had experienced it all.

He might have learned to live with the knowledge if he'd known from the start but the shock of finding out all at once had cut the ties that tethered him to himself.

If only he hadn't been alone. If only he'd rung me. If only Dora hadn't been away. There were lots of 'if onlys'. If only...

It should never have been kept secret. It should have been shrieked to the world. Part of me couldn't believe that nothing had changed since Vivian told me. People still walked slowly round the cathedral and gazed at its splendour. The tourists near us carried on with their tour and Vivian sat in front of me. Waiting.

'How could you agree to keep it quiet?' I said, in the end.

'Because everything Jean said made sense. The damage had been done and we couldn't undo it. If we'd made it public and people had lost faith in the vaccination process there would have been countless more deaths. We had the statistics from Cutter to prove that.'

She watched me take her words in. I thought of the crazies in the anti-vax brigade. The threat they posed to the children we treated who couldn't be vaccinated and who relied on herd immunity to protect them from diseases their broken systems couldn't cope with. She had a point.

'Jean wanted to do the right thing,' she continued, as the tourists moved away. 'Most of the others wanted to save themselves.'

She started talking about Richard but I wasn't listening. The rights and wrongs of the actions they'd taken didn't matter. I'd got what I wanted. I knew all about the secret and not one bit of it was any use to me. None of it was going to help me find Mat.

My phone vibrated with a text from Meghan.

Police hopeless. Mat not missing for long enough. What should I do?

I texted straight back.

Did you tell them about Michael Poulter and Philip Mason?

Yes. They thought I was a nutter.

'What is it?' Vivian asked.

'You have to come with me. To the police. And tell them all this. Someone killed Philip. Someone tried to kill me. And now my friend has disappeared. I need the police to take me seriously. I need to persuade them to investigate.'

I half rose from the chair, knocking my bag onto the floor in my haste, but when I stood from picking it up, she was still sitting. Her face had closed in, tight and expressionless, and her eyes no longer met mine.

'Please?'

I saw her answer in the eyes that wouldn't meet my gaze. In the fingers that drew circles on the back of the chair. She didn't want to be involved. She was going to disappear again. It was what she'd always done in the face of difficulty.

'Please,' I said again. I didn't know what else to say.

She turned away from me abruptly and buried her head in her hands. The crown of her beautifully cut hair settled back into loose curls. Earlier, I'd thought how much Dora could learn from her elegance and style. Now I wished she had a fraction of Dora's doggedness and determination to do the right thing and see it through to the bitter end.

Any ideas? Or should I come to the cathedral? Meghan texted.

Wait a minute…

What could we do? I thought of the *Coventry Telegraph*. Would they take us seriously? It was possible. They knew Mat. They knew he hadn't been in touch for a while. They'd have contacts in the police. Maybe they could exert some pressure.

Go to the Telegraph, I texted. *See if they'll help.*

Good idea.

Not really, I thought. But I couldn't think of anything better.

'I'm Vivian Reynolds.' Vivian's voice was low and bitter. 'This all happened to Victor Leadsom. By the time the police get their heads round me, it will be too late. I'm a distraction. Maybe if Victor had stayed…'

'The evidence,' I said. 'The evidence Philip mentioned in his letter. What was it?'

She sat up. 'The key bits of paper. The blood test results for the monkey infected with polio, along with the batch number of the vaccine it had been injected with. And the consignment notes from Harry's files showing the same batch had been delivered to the NHS.'

'Have you still got them?'

'No.'

The last hope that this meeting with Vivian was going to give me something tangible left my body in a shuddering sigh that disturbed the soaring nave's echoing acoustics and made the air around us vibrate.

I leaned forward to push myself up and leave.

'I know where they might be, though.'

It took a few seconds for the meaning of Vivian's words to penetrate my senses. I sat down again.

'After I told Richard Poulter I didn't agree with the decision, he asked me to wait in his office while he organised a few things. He said he'd like to have a little chat. I thought about refusing but... Well, there was something about Richard that made it difficult to say no to his face and I couldn't slip out after he'd gone because he locked me in.'

She ran her long, varnished nails over the skin of her forearms. They left no mark but the noise was like feet crushing dry grass.

'I try not to remember his exact words when he came back but he left me in no doubt that, if I breathed a word, I wouldn't like the consequences. Then he told me to collect my personal things and go. When I went back to my office, everything else had been removed: all my files; all the records of the research Jean and I had done; all the manufacturing paperwork for the vaccine, the tests, and the protocols. Everything. The speed and thoroughness of it terrified me. Michael found me. Richard had told him to collect all the documents that showed what had happened and put them in his car so he could destroy them. He was paranoid about them. He told Harry and Owen to make up some story and burn the entire week's consignment notes later. Michael was in a terrible state. We'd all of us ignored him. Richard never asked him what he thought and the rest of us just assumed he'd go along with his father. But Michael wasn't like that. He thought the decision was probably the correct one but he wasn't sure and he wanted the evidence to be kept. He just didn't know how.'

'What did you do?'

'I copied them for him.' She laughed at the expression on my face. 'You're quite right. Copying machines weren't commonplace then, but they did exist. Jean had got used to having one in Canada so we had an early model in the labs. However, we kept it quiet from the rest of the staff otherwise they'd all have been in using it. Michael left the copies with me and put the originals in Richard's car. And I hid the copies.'

I stared at her.

'I couldn't take them with me. Everyone was searched before they left, and in my case, it was very thorough. In fact, I didn't take anything with me. I think I knew everything had changed and I wanted a new start so I left everything behind.'

I understood.

'The papers are still at Berkswell House, aren't they?'

'I never went back, so unless someone's found them, they're still there.'

Berkswell House. It all came back to Berkswell House.

Meghan texted me as I raced out of the cathedral.

At Telegraph. Mat's boss out. Not back until tomorrow.

Shit. Can you get his number?

Tried. No chance. Dragon secretary. Who is Mr Knowles?

Mr Knowles. The name rang a bell but he was nothing to do with Poulters and the polio vaccine. Or was he? It came back to me. He was the gung-ho neighbour who lived by Berkswell House. The one who'd seen Grandad outside and helped Mat break in.

Why? I texted back.

He's been trying to get hold of Mat.

I thought for a minute.

Meet me at yours. We're going to see Mr Knowles.

Chapter Thirty-Seven:
Phiney Wistman

23 June 2017
Ten days after the reunion

Mr Knowles lived opposite the old entrance to Berkswell House. The one with the side gate I'd climbed over. He was tall and thin, with an awkward grace that reminded me of James Stewart in *It's a Wonderful Life*, Grandad's favourite film, and he wore a mustard yellow cardigan with leather patches on the elbows that seemed entirely in keeping.

'We're friends of Mat's,' I said. 'Mat Torrington.'

'Yes?' He frowned, as he looked us up and down from the top of the steps leading up to his front door.

'We think he's in trouble and I'm hoping you can help.' I had no time to beat around the bush.

The angles of his face sharpened but whether it was suspicion of us or concern about Mat I couldn't tell.

'You've been trying to get hold of him,' Meghan said. 'We wondered if you'd heard from him.'

Meghan too was in no mood for prevarication and neither, it seemed, was Mr Knowles. 'He was supposed to come and see me the day before yesterday but he never turned up. I've left messages on his mobile and at the *Telegraph*. Not like him at all.'

The day before yesterday was the last day Mat had been in touch. Since then, we'd heard nothing from him.

Mr Knowles raised a thin hand, clutching a pipe that leaked a thin trail of smoke, as he gestured towards Berkswell House opposite. 'Mat asked me to let him know if anything changed. That's why I was trying to get in touch. They're going to demolish the house.'

Meghan's mouth dropped open and my mind chased through ideas. Had someone realised the evidence must be hidden at Berkswell House? If so, what a brilliant way to get rid of it.

'Can they just do that?' Meghan asked. 'Don't you need planning permission? Or something?'

'Poulters got that before they put the house on the market. Increased the value no end as there was every chance whoever bought it would want to get rid of the old house.'

'When are they demolishing it?' I heard the panic in my voice.

'They're starting to strip the place out tomorrow and then the heavy machinery will arrive. All very hasty.'

Fear rose sharp and acid in me. They were prepared to go to huge lengths to keep the secret safe. Mat hadn't stood a chance against them.

'What sort of trouble?' Mr Knowles asked. 'You said Mat was in trouble.'

'He's missing,' I blurted out. 'And I think it's because of something that's in Berkswell House.' I made a swift decision. 'I need to get in. And I need to do it tonight. Mat said you helped him break in…'

Mr Knowles looked doubtful. Questions raced across his face as he scanned us. His eyes fell on Jack.

'That's his dog, isn't it? The man – what was his name? Mat told me his name. The one who –'

'Jumped off the bridge at Tile Park Station?' I said. 'Yes, this is his dog. He was my grandad.'

Another fraught silence only punctuated by the drift of smoke from Mr Knowles's pipe.

'Was his death to do with all this?'

'Yes.'

'Mat mentioned you.' He shoved his pipe in his mouth and sucked on its end. 'You'd better come in,' he said, at last. 'Not him, though.'

He pointed to Jack. 'I've got cats. You can shut him in the back garden if you want.'

Mr Knowles made us wait until it was dark. He told us the security service never went inside once night had fallen, contenting themselves with a quick drive round the exterior. I'd have free run once I was over the wall.

'I think I should come with you,' Meghan said to me as we wrestled Mr Knowles's ladder off the roof rack of her dad's car. The darkness made a mystery of her expression. She leaned the ladder against the wall enclosing the grounds of Berkswell House, dislodging a loose brick so it fell with a clatter, and split, throwing red dust over our feet.

'For God's sake, Megs. Be a bit more careful.'

'It's the bloody tree. It gets in the way of the streetlamp so I can't see what I'm doing.'

'I know. But this is the place Mr Knowles said.'

There were no houses opposite, he'd explained, only farmland, so the chances of being seen were remote.

'I'm sorry. Next time we go breaking and entering, I'll be more careful.'

I heard the wobble in Meghan's throat as I wrangled the ladder back upright and I hugged her.

'I'm the one who should be sorry. Thank you. Thank you for helping me. I'd have been stuck without you.'

'I'm still not happy about you going without me.'

I sighed inwardly. I'd already had to dissuade Mr Knowles from joining us and Meg, who hated the dark, wouldn't be much more help.

'Megs. Please. You know you won't cope. I'll be quicker without you. You'll be much more use keeping an eye out for the guards and warning me if they arrive.'

'You will look for Mat, won't you? Once you've found –'

'I said I would.'

Promising to search the house for Mat had been the only way to keep Meg from coming with me. I was sure Mat wasn't there, though. He'd have asked Mr Knowles for help breaking in and Mr Knowles hadn't seen him. And I wanted to get the evidence to the police as fast as possible.

Meghan stood on the bottom rung while I clambered up, swung one leg over the top and looked down into the gardens. Beneath me was a dark void although the light of the streetlamps penetrated weakly onto the open expanse of lawn between the wall and the house. I hesitated. Logic told me the ground was only a couple of yards below but it's hard to leap into a dark hole.

Instead, I turned and grasped the rough bricks and lowered myself down, digging my trainers into the wall as I went, then dropped the last couple of feet. It was enough to knock the breath out of me.

I looked up at the old, brick wall, softly crumbling in parts where ivy and wildflowers had colonised and grown, and realised getting out might not be as easy as breaking in.

'Phiney.' Meghan's voice came from above. She'd climbed the ladder too but her face was in darkness.

'Shhh,' I said.

'Why do I have to shush? There's no one around. You said, there was no one around.'

'There isn't. I'll see you back here. I'll be as quick as I can.'

'You sure you'll be OK?'

'Sure. The sooner I start, the sooner it will be over.'

Because I wanted it to be over. The dark, deserted grounds were spooking me and I was cold and shaky.

'Put the balaclava on.'

'I will.'

'No, do it now. You're so white! Your face gleams out of the dark.'

I pulled on the old black balaclava into which Mr Knowles had painstakingly sewn an old black scarf with holes for eyes and looked back up at Megs.

'Shit,' she said. 'It really does make a difference. With your black T-shirt and jeans, I can hardly see you.'

Nevertheless, I stuck close to the trees and bushes as I headed for the house, haring across the open expanse of moonlit lawn at its narrowest point and slipping straightaway into a dark corner between two outhouses. I waited there and listened, trickling breath in and out of my lungs as silently as possible. I heard nothing.

It felt safer by the house. Its stone façade sheltered me and its sharp outlines made it easier to orientate myself. I followed it round until I came to the back door, shut and locked with a big chain and padlock. Round the corner was the window Mat had spoken about. The one with the loose boarding. Mr Knowles had confirmed no one had repaired it.

He'd told me to look out for cameras near the house. They used infra-red light to see at night, so I should be able to spot them from the circle of gleaming red dots round their outside. Everywhere was pitch black, though, so I risked a quick flash of Mr Knowles's torch to check no one was waiting in the shadows. A gleam of metal and glass caught the light and held it for a few seconds. It was a camera, looking at me with a dark and empty stare.

Shit!

Except it had no red lights. I was in luck. For some reason or other, it wasn't working. Neither was the other one trained on the back door just a few feet away from the window with the loose board. I climbed in, dragging the board back behind me so a casual glance wouldn't reveal someone had got in this way.

The small room was empty although it smelled of stale air and rot. Enough moonlight came in through the cracks round the board to see where I was going but, once I went into the corridor beyond, it was pitch black. I flashed the torch round.

I was in a narrow corridor, its walls decorated by a pattern of cracks and black mould. To my right was the back door and opposite me a doorway revealed steps down to the cellar. A series of other doorways led to small rooms used by the footmen and maids for the invisible work that had kept the house running. In 1957, they were offices for the typists, according to Vivian. All the doors were long gone. To my left, an arch marked the beginning of the grander part of the house and the main staircase up to the floors above.

I took a deep breath and walked towards it. The torch's narrow beam caught odd details: loose cables hanging from the ceiling like vines in the jungle; a patch of damp on a torn piece of pink-and-white striped wallpaper; paint flaking off the spindling on the banisters curving up to the first floor.

The tightness of the beam worried me. It left acres of unlit space and, no matter how swiftly I raced the torch around, I had the feeling something was moving in the dark, hiding from me. Prickles of fear rushed up my spine as I tiptoed up the stairs. I was sure something was creeping up behind me, matching its footsteps to mine. But each time I paused, trying to catch it out, there was silence except for the creak of the wood on the stairs as it settled back to rest after the weight of my feet had disturbed it.

Too much time spent watching horror movies, I told myself. Get a grip. There's no one here.

Nevertheless, when I got to the top of the stairs, I forced myself to whirl round and shine the torch behind me.

There was nothing. Of course there was nothing. Yet my heart beat in heavy thuds as though I'd seen a horde of zombies clambering up the stairs after me, trailing tatters of bloodstained clothing.

Enough.

I scuttled along the corridor. Third door on the left, Vivian had said. Richard's office. The grandest room in the house and the least used. Where better to hide the papers than in there? So, sixty years ago, Vivian had waited until Richard had gone to oversee the clearing up process and slipped in.

I hoped the documents were still there.

The room was empty apart from a pile of plaster in one corner where the roof had crumbled, and there was a smell of mouldering wood. A thick layer of white, gritty dust coated the floor. Three large windows, although boarded up, still dominated the room. Most of their white paint had bubbled and chipped but the dilapidation couldn't disguise how striking they had been with their architraves and panelling. However, the panelling wasn't purely ornamental. Vivian didn't think anyone else had realised this.

The windows faced south, she'd said. Sun poured in during the afternoon. So, they had shutters, which folded into recesses at the sides. They looked like panels because the knobs to pull them out had long gone, even then.

I went over to the left-hand window, dug my fingers into the side of the frame and prised part of the panelling open. A shower of cobwebs and paint flakes fell around me when I dragged the shutter out of its box. The empty recess was dark with dirt and dust and my torchlight couldn't penetrate its depth. I reached in but my hand felt nothing apart from grit and powder. Shit. Had someone got here before me?

I forced myself to poke into the corners. A spider or two wouldn't kill me. My fingers met something. I pulled it out, raining dust and grit over my sleeve.

A brown envelope.

The papers were inside. Exactly as Vivian had described them.

Evidence of a terrible tragedy, buried sixty years ago. Evidence to stir the police and the *Telegraph* into action. My hands shook with hope.

Suddenly, the papers seemed all too flimsy. I was terrified they might disintegrate and disappear before I could show them to the police. Maybe I should take them back to Meg immediately.

Except it would be better to search the house for Mat first. I thought my nerve would fail me if I left and I might never come back. Philip's body haunted me. The thought of finding Mat's unpinned the tendons from my bones and threatened to break me in bits.

I made a decision.

The house itself was easy to search as the rooms were empty and doorless. All it took was a fast walk along each corridor and a quick flash of the torch round. They were all depressingly alike. Stained and grubby walls, crumbling plaster and the ghosts of old glory poking through in glimpses of oak panelling and tiled fireplaces.

The prefabs that sprouted from the original structure like malevolent growths weren't so easy. They smelled gross. People had dossed in them and they hadn't been fussy about going outside to pee. And worse.

Mat was nowhere.

Finally, I found myself back at the bottom of the grand staircase and facing the corridor leading through the servants' quarters to the back door. Fresh air and moonlight were a short way away.

A voice broke the silence. Rough and sharp. Security?

Shit! I peered down the corridor and saw that the back door was now wide open. Its chain was cut in two and lying on the ground with the padlock still attached and bolt cutters discarded by it.

Not security guards. They wouldn't have cut the chain.

The voice again. Louder. It was still outside but getting closer. A flicker of torchlight glanced in through the open door and lit up the red-tiled floor. Whoever it was, they were coming in. It was too late to dart down the corridor and hide in the room where the window board was loose, wait for them to pass and escape.

I turned, planning to slip back into the house. And heard footsteps running lightly down the main staircase.

Shit.

The footsteps on the stairs in the house stopped. Had they heard me?

I was trapped. Caught between someone inside the house and someone coming in from outside. Beside me, the doorway led down to the cellars. The smell of damp and rotting wood rose to meet me. I dug my fingers into the spongy frame and tried to think. Would I be better down there? I risked a quick flash of the torch. At the bottom of the steps, a passage twisted round the corner. *Go down*, I thought. *There'll be places to hide.* I tiptoed down and crept round the corner and down the passage which came to an abrupt end after a few feet.

Stumbling feet from the corridor above and the sound of muttering and angry murmurs. And then a wail pierced the dark.

I knew that voice. I'd have known it anywhere. It was Meghan's.

I stopped breathing although my heart beat blood round my body so loud I was sure it was pounding through the basement.

What had happened?

An angry voice barked indecipherable words and something tumbled down the steps, followed by the clump of heavy boots.

They were coming down here. I'd made the wrong choice.

There were two doors off the passage. One was padlocked, the other held shut by a bolt.

No choice.

I pulled the bolt open. It was old and corroded and the rasp it made sent tremors echoing through my nerves but the noise of Meghan's sobs covered it. And when it came free, I slipped in through the door, shut it behind me and shone my torch quickly round inside.

I was in a stone-floored cellar with low rafters overhead, coated with wispy white fungi. A small horizontal window high in the wall gave onto the ground outside but its panes were crusted with dirt and no light came through. The room was the dumping ground of last resort, crammed full of junk. My torchlight fell on a rusty iron mangle perched on top of rolls of what looked like carpet. In the far corner, stacks of books, swollen with age and humidity, formed a crazy tower that could topple at any time.

The torch lit up something white and round. A face. With dark eyes fixed on me.

It was Mat.

Sitting on a box.

Thick black tape over his mouth. His hands stretched behind his back and tied to something. Blood had trickled from a cut above his eye and dried in a purple stain.

Chapter Thirty-Eight: Phiney Wistman

23 June 2017
Ten days after the reunion

I turned the torch onto my face.

'It's me, Mat.'

More cries from Meghan. They were right outside the door now. And a slap.

'I'm not going in there,' she screamed. 'Please. Not in the dark.'

The sound of tape ripped from a roll.

Mat jerked his head towards the corner to the left of the door where the piles of junk were most impenetrable. He was right. I should hide. I stumbled over. An old metal drum, with a hole at one end and dials round its side, lay among the debris, under an old mattress which leaked stuffing out onto the floor. I kicked the mattress away from the end, reached down and slipped inside. Part of my brain registered it was an iron lung. Or half of one, anyway. The pumping mechanism and stand were long gone. The lung was built for someone lying flat with their head outside, not with their whole body rammed into it, with knees and elbows dug against the ridged surface, but at least I was out of sight.

The bolt on the door rasped. I waited for the exclamation that would mean they'd seen it was drawn back. It didn't come. Maybe they hadn't noticed. The bolt had been stiff and I'd only pulled it back far enough to open the door. I heard the thud of a body on stone as Meghan was shoved into the cellar. The door slammed and the bolt ground back into place. A smothered whimpering.

I waited until I heard the man's footsteps on the stairs and then the floor above before scrambling out and turning the torch back on.

Meghan was crouched in a ball on the floor; her mouth was taped and her hands tied behind her. Fear flared in her eyes as she twisted her head towards the light.

'Megs. It's me, Phiney,' I hissed, turning the torch on my face then shining it into the room. 'And that's Mat. We've found Mat.'

I hurtled through the clutter to them and ripped off the tape round Meghan's wrists. She tore the tape from her mouth as I examined the rope holding Mat's arms behind his back and to a brick pillar.

'Get the tape off his face while I untie him,' I said and rammed the torch in between my teeth, setting to work on the tight knot.

Meghan was as gentle as she could be, picking away at the adhesive, relying on touch rather than sight and murmuring apologies when she gouged the skin from his lips. He spoke as soon as she'd freed his mouth.

'Water.'

'I haven't got any. Have you, Phiney?'

'No.'

I'd brought the least amount of stuff possible. I finished untying him and he brought his arms round to the front of his body, crying out in pain.

'How long have you been here?' I asked and balanced the torch in a metal bucket so it bathed the cellar in a dim light. His face was dark with dried blood and dirt except for a white strip where the tape had been, faintly gleaming with the residue of glue. His lips were red and raw.

'Don't know.' Speaking was painful and his arms and shoulders juddered with cramps. 'Very thirsty.'

'He must have been here since the day he went missing. That's over two days, Megs.'

She took Mat's shaking hands in both hers, calmed them and felt his pulse.

Two days with his arms wrenched behind his back. No wonder he was in pain and his muscles were in spasm. But it was the time without water that worried me the most. He'd be seriously dehydrated. Initially thirsty and dizzy, then with a speeding pulse as the body diverted liquid to the essential organs. Followed by…

Meghan put a hand on my arm.

'His pulse is fine, Phiney. It's cold and damp down here. And he hasn't been moving. He's going to be OK.'

'My bag,' Mat croaked. 'Water in my bag.'

I looked around and spotted Mat's rucksack on top of a stack of old crates. There was a small bottle of water in it, half full. I held it out to him but his hands jigged too much to keep it still. In the end, I put it to his mouth and dripped the water through his lips while Meghan rubbed his shoulders until the shaking calmed.

'I'm sorry,' he said, after a while. 'I stink. I couldn't…'

'No worries. Meghan and I are used to all that. How did you get here? It was Arch, wasn't it?'

'He phoned me.' His voice croaked in fits and starts. 'Told me he had information but he needed to see me. He picked me up in town. Suggested we came here. Told me he knew the codes and where the cameras were. And –'

'It doesn't matter. Tell us later.'

I trickled water into his mouth again and he swallowed it thirstily. When he started speaking once more, his words came out more easily.

'I should have realised something wasn't right. Arch was twitchy, ranting at the slightest provocation. He told me there was something down here I should see and then he must have coshed me because the last thing I remember is falling down the stairs. I came to in here like this.'

I squeezed his arm and tried not to imagine what it must have been like waking in the dark, tied up and utterly alone.

'I heard the guards outside in the grounds from time to time and I tried to stamp but…'

'I'm going to call an ambulance,' Meghan said. 'And the police.'

She stabbed at her phone a few times.

'No fucking signal.'

'We're in a cellar.'

'How long will the torch last?' Panic nibbled at the edge of her voice.

'I don't know.'

She wrapped her arms around her head and crouched over the torch in its mop bucket. I knew she was willing the shakes to subside.

'How did Arch get you?' I asked her. 'It was Arch, wasn't it?'

'Yes,' Mat said. 'That was Arch.'

'What happened?' I asked.

Meghan uncurled a few inches. 'He appeared out of nowhere and asked me what I was doing, saw the ladder and grabbed me. I tried to scream but he had a knife. He held it against my neck, Phiney. He cut me with it.'

She put a hand to her neck, then held it to the torch. Blood stained her fingertips.

'He's dangerous. I don't know what he was like before, but he's lost it. Big time. I know the signs.' She shuddered. 'He dragged me into his van. He wasn't gentle.'

'I'm sorry,' I said. 'I'd never have got you into this if I'd thought he was around.'

Mat levered himself upright using the metal chest. His legs wobbled a little but he succeeded.

'Hold on to the pillar and shake your legs,' I said. 'Then try and walk a few steps because we need to be ready to overpower him when he comes back.'

'Do you think he will?' Meghan said.

'Yes. I think he came back because he found out people are coming tomorrow to strip the place out. They'll find Mat.'

'People? Coming here tomorrow?' Mat looked confused.

'Yes. They're starting demolition tomorrow.'

'So, he came back to –'

'Finish you off,' I interrupted him. 'I guess he thought he'd leave you to die in the dark. He didn't expect the place to be gutted. I think Arch is all for keeping his killing simple.'

'So, why didn't he?' Mat said.

I stared at him.

'Why didn't he kill us?'

I had no answer to this.

'He will,' Meghan said. 'The back of the van, it was full of plastic containers of liquid. They smelled like petrol. I think he's going to burn the place down.'

Above us, somewhere in the house, there was a sharp crack, like the splintering of wood, followed by a series of rumbling thuds overhead.

Then silence.

'It sounded like someone falling down the stairs,' Meghan said.

Another crack.

Then a long silence, filled out with the rustles and creaks of the old house settling. Mat staggered to the door and ran his fingers round it. Then froze as we heard the clatter of feet on the steps leading down to the cellar.

'He's coming back.' Meghan's voice shivered with fear.

'Shit. Go and hide, Phiney,' Mat hissed and rummaged through a pile of rusty garden tools, picking up a shovel whose blade was reasonably intact. He tested its weight. A shower of dislodged rust sparkled in the beams of the torch. He discarded it and chose an old mangle handle, long and unbroken.

'Go on, Phiney, he doesn't know you're here.'

Mat moved over to the door and stood to one side, the mangle raised above his head, ready to smash it down on Arch's head.

'But three of us against one,' I started to say.

'Please, Phiney,' he whispered urgently. 'Just do as I say. Meghan, get the torch. Stay behind the pillar but shine it in his eyes when the door opens.'

I ran to the lung and scrambled in feet first this time, bending my legs under me so I could peer out of one of the holes. All I could see was Meghan waiting behind the pillar.

The bolt scraped and the door creaked a little as it opened. A short silence and a click as Meghan turned the torch on.

'No, Mat,' she yelled. The light whirled around the room as she dropped the torch and ran out of my vision towards the entrance. I heard a heavy thud and a clang.

Then nothing but the sound of panting.

'Thank you.' It was a woman's voice but not Meghan's. Definitely not Arch's. The beam of another torch shone into the room.

'Mat, are you all right? I gave you quite a shove.' Meghan moved into view, helping Mat to the crate he'd sat on before.

Who was the woman?

I squirmed round, jamming my left leg painfully bent, until I could catch a glimpse of her face. It was framed by grey hair clipped short apart from a slice of fringe flicked to one side. The harsh light robbed any softness from her features and her skin had the fine, sharp creases of old silk. I thought I recognised her.

'It's Dr Storer, isn't it?' Mat's voice was shaky. 'Jean Storer.'

'We thought you were someone else. The person who locked us in. That's why Mat was going to cosh you,' Meghan said. She stuck her torch back in the bucket where its dim light created tentacles of shadow from every movement. And then she placed her hands on Mat's head. 'Tell me if anything hurts.'

'I'm fine,' Mat said. 'I'm fine. Let's get out. Before…'

Meghan gasped.

Silence.

Mat spoke first. In a voice of utter calm that sent trickles of ice-cold fear down my spine.

'Dr Storer?' he asked. And then in a louder voice. 'You know you're pointing that gun at us?'

Neither Meg nor Mat so much as glanced in my direction but I knew Mat's words were meant for me. My mind raced. Jean? Jean with a gun? The cracks we'd heard earlier. Were they gunshots? They must have been. I thought Mat had realised. And that was why he wanted me to hide.

'You might want to be careful with that.' Mat's voice was still devoid of emotion.

'I know what I'm doing. I've had it for years,' Jean said. 'We all had them when we worked in Africa and I've always had one since. In the flat. I know it's illegal in this country but London is almost as lawless as some of the African camps I've worked in.'

'Of course.' Meghan spoke. 'How sensible of you. I've often wished we had one in the hospital. Especially when I was working in A&E. It can be terrifying on a Saturday night.'

They might have been discussing some documentary they'd both seen if it weren't for the dark patches of sweat staining Meghan's T-shirt and the occasional swallow that punctuated her words. I knew the thoughts racing through her head must be the same as mine. Had Jean shot Arch? Why? What was going on?

'Let's go.' Mat said. He took a step towards the door.

'Stay where you are.'

He stopped mid-stride. I wished I could see what Jean was doing.

'Don't think I won't use the gun. I already have.'

'What do you want?' Mat's voice was tired.

'I want the papers, of course. The evidence that Vic— the evidence that's hidden here.'

I knew what had happened. Vivian had done this. She said she'd tried to get hold of Jean but failed. After our meeting in the cathedral, she must have tried again and succeeded. She'd told Jean everything, trusting her, like she had back at the beginning of all this, to do the right thing.

'The documents weren't there when I looked,' Jean went on. 'And then I heard you all and I knew I wasn't alone. One of you had got there before me.'

'You shot Arch,' Mat said. It wasn't a question. He'd given up all idea of pretending everything was fine.

'He was crazy and stupid. I had no choice.'

'You're quite right.' Meghan leapt in. 'You had no choice. He had a knife. He was threatening us all.' Fear frayed the edges of her voice and I thought she was wasting her time trying to talk to Jean.

'He thought it was funny when I took the gun out. He even laughed. Stupid, stupid man. And then he tried to take it from me. So, I shot him. In the kneecap, first. Easiest way to disable someone quickly.' She could have been advising a group of student nurses on best-practice wound dressing if it wasn't for the staccato jabs of her voice. 'And then in the heart.'

A long moment filled only with the sound of Meghan's jerky breaths.

Jean was as crazy as Arch. But twice as dangerous.

'But he didn't have the documents. I checked after I shot him. So, I knew you must. It's Phiney, isn't it?'

She waved the gun at Meghan, who flinched. Jean smiled.

'And you're going to give the documents to me. Once they're destroyed, it will all be over.'

'Of course, they must be destroyed. It would be a catastrophe if it ever came out.'

Meghan wasn't going to give up trying to distract Jean.

'Thousands more children would have died or been paralysed if their parents had lost faith in vaccinations,' she went on. 'After all, that's exactly what happened in the States after Cutter.'

'You know about that?' Jean's voice gleamed with excitement.

'I studied it at nursing college,' Meghan lied.

'Then you know I was right. I did the right thing. I made the others do the right thing.' Her voice took on a feverish intensity. 'And I did it for the right reasons. Unlike the others. Yet when Michael said he was going to tell everybody, I knew I would be the scapegoat. Not the stupid clods who made the mistake. Not the smug profiteers who've feathered their own nests ever since. No. It would be me. The female scientist. People don't like me. I've learned that over the years. I make them uncomfortable. They want their truth coated

281

with sugar and I've never been good at that. I was passed over time and time again for promotion, for honours, for the best research facilities.'

She moved further into the room as she spoke and completely into my view. Her right elbow pressed against her waist and her forearm shot out in a perfect right angle. The gun glinted in her right hand, caught by the torch she held in the other. It was small and dark, half-hidden in the caress of her palm and fingers.

'But for once the zeitgeist is in my favour. Finally, at the end of my career, everything is coming good. And I deserve it after all these years of being better than everyone but never getting the recognition.'

Mat and Megs were silent, their eyes locked on the gun, letting the torrent of Jean's bitter words flow out uninterrupted, but, behind his back, Mat's hands reached out for something in the shadows. He was watching and waiting for the right moment, I thought. The moment when the gun in Jean's hand was no longer trained on the two of them. Or when her gaze flicked away from them. Whatever he was planning would happen then.

And it occurred to me that I could help.

I'd shout. I'd come out. She'd look at me. Mat would go for it and I would rush her too.

'This is my moment,' Jean went on. 'And I deserve it. I'm not going to lose it. I can make something of it. Make it easier for the women after me.'

A smile flickered across her mouth and she stopped talking. I thought she was staring into the future, seeing all the things she wanted to do that were now within her grasp. For a brief moment, she resembled her younger self in the 1957 photo, when the world must have seemed full of possibilities, rather than the harsh-faced and disappointed creature she'd become.

'So, give me the papers.' She brandished the gun at them both.

In a moment, I thought, she'd realise she could shoot them and search their corpses for the documents like she had with Arch.

I took a great breath and screamed.

Jean's head spun round and Mat leapt forward. The torch swept in an arc over the ceiling, catching him as he lunged forward with some netting in his hands. Was that all he had?

She was too quick for him. Too sharp. Too desperate.

I saw the fire spurt out of the dark metal and push her hand back into her stomach. Heard the crack.

Meghan screamed. A long wail that went on and on and on.

And afterwards, all was still.

Jean pointed her torch at Meghan and then down at the ground.

'Mat,' Meghan said and went towards him.

'Don't move,' Jean said.

'But he's bleeding.'

'That means he's still alive.'

'He won't be for much longer unless I stop the bleeding.'

'He won't be if I shoot him again. This time in the head.'

Meghan was bent halfway down to kneeling by Mat. She stopped.

'Get up.'

Meghan did as she said.

'Phiney.' Jean said my name quietly. 'I was wrong, wasn't I? You're not Phiney. But she's here, isn't she? She screamed. Phiney,' she called. 'It's time to come out or your friend will bleed to death.'

She was right. We'd run out of options. I pushed my way out of the iron lung and emerged into the searchlight of the torch.

Painful tremors of fear ran down into my fingers. Would she shoot me here and now?

'Stand by your friend,' she said, waving the torch over at Meghan.

It lit up a terrible sight. Meghan clenching her hands open and shut, open and shut, and Mat, on the ground, unmoving in a slowly swelling puddle of deepest red, the only colour in the browns and greys and blacks of the cellar, the only sign that he was still alive.

I went to stand by Meghan.

Jean never twitched. The gun in her hand remained pointed at Mat, as though a steel hawser anchored it to his body.

'Give me the papers.'

I took them out of my bag and held them out without a word. Mat's life could be counted out in seconds if we didn't get to him.

Jean hesitated. Her hands were full.

'Put the torch down.' Meghan's voice was calm but I could sense the fury of impatience running beneath it, threatening to burst out at any minute.

'No, put the papers on the ground,' Jean said and she jerked the torch onto a space between us.

I did it and stepped back straightaway. I would have done anything. Anything to speed her out of that room and let us get to Mat. I could smell the blood now. An insidious, warm, rusty smell permeating the dankness of the cellar.

She put the torch in the bucket and seized the papers, bending easily despite her years, stuffed them in a pocket and left. She'd barely closed the door behind her before Meghan was kneeling beside Mat.

'Get a torch, Phi. Point it on him. His leg. It's his leg.'

The bolt ground into place on the other side of the door and a cold fury iced through my body, but my hands held the torch steady. While Jean and I had made our exchange, a few paltry pieces of paper concerning a sixty-year-old tragedy for the chance to save Mat's life, Meghan had been observing and planning.

She seized the blood-soaked material of Mat's trousers and ripped it apart, grabbed the scarf from round her neck and pressed it hard down onto the wound, kneeling up so all of her weight was behind her rigid arms. The flow slowed a little but too much blood still oozed through her hands and spread across the floor, soaking into the knees of our jeans and gleaming in the dimness.

'Shit,' she said.

'Tourniquet.'

'Yes. Got another scarf?'

'No. Long-sleeved T-shirt?'

'That'll do. Look around for something to tighten it.'

I gave her the old mangle handle Mat had found, wedged the torch in the bars of an old chair and took my T-shirt off. It took both of us to keep the pressure on his wound and apply the tourniquet. I followed Meg's lead in everything. And felt nothing except massive relief, truly massive, that she was here. Marvellous, wonderful, capable Meghan.

'OK,' Meghan said when we'd finished. 'Well done.' She dragged her phone out of her pocket, smearing blood all over her jeans and looked at it. 'It's ten twenty. We've got two hours.'

I knew all too well what she meant. After two hours, the tourniquet on Mat's leg would start to cause significant damage. Tissue death. Neurovascular failure. It meant amputation. Or worse. It wasn't over yet.

Chapter Thirty-Nine:
Phiney Wistman

24 June 2017
Eleven days after the reunion

Half an hour later, Mat came to, moaning and muttering. The torch battery had run out and Meg and I were taking it in turns to batter the door while the other held a phone to cast some light.

'Mat, it's all right,' Meghan called, then handed me the phone and went to him.

I used the pause to examine our progress. It was depressingly small. A few dents here and there. Nothing a good painter and decorator couldn't cover up. The door was made of tough stuff. I hunted through the heap of items we'd collected before the torch gave out. We'd already tried to jemmy the door with all the bits of metal and they'd been either too thick to get between the edge and frame or so thin they bent at the slightest force. I rested my damp forehead on the door and listened for noises beyond. At first, we'd been terrified our efforts to break out would bring Jean back but Mat's state meant we had no choice. All was still quiet except for Meghan telling Mat we'd be out as soon as we could and not to worry. He just needed to keep still and all would be well.

She didn't mention the two-hour deadline, after which he would probably lose his leg. I took a quick look at my phone. Three minutes to eleven. Eighty-three minutes left. And we didn't have eighty-three minutes to get out of the cellar. We had eighty-three to get Mat to a hospital, have him assessed and then treated.

'Phiney.' There was a tinge of desperation to Meghan's voice. 'He's passed out again. Keep going.'

'How is he?'

'Clammy skin. Pulse rate around 120. We have to get him out of here now.'

Haemorrhagic shock. Meghan didn't need to tell me.

I stared at the frame and willed my brain to work. Think, Phiney, think. Battering the door was getting us nowhere. Take a moment to work it out.

But something nagged at the edges of my thoughts. Distracting me. I took a deep breath and realised what it was.

'Meghan. Get over here.'

She came straightaway.

'Put your nose to the door. What can you smell?'

She inhaled a long breath. 'Nothing. Well, the place stinks and I stink. Of sweat. Of blood.'

'Nothing else?'

She rammed her nose against the edge of the door. 'Smoke,' she said quietly. 'I can smell smoke.'

'Jean. It must be Jean. Either Arch told her he was going to burn the place down or she found the stuff in his van.'

No wonder she hadn't bothered to finish us off. Corpses could tell no tales. Burnt ones gave even less away.

'How long have we got?' Meghan asked.

'Don't know.' I wrenched my thoughts back to Mat. 'But it doesn't matter. Mat'll be dead if we don't get him help very quickly. Keep out of the way.'

I threw myself against the door. Knowing it was useless but unable to stop myself. It thudded in its frame. Some vague memory of one of the firemen who'd spoken to us as part of my training came back. He'd talked about breaking into things. Mainly cars after RTAs but he'd digressed onto everyday doors. The weakest part of a door, he'd said, was the hinges, normally only held on by a few shallow screws. Kick that part of the door and the hinges would pop out. The trouble was he'd been talking from the perspective of someone outside kicking the door in. If I kicked I only slammed the door against the frame holding it firmly in place.

I looked at the hinges all the same. There were two of them. And he was right. They were puny. Held in place by a flap with three small screws. A screwdriver. If only I had a screwdriver. Or a Swiss Army type thing with lots of gadgets. If I ever got out of here, I'd buy one. Maybe two. And I'd never leave home without them. Never.

'Phiney,' Meghan said. The harsh smell of smoke was unmistakeable now.

'Just thinking. Working out the best way to get out.'

The answer had to be the hinges.

I tried to ram the edge of an old metal shelf bracket in and under to lever a hinge out but the stupid thing had been tightly sunk into the wood of the door on one side and was hidden by the doorframe on the other. The carpenter had done an excellent job. Fucker, I muttered. You fucker. Didn't you think that one day someone might need to get out in an emergency? When you were using all your neat little tools. Tapping away with a hammer on a sharp, sharp chisel. Glorying in the exactness of your work. Bastard. I realised I was muttering loudly. But I didn't care.

'Phiney,' Meghan's voice was full of alarm. 'No, Mat. No. Stay with me.' She grabbed the crate and shoved it under his legs, raising them and slapping his face. 'Come on, Mat, you can do this. We're going to get you out. Phiney, what are you waiting for?'

I slammed the hinge with the bracket. Drove it into the frame and shouted and swore. And cried. And smashed and smashed. Something splintered and the shelf bracket snapped and broke.

I pointed the phone at the hinge. It was intact but the force of my anger had dented it. Had made one corner of it curl away from the surface of the door. I tried to lever it off with the shovel but only succeeded in breaking the shovel's rusty edge.

Don't stop. Above all, I mustn't stop. No time. No time even to cast a glance at Meghan working on Mat. No time to pray she'd keep him alive.

I took an old brass coalscuttle and in a great swinging arc I drove it behind the curl. The impact juddered along my bones and knocked my jaw shut. I didn't care. I'd jammed it behind the hinge. It gave me a lever and I dug my feet into the wood and pulled with every last muscle. No screaming, this time. No noise except the crunch of the scuttle wrenching the hinge off the door and Meghan talking, talking, talking. And the grunt of someone's breath forced out of their body. My breath. My body.

The hinge came off.

It took minutes that felt like hours.

The door didn't open. It was still held in place by the lower hinge and the bolt but the top corner hung away from the frame. Smoke curled through the gap. A gap wide enough to wedge the tip of a poker in. To slam the poker through with the base of the scuttle. To lever the bottom hinges off and wrench the door open. Smoke billowed through the corridor.

'999,' Meghan said. 'You know what to tell them.'

I tore up the steps, my feet slipping and tripping, only the momentum of my speed keeping me upright as thoughts tore through my brain. The average ambulance response time in Coventry was good. Around seven minutes. Except Mat might not have seven minutes. If he was going into shock, he might not have two minutes.

The house was thick with smoke. Flames crackled nearby. I tripped and fell against the wall and screamed. A pipe, running down from the ceiling to the floor, carried the heat of the fire and burned a line of pain in my skin. No time. We had no time. The back door was shut but the padlock and chain still lay on the ground. I wrenched it open and staggered out into the dark.

Torches blinded me. Voices shouted. An ambulance swirled blue light. I was beyond caring how it was possible but screamed at the paramedics to get down to Mat and, as they rushed towards me, a dog thrust its nose into my hand and barked. It was Jack.

Dora's voice rose over the mayhem, calling him to her.

Chapter Forty:
Phiney Wistman

Afterwards

The ambulance took Mat to our hospital, where Mr Ahmad, the top surgeon, roused from sleep by Meghan's pleading but insistent call, met us and a cavalcade of doctors and nurses rushed Mat into theatre straightaway. The three of us – me, Meghan and Dora – paced up and down the relatives' room, watching the relentless light slide across the sky as day arrived.

In jerky snatches of conversation, Dora told us how, behind the scenes, police forces had actually been communicating, the Poulter name providing the link. Coventry police, looking into Michael Poulter's death, had been contacted by Derby Police and wanted to interview Dora. She'd been on her way down, deeply worried because she'd heard nothing from us, when Mr Knowles had rung her. When we hadn't returned with his ladder, he'd come looking and found it by the wall and Jack in the car nearby but no sign of us. He'd called the number on Jack's collar. Dora went to Berkswell House straightaway but, by the time she arrived, Mr Knowles had climbed the ladder himself. He'd seen smoke drifting over the stubbly, moonlit lawn and a glimmer of fire through a small, unboarded window so he'd called the emergency services.

We told her about Arch and Jean, and bits and pieces of the rest of it.

And in between, we waited.

We drank coffee and we walked up and down.

Meghan cried a bit. Then apologised for crying.

We waited some more. And walked some more.

A nurse, one I didn't know, told us politely the police wanted to talk to us. I told her to get rid of them. But less politely.

Still we waited. Now slumped over the chairs. Eyes gritty and sore with tiredness and smoke. Clothes stiff with Mat's blood.

And Mr Ahmad came in.

Mat was alive. He would stay alive. He still had two legs. And there was every chance they would both work. There was a lot more but none of us took it in. It was enough.

'Could we see him?' Dora asked.

Mr Ahmad shook his head. 'Later on today, maybe. For now, he is asleep and needs to be.'

Meghan crumpled to the floor.

Another stampede of nurses, porters and trolleys. Smoke inhalation, shock and exhaustion, they decided, but not severe. Nevertheless, a few hours on oxygen and a check-up tomorrow. Mr Ahmad looked me over too, found the burn on my arm and decided to admit me as well.

'Some of the burning is quite deep,' he said. 'I think we should keep an eye on it and you may need some pain relief.'

He was right. His probing, gentle as it was, had unleashed a whiplash of agony running up my arm. At the edge of my vision, Dora hovered, white and lost.

'Take my keys,' I said. 'Get Jack from the porters and go back to the flat. Get some sleep.'

She looked unsure.

'We'll be OK. None of this is serious. I'm a nurse. I know.'

I couldn't avoid the police the following morning. Not that I particularly wanted to. Once I'd checked that Mat was still doing fine I was determined that Jean wasn't going to get away with what she'd done.

'Dr Storer,' I said to the two police as I was ushered into the ward office where they were waiting. 'Jean Storer. She did this. She shot Mat and left us to die in the fire.'

A sudden wave of emotion choked me. One of them helped me sit down. The other, whose tired face made me wonder if she'd been at the hospital all night, spoke.

'We're looking for Dr Storer. Don't worry, Ms Wistman. I'm DI Blake. My colleague is PC Thomas. I appreciate this is a difficult time but I need you to confirm a few things for us. We spoke with Mrs Patterson last night –'

'Really?'

Poor Dora. They must have nabbed her as soon as she left the hospital. Of course they did.

'We had a burning house and gunshot wound to investigate, Ms Wistman. Naturally, we were keen to interview anyone involved as soon as possible.'

'Then you know about Poulters and the vaccine?'

'Your grandmother told us that an incident in' – she checked her notes – 'in 1957 was the start of this but, for the moment, I'd just like you to confirm what happened last night.'

I told her as best I could about breaking in, about Arch grabbing Meghan, how we thought Jean had shot him as well as Mat, and how she'd left us to burn.

'Is the fire out?' I asked, at the end.

'Yes. And I can tell you that we have recovered a body, although identification is going to be difficult. The fire was fierce in the centre of the house.'

'Was he shot?'

'We'll have to wait for the post-mortem.' She shot a glance over to her colleague. 'I think we can let you go now, Ms Wistman. We'll call you to come into the station and sign a witness statement in the next couple of days.'

They both stood but I didn't.

'What will happen now?'

'As I said we're looking for Dr Storer and we'll want to talk to your friends as soon as they're well enough. But you have nothing to worry about. It's unlikely we'll charge you with breaking and entering, and Poulters have already indicated that they have no wish to take any action against you.'

'But what about the contaminated vaccine and the cover-up? Didn't Dora, Mrs Patterson, explain?'

She sighed. 'Your grandmother told us about it in great detail, but it was a long time ago and it appears to have been an accident. I'm not sure an actual crime was committed.'

'But people have been killed because of it.'

'You're referring to Philip Mason?'

I nodded.

'We will pass on the information you've given us to our colleagues in Ullswater but there is no evidence that it was anything other than an accident. And, besides, if I understood correctly, you all think Simon Archibald was the perpetrator?'

I nodded again. I couldn't speak.

'Although we need official confirmation, I don't think there's any doubt that the body recovered is his. He's dead, Ms Wistman. We can't prosecute a dead man.'

Dora was waiting for me back in the ward with clean clothes and a tense, worried expression.

'I've been with the police,' I said and patted the bed.

She sat down, caught sight of herself in the window and started tidying the fuzz of hair that had escaped from her bun.

'They said they'd spoken to you last night.'

'They were waiting for me when I left. I wanted to wait but they said it had to be then. And I was so tired.'

She'd told them everything we'd told her, too shocked and exhausted to decide if that was right or wrong. About Arch and Jean. She'd tried to explain about the missing documents and the lethal vaccine but she only knew the bare bones of the story and the police had lost interest once they knew there was no immediate danger.

'They're not going to investigate, are they?' she asked.

'No.'

Her face contorted with a hundred emotions. I put an arm round her.

'I'm sorry,' I said. 'You must be angry because of Grandad but I don't know what else we can do. I'm too tired to think at the moment. The main thing is they know about Jean. I don't want her to get away with what she did to Mat.'

Three days later, as I was leaving the hospital, my phone rang and I found out about Jean. It had been three days of no information from the police, of waking nightly, convinced I could smell smoke or, worse, blood, and of sitting in the hospital holding Meghan's hand tightly every time Mat's temperature rose or he seemed confused.

'It's Susan Storer here.'

'Hello.'

'Aunty's dead.' Her voice was flat. 'Jean.'

'I see.'

'The police just came round to tell me.'

'I'm sorry.'

'They didn't tell me much. Just that it was suicide.'

I couldn't think what to say but Susan carried on regardless.

'So, I phoned a neighbour. The police found her. The local ones. He said they'd come to arrest her. Is that true?'

'It's possible.'

'She wasn't in the house, so they searched the land and they found her body. Leaning against a stone wall, it was, overlooking the hills. She loved the view there. There was a syringe next to her.'

She stopped again as though waiting for me to say something.

'Did she –'

'Leave a letter? No. Nothing. Just her will on her desk along with some more notes for me. I'm supposed to be writing her memoirs.'

A sudden spurt of rage took me by surprise. Jean had escaped. She'd never have to answer for what she'd done. I'd never get to stand up in court and accuse her to her face.

'This is to do with the meeting, isn't it?' Susan's voice rose a notch. 'What was it all about? Did you find out?'

I owed her. I knew I did. She'd done her best to help me when I'd gone to see her but I didn't know what to say. Above all, I didn't want to tell her that her aunt's last action had been attempted murder.

'Something happened years and years ago. Something she was involved in.' I crossed my fingers and lied. 'Maybe she regretted it.'

'Years ago? When she worked at Poulters?'

Susan would be able to work it out for herself. She knew who'd been at the reunion.

'Yes,' I said. 'But I can't tell you anything else. It's not really my story. I'm sorry.'

And I cut the call.

The words rang in my head. *It's not my story.* But it was. It was my story now.

Chapter Forty-One: Phiney Wistman

Afterwards

It rained the day of Grandad's funeral. A light rain that dampened the air and made the leaves gleam and little droplets sparkle on the petals of the flowers that lined the path to the crematorium. They were the only bright spots of the afternoon. That and the fact that Mat walked all the way from the car to his seat with only a stick to help him. He'd been out of hospital a few days, with Meghan calling in every day to badger him to eat properly and do the gentle exercises the hospital physio had prescribed. I was in Matlock, helping Dora with the arrangements for the funeral I didn't want to have.

A fierce kernel of anger and frustration had smouldered inside me ever since the police had told us that, with Arch and Jean dead, they'd closed the case. Dora had asked them what would happen about the contaminated polio vaccine and they'd said there was no one to prosecute as all those involved were no longer alive.

I spent a lot of time brooding over the 1957 photo of Richard Poulter – the fat-cat tycoon who'd profited most from the cover-up and who had evaded all retribution. It rankled. Something felt unfinished, unresolved, but I succeeded in tamping it down and keeping control of my grumpiness through all the funeral preparations.

I'd wanted something very quiet and private and been startled when Dora announced that it would be open to everybody and that we would have a hearse and flowers and a full service.

'Wilf was a wonderful man,' she said. 'I want him to have the send-off he deserves.'

'But people know he killed himself. How can you bear the unanswered questions in their faces?'

'It's not like that, Phiney. Wilf had a lot of friends. They'll want to pay their respects. If I stop them, they *will* think there's something wrong. Anyway, the funeral will be about his life, not his death.'

Most people had assumed Grandad had been unable to face some new phase of his polio and we hadn't contradicted them. It was easier that way although the injustice of that rankled too.

But now, as Dora and I walked into the chapel ahead of Grandad's coffin, I thought she might have been right. It was full of friendly faces and hands reaching out to clasp Dora's as she walked down the aisle. The service started and I stood and sat and knelt when required but my head was suddenly full of memories of Grandad's life. Of him reading the *Just So* stories to me when I was little and laughing in the face of Mum's outrage when I dyed my hair blonde. His patience when I failed my GCSEs after she died and his pleasure when I went back to school a year later and passed them. His pride when I finished my nursing training and, above all, I remembered the quiet happiness that showed in the ease of his movement and the smile lines that radiated from his eyes in the weeks after I'd lied about being tested.

'You were right to be happy, Grandad,' I whispered. I wasn't sure about life after death but I hoped, if any bits of Grandad were still paying attention, he knew my lie had become the truth.

That evening, Meghan, Mat and I sat in the backyard behind Dora's house in the dusk, listening to the shrieks of the neighbour's children as they lobbed balls through a basketball hoop fixed to the garage, and smelling the savoury aroma of a hundred barbecues. Dora, exhausted, had gone straight to bed after the funeral and it was the first time the three of us had been able to talk properly since the night of the fire. The muttered conversations in hospital, interrupted by nurses and doctors, had only been enough to fill Mat in on what had happened.

'So,' I said. 'What are we going to do?'

'About what?' Meghan said.

'The conspiracy. The polio vaccine. The fact that all those children were given polio by the very thing that was supposed to protect them.'

'What can we do?' Meghan said. 'The police aren't interested.'

'The police were never the answer,' Mat said. 'The solution was always going to be the press.'

'Well, then?'

'You want it out there?' Mat looked startled.

'Perhaps. I can't leave it like this.'

Mat kicked at the gravel with his good leg as he thought. 'I'm not sure what we can do. It's a good story but no paper would touch it without vastly better proof than we have. Especially not with Poulters' lawyers breathing down their neck and threatening libel suits. If we'd had the evidence, or if Vivian had been prepared to make a statement... I don't suppose...' He shot me a questioning glance.

I shook my head. We'd be able to track her down but I knew she'd never get involved. 'I do have this.' I handed him the letter Philip had written to Vivian and she'd left with me. 'Luckily, people like Philip still write things by hand, so there should be no problem proving it's genuine.'

Mat and Meghan read it.

'It mentions everybody,' I said. 'And Poulters. And that there was a cover-up. And we've got the list of people who attended the reunion at The Herbert. A lot of them conveniently dead. Susan Storer would help us. I told you she phoned me. She was there even if she didn't go in. And –'

But Mat cut me off. 'It's better than nothing. Much better than nothing. But it's not enough. If only we still had the evidence Vivian left in Berkswell House.'

I smiled and passed him my phone with the photos I'd taken in Richard Poulter's old office in Berkswell House, after I'd retrieved the documents from their hiding place in the window shutter box. Photos I'd taken with Mat's words ringing in my ears. *I've got a record on my phone. I photograph everything straightaway. It's much safer that way.*

Mat flicked back and forward through the photos. And when he looked back up at me, his face was filled with excitement. 'I think it's enough. With this and Philip's letter and the proof that these people met.'

'And don't forget the 1957 photo and article. If it does nothing else, it proves that all these people worked together at Poulters.'

He handed my phone back. 'Send me the photos, please. I need to think about the best way to handle it.'

Ideas raced across his face and his elation reached out and gripped me. It would be a big break for him and no one deserved it more. And I would get… what? I wasn't sure, but I knew I wanted it. Satisfaction? Revenge? A soothing of the rage I felt about Grandad?

'I don't think you should do it.' Meghan's words cut through the buzz of my thoughts.

'But, Megs. Why?'

'Because maybe Jean's arguments were right.' She leaned towards us, her face serious with the look of Meghan the ward sister. 'Revealing the truth would have caused more deaths in the long term. And it would do the same now. Phiney, you know parents are becoming more reluctant to vaccinate children. It's serious. You'd be thrusting ammunition into the hands of the anti-vaxxers.' Her deep-brown eyes softened. 'I know it would be a major coup for you, Mat. And, Phi, I get that you want… justice? But Jean and Arch are dead. So are Richard, Owen and Harry. They're the ones who bear the responsibility.'

She paused and I felt my excitement drain away. Was she right? I saw the same deflation on Mat's face.

'We need to be careful, anyway,' Mat said.

'Careful?'

'I've had time to think about what happened at Berkswell House. And before. There are things I don't understand.'

'Well, let's find out about them.'

He glanced at Meghan.

'Let's not rattle any more cages, Phiney,' she said. 'Mat's still recovering.'

'But they're all dead,' I said. 'There's no more danger.'

'We should talk to Dora first,' Mat said. 'She's as much part of this as we are.'

'I want it all to be over,' Dora said when we asked her. 'It was a tiny part of Wilf's life and I want to forget it.' She paused. 'But I do want justice too. It killed Wilf and he didn't deserve that.'

'No,' I said. 'You're right.'

'Mind you, I don't want people going round saying it was Wilf's fault so maybe we shouldn't do anything. Although, of course, Wilf wanted the tragedy to be out in the open. That's what Philip said in his letter, wasn't it? He said Wilf had voted for it all to be revealed?'

'Yes.'

'I'm sorry, none of this is very helpful. I think I'm going to leave it up to you. Is that all right?'

'We need time to decide,' Mat said. 'And I want to set a few things up.'

We agreed to talk soon and Mat and Meghan went back to Coventry while I helped Dora with the slow process of sorting through Grandad's things.

A couple of days later, a text arrived from Mat with a link to an article in *The Bookseller*.

Feodor & Fielding are to publish a biography of Richard Poulter, the charismatic founder of Poulters Pharmaceuticals, written by Susan Storer, author of biographies on figures as diverse as Eugene Vidocq, the world's first undercover agent, and Elizabeth Cromwell, queen in all but name.

Storer said: 'Richard Poulter was at the forefront of the UK pharmaceuticals industry during the post-war boom years. He is a fascinating and charismatic figure.'

James Poulter, CEO of Poulters Pharmaceuticals, said: 'We are delighted that Richard Poulter's contribution to the UK pharmaceutical industry is going to be shared with a wider audience.'

Theresa Irvine, commissioning editor at Feodor & Fielding, said: 'Poulters have given Storer unprecedented access to their archives to gather material for what promises to be an authoritative account...'

Mat rang me a couple of minutes later.

'Someone's been bought,' he said. 'And I think it's obvious who did the buying. When are you coming back?'

'Soon.'

Dora hugged me goodbye at the station.

'Please check in on Jack, if you have a minute? Make sure he's being looked after properly?' She caught sight of my expression. 'I'm sorry. I've already said that a few times, haven't I?'

'Yes, but it's OK. I will, though I'm sure he's fine.'

I remembered Jack's new owner, Mrs Oliver, in her wheelchair talking about her childhood polio. I'd like to see her again, when I wasn't as distracted as I'd been then.

The train appeared in the distance. Dora hugged me again.

'Phiney, you will come back, won't you? To see me, I mean. I know things haven't always been –'

I hugged her.

'I'll be back before you know it,' I said.

And I would, I thought. And not totally out of duty. We would still drive each other mad from time to time but... Well, just but.

As the train pulled out of the station, Mat phoned. The carriage was empty this time so I answered. He cut off my opening chat.

'James Poulter called me. He wants to meet us.'

'He can want all he likes.'

'Please, Phiney.'

'I'm not stopping you going. I wonder how much he'll offer you to keep quiet.'

'I just want some answers.'

'Like I said, I'm not stopping you.'

'It would be better if you came. I'll get more out of him. Please, Phiney.'

I couldn't say no to Mat.

'OK, if it's really that important.'

'It is. It's vital.'

'Why?'

'Phiney, I know you've had a lot to deal with over the last few weeks but you must see James Poulter could be involved in much of what has happened.'

Chapter Forty-Two:
Phiney Wistman

A few days later

We met James at Berkswell House. He'd suggested somewhere in town, but Mat had asked to meet here. I thought he wanted to lay a few ghosts to rest. It had rained the night before but today was hot and still. Mat levered himself out of the taxi and I stood by with the stick he still needed. However, nothing could distract our eyes from the sodden, black heaps of rubble strewn far and wide, nor the smell of acrid and damp ash.

James was leaning against his car and staring at the ruin, his eyes hidden behind dark sunglasses. He wore chinos and a short-sleeved shirt with a sweatshirt draped casually over his shoulders. Mat, to my annoyance, had worn a suit although I was in jeans. James seemed younger and more inoffensive than I'd expected. Not that I really knew what I'd expected. As he approached, I could see the heavy eyebrows and beginnings of jowls that marked him out as Richard's grandson. He came straight over to us and held out his hand.

'James Poulter,' he said. 'And you must be Matthew Torrington and Josephine Wistman.'

He took off his sunglasses and we shook hands. His eyes were a watery green with deep shadows under them. The harsh lines running between his nose and the sides of his mouth etched tiredness into his skin, which was the colour of someone who spent all his time away from natural light.

'You wanted to see it,' he said, gesturing towards the mountains of black-stained rubble and debris.

'There's nothing left,' I said.

He smiled. 'There was more – a few walls and part of the ground floor ceiling in the far side of the house but it wasn't safe so we had to knock it down. Have a look round if you want to. I'll wait for you in the lodge.' He pointed to the old building by the side gate Mat and I had used to get in the first time. 'There's coffee in there.'

He left us.

Mat told the taxi to wait.

'Really?' I said. 'It'll cost a fortune.'

'Yes,' he said. 'I want to be able to leave when I choose. Let's go and talk to him.'

But I hesitated. James had told Mat he wanted to know what had happened. The police had told him the outline but he would like to hear it from us.

'I still don't like the idea of telling him everything. Not if you're suspicious of him.'

Mat had been irritatingly unforthcoming about James, saying he wanted me to come to the meeting with an open mind.

'Let me do the talking. I won't tell him more than necessary and I suspect he knows it already.'

'Nothing about Vivian,' I said quickly.

'Of course not.'

'OK,' I said taking one last look at the remains of what had been Berkswell House. But Mat hadn't finished.

'Be careful. James is Richard's grandson. Everyone I've spoken to says he's a chip off the old block. Successful, dynamic –'

'I know.'

'But don't forget Richard was also ruthless, manipulative and utterly without morals.'

I thought back to the casually dressed and relaxed James who had met us. He seemed OK, really.

'You think he'll try to buy us. Like Susan?'

Mat looked at me. 'Possibly. Although he'll try to make it seem something different. I just want to get the answers to some questions from him and then –'

He broke off.

'And then?'

'And then we'll leave.'

The lodge windows were wide open although the smell of mildew lingered. The long hot summer had dried the damp but it had left stains on the patchwork of different wallpapers. Someone had put a mismatched set of stools round the old wooden counter that jutted into the room and James was sitting there with a jug of coffee and three Aston Villa FC mugs in front of him.

'Seen enough?'

We nodded.

'Coffee?'

The smell curled its way over to me. It was good stuff. I nodded again. I disliked what James Poulter stood for but I could drink his coffee.

'There's power here then,' Mat said. We took seats on the opposite side of the counter to James.

'Yes,' he said, as he poured coffee into the mugs. 'They ran it in for the security cameras, I think, and left this socket working too. This was your great-grandfather's office, Ms Wistman.'

So, Harry had worked in this tiny space. And Grandad during those few weeks in the summer of 1957. Forced to by Harry, despite being completely unsuited to the work. Despite being in pain. Having his photo taken as a not-so-subtle advertisement of how much Poulters was invested in the local community. My ever-present anger burned a little hotter. It was a mistake to meet James here. The place was too full of the past. We should have met him somewhere impersonal.

Mat tapped the counter as though drawing a meeting to order. 'You asked us to tell you what led up to the fire here. So, I might as well start.'

If James was startled by Mat taking control, he hid it well, merely nodding and taking a sip of his coffee.

Mat told the story with his usual flair but skated over a lot of the details. He didn't mention Vivian, merely saying that some notes Philip left had led us to suspect the evidence was at Berkswell House. Neither did he mention Mr Knowles nor Dora, and Meghan was merely referred to as a friend with a car. I watched James. He looked absorbed but it was impossible to tell what was going on behind his eyes.

When Mat finished, he offered more coffee. We waited while he made it, squatting down beside a socket in the far corner under a row of hooks. Then he settled himself back down, wrapping his hands round the mug.

'Thank you for telling me everything,' he said. 'You've explained some things that had been confusing me. I'm sorry, deeply sorry, that you had to go through what you did, although I know you'll think any apology from me is… maybe inappropriate.'

He paused as though expecting us to acknowledge the sensitivity of his words. Mat twitched but said nothing, and I hardened my face and stared at him. He was a Poulter. They deserved nothing from me.

He ignored the uncomfortable silence and went on talking.

'I was so shocked when my father told us what had happened in 1957 at the meeting at The Herbert that I stormed out. I should have stayed and spoken to Mr Patterson. I could see what a profound effect it had all had on him. I regret that very much. Along with regretting that my last words to my father were bitter. In the days after his death, I could think of nothing else.'

Again, he paused as though expecting us to react. I remembered Mat telling me he got more out of people by giving them a silence to fill than if he fired questions at them but this silence felt combative.

James pushed his fingertips into each other, stretching his hands in an arc as he appeared to think about what to say next.

'I think my father was murdered, you know?'

'We wondered,' Mat said.

'When the coroner told me she would have to refer his death to the police, I was appalled. She said it was probably nothing. Just a few signs that were unusual. But I think, deep down, I'd known his death was too convenient.' He placed his hands on the countertop. 'And when the police came wanting to interview Arch, I started to put it all together.'

This was news to me and, I saw, to Mat as well.

'The police came? When was that?' he asked.

'The morning of the night Berkswell House burned down. The police turned up at our London office. As a result, I think, of Mrs Patterson's insistence Arch was involved in your disappearance, Mr Torrington.'

Some of my faith in the police came back at that point.

'And what did Arch have to say?' Mat said.

'He wasn't there.' James sipped his coffee. 'After the meeting at The Herbert, he asked for time off. And, to be honest, I was happy to grant it. I never wanted to see him again.'

I remembered Susan's account of the reunion. What James had said didn't quite ring true. He and Arch had left together. Maybe Arch had asked for time off once they were alone.

'My father pulled no punches,' James continued. 'He told us Arch knew everything and that my grandfather had bought him off with a position as chauffeur. Grandad liked him, found him useful, but Dad couldn't bear the sight of him. I had briefly wondered why.'

Mat's leg jiggled under the counter. I glanced at him but he was utterly focused, on James.

'So, you had no contact with Arch after the meeting?' he asked.

'No contact? I'm not quite sure what you mean, Mr Torrington.' James smiled but there was an edge to his voice.

'I just wondered how Arch knew so much of what was going on?' Mat said. 'You'll know the police have traced Arch's car to Ullswater round about the time Philip Mason supposedly fell to his death. But I wondered how he knew Philip was a threat. Philip had voted against the truth coming out at the meeting. How did Arch know he'd changed his mind? How did Arch know Phiney had started asking questions?'

James's eyes flickered while Mat's words, with their suggestion of collusion, hung in the air.

'Jean, I'm afraid.' His voice was as calm and matter of fact as Mat's. 'I think Jean was giving Arch information and using him. She must have told him Philip was a threat. Philip spoke to us both, me and Jean, after Mr Patterson died. Did you know that?'

Mat nodded. 'I assumed he had.'

'Philip told me that your grandfather's suicide and Michael's death had made him change his mind. He wanted the truth out in the open. I'm sure he told Jean the same. He thought keeping it secret had turned it to a poison that was damaging us all. And now I wonder if he wasn't right. We all respected and trusted Jean. My father said she had something of Joan of Arc about her. Something pure and uncompromising that made you believe in her. But in the meeting, I wasn't so sure. I thought she'd hardened over the years. Her belief that they'd made the right and logical decision in 1957 had become a rigid refusal to see the human and illogical side of the affair.'

I didn't like James one scrap but he had a point. Something in Jean had warped.

'So you think Jean was behind everything Arch did?' Mat asked.

'I can't be sure but I agree with you that Arch was unlikely to have acted without help.'

Mat waited.

'And since hearing about her suicide, I've been wondering about Dad's murder.'

A shred of wallpaper with plaster attached to its back dropped off the ceiling and landed in the corner as a lorry rumbled past the lodge.

'Jean was in the same hotel as Dad,' James continued. 'I think Dad would have let her in if she'd come knocking. But if it had been

Arch? Probably not. There were possible traces of anaesthetic in his blood. Inconclusive. But I think that points to Jean as…'

His voice died away.

But he was right. It was unlikely Arch had done it.

Then another thought crawled into my mind. Jean wasn't the only person Michael would have let into his room without hesitation.

'And how did *you* feel about your father's determination to tell the truth?' Mat's voice was casual but I wondered if he too was thinking the unthinkable.

Or perhaps he'd thought it before we arrived.

'I wasn't happy about it. I cannot lie. But I think, if only Dad and I had had time, I would have been able to change his mind. Make him see how much damage it would have done, both to the vaccine industry as a whole and to Poulters.'

'Poulters, ha!' The exclamation came out before I could stop it.

'Yes, Ms Wistman, Poulters. Because Poulters isn't just me and my family. It's all the people who work for us. It's the suppliers who exist because of us. It's the pension companies who invest in us. They're the people who would suffer if scandal forced Poulters to close down. Dad would have realised how unfair that would be.'

James sipped at his coffee and watched Mat.

Mat gave a little sigh.

'What a pity your father didn't tell you in advance of the reunion so you could have said all that to him before he died.'

'Yes. It is a great pity. But this whole episode is a tragedy.'

James had just lied. I knew it. Mat knew it.

Arch had told Mat that James had had a long meeting with Michael a week before The Herbert reunion. He'd come out and stopped the sale of Berkswell House immediately. Why would he have done that if Michael hadn't told him about the vaccine then?

I felt as though we were playing a game whose rules I didn't understand no matter how hard I tried to make sense of them. And against an opponent who would break them without a second thought.

'Shall we go, then?' I knew I sounded rude and brattish but I didn't care. I had to get out.

'Sure.' Mat pushed his stool back and picked up his stick.

'Before you go, I wonder – I understand you're a journalist, Mr Torrington – would you feel able to tell me what you plan to do with the story?' James's voice was as bland as his beige chinos and matching sweatshirt.

Mat and I both spoke at the same time.

'We don't know what we're –' he began.

'We're going to publish it,' I burst out, my voice drowning out Mat's non-committal words. 'We're going to make sure Poulters' name will be forever associated with poisoning children.'

Actually, that wasn't true. I was still hopelessly unsure what we should do.

'We think justice needs to be done.' Mat backed me up.

'And Poulters need to pay the price.'

James narrowed his eyes at the word 'price', and I wondered if now was the moment he'd try to buy us.

'I see,' James said. 'I wonder if you've thought this through. It's an unsubstantiated story at best.'

He paused and sipped at his coffee again.

'You have no proof. No reputable newspaper or publisher will touch it. And if you do succeed in telling the story, I won't deny it. I won't take legal action. I won't give it the oxygen of publicity. I'll say I know nothing about it. That anyone who might have been involved is dead. Poulters will weather it one way or another, but you, Mr Torrington, it won't do your career much good, will it? Publishing dubious and unsupported stories is hardly top-rank journalism and I think that is what you aspire to.'

Mat smiled at the scorn in James's voice and shook his head. The fury simmering inside me over the last weeks broke through.

'And what if we do have the –'

Mat kicked me under the table.

'What happened to the security firm?' he asked quickly.

James's gaze flickered between the two of us.

'The security firm didn't patrol the night Phiney broke in, and the cameras weren't working,' Mat went on.

In the midst of everything else, I'd forgotten the blank eye of the camera by the back door of Berkswell House and suddenly I realised how odd it was.

'Why was that?'

'An administrative error,' James said smoothly. 'The demolition was due to start the next day with the clearing of the site. The demolition company provides its own security. It's much easier, with all their comings and goings, if they do it. But there was a lack of clarity and the security company ceased operations at the end of the previous day rather than the following morning.'

Mat nodded. 'I see,' he said.

'Anything else?'

'Yes.' Mat cleared his throat. 'As you pointed out, I am a journalist. You should know that I have already written the story about the lethal polio vaccine and Poulters' conspiracy to cover it up. My editor and various of my friends and family have copies, along with such proofs as we have and video recordings of Phiney, myself, and other people who witnessed what has been going on. It makes compelling reading and watching. And it would be even more compelling if something were to happen to either of us.'

He squeezed my hand under the table when he mentioned the video recordings, but he needn't have worried. My expression was fixed in stone.

He stood as he finished speaking, nodded politely and walked out. I followed him without a word and got into the taxi too.

'Let's get out of here,' I said.

'Well, he didn't try to buy us.' I said once the taxi had dropped us outside my flat.

'No.' Mat laughed. 'One look at your face would have told him he didn't stand a chance. I should have known I could rely on your grumpiness to win through. But he was building up to threatening us.'

'You can't think he'd get rid of us?'

'Of course he would. But only if he thought he'd get away with it. And I've made it clear enough he wouldn't. We should make those videos, though.'

He took his phone out of his pocket and turned it on. Messages and alerts started bleeping. Situation normal. But it felt good. The meeting with James had shaken me.

'Do you think he killed his father?'

'Let's talk about it in your flat.'

He followed me up the stairs, tapping at his screen as he went, and pulled his jacket off once we were inside, throwing it on the bed.

'Do you?' I repeated.

'Perhaps. I'm sure it was either James or Jean just as I'm sure one of them was using Arch. I thought it was more likely to be James behind Arch. The things Jean said to us in the cellar didn't seem right if she'd been using him all the time. And there are other reasons.' Mat sat down as I searched in the fridge for something cool to drink. 'You said the chains at the back door had been cut. Why? Arch knew the padlock code. He knew all the codes. He used them when he took me there. So, Jean must have cut them. But if she was in cahoots with Arch he would have given the code to her or let her in. No, I don't think either of them expected to see the other. I think Jean was there purely because of Vivian's call.'

I poured us both a glass of water. Mat drank his immediately. He hated being thirsty since his incarceration in the cellar. But when I put mine to my mouth, my teeth rattled against the glass.

'So, who killed Michael?'

'Jean or James. I don't know which.'

'He's an evil, evil man,' I said and put my water down because my hands were shaking too and wiped my eyes with a piece of kitchen roll. 'And I'm not crying because I'm unhappy. I'm angry. So, so angry.'

Mat nodded.

'He's going to get away with it all, isn't he? There's no point telling the police.'

'No.' His phone rang. He glanced at it but he didn't answer. 'But we could cause him a lot of grief.'

'You want to publish, don't you?'

'Of course I do. I'm a journalist. We believe things should be out there. And I believe the story of the vaccine and the cover-up is important. There will be consequences. Some of them will be bad. Meg is right. And James is too in that respect. But it's not my responsibility to worry about that. People deserve to be told the truth and make their own minds up.'

His phone bleeped and he looked at it again.

'And it's my job to put the truth out there. Honestly, you should be overjoyed that you live in a country where what goes on *is* written about, whether it's in the courts or in government or in business. Just the threat of the public knowing keeps the James Poulters of this world vaguely honest. They pay fortunes to try and control what's written about them but they'll never completely succeed. Not while the press is still free.' His voice throbbed as the words poured out of him in a torrent. 'So, every time some unfaithful footballer gets an injunction to stop us printing his name, you should be furious, because it's another tiny step towards controlling the press and, therefore, the truth.'

He paused for a few seconds, then laughed.

'OK. I've said my piece. Up to you now, Phiney. I told you I'd let you decide and I will,' he said. 'And now, I really need to pick up that message.'

I vaguely listened as Mat spoke to BBC Midlands Today. There'd been a major accident on the M6 and they needed someone to meet their cameraman at the scene and report. Matt said he could be there in thirty minutes and called a taxi.

'I should be driving again in a week,' he said. 'Short distances anyway. Which will be good because I'm spending a fortune on taxis. I'm sorry to go but...'

'It's fine. I'm going to meet Meghan anyway. Come and join us later. We're going to the Zanzibar.'

'Er, actually, maybe not this time. I don't know when I'll be finished.' And he blushed. 'I'll wait downstairs for the taxi.' He grabbed his jacket and left me to my thoughts.

Everything was a mess in my brain. The meeting with James had made things worse. What was the answer? What was the right thing to do?

No blinding flash of clarity came to me as I walked to meet Meg but I did realise two things. There wasn't going to be a right decision. I just had to go with my gut. And secondly, I needed to decide soon for my own sake. It was time to move on.

Meg was already at the Zanzibar, sitting out the back with two mojitos in front of her. I sipped mine cautiously. It had no alcohol in it. I smiled at her.

'Work OK?' I asked.

'Understaffed. Two agency nurses on today. We need you back.'

'Next week. I told HR.'

'How was the meeting with James?'

'Hasn't Mat told you?'

She didn't blush but she laughed.

'I asked him to come along tonight,' I said. 'But he said he wouldn't this time.'

'Yup. He wanted me to tell you about us without him being around.'

'Us?'

'Yes. Us,' she said. 'Us. Me and Mat. Like Romeo and Juliet. George and Amal. John and Yoko. Beyoncé and JayZ.'

'Yes, yes, I get it,' I said. 'Did you think I hadn't guessed?'

'I thought you might have. Mat wanted to be sure. How did you know?'

'Gut feeling,' I said. 'After the funeral, I just knew.'

She looked up at me. 'You don't mind?' she asked.

'Why should I mind?'

'I know you like him.'

'As a friend, Megs. A very good friend. Like a brother, and I've always wanted one. Besides, I prefer my men...'

'Sportier?'

'Yup, and smarter.'

'Oh, Mat will be.' A smile creased the corners of her eyes. 'You can be sure of that. Just give me a bit of time.'

I picked up the glass to hide my own smile. I wasn't at all sure Meghan would find it so easy to get Mat to do what she said.

'So? How did it go?' she asked.

I told her briefly what had happened.

'Mat wants you to publish,' she said.

'And you?'

'On balance, no.'

'I thought so.'

'So, have you decided?' she said.

I opened my mouth to say *No*, but realised that was no longer true. Something had settled inside me and I knew what I wanted.

'Yes,' I said.

Author's Note

The idea of a problem with the polio vaccine in the UK in the 1950s is entirely a figment of my imagination. The manufacture of polio vaccine in the UK was marked by an adherence to exemplary standards of care. However, the 1957 Coventry Polio Epidemic and the Cutter Incident are not my inventions.

The Cutter Incident took place in the USA in 1955. I am indebted to *The Cutter Incident: How America's First Polio Vaccine Led to the Growing Vaccine Crisis* by Paul A. Offit, MD, for a fascinating account of the tragedy as well as an explanation of the manufacture of polio vaccine and a host of other interesting facts and insights on the pharmaceutical industry.

Gareth Millward's article '"A matter of commonsense": the Coventry poliomyelitis epidemic 1957 and the British public' gives an interesting account of the tragedy, which saw more than a hundred children left paralysed or dead.

I am also grateful to the heritage archives at GSK for information about polio vaccine manufacture as well as some fabulous footage.

I started writing *A Quiet Contagion* before any of us had ever heard the word 'Covid' and, since the pandemic started, I've wondered several times whether I should be writing a book based on the Cutter Incident – a very negative episode in the history of vaccination. So, let me give you some other facts:

- *Between 1950 and 1957, the average number of paralytic polio cases per year in England and Wales was around 2,800.*
- *Mass vaccination against polio began in the late 1950s.*

- *Between 1960 and 1967, the average number of paralytic polio cases per year in England and Wales was around 166.*
- *There hasn't been a case of polio caught in the UK since the mid-1980s.*

Source: [https://www.gov.uk/government/publications/notifiable-diseases-historic-annual-totals].

Acknowledgements

I always enjoy researching my books, whether it's learning about climbing and sailing for my Jen Shaw series, reading about other people's experiences to inform my characters' actions or simply exploring the places where my stories happen. Some of my research is done through talking to experts, some of it through visiting places or trying things out for myself, but a huge amount relies on other people's words, images and videos, in books and on the internet. So I want to thank everyone who takes the time to share their knowledge, their opinions and their experiences. I'd particularly like to thank Jill Moretto, Heritage Archivist at GSK, for all her help.

A Quiet Contagion is my third book to be published by VERVE Books and, as ever, it's been a huge pleasure to work with the VERVE team. Thank you Sarah, Hollie, Ellie and Paru. Thank you also to Nick Rennison for his eagle-eyed attention to detail and the addition of a large number of commas and other punctuation that have made this book far easier to read. My editor, Jenna Gordon, has once again worked her magic on *A Quiet Contagion* with her suggestions and ideas.

I am very grateful to all my writer friends and non-writer friends who have read early and late drafts of *A Quiet Contagion* and told me what they think. It's always fascinating and helpful to hear their thoughts. I'd particularly like to thank Nikki Hughes, Debi Alper, Janette Owen, Sandra Davies, Thea Burgess, Jonathan Crowe, Madeleine Hill and Marion Silverthorne.

A big thank you to the people who are always there for me: my friends and family; my agent, Amanda Preston at LBA Books; and my husband, Alex.

Book Club Questions

1) Were you aware of the Coventry polio epidemic before reading this book?
2) Phiney is extremely health-conscious and yet has chosen a career in nursing, where she is surrounded by sickness. Discuss Phiney's attitude towards illness, and the reasons behind it.
3) Phiney harbours complicated feelings towards Dora, and this often shows in their interactions. Do you think Phiney's treatment of Dora is fair?
4) To what extent do you think Mat's motivation to help Phiney and Dora stems from his desire to write a good newspaper story?
5) If you had been present at the Poulter's laboratory on that night in July 1957, would you have chosen to keep the secret?
6) Was it wise to keep Wilf in the dark about the events of 1957 for all those years? If the secret had immediately been made public, do you think Wilf would have coped better?
7) In the end, Phiney regards Vivian as someone who 'disappear[s]… in the face of difficulty' (pp. 154) – do you think that's a fair assessment of her character and actions?
8) Do you think Phiney should make the secret public? At this point – in 2017 – would sharing the information cause more harm than good?
9) What do you think Phiney will decide to do, based on her character?
10) How relevant are the historical events of this novel to modern times?